KILL RIVER

a novel of slasher horror
by CAMERON ROUBIQUE

This book is for Mom and Dad.

Contents:

Chapter One: The Girl with the Headphones . . . 1

Chapter Two: Welcome to Camp Kikawa . . . 13

Chapter Three: Troublemakers . . . 24

Chapter Four: The First Night . . . 34

Chapter Five: Daily Activities . . . 38

Chapter Six: Swim Day . . . 49

Chapter Seven: The Punishment and The Plan . . . 61

Chapter Eight: The Escape . . . 74

Chapter Nine: The River . . . 93

Chapter Ten: The Rapids . . . 107

Chapter Eleven: The Park . . . 125

Chapter Twelve: All To Themselves . . . 134

Chapter Thirteen: The Missing . . . 163

Chapter Fourteen: The Lazy River . . . 172

Chapter Fifteen: The Fence and The Showers . . . 183

Chapter Sixteen: Trapped . . . 210

Chapter Seventeen: The Girls Alone . . . 223

Chapter Eighteen: The Man in the Mask . . . 256

Chapter Nineteen: The Dead Man's Drop . . . 284

Chapter Twenty: In The Tunnel . . . 298

Chapter Twenty One: The Second Escape . . . 311

Chapter Twenty Two: Coming Home . . . 328

Epilogue . . . 337

Afterword . . . 339

Chapter One:

The Girl with the Headphones

Cyndi was only vaguely aware of the background noise on the crowded school bus. All the laughing, screaming kids, road noise, and squeaks of the old bus were all but drowned out by the headphones blasting music in her ears. She was listening to her all time favorite song "Our Lips Are Sealed," by her all time favorite band, The Go-Go's, and watching the forest pass by endlessly with no real interest.

She was the very definition of a music junkie. Pop, punk, that weird new wave stuff, hard rock, the golden oldies, she loved it all. She decorated the walls of her room with pictures of musicians from magazines and posters. She dressed like a punk-chick most of time, wearing baggy, band T-shirts. She especially liked off the shoulder shirts where her right shoulder stuck out of the neck hole.

She had one of the new cassette Walkmans and had it playing at all times. She woke up and ate her Pac-Man cereal with her headphones on, while her parents talked about how much they wished they had gotten her the clothes for her birthday instead. Then she'd go upstairs, crimp her light blonde hair, and put on thick amounts of dark eye-liner and blue eye-shadow around her eyes while her headphones hung upside down under her chin. She kept her headphones on while she walked to school, waited for her classes to start, and ate lunch by herself. After school she finally took the headphones off, only to turn on some tapes or records on the big stereo in her room while she did her homework. Later, she would go downstairs and watch some music videos on MTV. Her parents would sit downstairs, try to ignore the loud music, and worry about their quiet, antisocial daughter.

One night in April, Cyndi's mother came into her room to have a serious mother-daughter talk with her. She had started out by making Cyndi turn off all her music, which made things ten times more uncomfortable for her. She hated the silence, it made her all nervous and fidgety.

"Now I'm not trying to judge you or bring you down, but your father and I are worried about you, dear," her mother explained. Cyndi felt an itch inside her ear and glanced over at the headphones sitting next to her on the bed. "I know it's really difficult growing up and...adjusting, but I'm just worried that you spend too much time listening to music and not enough time with your friends."

"Mom..." Cyndi mumbled in protest. Most of the words she said were mumbled, except for the occasional, 'HUH?' whenever she heard someone talking to her and pulled one headphone back to listen.

"Cyndi, you're thirteen-and-a-half years old and you need to start learning how to socialize and get along with your peers better. One of these days a boy is going to come along and then what will you do? Turn away from him and turn your headphones up louder?"

"Mom, please!" This was too much. As soon as Mom awkwardly pulled the Boys Card it became overwhelmingly uncomfortable. She stood up and reached for her Walkman, but her mom snatched it away.

"Please try to be more social," her mom pleaded. "For me."

Cyndi rolled her eyes and nodded. She held her hand out for the Walkman. Her mom handed it to her, leaned in, and kissed her on the cheek.

"I love you, Cyndi," she said.

"Love you, too," Cyndi muttered.

Her mom walked out of the room and Cyndi put her headphones back on, immediately getting the Ramones tape she'd been listening to, going again. Her mom turned at the doorway and called back to her. She pulled her one headphone back and yelled, "Huh?"

"Maybe you should invite Jennifer over. It's been so long since we've seen her," her mom suggested eagerly. Cyndi just shrugged and her mom's eager smile left her face. She walked out. If only she'd known that Jennifer, her former best friend from elementary school, was a total conceited bitch, she never would have brought her up.

Cyndi didn't take her mother's advice at all, so her parents decided on Plan B. If she wouldn't get out of the house once in a while and get her feet wet, they'd have to throw her in the deep end. They decided to send her to summer camp.

They broke the news to her on her last day of school. With eager smiles they told her, "you're leaving in two weeks for Camp Kikawa." Her mouth dropped open in shock as they tried to hand her a brochure with a smiling group of little kids and the words, *Camp Kikawa, Summer 1983*, on the front.

"It'll be great! You'll get to be outside all summer. You'll get to play all kinds of games and do fun activities. The camp's on a big lake too, so you can go canoeing and rafting."

3

They tried opening up the brochure and showing her pictures. Cyndi only gave them brief horrified glances.

"Well, what do you think?" her mom asked.

"Camp's for babies. I'll be, like, the oldest kid there," Cyndi said in a uncommonly loud and clear voice. She could speak like normal people, she just chose not to most of the time.

"No you won't, sweetie. See, it says right here, ages eight to fourteen," her dad said pointing at the brochure. The pictures mostly showed younger, pre-puberty kids, and a few camp counselors that were closer to her own age. Every kid in the brochure looked at least two years younger than she was, grinning their goofy loose-tooth grins.

"You can't be serious," Cyndi said. Her mother and father glanced nervously at each other. "I'm *not* going to that little kid's camp."

"I'm sorry, honey, but your father already paid for it," her mother said apologetically.

"Dad! How could you?" Cyndi nearly screamed at him. He was taken aback by her outburst. It was the loudest they'd both heard her speak in the last two years.

"Come on now, Cyndi. Don't be like that. You'll have a great time," her dad reasoned.

She looked down at the smiling little kids on the brochure.

"For how long?" Cyndi asked.

"It lasts June ninth through..." he grabbed the brochure and read over it briefly, "July seventeenth."

Cyndi felt tears suddenly sting her eyes. "Dad! That's over a *month!*"

"It'll be good for you, dear," her mother said.

"Look Cyndi, you need to get out and learn to be with people. You're going to camp, and that's final," her father said sternly.

4

Cyndi got up from the table and ran to her room. She slammed the door behind her and blasted her music as loud as she could. Her parents didn't protest.

Cyndi resigned herself to the fact that she was going to camp. The apathetic disinterest she usually gave her parents now turned to cold, rebellious bitterness, but she didn't argue. In fact, she ignored them almost completely, plunging herself even deeper into her music.

She packed her bags the night before leaving for camp with an assortment of her off the shoulder band T-shirts. She filled her thin purple backpack with tapes, and batteries for her Walkman.

When she finished packing, she sat down on her windowsill and stared out, feeling like a prisoner on death row. It was a beautiful summer evening and the sun was beginning to set. Over the sound of "We Just Don't Get Along," by the Go-Go's, blasting out of her big speakers, she heard a lawnmower somewhere outside. Just then, a boy came into view pushing a clunky old gas powered mower across her own front lawn. He was about a year or two older than Cyndi, and looked like a surfer with his sun-bleached blonde hair flipped over to one side. He wore a green Hawaiian shirt unbuttoned half-way down his chest, tucked into his acid-washed jeans. His white high-tops were turning green with grass stains.

The boy suddenly turned his head and looked directly up at Cyndi, as if he had sensed that she was staring at him. He had arresting blue eyes. As soon as he saw her, he gave her a crooked smile that all of the cute guys she had ever seen seemed to master. She immediately spun around awkwardly and walked away from the window.

Oh, real smooth, Cyndi, she scolded herself. *Now he probably thinks you're a total weirdo.*

5

So what if he did? She didn't know him. He was just some boy that her parents paid to mow the lawn. She had never seen him in her life.

She sighed and collapsed back on her bed. Maybe her parents were right. Maybe she did need to learn to be more social. She turned her head and saw her packed suitcase sitting on the floor next to her bed. It seemed to mock her, reminding her that she was being shipped off to Kiddy-Camp tomorrow as punishment for her antisocial tendencies. She sat up and kicked over the suitcase, then walked over to change the record.

*   *   *

The big yellow school bus stopped at her house and honked for her around 9:45 in the morning. Cyndi's mother had to run up to her room to get her attention. She opened the door and found Cyndi lying on her bed on her stomach with her bare feet in the air.

"Hurry, sweetie, your bus is here," her mother said.

Cyndi looked up but didn't even pull off her headphones. She grabbed her backpack and her suitcase and left the room without a word.

At the front door, Cyndi looked out at the yellow school bus. It was packed with screaming, wild, younger kids. Cyndi stared at them with disgust. Her mom hugged her goodbye and kissed her cheek. She pulled off Cyndi's headphones and said, "I know you don't think so, but you'll have a great time. And you'll make all sorts of new friends. Just wait and see."

Cyndi simply put her headphones back on and walked away from her house without smiling. She handed the bus driver, a surly unshaven guy in his mid-fifties, her suitcase and he stowed it in a compartment underneath the seats. She got on, and the bus driver followed behind her.

The bus was filled with little kids mostly between the ages of eight and eleven. It appeared that the younger they were, the more of them were here. Three quarters of the kids on the bus were age ten or younger. The younger kids all seemed to peer up and giggle at the alien teenage creature entering their territory. She saw an open seat on the left, the second row from the back, and made her way toward it. The bus took off before she was even a few steps down the aisle and she stumbled forward. Several kids nearby giggled at her. Even though she couldn't hear their laughter, she could feel it.

As she walked up to the open seat, she saw an older boy sitting in the seat directly behind it. The boy was punching the back of the open seat where Cyndi was headed. He had black greased hair that slicked to one side and hung down in shiny curls. He had a smooth olive complexion and a skinny, mischievous look to him. He wore a black sleeveless T-shirt, faded jeans, and dirty old Converse sneakers. He was the kind of guy you'd see in one of those rock bands on MTV and he looked like he had to be at least fourteen. She thought he was cute. He stopped punching the seat, looked up at her with wide, dark eyes, and gave her a lazy smile. She immediately looked away and sank down into her seat, instantly regretting the fact that she hadn't returned his smile.

He was cute, damn it. Why is it so hard for you to smile at cute guys? She guessed she just wasn't the smiling type.

She stared out the window and felt the cute guy behind her lean on the top of her seat, looking down at her. She turned her Walkman up louder and leaned forward. She stared out the window, trying her best to casually ignore him. Eventually, the boy behind her sat back in his seat and left her alone.

The bus drove into a rich neighborhood where the houses were as tall as the thick trees lining the street. They pulled up to a big white house with columns lining the front porch. A popular looking fourteen-year-old girl came out. Her mother came out arguing with her about something. The mother wore too much jewelry and too much makeup, and had a snooty look about her. Cyndi supposed the girl did too. She had a rich-popular-girl way about her, but Cyndi could tell she had a wild side too. She wore a bright colored low-cut shirt showing too much cleavage and too much of her midriff to earn parental approval, and a tiny short sleeve jean jacket. She had a frilly skirt and bright pink tights that ended below her knees. She wore her blonde hair in a side pony-tail and had a thick white headband just above her forehead. Her jewelry consisted of big hoop earrings, a few long pearl necklaces, and a ton of bracelets covering most of her forearms.

The girl got on the bus and came down the aisle toward the back. She gave Cyndi a quick smile with her perfect white teeth and sat down next to her. Cyndi gave her a brief smile and immediately turned back to the window. She heard the girl say something to her and she pulled back a headphone.

"Huh?" Cyndi asked.

"I said, thank God I'm not the only teenage girl on this bus," she said. "I'm Stacy."

Stacy held out her hand, and Cyndi slowly shook it.

"Cyndi."

"My dad is this executive for Bright Smiles toothpaste and he makes me go to this stupid fuckin' camp every year because they own it. It's total bullshit."

Cyndi couldn't really believe that this Stacy girl was talking to her. This was the type of girl her ex-best friend Jennifer aspired to be. Rich, beautiful, and a total spoiled brat. She had a perfect Barbie-doll face and bright blue eyes. She was tall too, close to five foot six. She wasn't just pretty, she was supermodel pretty. This was exactly the reason why Jennifer and her new group of friends had shunned Cyndi over a year and a half ago. Jennifer wasn't as pretty as Stacy, but she was easily the prettiest girl in class at their school. She liked to hang around with all the other pretty girls in their class. Cyndi was pretty too, but in a more wild rock-n-roll girl way. She had a smaller round face, with big green eyes and full pouty lips. Plus, she had big goofy ears that she hated, they poked out of her hair no matter what she did with it, giving her a slightly elvish look. She was only five feet tall and that was about as tall as she'd ever get, according to her mother.

Whenever Cyndi hung around with Jennifer and her new group of pretty friends she frequently fell silent. She didn't really know what to say in their conversations about boys, gossip, makeup, and clothes. She didn't really care about any of that trendy stuff, what she really cared about was music. Jennifer started intentionally avoiding Cyndi, and eventually convinced her whole group turn their backs on her. If Cyndi sat down at their table for lunch in the cafeteria, they would all get up and find another table. So Cyndi had flung herself into her music and quit trying to socialize with other girls. She also began to dress and do her makeup more like the girls she saw on MTV instead of the snotty girls at school. Screw them if they didn't want her to be a part of their group. The girls on MTV, like Belinda Carlisle or Pat Benatar, were much cooler anyway. Their songs never made you feel bad or unpopular. They made you feel like those artists were just like you, and that they didn't give a shit about the rest of the world.

Stacy was the first girl who had willingly talked to her in public in months and Cyndi was at a total loss for words. Her mom's voice echoed in her mind, *you'll make all sorts of new friends. Just wait and see.*

Shut up, Mom. She wasn't going to let her mother win that easily.

All she said back to Stacy was, "Yeah." Then she immediately turned back to the window. She felt totally stupid, but what could she say? Stacy looked at her for a moment, then shrugged and pulled a nail file out of her own purse. She began working on her hot pink nails as the school bus rumbled on.

Before long, the bus stopped again in front of another huge house and a jocky athletic looking guy with blonde feathered hair came out. He had a handsome smooth face and the look of an All-American baseball hero. He also had to be at least fourteen. He wore a pair of high athletic shorts and a tight polo shirt with the sleeves rolled up almost to his shoulders.

The boy in the seat behind Stacy and Cyndi immediately stood up when the bus pulled up and yanked his window down.

"Ay Bradley, Bay-Bay!" the boy on the bus screamed out the window to him in a playful tone. The kid looked up and smiled.

"Ay Zacky, Bay-Bay!" he replied as he tossed his gym bag at the bus-driver and jogged on board. A little kid threw a crumpled paper airplane at the boy, it hit him in the face. This cracked up most of the younger kids on the bus. Without missing a beat, the jocky Brad kid leaned in and punched the little kid hard on his skinny forearm. The kid gasped and began to cry loudly, and most of the other little kids stopped giggling immediately. He turned to another little kid and lunged at him.

"What the FUCK are you looking at?" He said the word FUCK loudly right as he lunged toward the kid. The kid shrank back. Brad laughed lazily and continued walking toward the back of the bus. Stacy stood up as he approached.

"Hey, Stace," he said as she flung her arms around him and gave him a big kiss right on the lips. Several little kids made *ooooooh* noises from the front. Cyndi watched all this with mild interest. The Zack kid with the greasy hair grabbed Stacy by the shoulders and turned her around.

"My turn, baby," Zack said leaning in to kiss her.

"Get the fuck off me, Zack," Stacy said pushing him back down in the seat. Brad punched Zack in the arm and they both laughed and gave each other a high-five. Stacy turned around, putting her knees up on the seat next to Cyndi and spent most of the ride turned that way, talking to Brad and Zack.

So much for new friends. At least I don't have to try to talk to anyone anymore, Cyndi thought dismally.

For most of the three hour bus ride Cyndi sat in her own world. She listened to her Go-Go's tapes and watched the woods pass by. About halfway through the ride, Brad, Zack, and Stacy's conversation had shifted onto the topic of Cyndi.

"So who's this chick, Stace?" Zack asked her, pointing a thumb toward Cyndi.

"I don't know. Her name's Cyndi, I think," Stacy said.

"She's pretty hot. Think I have a shot with her?" Zack asked.

"Go for it, dude," Brad said.

"No, leave her alone, Zack," Stacy protested, but it was already too late. Zack was up leaning on the seat and grabbing the headphones off Cyndi's head.

"Whatcha lissnin' to, babe?" Zack asked putting the headphones on his own ears. Cyndi immediately grabbed for her headphones, but Zack was out of reach, sitting back in his own seat.

"Hey! Give me those," Cyndi said seriously.

"The Go-Go's? Aww man, all they ever do is chick songs," Zack said pulling the headphones off. "Still that singer chick is pretty hot."

"Give her those, dick-face," Stacy said, grabbing the headphones out of his hand. "Here. Don't mind Zack. He's a total idiot." Cyndi gave her an uncomfortable smile then put her headphones back on. Stacy turned back to Zack and shoved him. "Asshole."

"Ay! What'd I say?" Zack yelled indignantly.

"Ah, don't sweat it, man. She seems like a prude anyway," Brad said laughing.

"Don't be such jerks. Both of you," Stacy scolded. "She's just quiet. Leave her alone."

Cyndi listened to this whole conversation. She pretended to listen to her tape player, but had the volume on her Walkman all the way down. She turned the volume back up as their conversation shifted back to other topics.

Well, we may not be friends, but at least she stood up for me, Cyndi thought. She watched a river run along the side of the road as they neared Camp Kikawa.

Chapter Two:

Welcome to Camp Kikawa

The bus turned off the main highway onto a dirt road and the noise level of the excited younger kids went up a few more notches. Cyndi turned away from the window and looked around as the noise began to creep into the music blasting from her headphones. Stacy noticed Cyndi and gave her a smile. Cyndi smiled back a little uncomfortably and turned back to the window. She had a feeling she was going to like Stacy, but her prettiness and slightly snobby demeanor made Cyndi wary of her. She would not let Stacy humiliate her the way Jennifer had.

Thick woods surrounded the dirt road.

Jeez, this place must be in the middle of nowhere, Cyndi thought and turned up her Joan Jett tape a little bit louder to drown out the elevated kids and road noise. The bus hit a deep pothole and everyone bounced off their seats. Stacy and Cyndi looked at each other briefly and laughed. Brad leaned forward and pointed at a little red-headed boy a few rows up.

"It was Carrot-Top up there," Brad yelled. "He went up at least three feet!"

"I know. His head almost hit the fuckin' ceiling!" Zack chimed in. They both laughed uproariously. Stacy couldn't help but laugh with them. The kid turned back to look at them. He must have been barely eight years old.

"Whatcha' lookin' at?" Zack yelled at the kid.

"That's right. We're talkin' about you!" Brad yelled pointing at him. The kid gaped at him with wide eyes. "Turn your ass back around!" The kid immediately turned away.

"Brad. Be nice!" Stacy scolded.

"What? Little fucker was starin' at us," Brad cried defensively, then gave her a sly grin.

The bus rounded a corner and the entrance to Camp Kikawa came into view. Two totem poles with carved, brightly painted Indian symbols and faces stood on opposite sides of the road. One brightly colored eagle wing poked out into the woods at the top of each totem pole. A high wooden arch bridged the tops of the two totem poles with the words *Camp Kikawa* rustically spelled out with thin tree branches.

Just past the totem poles, the woods opened up into a huge clearing. The cabins were off to the right of the road, clustered near the woods. The activity areas like the volleyball nets and a baseball field were off to the left. Straight ahead was the lake and a large wooden building that Cyndi guessed must be the main lodge. The entire camp was built on a slight downward slope that ended at the lake.

All the little kids on the bus cheered and jumped up and down as the camp came into view. Everyone was standing and moving into the aisle before the bus came to a stop. Cyndi saw everyone getting up and stood up herself. She grabbed her backpack from under the seat and swung it around on her shoulder. Her headphones cord got snagged and the headphones pulled down off her ears, hanging loosely from the back of her neck. She reached for them and began to put them back on her ears instinctively, then thought better of it. She might need to hear where to go and what to do. She let them drop and hang down around her neck.

The bus came to a stop and the front doors flew open. Even though the younger kids were making a mad dash off the bus, it still took forever for the line ahead of them to move.

Zack had his head hanging out the window and pulled it in. "Uh-oh. Look who came back for more summer fun," he said sarcastically. Brad and Stacy leaned over and looked out the windows. Cyndi couldn't help but crane her neck to see who they were looking at. She saw a tall muscular man with a whistle around his neck holding a clipboard, directing kids off the bus and barking out orders.

"Ewww, Counselor Sheehan," Stacy said. She turned away from the window and allowed Cyndi a better look. The guy was in his late thirties but was trying his best to look younger. He had dark feathered hair that went down to his shoulders, and a deep tan. He had the muscles of a body builder and the macho attitude of a kid who had been picked on a lot in school. He wore a white Camp Kikawa T-shirt that was two sizes too small, tight fitting shorts that went up way too high, Adidas sneakers, and athletic tube socks pulled up most of the way to his knees.

The line started moving and they all hurried off the bus. Counselor Sheehan yelled and motioned with his free hand.

"Boys cabins to the right. Girls cabins to the left!" he shouted and quickly repeated himself two more times. Stacy quickly grabbed Cyndi's arm and pulled her off toward the cabins, avoiding eye contact with the counselor.

15

"Come on," she said. "I'll show you where the girls cabins are."

Brad and Zack sauntered off the bus.

"Well, look who it is," Brad said in a condescending tone and pointed to the counselor. "It's She-Man." Zack immediately burst out laughing, and Sheehan looked over. Brad held out his hand for a high-five from Zack without breaking his eye contact with the counselor. The counselor gave them a sardonic smile and walked over to them.

"Hello, boys," the counselor said, ignoring their comment. "I hope you brought extra toothbrushes this year. I have a feeling you're gonna need 'em."

"Oooh," both Brad and Zack mocked, pretending to shiver in fear. They began to saunter past him without stepping aside, but he quickly put his hand firmly on Brad's shoulder.

"You boys better watch yourselves," Sheehan said sternly. "You pull any of that same crap like last year and I'll throw you outta here. I mean it! And I don't want you causing anymore trouble for the little kids either. I catch you beating up on one kid and your punishment is gonna be triple what it was last year, got it?"

Brad simply gave him a quick smile dripping with sarcasm. He picked Sheehan's hand off his shoulder with two fingers as if it were some nasty specimen. "Sure thing, She-Man."

"That's Counselor Sheehan! Get it right or you'll be cleaning out toilets!" he yelled to them.

"Yeah, yeah," Brad muttered, without turning around.

Sheehan turned back to his clipboard shaking his head in frustration. He looked back up and then yelled to the bus driver. "All right, let's get those suitcases down to the lodge!"

Cyndi and Stacy walked down the slope toward the girl's cabins in the fading afternoon sunlight.

"God, I hope we get Ashley as our bunk leader, she's the best," Stacy said. "I had her last year. She lets the older girls like us stay up late, instead of that stupid nine-thirty lights out. It's like, we're not babies, right?"

"Yeah. Right," Cyndi agreed quietly, smiling.

"If we get Morgan, it's really gonna suck. She is a total bitch," Stacy chattered on. "She's such a rule-Nazi. I don't think she's ever broken a rule, or, like, had any fun in her entire life. She's way too uptight."

Cyndi nodded, staring at the Walkman attached to her belt and wishing she could turn her music back on.

"You don't talk much, do you, Cyndi?" Stacy asked. Cyndi looked up, caught off guard.

"No, I guess not," Cyndi said, laughing a little shyly.

"Well, I hope you're not gonna be all quiet all summer," Stacy told her. "Because we're probably the two oldest girls in camp and we gotta stick together, y'know?"

Cyndi suddenly realized she was being socially accepted for the first time in almost two years. After a shocked second, she felt so happy she wanted to reach out and hug Stacy, but instead she held out her hand.

"Yeah. Stick together," Cyndi said confidently.

"Awesome," Stacy said. They shook hands, then both laughed a little to break the silence and continued down the slope toward their cabin.

Maybe this summer won't be so bad after all.

The smile didn't leave Cyndi's face until they reached a small cabin near the woods. A pretty girl in her mid-twenties was standing on the porch of the cabin holding a clipboard. She had light brown hair up in a ponytail and a whistle around her neck.

"What's up, Ashley?" Stacy called to her.

Ashley turned and smiled warmly.

"Hi, Stacy," Ashley said. Stacy ran up and hugged her. "It's really good to see you."

"It's really good to see you too!" Stacy said and started to walk toward the cabin. Ashley stepped in front of her and the smile left her face.

"Actually...uh...they told me they want me to be in charge of all the little kids this year," Ashley said uncomfortably. "And they wanted all the older girls with, uh, Morgan."

"What?!" Stacy cried.

"I'm sorry, Stace. Counselor Sheehan just told me this morning. He says he's trying to cut down on all the pranks and trouble because of what happened last year."

"You've got to be kidding me. That was all Zack and Brad. Not me," Stacy protested.

"I know. I'm really sorry, Stace. I was looking forward to having you in my cabin again too. But hey, we'll see each other at activities and at meals and stuff, right?"

"Yeah, yeah, okay." Stacy sulked off toward another cabin. Cyndi looked at Counselor Ashley who gave her a disappointed shrug, then hurried off after Stacy.

"This sucks!" Stacy yelled. "Morgan's gonna be on our asses all summer."

Cyndi didn't say anything but stared at her sympathetically. She knew better than to try to console another teenage girl. They walked past two more of the girl's cabins to the one closest to the lodge and the lake. A chunky girl with really curly auburn hair and a stern expression stood on the porch with a whistle and a clipboard. Cyndi took one look at her and figured that this was the infamous Morgan.

"Stacy," Morgan said solemnly as Stacy trudged

up the steps into the cabin.

"Hey, Morgan," she replied without stopping to talk. Morgan glanced down at her clipboard.

"And you must be Cyndi Stevens," she said to Cyndi. "Welcome to Camp Kikawa." She gave her a perfunctory smirk that passed for a smile. Cyndi returned it with an equal lack of enthusiasm and followed Stacy in.

The bunkhouse was essentially one giant room and a big bathroom. There was a small sitting area near the entryway with a couch and a bookshelf filled with old books and magazines. Two rows of bunk beds lined the walls at the end of the room. There were already four other eleven and twelve-year-old girls in the cabin chattering excitedly and sitting on two of the bunk beds. Across from the girls, there was a normal sized bed reserved for the counselor.

Stacy walked down the middle aisle and went for the bunk bed in the far corner, the farthest one from the counselor's bed. She threw her purse up top, and Cyndi watched with a little disappointment as Stacy climbed up the side to get onto the top bunk.

What's wrong with you, Cyndi? She thought to herself. *Are you really gonna be jealous that she got the top bunk? I mean, come on, how old are you?* She shrugged off her jealousy and tossed her pack onto the bottom bunk.

Cyndi looked out the window on the side of the bed. It faced the woods behind the bunkhouse. She turned back, saw the other girls chattering away across the room, and felt the quiet of the back corner closing in on her. She leaned back, opened up her pack, and began sifting through her tapes for a new one to listen to. Suddenly, Stacy's head poked down from the top bunk.

"BOO!" Stacy said, her side-ponytail hanging down. Cyndi smiled up at her. "God, you really are quiet."

"Sorry," she apologized quietly.

"Huh?" Stacy asked.

"I said sorry," Cyndi said a little more clearly.

"What?" Stacy asked again.

"Sorry," Cyndi said a little louder.

"Hang on I can't hear you. I'm coming down there," Stacy said and her head was replaced by white Keds tennis shoes and pink leg warmers. She lowered herself down onto Cyndi's bunk, her arms still hanging onto the top bunk. "Okay, now what did you say?"

"I said, I was sorry," Cyndi said loudly and clearly.

"Oooooh, I get it," Stacy said sarcastically, then smiled at her. Cyndi looked at her puzzled. "I'm kidding, Cyndi. I can hear you fine. Just promise me you won't be this quiet all summer. I hate silence."

"Really? Me too," Cyndi said.

"Is that why you listen to tapes all the time?" Stacy asked.

Cyndi looked down at her cassette player, honestly considering the question. She had never made the connection before, but it made perfect sense.

"I guess so," she said after a moment.

"I'm the total opposite. That's why I'm always talking to people," Stacy began. "My dad got me a separate phone line for my room because he said I was tying up the phone too much. He says I should be one of those talk radio DJ's." She imitated her dad in a low stern voice, "Might as well get paid for all that talkin,' girl."

Cyndi laughed. "You know what? Working at a radio station sounds like a great job! I always know all the best music that comes out."

"Yeah, I bet you probably do," Stacy said laughing and picking up Cyndi's pack. "Is this whole thing filled with tapes."

"Pretty much. Tapes and batteries," Cyndi said as Stacy sifted through them. "And my toothbrush."

"Alright then, here's what we're gonna do," Stacy said. "We are gonna move to Hollywood and take over the radio business. I'll be the DJ and you can, like, play the records and stuff."

"Or we could be on MTV," Cyndi said.

"Oooooh, even better!" Stacy shouted. "I'm gonna be an MTV star!"

The door to the bunkhouse opened up and Morgan walked in with the rest of the girls. They quickly ran over to their bunks and Morgan stood at the front of the aisle in between the rows of bunk beds.

"All right, listen up, ladies," Morgan shouted in a commanding voice. It only took a second for the younger girls to silence themselves. "All right. Now, for those of you who don't know me, my name is Morgan. And for those of you who do know me, it's nice to see you all again." She didn't sound happy to see anyone at all, speaking in a dry, bored, I-Hate-Life voice. She sounded like she was delivering lines from a script that she didn't want to read, delivering them badly. Stacy gave Cyndi a sideways look.

Morgan started slowly walking up the aisle between the bunk beds, looking at each of the girls as she continued her speech. "Now I'm gonna go over a few basic rules. First off, no food in here. If I catch you with it, I'm throwin' it out. And can someone tell me why?"

She stopped walking and held her hands out expectantly, waiting for some girl to fill in the blank. After a moment of awkward silence, one short eleven-year-old girl with huge red rimmed glasses piped in, "because of bears?" She looked like she was probably the youngest girl in the whole cabin.

"Bingo!" Morgan pointed at the little girl.

21

"What's your name?"

"Umm, Stephanie."

"Congratulations Stephanie, you seem to be smarter than all the other girls in here, so far," Morgan said with a fake smile and a voice dripping with sarcasm. "There are bears, and mountain lions, and raccoons, and all sorts of other animals we don't want coming in here."

Stacy turned toward Cyndi, put two fingers up to her temple mimicking a gun, and pulled the trigger. Cyndi smiled and turned back to Morgan.

"Second rule is we're gonna keep this bunk clean," Morgan continued and resumed walking slowly down the aisle. "Every morning we're gonna make our beds, pick up all our junk, vacuum the rugs, and clean the bathrooms." Stacy and several other girls groaned at this. Morgan immediately deflected all the complaints, raising her voice and putting her hands up defensively. "I don't wanna hear it. Vacuuming and bathroom clean up schedules will rotate from bunk to bunk everyday. We're gonna keep this cabin clean and that's that. End of story. Got it?

"Third rule, and this is more for you older girls, absolutely no boys are allowed in this cabin." Several younger girls began to giggle. Morgan turned to them and added, "And I mean it." They immediately fell silent. She resumed her walk up the aisle and stopped near the back corner.

Morgan stood a few feet in front of Cyndi and Stacy's bunk bed. Her beady eyes bore down into Stacy's as she said this last rule. "Now the last and most important rule. In this cabin, it's lights out at nine-thirty. No talking, no sneaking out, no pranks. If I catch you outside this cabin, sneaking around after lights out even one time, it's bathroom duty for the rest of the summer. Twice, and you're going home. Understand?" Stacy glared at her defiantly without answering. Cyndi, watching the exchange, felt extremely uncomfortable. She wished she could just put on her headphones, blast some music, and look the other way until this was over.

"Do you understand that, or do you want bathroom duty for the next week, Ms. Weston?" Morgan asked in a quieter, more threatening voice.

Stacy took a deep breath and said one word in a monotone voice, dripping with attitude, "Gotcha." She never broke eye contact with Morgan. They stared each other down for another second, then Morgan turned back to the rest of the girls.

"You're all older girls. The rules aren't hard to understand. Just follow them, and we'll have a great summer, simple as that. You don't follow them, well, your summer's gonna suffer, okay? Now that we got that out of the way, let's all head up to the lodge where you can pick up the rest of your bags and Head Counselor Sheehan will have a few words to say to everyone."

Stacy made a face behind Morgan's back and turned to Cyndi smiling. "Come on." They headed out of the cabin.

Chapter Three:

Troublemakers

The lodge was a huge log cabin facing the lake. The girls walked up a short flight of steps, onto a big beautiful deck. They went inside into the main sitting area, which was as big as a large living room. It had comfortable couches and chairs, and huge windows. There was a gorgeous view of the sprawling blue lake, the thick green surrounding woods, and the spectacular, cloudless orange afternoon sky. There were several bookcases loaded with books. Hung from the walls were mounted deer heads and Indian masks and decorations. On the far wall across from the couches was a big stone fireplace, and a mantle covered with pictures and awards from past summers. Hung above the mantle was a big painting of a middle aged man with slicked back black hair and a big perfect smile on his face.

Down a side hall was the nurse's station and the Head Counselor's office. Morgan pointed this out to them for the benefit of the new kids as they filed into the lodge toward the mess hall.

A staircase led down from the main level with rustic wooden tree limbs as the railings. If you went all the way down the stairs and took a left, you'd wind up in the Rec Room. There were two Foosball tables, several dartboards, and card tables. There were several ground level windows and a doorway leading back out toward the cabins. There was a radio with big speakers and a big space for spread out games like Twister and Duck Duck Goose. All of their suitcases were lined up neatly in this space. Morgan showed them the Rec Room, again for the new kids benefit, and had to yell when several kids went for their bags.

"Ah-ah-ah! You'll get your bags after Counselor Sheehan's speech! Don't worry they'll still be here."

On the other side of the Main Lodge Area a short set of steps led down into the big ground level mess hall. To Cyndi, it looked like a log cabin version of the cafeteria at her school. Rows of long tables filled the huge mess hall, divided by an aisle in the middle. At the far end, there was a buffet-line with open windows leading into the kitchen where you picked up your food. At the front near the food line, Counselor Sheehan stood with another counselor talking quietly and watching the kids file in. Most of the other kids were trying to come into the mess hall all at once and there was a big crowd around the door.

Brad and Zack snuck up behind Stacy and Cyndi as they walked in. Brad threw his arms around both of their shoulders, sliding smoothly in between them. Cyndi jumped a little at first, but then relaxed as she recognized him.

"Lllllladies," he said in a mocking Mister Smooth voice.

"Hey, you," Stacy said happy to see him. "How's the cabin?"

"Ugh, don't remind me," Zack said from the other side of Stacy. "They put us in with James." He said James name in a nasally uptight voice.

"You think *that's* bad? They stuck us with Morgan," Stacy said.

"Oooh, tough break," Zack said.

"Yeah, they're being really strict about their stupid rules this year," Stacy said.

"Ah, they don't scare me," Brad said.

They sat down at one of the tables in the back. Zack sat next to Cyndi and gave her a big smile, which Cyndi returned nervously. Most of the kids had taken their seats, so Sheehan began his speech in a loud carrying voice.

"Okay. First, I'd just like to welcome you all to Camp Kikawa and tell you how glad I am that another summer is *here!*" he yelled enthusiastically. Most of the kids cheered, Brad and Zack joined in, a little too enthusiastically to be serious.

"YEAH SUMMER!!! WOOOOO!!!" Brad screamed jumping up and down and pounding his fists on the table like a drum roll.

Sheehan put his hands in the air to signal for quiet. "Now for those of you who don't know me, I'm Kirk Sheehan, and I'm your head counselor."

"She-Man!" Zack coughed loudly into his hand. Brad smirked, stifling a laugh. His gaze never left Sheehan.

Sheehan either didn't hear or didn't respond. He pointed to an old black and white photo that hung on the back wall. In the photo was an older man with white hair, piloting a sailboat and smiling with big white teeth. Cyndi noticed it was the same guy from the painting above the fireplace in the main lodge, only he was about twenty years older. "And this guy behind me, is our founder, and the President of Bright Smiles Inc., Mr. Kent Carver. Now Kent Carver started his career making the Bright Smiles Toothpaste Company in 1937. His dream was to make the world a brighter place by making

26

everyone all over the world smile with the products he made and the things he involved himself in. One of his side projects was this camp. He opened Camp Kikawa in 1954 and we've been here ever since."

Sheehan talked about all the fun things they'd be doing all summer. At one point, Zack began to snore loudly, keeping a straight face. This caused several kids to giggle and turn toward him. Stacy looked down, tightening her lips together and trying not to laugh. Brad had to cover his mouth with his hand to keep in his own laughter. A hand clamped down on Zack's shoulder making him jump, choke on one of the snores, and spin around coughing for real.

"One more time, and you're mopping up in here after dinner," Morgan whispered threateningly to him. He nodded seriously and turned back to Sheehan. After Morgan left, he looked over at Cyndi and gave her a tight-jawed That-Was-A-Close-One look.

Sheehan droned on about rafting and canoeing on the lake, before moving on to safety. Cyndi thought he was a better public speaker than Morgan. At least he showed real enthusiasm for the camp and the upcoming summer. He even got a few genuine laughs out of the kids. As he went on, he talked about a lot of the same stuff Morgan had already touched on back in the cabin.

"And finally on a more serious note," Sheehan said. "We have a new rule in place. If anyone is caught with any lighters, cigarettes, fireworks, or any other incendiary device, you will be immediately sent home. Furthermore, if anyone is hurt or any camp property is damaged because of anything fire-related, you'll be sent home, and not ever allowed back at this camp again. Your safety is my biggest concern, okay? We take this stuff very seriously and I don't want any repeats of last year, got it?" He looked directly at Zack, Brad, and Stacy as he made this last remark. All the counselors' eyes seemed to be on them. Brad and Zack looked at each other, then shrugged and looked around at everyone else with fake innocence on their faces. "I'm serious, guys," Sheehan added. Brad and Zack turned to him and they both gave him a sarcastic salute. He glared at them for another second, then turned back smiling at his audience. "Well, that's about it, have a great summer everyone." The kids all cheered and got up from their spots at the tables.

Stacy grabbed Cyndi's arm and pulled her up quickly. "Come on," she said. "If we don't hurry, it'll take us forever to get our bags."

Brad and Zack shoved their way through the mass of kids that were already gathering at the door. Sheehan motioned to one of the guy counselors to stop them.

"Comin' through, comin' through," Brad and Zack yelled as they shoved past several little kids. Just before they reached the door leading out of the mess hall, a counselor wearing a white baseball cap shoved his way in front of them. He was in his early twenties and looked like a jock.

"Hold it right there, you two," the counselor said. "Counselor Sheehan wants to have a little chat with you."

"What'd I do?" Brad asked incredulously.

"I don't know, you tell me," the counselor said.

Stacy snuck past the counselor, still holding Cyndi's arm. Cyndi was almost shoved into the counselor by the crowd of kids.

"Hey, watch it," he said.

"Sorry sorry," Cyndi mumbled as she was dragged away by Stacy.

"And you slow down!" he shouted back at Stacy.

They found their bags easily enough and left

through the exit doors in the game room. They lugged their suitcases back up the hill toward their cabins.

"I don't know why they don't just bring them to our cabins. Oh my God, this thing is heavy," Stacy complained breathlessly. Her suitcase was almost twice as big as Cyndi's.

"Yeah, I bet," Cyndi said laughing at her. This got Stacy laughing too.

"Hey, shut up," Stacy said giggling. "You just wait 'til we've been here for three weeks and you're sick of all your outfits. Then we'll see who's laughing."

"Sure. Hey can I ask you something?" Cyndi asked. Stacy was taken aback.

"Wow, I've never heard you say so much in one sentence. She speaks!" Cyndi smiled and looked down embarrassed. "Ask away."

"Well, what's the deal with you and Brad and Zack?" she asked, quickly realizing that it came out the wrong way. "I mean, what happened with you guys that made all the counselors so...."

"Suspicious of us?" Stacy filled in.

"Yeah."

"Well, me and Brad and Zack go way back. We've gone to this camp together since we were all, like, eight years old," Stacy explained. "Brad and Zack have always been...troublemakers. But the thing you have to understand about them is that they're good guys. They really are."

"So...what happened?" Cyndi asked.

"Last year, we used to sneak out of our cabins, like, almost every night," Stacy continued. "It was me, Brad, Zack, and this girl Katie who doesn't go here anymore. Last year Counselor Sheehan had just gotten promoted to *Head Counselor*," she said these last words in a macho accent. "If you haven't noticed he takes his job waaaaay too seriously."

29

"Seems like it," Cyndi agreed.

"Yeah, he's a total power-tripping moron," Stacy said with some anger. "So Zack had these firecrackers that he had gotten from his cousin or uncle or something, I don't remember, and we thought it'd be really funny to pull a prank on Sheehan. We were gonna light off a ton of them near the lake, so everyone would wake up and see all the fireworks, y'know? And, well...things got kinda out of control."

"Out of control?" Cyndi asked curiously.

Stacy looked around, then shook her head reluctantly at her. "I'm really not supposed to be telling you this. Brad would kill me if he knew I was telling you."

"I won't tell anyone."

"You promise? Pinky swear?"

Cyndi held up her pinky finger, "Pinky swear."

Stacy grabbed Cyndi's pinky finger with her own and continued in a low voice, "One of the fireworks went straight for Sheehan's cabin and exploded on the door. All the grass around it caught on fire, and it almost burned down the cabin. Luckily, they all woke up and poured glasses of water all over it."

"Well, at least no one got hurt," Cyndi said.

"Yeah, I know."

"Did you get in trouble?"

"*Oh* yeah. Brad and Zack got sent home early and we all almost had the camp press charges against us. But all three of our dads work for Bright Smiles, the company who owns this camp, so they talked them out of it."

"Gee, you guys got lucky," Cyndi said.

"Well, what were they really gonna do to us?" Stacy said arrogantly. "My daddy is the VP of the company. I mean, we practically own this camp. They don't scare me. Not Sheehan or Morgan or any of the other stupid counselors."

Cyndi nodded in an agreement that she didn't really feel. She wanted to relate and build a friendship with Stacy, but deep down part of her wanted to tell Stacy that she was a rich spoiled brat. It would've served her, Brad, and Zack right if they'd had criminal charges pressed against them. Instead, she just nodded.

"Anyway," Stacy said. "Let's get back to the cabin." They smiled at each other and continued up the slope.

*   *   *

Brad and Zack sat in front of a big wooden desk covered with sports trophies. They stared at the name tag facing them, Head Counselor Kirk Sheehan. James, the counselor who had stopped them, stood outside the office door and watched the kids file past to get to their bags down in the rec room. He glanced back at Brad and Zack every few seconds.

Brad and Zack had protested vigorously as they were escorted to Sheehan's office by James.

"Dude, we haven't even done anything. We've been here for two hours," Brad said.

"Yeah, what's the big deal?" Zack asked.

"Just come with me," James said in a deadpan tone. He tried to sound like a hard-ass even though he knew Brad and Zack really weren't intimidated by him in the least. "Counselor Sheehan just wants to talk with you."

Now they sat waiting. Zack turned and tapped Brad on the arm to get his attention. Brad looked over and Zack gave him a shrugging gesture that said, *what the hell?* Brad gave him an incredulous shrug in response that said, *I don't know.* Zack shook his head and they both faced forward again.

Sheehan walked in a moment later and clapped James on the shoulder. "Thanks James. I'll take it from here."

"No problem, Counselor Sheehan." James walked off and Sheehan shut the door behind him. He made his way around the desk and sat down.

"I love doing that opening speech, it just makes the summer feel...official, y'know?" Sheehan said to them in a bright tone. Brad and Zack were not amused, they both stared at him waiting for the important part of whatever it was he had to say.

"You didn't like my speech?" Sheehan asked them with mocking curiosity.

"It was a great speech, dude, soooo awesome," Zack blurted sarcastically. Brad cracked a smile.

"Really? I'm surprised you even heard it over your own snoring," Sheehan said. This caught them both off guard and they both burst out laughing. Sheehan smiled at them and shook his head. "You guys think you're sooo funny, don't you? Well, if you had such a good time laughing it up in the mess hall, then I guess I'll put you on cleanup duty for the rest of the week. Sound fun?"

Their laughter trailed off immediately and the smiles were wiped from their faces.

"Dude, I didn't even do anything," Brad protested, glaring at him.

"I'm not your dude," Sheehan retorted seriously. "Look, this year I'm gonna make it real simple. If you two make *my* life harder, I'm gonna make *your* lives harder, okay? That's how it's gonna work this summer. Are we clear?" Brad and Zack glared at the floor without answering. "You got cleanup duty for one week. Get outta here."

They got up and Brad gave Sheehan a cold look. They opened the door and let it swing shut behind them.

Before they were even ten feet from the door Brad gave Zack a hard punch on the arm.

"Oww, what the fuck?" Zack said grabbing his arm.

"Thanks, dumbass," Brad snarled. "I didn't even *do* anything and I gotta do this cleanup shit with you!"

"I didn't know that was gonna happen," Zack shouted defensively.

Brad walked ahead of Zack and yelled, "FUCK!"

Zack shook his head and gave up the tough guy act. "I'm sorry, man."

"Whatever. Let's just go get our fuckin' bags," Brad said as they turned and went down the stairs into the rec room. His anger at Zack was already melting. Zack had been one of his closest friends since they were little, and they'd been through too much for Brad to really hold a grudge against him over something as stupid as getting roped into a punishment. The real problem was Sheehan, the She-Man. Brad realized right then that he was too old to be at summer camp. And he had a feeling that before the summer was up, one of them would have to go, either him or Sheehan.

Chapter Four:

The First Night

Cyndi sat up in bed and reached for her pack. She had gotten tired of the Duran Duran tape she was listening to, and thought she'd put on one of her mix tapes instead. She pressed stop on her Walkman and heard just how quiet it was in the cabin. Several of the other girls were breathing loudly through their mouths, and one of them (she assumed it was Morgan) was snoring loudly into her pillow. One of the girls in the bunk directly across from hers turned over and the cheap metal frame squeaked loudly. Despite all the night noises inside the cabin, it was quiet, uncomfortably quiet. She could hear a ringing in her ears that was only noticeable whenever there was complete silence.

Over the ringing in her ears, she still heard the crickets chirping loudly outside. She turned to look out the window and saw the thick dark woods behind their cabin. The trees were completely black and their knobby branches looked like arms.

Suddenly, there was movement back in the trees. She could see the outline of a man standing out there in the woods. He stood in the trees staring at the cabin. In fact, he seemed to be staring directly at her window. She shrank back away from the window, suddenly afraid. The man stood still for another moment, then the wind gusted making all the limbs in the surrounding trees sway. She craned her neck, her eyes searching for the man's outline again, but once the wind died down she couldn't see it anymore.

Maybe it was just her eyes playing tricks on her. To be completely honest, it was dark out there. Even if it was a guy, so what? Maybe it was just Counselor Sheehan walking around and making sure there weren't any kids, like Brad and Zack, out of bed.

Just then, Stacy turned over above her and the whole bed creaked. Cyndi looked up and saw the bulge of Stacy's body shift to the right. She shook her head and went through her pack looking for that mix tape. She wished she could sleep as easily as Stacy and every other girl in this cabin. She just never slept well in unfamiliar places. During sleepovers at her ex-best-friend Jennifer's house, they would stay up until two, three, sometimes even four in the morning. Then Jennifer would doze off, and Cyndi would find herself alone, bored, and awake all by herself in Jen's house. That was torture.

Cyndi found the tape she was looking for and popped it in, immediately "Tonight" by the Go-Go's started playing and she lost herself in the music, letting her thoughts wander.

Earlier, she and Stacy had gone down to dinner where they met up with Brad and Zack. After they got their dry turkey, instant mashed potatoes, and flaky biscuits (which actually weren't half bad) they found themselves an empty table near one of the windows. The dining hall was extremely noisy, especially from all of the chattering younger kids loud voices reverberating off the walls.

The boys told them about how they had gotten

cleanup duty for the next week. Stacy sympathized and told them about the suspicious treatment Morgan had been giving her all day.

"They'll probably get over it as the summer goes on," Zack said, his mouth full of food, trying to make the best of the situation.

"They better or I'm bustin' out of here, dude," Brad replied.

For the rest of the meal, they went on insulting Sheehan and creating scenarios about how he was a She-Man and turned into a dainty, ugly woman at night. Cyndi and Stacy couldn't get much of a word in edgewise. They smiled politely and laughed a little at the boys' jokes. Whenever their jokes reached an outlandish or disgusting peak, usually by Zack, they turned and gave each other strange looks that said, *oh my God, what are we doing sitting with these two?*

Counselor Sheehan finally came over near the end of the meal when kids were beginning to file out of the mess hall.

"Better get to work, boys," he said in a condescending voice meant to wipe the smiles off their faces. Instead they both looked at each other and burst out laughing. "What's so funny?" They looked at him and laughed even harder. Sheehan looked at Stacy and Cyndi for support.

"Boy humor," Stacy explained. She and Cyndi got up, leaving Counselor Sheehan with a puzzled frown. Finally he got the hint that the joke was on him.

"All right, that's enough! Get to work!" he burst out. He pointed to the storage closet where they kept the mops and trash bags. They both got up, still giggling, and carried their trays back to the kitchen area.

Cyndi and Stacy had walked back to their cabin and continued unpacking their things. Afterward, they listened to some of Cyndi's tapes on a little stereo that they found near the sitting area in their cabin. A short time later, Morgan got up and yelled that it was time to get ready for bed. Stacy and Cyndi looked over at a cat clock hanging on the wall and saw that it was only nine-fourteen.

"Are you serious?" Stacy rhetorically asked Cyndi. Cyndi sighed and rolled her eyes. Morgan walked over to the stereo and turned off the tape player.

"Time for bed, ladies," she said in a dry voice. Cyndi and Stacy glared at her for a second, then trudged off to their bunks to grab their toothbrushes.

The lights had gone out sharply at nine-thirty and Cyndi laid there looking back on the day and trying to get to sleep. She was really grateful to have found a friend like Stacy so easily, but she wasn't sure if she liked Brad or Zack yet. Brad seemed like a complete asshole a lot of the time, but sometimes he said things that were unexpectedly nice. He was cute in a popular-jock sort of way, and he could also be really clever and funny. He was a lot funnier than Zack anyway, who tried too hard to be as funny as Brad. Although Zack was pretty cute, she had to admit. She didn't know if she liked them, but she did agree with them totally on one point: they were all too old to be here. Plus, with all the counselors keeping a sharp eye on them, it was going to be hard to have a good time this summer, unless they did something drastic. With Brad and Zack, drastic might be too far for Cyndi. The last coherent thought she had before drifting off to sleep that night was that she would have to be careful around them.

Chapter Five:

Daily Activities

The first week in camp was pretty uneventful. The daily activities schedule dictated the majority of their lives at camp. Every morning, Morgan would wake the girls up at seven o'clock, yelling for them to get up and get ready for the day. The first morning Cyndi got up slowly, while Stacy simply turned over and put her pillow over her head. Morgan saw her still asleep and stormed over. Cyndi quickly got out of her way. Morgan walked right up to Stacy's head, pulled her whistle out, and gave Stacy a loud blast. Stacy jerked awake, her makeup smeared and her hair all messy. Her pillow went flying to the foot of the bed.

"Wake up, Weston!" Morgan yelled at her. "You're wastin' daylight!"

Several of the younger girls giggled and Morgan walked away from the bed with a satisfied smile on her face. Stacy was still breathing hard from the shock.

"You gotta be fucking kidding me," Stacy wheezed. Cyndi looked up at her and smiled sympathetically. Stacy rubbed the sleep from her eyes and dragged herself off the top bunk.

Every morning they got dressed and fixed their hair and makeup in the bathroom as quick as they could. Morgan only gave them a half-hour to get ready for the day and if they were still in front of the mirror, which they always were, Morgan would poke her head into the bathroom and scream at them.

"Pretty Time's over ladies. It's time to get this cabin in shape!" If they didn't comply within sixty seconds she would pop back in and threaten them with, "If you like the bathroom so much, you can clean it up!"

"Hang on! Jesus!" Stacy yelled back at her.

"Move it!"

This exchange happened daily with essentially the same dialogue. Cyndi then rushed out of the bathroom and made her bed. Stacy would usually stay in longer and ended up cleaning up the bathroom three times during the first week.

While they walked to breakfast, Stacy would ramble on and on about what a total bitch Morgan was. Cyndi completely agreed.

Brad and Zack would meet up with them at breakfast, which was always the tastiest meal of the day. They would all laugh and joke with each other, sharing stories about how the counselors were all coming down on them. Brad and Zack seemed to be having a rougher time with the counselors than Stacy and Cyndi were.

After breakfast they headed back to their bunks and quickly brushed their teeth, then Morgan rushed them off to their various activities. It was a rotating schedule involving different kinds of games, sports, other outdoor activities, and arts and crafts. Cyndi actually didn't mind the activities schedule. She wasn't naturally inclined towards sports, but Stacy was. Cyndi and Stacy were both older and bigger than a lot of the girls they were playing against, so it was usually easy to win most of the games. Another nice thing about the activities schedule was that they were away from Morgan a lot of the time. Their activities would be led by the other counselors; like Christina, another girls counselor who constantly wore her dark hair in braided pig-tails, and Ashley, who was easily the nicest counselor in camp.

One day they played volleyball in the morning, beating the younger girls' team easily. They played in a sandy pit near the lake on the other side of the lodge. Morgan, who ran the volleyball activity, actually gave a shocked Stacy words of praise for her volleyball skills.

Brad, Zack, and a bunch of the other boys were off playing baseball in the field near the woods. Counselor James had a no-win situation with baseball. Brad and Zack separated made for a really fun intense game, but the trash-talking and competitive squabbles that ensued between Brad and Zack made the baseball field a bad place for younger ears and eyes. Roughly every thirty seconds you would hear a "*fuck you*," a comment about someone's mother, or see an inappropriate hand gesture. On the other hand, with Brad and Zack together on a team the trash-talking went down to a minimum, but the team was virtually unstoppable. They were also sore winners, rubbing their victories in the younger kids' faces and getting them all riled up and cranky.

Arts and crafts were an unexpectedly fun part of the activities schedule for Cyndi. It was usually led by Ashley or Christina and it was a boys and girls activity, so Cyndi and Stacy got to hang out with Brad and Zack. One day they made name badges out of circular strips of leather. Another day they constructed a giant tipi in the middle of the grass near the lodge. It was definitely a more laid back activity and, to both Cyndi and Stacy, it seemed more fun when the boys were around.

On their fifth day in camp, the four of them and some of the other older kids packed a huge lunch and went on an all-day nature walk with Christina and Bobby, another boys counselor with dark curly hair. The two counselors pointed out various plants and told them tips on what to do if they ever got lost in the woods; things like moss always grows on the north side of the tree, you can tell which direction you're going by the sun. The group went up into the hills surrounding the camp and came around a cliff onto a high clearing that had a great view of camp and the surrounding forest. Even Brad and Zack were speechless. They looked down at the camp and saw a lot of the younger kids in the middle of their activities.

"Now I want everyone to look to the south of the camp. See the river down there?" Bobby asked. Several of the kids nodded. "That river runs along Highway 85 for over twenty-five miles. If you ever happen to get lost in the woods, you need to look for the moss or look at the direction of the sun and make your way south. You should come across that river and the highway. State Patrol usually drives down that stretch pretty often and they'll help you. Okay?"

"Oh, so if we wanted to ditch this camp and hitchhike back to civilization that's where we'd go. Good to know," Zack joked in a solemn voice, then grinned. Everyone laughed at that, even the counselors.

"Seriously though, remember that. If you guys ever get lost in the woods around camp. Head south, okay?" Christina explained.

"South. Gotcha," Zack said.

They ate lunch on the cliff while enjoying the view, then headed back to camp. The sun began to go down on their way back and the thick trees in the woods cast long shadows. They were almost home when Counselor Bobby stopped and looked off toward the south.

"Sh-sh-sh-sh you guys. Be quiet a second,"

Bobby whispered. Everyone stopped and looked in the direction Bobby was looking. "You hear that?"

Something was running through the woods about a hundred yards to the south of them. It was too far away to see, but they could all hear the twigs snapping and the underbrush crunching as something ran off away from them.

"Is it a deer?" Christina asked.

"I don't know, maybe," Bobby said. "It sounds too loud to be a deer."

"A bear?"

"God, I hope not," Bobby said.

"What? A bear? Oh my God!" some of the younger kids cried out.

"It's all right. It's all right. Relax," Bobby said loudly and confidently. "Whatever it was, we scared it away. And we're not far from camp so just cool it, okay? Let's keep going."

They began walking again and Zack turned to Brad. "A fuckin' bear, man!" he whispered excitedly.

"I don't think it was a bear," Brad said skeptically.

"What?" Zack asked in disbelief. "What else could it be?"

"I don't know. Maybe a deer. I doubt it was a bear though."

"Whatever, man. That was totally a bear."

Brad and Zack continued to argue almost all the way back to camp, while Stacy rolled her eyes at Cyndi. They made it back without seeing or hearing anymore wildlife.

*　　　*　　　*

Everyone at camp was excited for the next day: swim day. Brad and Zack were also particularly eager to

42

be done with their week of cleanup duties in the mess hall. For the younger kids, the daily activities were swimming lessons and sand castle building on the sandy lake shore. The older kids got to go canoeing and rafting on the lake with Counselor Sheehan and Counselor James.

Sheehan made the announcement at dinner the night before and a resounding cheer echoed through the entire lodge. The whole camp was buzzing with excited conversations about their swimsuits and how they couldn't wait to get into the water.

"Swim days are hands-down *THE* most fun days in camp," Stacy explained to Cyndi.

"Yeah, they bring the barbecue grills down to the shore and make some actually decent burgers," Zack said with wide excited eyes.

"And they build a huge campfire when the sun goes down, and we all tell ghost stories," Stacy said.

"And we get to bring the canoe and the raft way far out on the lake," Brad said. "Only it's too bad we have to go with She-Man."

"Yeah, that does bite," Zack said.

"*Please* try not to piss him off tomorrow," Stacy pleaded to both of them. "I really do not want to deal with him."

"Hey, you think we try piss him off *on purpose?*" Brad asked incredulously.

Cyndi and Stacy shared a look, then said in unison, "YEAH!"

"No, *he's* the one who singles *us* out, okay?" Zack explained.

"You know he's had a stick up his ass since day one," Brad said.

"Since *before* day one," Zack added.

"Yeah!" Brad agreed holding up his hand for a high-five, which Zack roughly returned with an ear-shattering slap. "How's that our fault?"

"All I'm saying is, if you two decide to do something stupid, don't drag me down with you," Stacy warned.

"Me either," Cyndi said. Brad and Zack shrugged.

"Okay, but I'm tellin' ya, no guarantees. The guy's a basket case," Brad said as he began to shovel food into his mouth again. He then turned and looked at Cyndi. "And what the fuck are you complainin' about, Headphones? You barely even talk, how could we get *you* in trouble?"

Cyndi immediately turned red and looked down at her plate.

"Hey!" Stacy immediately shouted, kicking Brad under the table. "Leave her alone, asshole!"

Brad made a sarcastic mocking face at Stacy. Zack began to giggle, and Stacy kicked him too, glaring at him. Zack immediately stopped giggling and concentrated on his dinner.

*　　　*　　　*

After dinner, as they all left the mess hall and headed for their cabins, Stacy held Cyndi back.

"I'll meet you back at the bunk, okay?" she said. Cyndi looked up at Stacy questioningly as she rushed ahead, toward Brad. Zack's hand grabbed Cyndi's shoulder.

"Hey, uh, Cyndi. Right?" he said in a uncharacteristically mature voice.

Cyndi nodded at him mistrustfully.

"Look, I..." he struggled with his words. "I'm sorry about back there. Brad can be a real dick sometimes. Believe me, I know." He smiled sheepishly at her. She gave him a slight smile and started to turn back towards her bunk.

"Wait! Cyndi!" She turned back to him. He ran his fingers through his shiny black hair again and as he struggled for words. "And I'm sorry I...I laughed at you. That was fucked up."

Cyndi could feel her cheeks starting to burn again. She had thought he was kind of cute before, but the times when he was trying to be serious, which were few and far between, he was even cuter. Not only that, he was talking to her *alone*. No cute guy had ever given her this much attention before. She struggled to find her own words.

"Don't worry about it, Zack," she mumbled. She met his eyes for a quick second and saw his warm, crooked smile. Her eyes immediately went to the ground.

"And for what it's worth, I think you're really cool, Cyndi," Zack said to her, with no hesitation at all. She was too embarrassed too respond. "Well, see ya." He turned back toward the lodge and she quickly rushed towards her cabin. She desperately needed to listen to some music and get back into her own comfort zone.

Stacy met up with Brad just after Cyndi and Zack began to talk. She grabbed him by the shoulder and yanked him toward her.

"What's your problem, Brad?" she scolded him.

"What the fuck did I do?" he yelled back.

"You're being a total jerk, that's what! Cyndi's a really cool girl and you keep treating her like shit. Like she doesn't even exist."

"Well, what do you expect? She barely even says one word half the time!"

"She's just shy, okay? And she's my friend."

Brad's only response with a stare full of attitude.

"You know what, I was gonna see if you wanted to hang out tonight, like we *used to* last summer. But now, forget it."

She turned to walk away but Brad grabbed her hand, spinning her back around. She met his stare without a trace of fear.

"I'm sorry, all right? I was just messing around with her, that's all," he said in a sly voice.

"Sure," Stacy said sarcastically, her voice full of disbelief.

"Really," Brad said. He wrapped his arms around her, holding her close. "We can still hang out."

"You gotta apologize to Cyndi first," Stacy said without breaking her stern gaze.

Brad rolled his eyes and sighed, "Fine."

"And you gotta start being nice to her. She's part of our group now."

"Okay, okay!"

"Come on then."

Stacy gave him a quick kiss, broke away from his arms, and pulled him toward the girls' cabin. Cyndi had passed them a short while back, but they caught up with her as she was about to open the door to the cabin.

"Cyndi!" Stacy called out. Cyndi turned around and watched as Stacy practically dragged Brad to the front steps leading into the cabin. She shoved Brad in front of herself and nudged him in the back.

"Hey look, Cyndi," Brad began, glancing back at Stacy. "I was just messing around with you, okay? I didn't mean anything by it."

Cyndi nodded solemnly. Stacy nudged him in the back again. "And you're part of our group now. You, me, Stacy, and Zack. So...if I say mean things to you...you know I'm just kiddin.' Okay? So, we cool?" He held out his hand to her.

Cyndi wasn't convinced at all by his insincere excuse for an apology, but she reached out and shook his hand anyway. "Okay, Brad. We're cool." Frankly, she

46

didn't give a damn if she won Brad over or not. She knew she had a good friend in Stacy, and now Zack also.

Brad smiled at her and turned away from the cabin. Stacy looked at her and rolled her eyes.

"Boys," Stacy sighed. Cyndi laughed a little. "Well, hey, me and Brad are gonna go hang out by the lake for a little while. But if you're bored I think Zack went back to the rec room at the lodge." She said the last sentence in an elbow-nudging voice.

"Yeah, Zack totally has the hots for you," Brad blurted to Cyndi. "He made me promise not to tell you but, fuck'im.'" Cyndi turned red again and laughed nervously.

"You say the nicest things sometimes, you know that?" Stacy said sarcastically to Brad, who only shrugged. "Anyway, you should go down there."

"That's okay. I think I'll go to bed a little early tonight to be ready for Swim Day tomorrow," Cyndi said.

"All right. Be back in a little while."

"Have fun," Cyndi said, mimicking Stacy's previous elbow-nudging tone. Stacy grinned as she and Brad walked off toward the lake with his strong arm around her waist. Cyndi turned and went back into the cabin. She got ready for bed and turned on some tapes, replaying the day's events in her head again and again. She caught herself thinking about Zack over and over and realized she was starting to develop a crush on him, God help her. The rest of the girls came in eventually. Morgan had to practically drag an annoyed Stacy in at the last minute before lights out.

"Move it, Weston," Morgan yelled. "You can continue your make out session in the morning." Some of the younger girls gave Stacy an, "Ewww."

Cyndi giggled at her as she walked up. Stacy just smiled, shook her head, and climbed up to her top bunk out of sight. Within a minute, the lights were out and Cyndi was back to her music, letting it carry her off to sleep.

Chapter Six:

Swim Day

Brad and Zack were really nice and talkative with Cyndi all through breakfast. They talked to her about music mostly, asking if she had heard of rock bands that they liked. They tried their hardest to stump her with a band, artist, or song that they knew, but were unsuccessful. She knew all of the bands they brought up, and liked most of them. Then, she flipped their game around on them and recited a long string of band and artist names that completely stumped them.

"Damn. When it comes to music, you really know your shit," Brad said honestly impressed. She smiled at him and shrugged.

Counselor Sheehan stood up and announced that anyone over the age of twelve was to meet with him on the deck outside the lodge after breakfast so they could get started on their canoe/raft trip.

After breakfast, they all changed into their swimsuits and gathered on the deck. Cyndi felt self-conscious in her new white polka-dotted two-piece swimsuit. Stacy came out in her own bright pink two-piece swimsuit looking gorgeous and confident. Cyndi silently wished she could look as good as Stacy. Brad and Zack came up in their own brightly colored swim trunks, ogling them and making lewd gestures. Cyndi blushed bright red and let her crimped hair hang low over her eyes. Stacy rolled her eyes and laughed at the boys.

Counselor Sheehan came out of the lodge wearing a tight yellow muscle-shirt that showed off his considerable pecs and arms. He lectured them about the importance of sunscreen and made them all take a few squirts of generic sunscreen from a dirty old bottle that looked suspiciously like a recycled ketchup dispenser from the mess hall. Stacy, who was grossed out by the thought of a communal sunscreen bottle, only took a pea sized amount. Cyndi didn't think Stacy would get much of a sunburn anyway, she was already pretty tan.

Once they were all sunscreened up, Sheehan led them over to the equipment shed, lecturing them the whole way. The shed looked like a miniature barn made of rusty old sheet metal. He unlocked the padlock and pulled away the chain on the doors. The doors slid open with an agonizing metal screech that made all of the kids wince. Without hesitating or pausing his sermon, he strode in and began handing life jackets back to the kid behind him.

"Now everyone is going to wear a life jacket at all times," Sheehan droned. "Once we're out on the water, you do not take your life jacket off for any reason. I don't care if we're in the middle of the lake or if we're five feet from the shore."

The life jackets came down the assembly line and Stacy was handed a faded yellow life jacket that looked like it may be on its final voyage. She held it away from her as if it were a dirty old sock she'd found on the side of a road.

"Gag me with a spoon," she said disgustedly.

Cyndi looked at it and shrugged.

"Brad and Zack," Sheehan yelled back to them. He walked out of the shed with a stack of paddles in his arms.

"Sir! Yes, Sir!" Brad yelled in a military voice. Zack saluted, and Sheehan ignored the jokes. Sheehan walked out of the shed and over to the wooden canoe rack next to the shed.

"Help me pull the canoe off the rack." The raft was on the bottom of the rack below the canoe. Sheehan handed the paddles to some of the younger kids, then unlocked the bike lock that had been looped around one of the canoe's seats. He lifted it from the bottom and tilted one end toward Zack, who grabbed it and began dragging it off the rack. Sheehan guided the other end down to Brad and instructed him to bring it down to the dock near the main lodge. They did so without a joke or complaint. Sheehan unlocked another bike lock from the old orange raft, had two other younger boys in their group carry it down to the dock, and led the rest of the group down.

Once they were all down at the docks, he tied up the canoe and the raft, showing them how to tie figure-eight shaped cleat hitch knots that would properly secure a boat to a dock. Everyone was getting antsy to get onto the water and chattered excitedly over Sheehan's lecture. He finally stopped talking and waited for a second while the noise level from the group escalated.

Finally, in a loud voice he said, "The longer you keep talking, the longer we'll wait to get out on the lake." A classic teacher trick, the chattering ceased almost instantly. "Okay then, Zack you're in the raft, Brad you're in the canoe."

"Awww," Zack whined.

"Come on, man," Brad protested. Sheehan ignored their protests and continued his lecture.

51

After a life jacket check and an awkward wobbly boarding, they were out on the lake. Cyndi and Stacy had opted to stay near Brad in the canoe. Zack asked Cyndi if she wanted to ride next to him in the raft, but she shyly declined in order to stay near Stacy. Stacy nudged and pushed her toward the raft and Zack.

"Go with him," she said softly through clenched teeth.

"No," Cyndi laughed nervously.

Sheehan never stopped droning from the head of the canoe. He went completely overkill with directions as if he were talking down to them.

"Now, if the canoe is turning too far to the left, you paddle on the left side, got it? Paddle on the opposite side you want to turn. Good, now stroke, stroke." Several kids began to giggle and snicker at this but Sheehan was oblivious. He looked back at Brad, who was seated at the back of the canoe and paddling diligently. "Nice stroke, Brad." Cyndi and Stacy, sitting in front of Brad, looked back at him. He gave them a horrified expression and they burst out laughing.

They paddled out onto the middle of the lake. At one point Cyndi looked back and saw that the main lodge and the kids playing on the shoreline looked tiny from this distance. As she turned to face forward again, she caught Zack looking at her from the back of the raft. His face suddenly took on an exaggerated strained expression and he pretended to struggle with his paddling as if he were in the middle of a huge body-building workout. She laughed at him and he smiled back at her. He was such a goof. Then he lifted his paddle out of the water and laid it on his lap. He leaned back, stretched his legs out, and reclined with his hands behind his head. Counselor James, who was at the head of the raft, looked back and saw Zack joking around.

"What are you doing, Zack? You're holding us

up!" James yelled back at him. Zack immediately jumped and put his paddle back in the water.

"Sorry, sorry, sorry," Zack mumbled as he started paddling again.

Sheehan turned around and looked at him. "You getting too tired back there? I can get one of the girls to cover for you," he said condescendingly. Several of the kids started to laugh at Zack.

"I'm fine, I'm fine," Zack yelled defensively.

"Then quit slacking," Sheehan yelled as he turned back to his own rowing.

Zack made a face mocking Sheehan and the kids that laughed at him.

They rowed out to a small cove near the south side of the lake. Thick woods surrounded the cove and it was really quiet. Sheehan had everyone turn and look back at the camp which was now only a tiny speck, barely discernible in the distance.

While everyone marveled at how far away they were from camp, Brad looked around at the cove. He had noticed a stream that branched off from the cove and flowed far back into the woods.

"Hey, where does that stream go?" Brad asked interrupting Sheehan in the middle of a speech about the camp's history and founder Kent Carver.

"What? Oh that? It's just a little stream. Probably leads off to the river along the highway," Sheehan said dismissively. "Anyway as I was saying..." Sheehan continued but Brad wasn't listening. He was busy staring at the stream, trying to see where it went.

A few minutes later, they were paddling straight across the lake toward some steep rock cliffs that jutted out almost all the way to the water's edge and went up thirty feet into the air. Sheehan told them about the various Indian tribes that were said to have lived in this area hundreds of years ago.

They reached the shore and paddled right up to the sand. The counselors allowed the restless kids to get out and stretch their legs in the woods for a minute before heading back to camp. And that was where the trouble started.

Brad and Zack rushed around the back of the cliffs and began climbing their way up, despite the fact that they were only wearing flip-flops and not their regular tennis shoes. They made their way up the jagged, lichen covered backside of the cliffs and reached the small plateau at the top.

"Check it out!" Brad yelled. They looked around in amazement at the surrounding woods and the lake. They could see several coves dotting the opposite edge of the lake. On this side of the lake they could only see the treetops surrounding the cliffs. Zack picked up a golf ball sized rock and heaved it far out into the lake. He made sure to throw it where none of the counselors could see. The rock sailed out and made a tiny plunk in one of the small, choppy waves.

Brad looked down and saw Cyndi and Stacy walking along in the woods in the middle of some girl talk conversation.

"Hey, Stace! Cyndi!" he called down to the girls.

Stacy and Cyndi both looked around for a second before realizing they had to look practically straight up.

"Hey! How did you get up there?" she yelled back, shielding her eyes from the sun.

"Come on up here! You gotta see this view!"

"Yeah, come on!" Zack yelled out in agreement.

"Are you crazy?" she yelled up at them. "I'm not going up there!"

"Come *on!*" Brad insisted.

"Sheehan's gonna kill you guys!"

54

"Is he down there?"

Stacy looked around and pointed to the other side of the cliff near the shore.

"Go around back, you can make it up!" Brad pointed to the backside of the cliffs.

"No way!"

"Fine! Your loss!" They turned back to the view.

"Man, it gives me the heebie-jeebies looking down," Zack shuddered.

"You see Sheehan down there at all?" Brad asked.

Zack took a small step toward the edge and peered down, looking for Sheehan. Brad crept up behind him and Zack didn't even see it coming.

"No, I don't see him. He must be--"

"OOPS!" Brad yelled as he suddenly grabbed Zack by the shoulders, pushed him forward a foot, then immediately yanked him back away from the edge. Zack screamed in terror and fell back onto his butt on the plateau, while Brad erupted with laughter.

Zack sat in shock for a minute, breathing hard. All the color had drained from his face and he gazed up at Brad in white shock.

"What the *FUCK*, man?!" he gasped.

Brad used two fingers to mime Zack's legs as he fell off the cliff. He mocked Zack's scream in a high falsetto, and his fall with a fart noise from his tongue. Zack was outraged.

"*What the fuck is wrong with you?! You could've fuckin' killed me!*"

Zack got to his feet and immediately went for Brad.

"Uh-oh, what are you gonna do?" Brad mocked.

"*It's not fuckin' funny!*" Zack screamed at him with real anger. He grabbed him and they started

55

struggling.

"HEY!" Sheehan's voice suddenly boomed from the ground. They immediately stopped and looked down. "YOU TWO! GET DOWN HERE, IMMEDIATELY!"

They both sheepishly made their way down the jagged cliff side without talking to each other. Sheehan waited on the ground, his face growing red and his jaw clenching.

"James, can you get everyone back on board please?" Sheehan asked in a calm voice.

"Sure," James said quietly. He looked nervously at Sheehan, then began rounding up kids. "Okay, okay, everyone back to the boats."

Brad and Zack came around the corner of the cliffs with sulking faces and walked up to Sheehan.

"Do you have any idea how dangerous that was? Why do you two *insist* on trying to get yourselves killed?"

Stacy and Cyndi walked by at that moment, watching them and listening to their conversation. Stacy saw how angry and red in the face Sheehan was. Without thinking, she let the words bubble up out of her mouth.

"To be fair, Counselor Sheehan, you didn't say we *couldn't* go up there," she blurted.

"Stay out of this, Weston!" he yelled at her without missing a beat.

She immediately wished she hadn't blurted out that last remark. She felt like cupping a hand over her mouth. At the same time, she was angered by his sudden outburst on her. Cyndi stared up at her in amazement.

"Just sayin,'" Stacy grumbled under her breath.

"You want cleanup duty?" he snapped. Apparently she hadn't said it quiet enough.

Stacy shook her head violently. Cleanup duty in

the kitchen was the most disgusting punishment she could imagine. Sheehan gestured toward the boats with an angry swipe of his hand and she rushed off toward them with Cyndi close behind.

Sheehan took a deep breath and stared at them for a moment. When he finally spoke he struggled to keep his anger in, keeping his voice low and calm.

"I'm not gonna yell at you. I don't want to hear your excuses. I just want you two to go for one day without doing something *stupid*, okay?" He said the word *stupid* through a tightly clenched jaw and white knuckled fists. Brad noticed a vein popping out on Sheehan's forehead as he and Zack nodded. "Why do you-- How many times--" He struggled to find the words but realized it would be useless. He let out an exasperated sigh and motioned for them to get on. "Just get on board." They looked up at him surprised, then cautiously walked to the shoreline. Zack kicked Brad in the shin as they walked. Brad shoved him back.

"Hey!" Sheehan cried. "One more screw up and there's gonna be serious consequences!" They continued walking toward the boats.

Sheehan was unusually quiet as they all rowed back to camp. Some of the younger kids were chattering but the four oldest kids stayed quiet. They were out in the middle of the lake when Brad leaned forward and kissed Stacy on the cheek.

"Thanks for sticking up for us back there," he said smiling at her.

"I can't believe you said that," Cyndi told her in a low voice.

"I can't either," Stacy said, angrily turning towards Brad. "You're gonna get me in big trouble, you know that?"

"Uh-huh. I love you, too," he said, kissing her again.

Stacy faced forward again. Brad and Zack were just magnets for trouble and she hated how she always somehow got mixed up in it just by association. Nevertheless, she already felt herself warming back up to him, like she always did.

Zack felt alone at the back of the raft. He was still pissed at Brad for nearly pushing him to his death, and was desperately trying to think of a prank to pull to get his revenge. Brad was a cool guy but sometimes he took things too far. Zack looked over, saw him kiss Stacy on the cheek, and was immediately jealous. *Brad* was the one who started this, *Brad* was the one who didn't have to be separated from the girls, and *Brad* was also the one who just didn't give a shit.

Zack pushed his paddle angrily against the water and it sent up a small splash behind the raft. He watched the splash and the wheels in his head started turning. He pushed down harder and a bigger splash went up. Over in the canoe, he saw Brad paddling and smiling smugly.

How awesome would it be to splash some nice cold lake water on that smug face? he thought maliciously. The plan was instantly cemented into his mind.

Zack paddled harder, pushing the raft ahead to catch up with the canoe. It took a few minutes but the raft finally pulled up next to the canoe. He glanced over at the canoe, aiming his splash. They pulled ahead of the canoe slightly and Brad was in splashing range. Zack tensed, feeling his heartbeat speed up nervously.

All at once, he yelled out, "OOPS!" the same word Brad had used on him. He shoved his paddle against the water with all his strength, meaning to spray Brad with so much water that he would be left completely soaked. Instead, he put too much strength into it and compromised his aim. A wave of cold lake water splashed up onto an unsuspecting Stacy.

Stacy immediately gasped deeply and stood up out of her seat. The canoe began to rock unsteadily.

"Zack!" she screamed at him. "I'm gonna kill you!"

In a dripping wet rage, Stacy yanked Brad's paddle out of his hand and began swinging wildly at Zack. Sheehan turned around and began shouting at her.

"STACY! SIT DOWN!" But she was past the point of no return. Sheehan continued to scream while Cyndi and several of the other kids hung on for dear life in the violently rocking canoe. Zack also stood up, trying to defend himself from Stacy's attacks, and the raft started to rock unsteadily.

"KNOCK IT OFF! BOTH OF YOU!" James yelled.

Stacy swung wildly and the paddle connected with the palm of Zack's hand. He clapped his other hand instinctively on the other side of the paddle and tried to yank it away from her. They both suddenly gave a great yank. Both the canoe and the raft tipped over. Kids screamed as they flew into the air and crashed down into the cold lake water.

On the far side of the canoe, Cyndi went flying. Her arms pinwheeled wildly before she plunged into the water. She went down face first and paddled wildly, but her life jacket was already bringing her up to the surface again. She came up along with the rest of the campers and counselors, coughing and sputtering, gasping for breath. She felt the sting of water up her nose.

Stacy was a few feet away, gasping and screaming at Zack. "ZACK, I HATE YOU!!!"

Sheehan was still near the front of the canoe screaming, "EVERYONE STAY CALM! STAY CALM!" James hung onto the raft, trying to flip it over, but several of the younger kids were clinging to the sides and weighing it down.

Brad began to splash a very disoriented Zack. "Nice going, dumb-shit!" His first big splash hit Zack in the mouth right as he gasped for breath. He began to cough violently. He splashed Brad back defensively. Cyndi, Stacy, and several other kids were caught in the crossfire of their splash war. Stacy joined in and began splashing at Zack.

James flipped the raft over and climbed in. He held out a hand to Sheehan, and pulled him up also. Sheehan looked down at the splash war and suddenly bellowed, "ENOUGH!!!"

Everyone stopped splashing and looked up at him with wide eyes.

"YOU THREE!" He pointed down at Brad, Zack, and Stacy, they looked up at him stunned. "KNOCK IT OFF RIGHT NOW! You're gonna flip the canoe over, bail out all the water, and paddle us back to camp right now! And if I hear just one peep out of either of you, you'll be swimming back to camp. I mean it!"

Brad and Stacy glared at Zack. Sheehan watched them with fire in his eyes as they slowly swam around the canoe and began to turn it upright again. James helped some of the younger kids back onto the raft.

Zack felt all eyes glaring down at him, and the beginnings of a nervous stomach ache as he tried to turn the canoe over. This time, he knew he had pushed things too far.

Chapter Seven:

The Punishment and The Plan

It was a long silent ride back to the shore. Brad and Stacy did all the paddling in the canoe, while Zack paddled the raft. All of the other kids were too afraid to talk, they didn't want to upset Sheehan who stared out angrily at the water ahead of him and said nothing. Cyndi tried giving Stacy a few consoling looks. Stacy only glanced at her, shook her head, and sighed in frustration.

They pulled the boats up to the dock and began to tie them down. The kids rushed off the boats, eager to get away from the fuming Sheehan.

"You three wait up on the deck and dry off, then you get into my office pronto," Sheehan barked out at them. The three of them sauntered away looking down at their feet. Cyndi watched them go and reluctantly followed the other kids over to the shoreline where the younger kids were playing.

Counselor Ashley was sitting on the sand, acting as one of the lifeguards for all the young kids playing in the shallow water. She watched as Brad, Zack, and Stacy stormed off toward the lodge. Cyndi and the others walked off the dock and most of them immediately went right back into the water with the younger kids.

"Hey, Cyndi," Ashley called out to her, waving her over.

Cyndi looked up surprised, then smiled and walked over.

"What happened?" Ashley asked her in a low voice, the kind of voice she used when she knew there was major gossip.

Cyndi shook her head, "They're in trouble. Big trouble."

"What'd they do?"

"They flipped over the canoe and the raft."

Ashley began to laugh, then suppressed it as she saw Sheehan stomping down the dock toward the lodge. She didn't want to get on Sheehan's bad side, especially when he looked mad enough to tear down the whole main lodge.

*   *   *

Zack tried apologizing to Stacy as they went up the stairs into the main lodge.

"Look, Stacy. I'm sorry," he pleaded with her. "I meant to hit Brad with the water, not you. I'm sorry, okay?"

She simply ignored him and marched into Sheehan's office. James followed them to the outside of the office and stood there, guarding them.

"Have a seat, you know the drill," James said.

Stacy sat down in the chair on the left, Brad sat in the middle, and Zack sat on the right. Stacy crossed her arms over her chest and tried to rub away her goosebumps. She was still cold from the splash and the plunge into the lake.

While they waited for Sheehan to come in,

62

Stacy glanced over at Brad. He kept a defiant nonchalant look on his face and stared around the room idly, as if he were simply bored with the whole thing. She looked past him at Zack and saw him mouthing the words, "I'm sorry," to her.

"Didn't I tell you morons not to get me in trouble?" Stacy growled at him through clenched teeth.

"No talking!" James snapped from outside. Stacy glared at Zack for a second then faced the front of the room again.

Sheehan walked in slowly and shut the door with a quiet click. Brad knew that was a bad sign. He had dealt with Sheehan enough over the years to know that if Sheehan acted, or at least *tried* to act calm and collected, it usually meant that he had some harsh punishment up his sleeve. When he was mad and raging, all he usually did was yell, which was nothing Brad couldn't handle. That tiny click of the office door closing told Brad everything he needed to know, this was gonna be bad.

Sheehan sat down at his desk and folded his hands calmly in front of his face. He looked back and forth at them individually, savoring the questioning fearful looks on their faces.

"You know, I'm glad that happened out in the middle of the lake, instead of near the shore," he began in a polite conversational voice. "The nice long ride back really gave me a chance to cool down. Gave me a chance to think. I thought to myself, what is wrong with you three? And the answer is simple. You're spoiled. And all you really need is the right punishment. Now if that had happened near the shore, I'd probably be on the phone calling your parents right now and you'd probably be going home. And once you got there you wouldn't be punished at all. You'd just go off Scot-free and have a nice rest of your summer. So the question is: am I gonna call your parents? No. I'm gonna let you spend the rest of your time here at camp."

Brad and Zack glanced at each other suspiciously.

"But instead of going off to your daily activities, you're gonna go off to work," Sheehan continued cheerily. "You will have cleanup duty in the mess hall every day after every meal. You will clean the bathrooms in your cabins every day. And you're gonna clean the lodge everyday. Whenever we have fun days like Swim Day or Game Day, you get a nice relaxing day off, sitting up in the mess hall. Get the picture?"

Brad, Stacy, and Zack were all taken aback. Their mouths had dropped open listening to Sheehan's punishment.

"I know this is your last summer here, and I really want to make it count," Sheehan said with fake enthusiasm. He clapped his hands together, "So, since this is swim day, that means you get a day off from your work. Lucky you! But starting tomorrow, you better get ready because it's gonna be a long summer."

They were all speechless. Sheehan smiled at them, then the smile dropped off his face and he let his true expression show through the facade. "Now get up to the mess hall. And if I catch you outside at all, the septic system has been acting kinda funky lately, and I'm sure you won't mind digging it up. Now get out."

He pointed toward the door, his eyes blazing. They all sat there for a shocked second, then Brad got up to leave, scraping his chair loudly against the floor behind him. The others snapped out of their trances and they followed Brad out. James went in after they exited and Brad heard Sheehan begin to laugh from behind the door. Brad's fists clenched and his blood began to boil.

*   *   *

Cyndi left the beach and snuck away to see what happened to Stacy and the boys. She had been sitting out on the shore with only her feet in the water, desperately wishing she had her headphones on. She felt like such a loser just sitting out here in her swimsuit all by herself. She kept glancing back up toward the lodge every few minutes to see if Stacy, Zack, Brad, or anyone would come out. No one came.

She heard secretive giggling off to her left, and turned just in time to see two slightly younger girls pointing at her and whispering some snide comment to each other. A second after they noticed Cyndi looking at them, they immediately turned around, trying to act casual.

That did it, she got up and began walking toward the lodge.

"Where you going, Cyndi?" a harsh female voice burst out suddenly. Cyndi jumped and turned to see Morgan sitting a few feet away in a plastic lawn chair with a suspicious look on her face.

"Uh...bathroom," Cyndi mumbled and immediately ran up to the lodge. She knew Morgan wouldn't be able to argue with her about that. Morgan's eyes narrowed as she watched her go. Then there was a sudden splashing and several little girls screaming. A group of little boys had decided to start splashing them wildly. Morgan immediately forgot about Cyndi, put her whistle up to her lips, and ran toward the boys in full-on disciplinarian mode.

Cyndi walked into the lodge, looking around cautiously. She crept into the main room quiet as a cat, and looked toward Sheehan's office. The door was closed and she couldn't hear a thing behind it.

All of a sudden, she heard a muffled voice, either Brad or Zack's, saying, "Okay, okay!" It came from the mess hall.

Cyndi walked toward the noise, and looked down into the mess hall. Brad, Zack, and Stacy were all in there just sitting down at one of the tables. They all looked miserable. Stacy looked up and saw Cyndi standing there. Her eyes went wide like she wanted to warn her about something. Without warning, Sheehan stepped in front of the doorway and stopped. He looked just as surprised to see Cyndi as she was to see him.

Stacy gave her one last hopeless look as he closed the door tightly behind him with a resonating boom.

"Can I help you?" Sheehan asked in a commanding voice meant to intimidate her. It worked. She glanced up at him and shook her head no. "Let me give you some advice: stay away from those three. They're only gonna get you into trouble." His eyes were big and he spoke clearly and slowly, talking down to her as if explaining something important to a small child. Every word he said to her was dripping with condescending, power-tripping authority, and for the first time she got a little taste of why her friends hated this man so much.

Cyndi nodded at him and walked back up the stairs heading out of the lodge. He stood by the doorway and watched her leave, waiting until he heard the lodge door open and close quietly as she went back outside. With a sigh, he walked back up to his office.

Cyndi looked for Morgan as she went down the steps. She was out on the far end of the docks whistling at some rowdy boys. The coast was clear. Cyndi turned and sprinted back to her cabin for her Walkman. There was no way she was going to spend the rest of the day by herself with no one to talk to and no music to blast away all the inner voices that wouldn't stop telling her how awkward she looked and felt.

*   *   *

The hours dragged by painfully for them that day. They sat in silence in the mess hall for what felt like forever. Stacy stared down at the swirling patterns in the wood on the table. She brooded and listened to the noise of kids playing outside at the lake. When she finally looked up at the clock, she saw that they had only been in here for forty-five minutes. Her eyes stayed on the second hand of the clock, watching time drag by.

Sometime later, Brad got up and Stacy watched him walk over to the window. She hated him and Zack for getting her into this trouble. She hated how they always had to be joking around and acting so stupid. And she especially hated the detached, unaffected look on Brad's face as he stared out the window. How could he not be the least bit affected by this? The whole rest of the summer was ruined for all of them, and it was all his fault. He just sat there solemnly staring out at the lake. He stared out for about fifteen minutes, then sat back down again.

Now the sun was starting to go down, giving off that warm, slanting, afternoon glow that Stacy loved. It depressed her even more. She heard kids still playing outside, and wondered what Cyndi was doing right now. *Probably listening to her Walkman*, she guessed.

Zack, who was tracing the wood patterns in the table with his finger, suddenly began whistling an Ozzy Osbourne song, "Crazy Train," through his teeth. He barely got past the part about the *millions of people* before Stacy snapped at him.

"Will you please shut up?" she said in a low voice, giving him an icy glare.

He stared at her, trying to think of some witty comment. Then he sighed and shrugged, deciding it wasn't worth it to fight with her.

Brad got up and stared out the window again. Stacy saw him narrow his eyes a few times, like he was thinking about something. There was something cute about the way he looked when he was thinking really hard, and despite the anger she had for him, she felt herself reluctantly warming back up to him all over again.

Zack started whistling again, this time "Mr. Crowley." Stacy, who had been resting her head in the palm of her hand, suddenly slammed her hand down on the table again and glared at him.

"What? You don't like Ozzy?" Zack asked, smiling.

She glared at him for a moment. "You're an idiot," she finally said dryly.

"Cyndi likes Ozzy," he said dreamily and sighed, looking up at the ceiling. Stacy rubbed her hand over her face, exasperated.

"Oh my God, I hate you so much, Zack," she muttered.

"Oh, come on, Stacy. It's not that bad. It could've been way worse," he said.

"Don't even talk to me right now, okay? I don't even want to hear your stupid voice," she blurted at him.

"Look, let me talk to Sheehan," he said. "I'll...I'll talk to him...Set things straight, y'know? Tell him to go easy on you...I'll tell him--"

"It doesn't matter *what* you say to that motherfucker," Brad interrupted, still facing the window. His tone was cold and full of hatred. He turned from the window and faced them. "He won't listen to you, or me, or anyone else. And if you do say anything to him, it'll only make it worse, for all of us."

"Why do you say that?" Zack asked, honestly curious.

"Because this time, we've pushed him too far," Brad replied sitting down. "I've been messing with people all my life. You know I love to mess around with people, just really get a rise out of 'em. Most of the time all they want is for you to just leave them the hell alone. That's just the way it used to be with the She-Man. It was always, 'I'm calling your parents,' and, 'I'll have your ass thrown out of this camp so fast...'" Brad did a pretty good imitation of Sheehan's voice, which brought a smile to Zack's face. He copied his mannerisms, like his wide eyes and hand gestures, and his condescending vocal inflections perfectly.

"But this...this is different. He doesn't want us to leave him alone anymore. He wants to make us suffer, and he'll do it too. Because to him it's not about just getting out of the game anymore. It's about winning it. You watch, he'll make sure the rest of our summer here is Total. Complete. Hell."

"Yeah, and because of you, I get dragged into it too. Thank you so much! Way to go, guys!" Stacy said sarcastically.

"That's true. I *did* get you into this, but what if I told you I have a way I could get you out?"

"How, Brad? How can you possibly '*get me out*'?"

"By getting us *out*. Tonight we pack up our things and we just get the fuck outta' this camp."

Stacy and Zack sat in stunned silence for a second.

"You're out of your mind, Brad," Stacy finally said with a dismissive wave of her hand.

"Yeah, what are you talking about, man?" Zack chimed in skeptically.

"It's real easy, I got it all figured out," Brad began. "Tonight while they're all out at the campfire, we sneak into She-Man's office and take the keys for that

69

canoe rack--"

Zack sighed reluctantly, "Yeah, I don't thin--"

"Hear me out, hear me out! We take the key, then go to bed just like everyone else. We wait till late, late tonight after everyone's asleep. Then we'll take the raft off that canoe rack and some paddles, and go out onto the lake--"

"Being stuck out on the lake isn't exactly--"

"Shut up! Let me finish! We're *not* gonna be stuck out on the middle of the lake. You remember that stream we saw earlier today? The one that drained out of the lake in that little, uh, cove area? We'll paddle down that and it'll empty out into the river. She-Man even said so. And you remember what Bobby said about the river? It flows along the highway. From there we can get off the raft and we can either walk or hitch a ride to the nearest town and call our parents to come pick us up."

Brad finished and sat there grinning at Stacy and Zack, who shared a skeptical look. The smile slowly left Brad's face as he realized he hadn't sold them at all.

"What do you not understand about this?" Brad asked.

"Umm, well...it's--" Zack started carefully.

"It's insane," Stacy said flatly. "You can't be serious."

"Oh, I'm serious. You bet your ass I'm serious."

"Why don't we just call our parents from here? Why go to all that trouble?"

"You wanna try calling your parents? Go ahead. But hey, save your quarter, because here's what they're gonna say. 'Now Stacy, you're just being silly. We'll see you at the end of the summer, mm'kay? Bye.' Stace, they sent us here for the past six years to get rid of us. We have to do something drastic or they'll never come get us."

"And you think we'll just be in no trouble at all

once we get home? I don't think s--" Stacy started.

"I've got news for ya, babe, you're already in deep shit," Brad interrupted. "Here's the situation we're all in right now. You've got two choices. You can stay here in kiddie-camp for the next few *weeks* and clean up everyone else's shit, literally. Sheehan and all the other little fuckers'll be laughing their asses off at you the whole time. Or you can come with me, *tonight*, and we can all go home. Back to our normal lives. Think of how nice it would be to just spend the summer at home with your friends and all your stuff. To not have to wake up at the ass-crack of dawn and go play a bunch of kiddie games and do little sissy arts and crafts projects. Come on, you guys, we're too fucking old to be here!"

"I know, man, but my parents will kill me," Zack protested. Brad saw Stacy looking down at the table considering his plan, the wheels turning in her head. Zack still needed some convincing.

"Your parents won't do shit to you," Brad countered. "Neither will yours. What's the worst they'll do, ground you for a week? Oooh! Personally, I'd rather sit in my room at home for a week than spend a day being Sheehan's little slaves." Zack shrugged. Brad knew he was winning him over.

"And as for Sheehan," Brad continued, beginning to laugh. "We'll never have to see or deal with his sorry ass again. He can spend the rest of his pathetic life here, remembering how *we* got the best of him. Knowing that no matter how much power he gets at this dump, there'll always be those few kids that just won't put up with his shit. I mean it, guys. Let's go home."

Zack and Stacy looked at each other again, less skeptically than last time. If Stacy had looked totally convinced, that would have done it for Zack. He would be all for Brad's crazy escape plan. But Brad saw a flicker of doubt in the way Stacy narrowed her eyes, and

Zack turned back to him.

"You're crazy, man," he laughed at him, partially believing this was one of Brad's classic jokes. Even after all the years he'd spent with Brad, he still never really could tell when Brad was joking or not. Brad was a great liar, and he could still frequently get Zack to believe some of the crazy things he told him. Last summer, Brad actually convinced Zack that he saw an alligator in the lake. It took an hour of Brad telling the same convincing story over and over. Once Zack finally gave in and said, *'Really?'* in a completely convinced tone, Brad burst out laughing.

"You don't think I'm serious?" Brad asked. "Okay." He shrugged, got up from the table, and walked toward the door leading back out into the lodge.

"Where you goin'?" Zack asked still laughing.

Brad opened the door a crack and peered out, checking both ways quickly. He slipped out before Zack could even yell, "Hey!" The door closed with a soft click.

"You think he's really serious?" Zack asked Stacy. She shrugged.

"If he gets us in more trouble today, I *will* kill him," Stacy said gravely.

"I'll help," Zack chuckled. He thought silently for a second. "You know what I think? Maybe Sheehan pushed *him* too far this time. Maybe they both pushed *each other* too far, y'know?" That caught Stacy off guard. It was probably the most insightful thing she had ever heard Zack, the king of fart jokes and other vulgarities, say in the entire six years she'd known him. She stared at him with a bit more respect than she had ever given him before, thinking that maybe he was smarter than he let on.

"Yeah, that's what I'm afraid of," she muttered.

A few minutes later the door clicked open again

and Brad snuck in. He glanced over his shoulder one last time and pulled the door shut with an almost inaudible click.

"What was that all about?" Zack asked.

Brad walked back to the table without a hint of a joke on his face. He walked right up and laid two small copper colored pieces of metal on the table. He looked back up at Stacy and Zack.

"Still think I'm not serious?" he asked.

Zack recognized the unmistakable shape of the key to the equipment shed and the key to the bike lock around the raft. He stared at Brad in disbelief.

"Did you just *steal* this from Sheehan's office?" he asked amazed.

"Two A.M. Tonight. I'm gettin' the fuck out of here, with or without you guys," he said. He snatched the key out of Zack's hand, then went back to stare out the window at the lake and the setting sun. He went over the escape plan in his mind. Zack and Stacy sat in silence, trying to decide whether or not to follow him tonight.

Chapter Eight:

The Escape

Cyndi felt the bed moving and woke up groggily. She looked around squinting, trying to get her bearings. Even after a week she still wasn't used to waking up here at camp instead of in her own bed at home. She remembered where she was and realized it was only Stacy moving around up there. Sometime during the night her headphones had slipped off and the thin metal band had dug into her ear. She had no idea what time it was, but figured it must be late because her Walkman had finished its tape long ago.

She remembered how painfully boring and awkward her afternoon and evening had been. They had all eaten burgers on the lake shore, and Counselor Sheehan had built a big campfire right on the beach. Everyone hung out in their own little groups talking and playing, having a great time as the sun set across the lake. She hung out near counselor Ashley, tried to blend in, and thought over and over how much fun the night would have been if Stacy, Zack, and Brad were there with her.

All of the counselors had told ghost stories as

the campers all sat around the campfire on the sandy shore of the lake. Most of the stories had been totally cliché, and kept clean for the benefit of the little kids who looked absolutely terrified. Cyndi stared into the fire as Counselor Bobby finished a badly told Hook-on-the-Door-Handle story.

"Okay, okay, I've got one," Counselor Ashley spoke up. "And this one is true. It happened a long time ago, right here at Camp Kikawa. There was--"

Counselor Sheehan suddenly cleared his throat loudly and she stopped in mid-sentence. Cyndi looked up and watched suspiciously as Sheehan gave her a slight scolding shake of his head.

"Umm..." she continued, trying to think up something fast. "There were some bad kids who didn't do what they were told and got sent home. So they had to miss all the fun. The end." She finished with a smile. Several of the older kids booed her. Cyndi narrowed her eyes, watching Sheehan suspiciously.

He spoke up then, starting a predictable, unemotional rendition of the Calls-Are-Coming-From-Inside-the-House story. Cyndi stood up and whispered to Morgan that she felt tired and was heading back to her bunk. She walked back alone, settled into her bunk, and listened to some tapes.

A few minutes before lights out, Stacy was finally escorted in by Morgan. She trudged back to her bunk with her head down. She glanced at Cyndi as she climbed up to her own bunk. Cyndi immediately set her headphones down and stood up to talk to her.

"What happened to you guys?" she asked, intensely curious.

"You don't wanna know," Stacy mumbled to her.

"LIGHTS OUT! No talking!" Morgan yelled from the front of the room, looking directly at Stacy and Cyndi. Several of the younger girls grumbled. Stacy shrugged at Cyndi and turned over to face the window. Even if she had been able to talk to Cyndi, she wasn't really in the mood. She was deep in thought, contemplating whether or not to sneak out of camp with Brad and Zack.

Cyndi, feeling dejected, had put her headphones back on and laid back down.

Now Stacy was climbing down carefully, trying hard not to wake anyone up. She managed to get down without shaking the creaky old bunk bed too much. Cyndi watched her climb down and noticed that she was fully clothed with a tiny pair of shorts and her pink mesh shirt on over her pink swimsuit top. Her big hoop earrings, head band, and bracelets were also already on. Stacy stood in front of the bed watching Morgan. She stood there for a full minute, listening to Morgan's rhythmic snoring, then she reached back to the top bunk and silently took her backpack off the top bunk. Holding it in front of her, she began tiptoeing toward the bathroom.

"Hey," Cyndi whispered loudly at her. Stacy nearly jumped out of her skin, spinning around to face her. She put her hand over her chest and sighed silently.

"Shh," she whispered.

"What are you doing?" Cyndi whispered at her. Stacy glanced back at Morgan, then leaned in and cupped her hand over Cyndi's ear.

"You never saw me," Stacy whispered in her ear. "I'm leaving."

"What? Where are you going?" Cyndi asked her shocked.

"The less you know the better, okay?" Stacy said. She handed her a ripped piece of notebook paper with her phone number written on it in her own flowery penmanship. "Look, Cyndi, you've been a great friend. When you get outta' here this summer, call me and we'll go to the mall or something, okay? I gotta go."

"Wait? What? Tell me where you're going!"

"Just...Quiet, okay? I'm going off with Brad and Zack. We're getting outta' here before they make our lives a living hell." Cyndi stared at her shocked and disappointed. She felt the rest of her summer crumbling.

"You guys are leaving?"

Stacy nodded.

"You can't."

Stacy only shrugged at her.

"But what am *I* supposed to do all summer?"

Stacy glanced back at Morgan. "I'm sorry, Cyndi. I really have to go. The boys are waiting. Call me later this summer, 'kay?"

Stacy turned and began walking toward the bathroom again. Cyndi wanted to grab Stacy and stop her. Her mind reeled, thinking about how awkward the rest of the day had been without them. It wasn't just Stacy, it was also Brad and Zack. Without the three of them, she would be the oldest girl in camp. She grimaced at the idea of spending the rest of the summer tagging along with the goofy younger girls. Just like in school, she would be ostracized, but this time it would be by girls two, three, and even four years younger. She felt humiliated to even imagine it. Stacy, Zack, and Brad had accepted her. They were a group, and now that was--

An idea clicked into her head.

"Wait, let me go with you."

Stacy turned to face Cyndi again, shaking her head.

"Cyndi, we're all gonna get in huge trouble when we get home. You're better off just staying here."

"I don't care. I wanna go with you guys."

Stacy considered it for a moment.

"No, Cyndi. I don't want to drag you into this."

"What happened to, 'we have to stick together?'"

Stacy sighed, she knew her argument was beaten. She glanced at her watch and saw that time was wasting. Brad and Zack were probably already getting the raft down now. She saw Cyndi's pleading expression and felt her mind giving in. They had only known each other for a week, but Stacy had already grown close with Cyndi. She was almost like the little sister Stacy never had.

Stacy sighed and gave in. "Quick. Pack as much as you can in your backpack and get your swimsuit. We don't have much time."

Cyndi immediately sat up and flung the covers back, causing the bunk bed to creak loudly. Stacy gave her another *shh* and glanced over at Morgan, making sure she was still asleep. One hearty snore from Morgan's open mouth reassured her. Cyndi quickly threw a few pairs of clothes and her swimsuit into her pack. She counted, making sure she had all of her tapes and batteries.

"Hurry," Stacy insisted.

"Hang on, hang on," Cyndi whispered back at her as she tossed the last of her essentials into her backpack and began to zip it up as slowly and quietly as she could. She grabbed her Walkman off the bed, hung her headphones around her neck, and stood up.

"Okay, come on. Hold onto your shoes, and keep your backpack in front of you. Whatever you do, keep quiet," Stacy whispered forcefully.

Stacy led the way between the aisles, looking at each and every one of the sleeping girls to make sure no one was watching their escape. They all slept like babies. Stacy and Cyndi both held their backpacks out in front of themselves to control any potential noises.

As they approached Morgan's bed, Cyndi's heart began to pound so loudly she could hear it. She stared down at Morgan as they crept around the corner of her bed. Her palms felt all sweaty, and she could feel the backpack starting to slip out of her grip.

Just keep it together, Cyndi. Just hold onto it for a little longer, she thought to herself.

She held the backpack with one hand and got a tighter grip with the other. A few tapes fell inside the backpack with a plastic clatter. Cyndi and Stacy stopped dead, their shoulders instantly tensed. They stood silently at the foot of Morgan's bed waiting to bolt back to their beds at any sign of movement from her. Morgan continued to sleep like the dead. Her mouth hung open, and she uttered a few nasally snores.

Stacy turned back to Cyndi and gave her an exasperated look. Cyndi returned it with a defensive shrug, and they continued on.

Stacy led the way into the bathroom, pushing the door open slowly and quietly. They both walked onto the tiled floor silently. Stacy held the door open for Cyndi, then slowly closed it. When she heard an infinitesimal click, she let go and turned back to Cyndi.

"Okay, quick get changed into your swimsuit," she said in a low whisper. "We're already late as it is." Cyndi pulled her swimsuit out of her bag without question, and went into a stall to change.

Stacy went over to the narrow pebbled glass window at the back wall and slid it open slowly to mask the noise. The sound of crickets outside instantly flooded in. She looked around outside, checking for signs of Sheehan or any of the other counselors. Once she was satisfied that the coast was clear, she began pulling the window screen out from the notch it rested in. To her surprise, it popped out easily. Stacy leaned out of the open window and lowered the screen quietly to the ground, leaning it up against the outside wall of the cabin.

"Okay, Cyndi. You ready?" she whispered.

Cyndi came out of the stall. Her white polka-dotted swimsuit showed underneath the drooping shoulder of one of her big Go-Go's T-shirts. She wore a pair of shorts over her swimsuit bottom. The sight of Stacy standing at the open window and lowering her own backpack down to the ground sent her into a panic. Her heart began to pound again as it did when the tapes in her backpack had clattered.

A million voices suddenly spoke up inside her head. *This is really happening. If I go out that window, there's no turning back. This is crazy. How did I even end up here at this moment, facing this decision?* All at once she felt like telling Stacy, *Never mind, I changed my mind. I'm just gonna go back to bed.* Then she would bolt from the bathroom.

Stacy walked over to her and put her hands on her shoulders. Suddenly all the voices stopped.

"Cyndi, you don't have to come with me if you don't want to," she said in a low calm voice. "But I need to know now if you're staying or going."

Cyndi suddenly thought of her parents and how they had forced her to come to this camp, without a choice. How they didn't realize that she was old enough to make her own friends, listen to her own music, and make her own decisions. She thought of Jennifer, who had just ditched her without a second thought. But here was Stacy, who stood up for herself, and made her own choices. Stacy, who looked out for her ever since they had first met on the bus. Stacy, who had stood up to Brad and Zack for her. She was everything Cyndi wished she could be. She cared enough about Cyndi to give her her own choice.

We're probably the two oldest girls in camp and we gotta stick together, y'know?

"I'm going with you," Cyndi said confidently. "We gotta stick together."

Stacy smiled. "Yeah, stick together. Now come on."

Stacy went over to the window and climbed up on the windowsill. It was a tight fit, she had to squeeze her body through sideways. Once she was through, she rested her weight on her hands and lowered herself down a few feet before dropping to the ground. She got up and dusted off her hands and knees before turning back to the window.

"Give me your backpack," Stacy whispered up to Cyndi. Cyndi lowered her backpack down and Stacy rested it on the ground next to the screen. She glanced back and forth for any signs of camp counselors, then turned back to Cyndi. "Okay, I'll help you down."

Stacy held up her hands and glanced around nervously as Cyndi hoisted herself up on the windowsill. She was still looking over to the side when suddenly Cyndi flew from the sill, crashing down on top of her. They both fell to the ground.

"I said I'd help you. What--"

"Someone's coming!" Cyndi whispered frantically.

"Shit!" Stacy immediately jumped up, grabbed the window screen, and held it up against the open window.

A bleary eyed eight-year-old girl in pink pajamas and furry slippers shuffled into the bathroom, pushing the door open and rubbing sleep out of her eye. She walked over to one of the stalls and stopped before going in. Something had caught her attention. The window was open.

Below the window, Stacy and Cyndi pressed tight against the wall and held onto two corners of the window screen with only the tips of their fingers. Even though they had only held the screen up for a few seconds, their arms began to throb because of the awkward angle.

As the girl came closer, her shuffling slippers got louder. Cyndi and Stacy both held their breath and braced themselves for discovery. The little girl walked up to the window and stared out for a few seconds. It felt like an eternity to their aching arms and wrists. The little girl yawned.

Come on, come on, what the hell are you doing? Just go away! Stacy wanted to scream out to her. Then the little girl casually shut the window and walked back to the stall. Through the closed window, they still heard the muffled sound of the stall door closing and the lock latching with a click.

Stacy immediately stood up and worked the screen back into its notch in the window frame as silently as she could. She pulled it tight just as the toilet flushed loudly. Both Stacy and Cyndi collapsed onto the ground, sighing with relief.

"That was way too close," Stacy whispered breathlessly. Cyndi nodded, rubbing her sore wrists. "How did you even hear her coming?"

"I could hear her slippers on the floor coming towards the bathroom door," Cyndi said. "You're pretty fast with that screen thing."

"Yeah, well, I've had a lot of practice," Stacy said nonchalantly. "I've snuck out of these cabins more times than I can even count." Cyndi smiled at her. Stacy picked up Cyndi's backpack and handed it to her. "We better get out of here before Morgan gets up and notices we're gone."

Cyndi slipped on her flip-flops and pulled her favorite baggy off-the-shoulder sweatshirt over her head. The oversized neck hole draped down exposing one of her shoulders. They looked back and forth, making sure the coast was clear. This late at night the camp was as quiet as a tomb. They slipped their backpacks over their shoulders and took off.

Stacy led her around the back of the cabin, ducking low so no one could see them out the windows. As they passed the corner window near where their bunk bed had been, it occurred to Cyndi that she had never been on this side of the cabin before. For a second, she had the urge to look in the window and get the complete opposite perspective of what she'd had for the last week.

They stopped at the corner of the cabin and Stacy peered around the side. This was going to be the riskiest part. They had to make it from the girls cabin all the way across the grassy clearing to the main lodge. Then they had to sneak around the side of the lodge and get to the end of the white plank board dock without anyone seeing them. Brad and Zack would be out there waiting, unless they had already taken off and left them behind.

"You ready to run?" Stacy asked.

"Wait, you haven't even told me where we're going!" Cyndi whispered.

"Brad stole Sheehan's keys this afternoon. We're taking the raft out across the lake, to that far cove we were at earlier today on the canoe trip. Then we'll go down the river and get off when we reach the highway. From there, we'll hitchhike to town and call our parents."

"That's your guys' big plan?"

"I didn't make it up, okay?"

"Why don't you just call your parents and tell them to come get you?"

"They'd never go for it."

"Well, then why don't we just walk out on the road?"

"Because this is faster. Besides, that's the first place they'll look when they find out we're gone. Look, do you want to just go back?"

Cyndi thought about it and shrugged, "Too late

now." She still wasn't convinced that it was a great plan but she was in it now. God help her, she was in it up to her neck.

"Okay, this is gonna be the trickiest part. We have to make it all the way across the field and behind the kitchen over there." Stacy pointed to the woodsy side of the lodge where the trashcans were. The cooks took their smoke breaks there. "Stay low and keep up."

"You got it."

Stacy looked around one last time, then began the countdown. "One, Two, *Three!*" Stacy took off in a crouching sprint. She ran so fast that Cyndi had a hard time keeping up. Her backpack bounced and jostled on her back. She had to keep pushing it back up as it repeatedly slipped off her left shoulder. The mad dash to the lodge felt three times farther than it actually was.

The girls gasped for breath as they reached the side of the main lodge. They slammed up against the wall just past the back door that led into the kitchen. They both looked out across the field again, searching for faces in windows or bouncing flashlight beams. Except for the hundreds of crickets and mosquitoes buzzing around, the whole camp was quiet.

"Looks like we made it," Stacy exhaled. Cyndi immediately thought of that old Barry Manilow song her mother always listened to on the downstairs record player back home. Stacy turned toward the lake and began sliding along the side of the lodge. "Hopefully they haven't already left without us."

"Why would they leave without us?" Cyndi asked.

"I've known Brad since we were eight years old. Believe me, when he says he'll do something, he means it."

They crept along the backside of the lodge past the smelly trashcans. Stacy stopped them once, thinking she heard something back the way they came. Cyndi immediately froze, trying not to even breathe. Stacy watched in silence for what felt like a full minute, then relaxed her tensed shoulders. "It's nothing, let's hurry."

Cyndi followed her, looking back over her shoulder. She watched the woods and the cabins from which they had just fled with a paranoid intensity. Stacy cautiously watched where she was stepping. They approached a long rusted piece of grooved sheet metal that Stacy figured was probably a leftover from building that rusty old equipment shed roof. She stepped around the sheet metal, glanced back, and noticed Cyndi's inattention. Cyndi was about to walk right onto it, and it would make a loud rusted screech that could be heard all the way to the boy's cabins.

Stacy shot out an arm and Cyndi crashed into it hard, turning forward immediately. She looked like she had been shocked out of a daze.

"Watch where you're going, will ya?!" Stacy whispered, pointing to the sheet metal.

"Sorry, sorry," Cyndi mumbled so quietly Stacy almost couldn't hear her over the drone of the crickets.

"There's no one back there, don't worry," Stacy said. "Just watch where you step."

Cyndi nodded, she felt like she was in way over her head here. She had no idea what she was doing sneaking around in the middle of the night, and Stacy had made it clear that she was obviously terrible at it.

They came to the edge of the main lodge and looked forward at the lake shore. The blackened rocks circling the fire pit were all that remained from the Swim Day's activities. Stacy looked around for Zack and Brad.

What if they set this whole thing up just to get me to try and sneak out as a huge joke? Stacy wondered. That was ridiculous, of course. The dead set look on Brad's eyes, his speech, and the keys he stole from

Sheehan's desk had to be serious.

"Are they even out here?" Cyndi asked.

"Shit, Brad," Stacy mumbled mostly to herself. "I swear if you left without me, I will--"

"There!" Cyndi hissed pointing out the far end of the dock.

Stacy immediately looked in the direction of Cyndi's pointing finger. She could see Zack in his dark gray muscle shirt poking his head out from the bottom of the dock. He saw them and gave an anxious, tiny wave, trying not to attract too much visual attention to himself, should anyone be watching from up at the lodge.

"Oh, thank God!" Stacy sighed, waving back at Zack. He motioned them over. "Come on."

Zack watched from the edge of the dock as not one, but two girls came around the corner from the lodge. In his adrenaline pumped state his first assumption was that the other girl with Stacy was a counselor and they were busted. His heart went cold with fear for a second, but then his mind put the pieces together and he realized who the other girl was. He couldn't help but smile, and felt a flush in his cheeks immediately rushing in.

"They made it," Zack whispered. Brad crouched in the raft tying the drawstring on his neon blue and green swim trunks tighter. He immediately looked up at Zack.

"Finally. Wait, what?" He glanced over and saw not only Stacy, but the mousy little headphones girl running with her. His blood began to boil. "Oh, shit," he said. This was not part of his plan.

Stacy led Cyndi toward the shoreline of the lake. They ran with their heads low and glanced up at the windows in the lodge every few seconds. Zack also kept an eye on the windows, but they were all dark. They were completely in the clear.

The girls made it to the edge of the dock, crouched down and took one last look around at the lodge and the camp.

"Come on, you guys. It's fine," Zack said out loud.

"*Shhhhut up,*" Brad hissed. He punched Zack in the arm.

Stacy stepped up onto the smooth white planks of the dock and walked softly towards the boys. Zack stood with his arms open smiling at them.

"You made it!" he whispered. Stacy smiled back at him.

"What? You honestly thought I wouldn't?" Before she could even finish her sentence, Brad climbed up out of the raft and rudely shoved Zack out of his way. He wore his white football jersey with the number 00. Stacy saw his fuming expression and braced herself.

"What the fuck is *she* doing here?" he said in as low of a voice as he could manage. "What the fuck do you think you're doing?"

Cyndi braced herself for a long argument, the kind that would escalate and get louder and louder until one of the counselors woke up and saw them all out on the dock screaming at each other. Stacy didn't miss a beat. As the last word came out of Brad's mouth, Stacy was already pushing her way past him.

"Cyndi's coming with us, Brad," Stacy said, holding her ground.

"No, she's not," he protested.

"What are you gonna do? Send her back?"

"She can't..." Brad struggled to find his words. His mind reeled trying to re-envision the plan that he had gone over all day in his mind. A plan he had envisioned for *three*, not four.

"She's coming, Brad. Deal with it," Stacy whispered in a tired yet authoritative way that sounded eerily like her parents. Hadn't she heard her father use that exact expression on her more than once?

Brad immediately stepped in front of Stacy, blocking her path onto the raft. She stopped and glared into his eyes with her coldest strongest stare. His eyes flicked back and forth from her left eye to her right, as if he were trying to read her expression and figure out what to do. Cyndi and Zack's eyes met nervously for a second as they all sat in tense silence.

"This wasn't part of the plan," Brad said in a weaker voice than he had intended. He immediately regretted not using a stronger voice.

Stacy did not back down the slightest bit. "We gonna sit here and argue about this, or are we gonna get going?"

Brad stared at her for another second, then glanced nervously at Cyndi and Zack.

"It's fine, man. Relax. She's cool," Zack said to him.

Brad glanced back at Stacy, then looked around nervously at the camp again. Finally, he sighed in defeat.

"Fine, whatever," he muttered, stepping back down into the raft.

Cyndi felt another surge of love and admiration for Stacy. She seemed completely unstoppable, and she always had Cyndi's back. Stacy continued to amaze her.

Zack held up a hand to help Stacy and Cyndi down into the raft. Stacy went first, casually sitting in the back row. Cyndi took Zack's hand and gave him a nervous glance as she stepped down into the raft on wobbly legs. Zack easily held her up and steadied her. She looked up at him and smiled.

"Thanks," she whispered to him.

"No sweat," he said smiling back at her. "Welcome aboard."

Brad stood up and looked down at the others.

"Last chance, everybody," he said seriously. "If any of you wanna go back, now's the time. Once we're out there, I ain't turning around for nothin.'"

They all looked at each other, but no one gave any objections. Stacy had gone too far to back out now, even though she had a sick nervous feeling in her stomach. Cyndi would go wherever Stacy went without question. And now that Cyndi was here, all Zack really wanted to do was be close to her.

"Okay, let's ditch this fuckin' place," Brad said with a rebellious smirk.

Zack began to laugh crazily as he untied the rope holding them to the dock. All three of them immediately shushed him.

"Sorry, sorry. Got a little carried away," he whispered, still giggling. He flung the last loop of rope off the dock and tossed it into the raft. He put his foot up on the dock and kicked off with a rush of adrenaline. Cyndi watched as he kicked, and almost fell back as the raft sprang forward.

"Shit, Zack!" Stacy whispered annoyed. He ignored her and sat down in the front row, grinning.

"You two watch the camp and tell us if you see anyone coming," Brad said in a low voice to Cyndi and Stacy. He turned to Zack, "Remember, paddle slow 'til we get far enough away."

"Gotcha."

Zack and Brad both began paddling in slow powerful strokes, trying to keep the sloshing sounds on the sides of the raft as quiet as they could. Stacy and Cyndi watched the main lodge intensely. Their minds raced feverishly, but one thought rang true for all four of them, *I can't believe I'm actually doing this.*

They watched the camp dwindle away in the distance for what felt like a very long time. As they went farther and farther, the camp faded into the dark shoreline and the surrounding woods. Out in the middle of the lake, the shoreline was so pitch black it made the starry moonlit sky seem bright in comparison. Cyndi looked up and saw more stars than she had ever seen in her life. The small choppy waves glinted in the moonlight and slapped against the plastic sides of the raft.

All four of them were silent, afraid of being reprimanded by Brad, although he wouldn't have cared if they made small conversation. He was at a total loss for words himself. A few doubtful thoughts kept trying to work their way into his mind, but he quickly shoved them back. He needed to focus on the task at hand.

They had paddled long enough so that camp was now no longer visible against the black shoreline. Stacy squinted into the distance trying to make it out, then decided it was no longer discernible. She glanced at everyone impatiently, looking for someone to break the silence. Cyndi looked back at her and they both shrugged. Neither of them could see the camp anymore, and neither knew what to do next. Stacy didn't want to break the silence, to do so seemed like some forbidden act. Cyndi sure as hell wouldn't break it, she'd wait until the lake froze over for the winter before she'd utter a peep. Stacy looked over at Zack and motioned to the camp with her hand. He looked back and scanned the shoreline briefly, then turned back to her and shrugged. She rolled her eyes, thinking, *Do I have to do everything myself?*

"Uh, Brad?" Stacy said in a normal volume that seemed awkward and loud after the silence. She thought briefly that this must be what it feels like to be Cyndi, not ever wanting to break the silence, feeling like your own voice was an uncontrollable thing that would get you into trouble. "I think we're far enough away now we can talk."

Brad turned around and scanned the horizon. "We made it," he said solemnly. The three of them watched him with uncertainty.

Suddenly, a smile lit up Brad's face. He began to chuckle, then it became a full blown laugh. They all felt smiles creeping onto their own faces as Brad began to laugh hysterically.

"We made it, you guys!" he said between laughs. He stood up in the raft and shouted back at the camp. *"You hear that, She-Man? We made it! So fuck you, m'man!"* he shouted back at the camp. His index finger pointed as he shouted, accenting every other word.

Zack got up and cheered Brad on. The girls quickly followed. They all laughed and cheered. Brad grabbed Stacy and gave her a rough, triumphant kiss on the mouth. Cyndi pleasantly surprised both herself and Zack by reaching out and hugging him. At first he was so shocked he didn't know what to do, then it became real for him and he hugged her back fiercely, lifting her up off her feet.

The raft started to rock dangerously from side to side and Zack put Cyndi down clumsily. Water splashed up into the raft on the right side, soaking their feet and sobering their cheering moods immediately. They all sat down quickly, held onto their few backpacks, and tried to steady the raft. After a few seconds of precarious rocking, the raft steadied itself and the smiles returned to their faces.

"Shit, that was close," Zack sighed. They all nodded and murmured in agreement.

"Well, what now?" Stacy asked.

"First the cove, then the river, then...home," Brad said with a smile.

They all smiled at the comforting thoughts of their own warm beds in their cozy bedrooms. Brad continued to smile as he picked up the paddle and began rowing at a normal, quicker stroke. He thought about his room, and how nice it would be once he made it home. It didn't cross his mind that he would never make it home again.

Chapter Nine:

The River

It was so dark out on the lake that it was hard to tell how far they had gone, or how much time had passed. Conversation had been scarce ever since they left the dock. Brad and Zack concentrated on their paddling, and Cyndi was more reluctant to say anything while they were in close contact with the boys. Stacy didn't try to force conversation, but she did wish someone would say something for God's sake. She looked over to the shoreline and saw something huge and gray jutting out into the lake. It was the cliff where they had stopped earlier that morning.

"God, are we that far out already?" she asked out loud.

"Huh?" Brad asked.

"Isn't that the cliff where you guys were screwing around this morning?"

Brad wiped sweat from his forehead and pushed his feathered hair back, squinting over at the cliff. "Wow, I guess you're right. That means we gotta be close to the cove. Zack, get me that flashlight out of the pack."

"Alright, hang on," Zack said. He put down his paddle and lifted up the pack from the bottom of the raft. He unzipped it and after a minute of fishing around inside, he yanked it out from near the bottom. He clicked it on and put it under his chin, as if he were at a campfire telling a ghost story. He spoke in a low spooky voice. "And all they ever found from the four campers that went out on the lake that night, was this paddle...covered...in *BLOOD*!" He lifted up the paddle and began an insane spooky laugh. Stacy gave Zack a raised eyebrow, and Cyndi giggled a little nervously.

"Gimme that," Brad chuckled yanking the flashlight out of his hand. He clicked it on and pointed it across the lake at the shore. The beam of light seemed very weak, only illuminating a small portion of trees. He slowly scanned the shoreline until the beam of light dwindled so much that it didn't really make a difference. He handed the flashlight to Stacy. "We're not there yet. Let's keep movin.' Zack, steer us closer to the shore, okay?"

"Aye aye, Cap'n," Zack said with a salute.

They paddled on, slowly leaving the middle of the lake and moving closer to the shore. They all began to make out details in the dark trees under the moonlight. Brad thought he noticed an indent in the shoreline where the trees broke off and there was only water. The farther they went, the clearer it became.

"Okay, I see it. We're almost there," he said.

They paddled the raft around the corner and into the cove. It had been a shady little cove during the day. Thick pine trees and cottonwood limbs reached far out above the water, shielding it from the sun. At night it was a black bottomless pit of darkness. The pine trees blocked out almost all of the dim moonlight. The crickets were louder here, and the clouds of mosquitoes and gnats were thicker. Stacy smacked one that landed on her arm and gave a small cry of disgust. The cove seemed foreboding and secretive. Cyndi thought, *I shouldn't be here, I should be back at camp asleep*.

"Okay, give me the flashlight," Brad said quietly to Stacy. She handed him the flashlight and another mosquito dropped down on her outstretched hand. She slapped it away.

"Eww, bugs! Eww," she mumbled, shuddering in revulsion.

Brad clicked on the flashlight and a pair of gleaming eyes in the woods suddenly reflected back, staring directly at them. They all gave a startled cry. The deer promptly turned and leaped off into the woods.

"Just a deer," Brad sighed shaking his head. "You girls all right?" Cyndi nodded.

"Yeah, I could use some bug spray though," Stacy said, smacking another mosquito that landed on her neck.

"Yeah, totally," Zack agreed.

"Sorry, fresh out," Brad said.

Brad turned the flashlight beam back to the cove and scanned the shoreline for the little stream trickling away from the lake. His flashlight beam stopped and he saw the small gathering of limbs and algae that had piled up and clogged the stream's entrance.

"There, that's where we're going. Keep the light on it," Brad handed the light back to Stacy and he and Zack began to paddle.

They moved slowly toward the stream. Small waves began to slap against the sides of the raft as they moved in toward the shallower water. The sound made Cyndi suddenly imagine dead wet hands all pruney and purplish-white smacking against the side of the raft. The image was so strong she suddenly felt sure it was going to happen, and she gaped down at the water in anticipation. Her heart began to race, and she felt a sick ache in her stomach.

Just stop it, Cyndi thought to herself. *This is not helping.* She forced herself to look away and not think about what may or may not be floating in the dark water below. She watched the approaching stream lit up by the flashlight in Stacy's hand, but the sick feeling in her stomach remained.

This is not a good idea. We should not be here. These woods don't belong to us. That was a funny thought. If the woods didn't belong to them, then who did they belong to? She decided it was better not to think about it. She scooted closer to Stacy on their seat in the raft.

The raft bumped up against the gathering of debris that had piled up. Brad pushed at the limbs with his paddle, trying to clear a passage. The front end of the raft sunk a little lower into the murky water as he put his weight into it. Brad grunted with effort as the paddle slipped off the slimy, algae-covered limbs with every attempt he made.

"Shit," he growled under his breath, tossing the paddle back into the raft. He reached down to lift the branches up with his bare hands.

"Uh, do you need any help, man?" Zack asked tentatively.

"Almost got it," Brad said in a strained voice. "It's giving...Hang on."

A thick gnarled limb covered with river mud and algae suddenly jolted up out of the water and splashed back down a little farther along the stream. Almost immediately, water began coursing through the opening and the raft inched forward.

"Okay man, push us through," Brad said quickly to Zack. Both of them grabbed their paddles and stuck them down deep into the soft mud on the bottom. They shoved the raft through the narrow opening. Branches and twigs scraped the sides of the raft and Stacy worried that it might get punctured. The last twig gave way with a final scrape and the raft floated forward unscathed.

The stream was only fifteen feet wide and maybe a foot deep, with grassy banks that gradually rose up on either side. The trees closed in thickly around them, and Stacy kept the light on, looking around into the woods. Brad and Zack paddled lightly, keeping them from drifting to the sides.

"Whoa, creepy," Zack said in a low voice filled with awe. He looked back at Cyndi and gave her a smile. She smiled back, then turned and looked back at the moonlit lake, which now seemed bright by comparison. Zack looked back and noticed the bright lake too.

"No turning back now," he said with a touch of nervousness that Cyndi didn't care for. She gave him a quick smile, then faced forward again. She would somehow have to make it through this dark night on the river. Then it would be daylight again and she'd be able to figure out how she would explain all this to her parents.

They drifted slowly down the river for a while without saying much. Zack's mind kept returning to his joke about the four campers who were never seen again. The more he thought about it, the less funny and more real it became.

He opened up the pack and dug around for one of the Twinkies they had stolen from the mess hall earlier. He pulled out a smooshed but still (always) edible Twinkie, unwrapped it, and took a bite. They all turned at the sound of the wrapper and stared at him. Stacy shone the light on the Twinkie.

"What? You guys want one?" he asked with his mouth full.

"Can't you save that shit for tomorrow? We

97

might need it," Brad asked annoyed.

"I'm hungry," Zack said unflinchingly.

Brad rolled his eyes and turned forward again.

"No more tonight," he said with authority.

The stream went around a bend, changing directions. Then another bend immediately came, sending them around in an S shape. Brad was trying desperately to hold onto his sense of direction in the pitch black woods, but it was a losing battle. After they rounded the last curve of the S shape, he thought they must still be on the right track. A tiny streamlet, no more than two feet wide, branched off from the left side of the stream. That was the side Brad thought would lead to the main road, the direction they wanted to go. But the main stream curved off to the right, away from the direction he felt they should be going.

As if reading his mind, Stacy said, "Uh, Brad do you know where we're going?"

"Yes," he said solemnly.

"Are you sure, man?" Zack piped in, popping the last bite of Twinkie into his mouth.

"Look, you heard She-Man earlier. He said this river eventually winds up alongside the main road."

Zack shrugged and crumpled up the Twinkie wrapper into a tight ball. He absentmindedly tossed the wrapper into the water where it uncrumpled slightly and floated alongside the raft. The current picked up the wrapper as they passed the bend in the river, and it floated off along the tiny streamlet, away from the four runaways. None of them noticed as it passed away from them and went off on its own path.

The wrapper continued down the little streamlet and it began to pick up speed. The streamlet wandered around several meandering bends of its own before it began to widen out and join with other small streamlets. After another fifteen minutes of travel, the stream had widened out into a full river and went around a final bend. The Twinkie wrapper washed up on the shore only a few yards from the main road that the four of them had been hoping to float to. The discarded wrapper lay there with water and mud washing over it as another river carried the four runaways farther and farther away from where they had hoped to wind up.

*   *   *

An hour had passed with them slowly drifting down the creek (it really wasn't big enough to be called a river), and the woods around them grew steadily darker and thicker. More than once, a deer or raccoon would appear in Stacy's wandering flashlight beam, its pupils glowing back and startling them. A few times some animals scampered away deeper into the underbrush without ever having been seen, and all four of them would gasp and turn in the direction of the noise. They sat mostly in tense silence, looking to Brad as their makeshift leader.

Brad felt like he was far from a leader. He was in over his head now and he knew it. On the outside, he remained collected and silent. He tried not to turn his head too sharply whenever a twig would snap near the shore, or look around too much, giving off the impression that he didn't know where the hell they were. The animal noises and glowing eyes frightened him more than he would ever admit. He glanced to the right and saw a pair of wide glaring eyes set back in the brush, calmly watching them. They seemed to say, *What are you doing trespassing in our woods? You're not from here, you don't belong here. And you better just keep floating down that river because the next one of us you see may not be as passive as I am. You might just see one of my bigger brothers; a badger, or a mountain lion, or something even bigger, with sharper teeth....*

The creature scampered away, breaking off the trail of Brad's thoughts. He looked back around and saw Stacy, Cyndi, and Zack peering up at him with wide eyes and tensed shoulders.

"You guys all doin' okay?" he asked in a low voice. They all nodded slowly, the lack of confidence in his voice made them even more nervous. If they had no one to turn to, no one to look out for them and tell them it was going to be all right, then what? He immediately faced the front of the raft again, regretting saying anything at all.

Brad had to face the facts, he was just plain scared. What had he gotten them into? Thoughts of anger, Sheehan, and cruel punishments were the farthest things from his mind now. Now he silently prayed that some hungry, predatory animal wasn't just across the creek, waiting and watching them, figuring out the best plan of attack in its vicious primitive mind.

"Brad?" Stacy spoke up. He turned to her without saying anything. "Are you sure you know where we're going?"

"What? Am I sure I know where we're going?" he asked stalling. "Why?"

"Where are we, man?" Zack asked. Something had finally broken for Zack. He was just as scared as any of them, and had sat back quietly, letting Brad take the dominant role he'd had in their friendship for years. But enough was enough.

"We're on the river going away from the camp, where do ya' think?"

"Yeah, but where?"

"Well, how the *fuck* should I know?"

Another animal scurried off at Brad's sudden outburst.

"You said you knew where we were going,"

Stacy said again, her voice dripping with disappointment.

"No, no, no. I said, that *Sheehan said* that this river would eventually lead out toward the main road, okay? I never said I knew where we were going."

"Oh my God," Stacy mumbled, sounding sick. Cyndi looked at her with huge eyes, then down at her feet shamefully.

"Look, this should turn into the river by the main road any minute now, okay? Just shut the hell up and be patient."

"And what if it doesn't?" Zack countered gravely.

"It will," Brad replied.

"But what if it doesn't?" Zack insisted.

"Shut the fuck up, Zack," Brad said after a pause.

"No, *you* shut the fuck up," he said with more confidence than he had ever mustered in his whole life. He was beyond thinking. They were in a potentially dangerous situation now, and Zack was on autopilot.

"What did you just say to me?" Brad asked disbelieving.

Zack ignored him. "I say we stop, get off the river, and get some sleep. And tomorrow when it's light out, we try to figure out just where the fuck we are."

"Yes, I'm with Zack," Stacy said immediately.

Brad gaped at them. "I can't believe you're on his side."

"I'm not against you man, but this is crazy, going in the middle of the night when we can't even see if we're on the right river or not."

"I'm telling you we'll be going along the main road any minute," Brad said.

"Fine. Then what the hell is the difference if we get off and get a couple hours of sleep?" Stacy reasoned. She reached out and put her hand on his arm softly.

"Come on, seriously. You look exhausted."

Something in Brad melted at her touch. Cyndi watched her do this with fascination, thinking, *she knows just how to make him do exactly what she wants.* She wondered if she would ever have that kind of power over a boy, or if she would even want to use it.

"All right, fine. But someone's gotta stay up and watch. There could be mountain lions, or badgers, or...who the fuck even knows what's out here."

"Thank you," Zack said with relief. In a badly executed Jewish accent he added, "Finally, the boy sees reason!"

Cyndi smiled back at him as he helped Brad steer the raft to the side of the river. They stopped the raft at a small point just ahead of them that jutted out, sending the river around in a wide bend. Once they reached the river's edge, the boys struggled against the current and held the raft steady as Cyndi and Stacy stepped out onto the grassy bank. They carried their packs up the little sloping bank and onto the point which was a flat little clearing encircled partially by a tree trunk that had grown horizontally along the ground. The clearing was covered in long green grass that made a soft mat under their feet.

Brad and Zack tossed the paddles up onto the clearing and yanked the raft up out of the water. They pulled it up the bank and tossed it down at the edge of the clearing. It bounced and settled softly on the grass, still dripping with river water.

"Turn that flashlight off, we gotta save the battery," Brad said to Stacy.

"I'm not gonna sit here in the dark," Stacy insisted.

"Relax, we'll build a little fire. Besides, it'll help scare away the animals."

"Actually hand me that flashlight, I'll see if I can

find some dry wood," Zack said, holding his hand out.

"Sure," Stacy said handing it to him. He clicked it on, then stepped a little farther back into the woods. There was a dead tree with a bunch of gnarled, dried out limbs only a few yards farther in, and he easily gathered enough kindling.

Cyndi opened her pack and methodically checked through her tapes and batteries to make sure they were all still dry. Everything was still intact. She held a few batteries in her hand and an idea popped into her head. Maybe she could make herself useful on this trip after all.

"If you guys need batteries for the flashlight, I got plenty of double A's," she suggested. They all turned, surprised at the sound of her voice.

"Uh, I think this thing only takes C Cells. And we've got a couple extras," Zack said from the dead tree. Cyndi nodded and lowered her head. Zack felt bad for shooting down her offer and was compelled to add, "But thanks anyway." She smiled at him, thankful for his gesture, and pulled her headphones up over one of her ears. She needed a little shot of some music after that painfully long silent trip in the raft.

Brad dug through a blue gym bag they had brought along, and fished out a metal lighter. He flicked it open and watched the small yellow flame dance in front of his eyes.

"You brought a lighter to camp? Even after last year?" Stacy asked.

"No, I swiped this from the She-Man's office when I took the keys. Thought it might come in handy," Brad explained with a mischievous smile, flicking the cap closed on the lighter and dousing the flame. He flicked the lighter open and closed. "Come on, I'm not *that* stupid." Stacy smiled despite her earlier anger at him. He could be such a dick, but sometimes she wondered how she ever got mad at him in the first place.

Zack walked back into their makeshift camp and dumped a pile of small dry twigs and limbs on the ground.

"You think that'll be enough, dude?" he asked.

"Probably," Brad replied. He immediately began working on stacking them up against each other, building a mini campfire. Zack crouched down and helped. Stacy collapsed down in the raft. After a moment of lying there exhausted, she pulled over her pack and yanked a baggy sweatshirt out. She pulled it over her head and let it drape down off of one shoulder.

"God, I'm tired," Stacy sighed. "It's gotta be, what? Three? Four in the morning by now?"

Brad flicked the lighter open and began trying to set the little fire ablaze. Zack held his wrist near the light from the lighter to check the time on his wristwatch.

"It's four-seventeen actually," he told her. The flames caught and a bright orange flickering glow lit up their little clearing.

"That explains a lot," she said rolling over on her side near the bottom of the raft. "I'll catch you guys in the morning."

Cyndi sat down in the raft next to Stacy and let her tape player roll on, "This Town," by The Go-Go's, from one of her mix tapes was blasting into her right ear. Brad and Zack sat on opposite sides of the fire, staring into it silently. After a moment Brad spoke up in a very soft, uncharacteristic voice.

"I'm sorry, guys. I didn't mean to get you into this. I just--" he trailed off for a second while everyone watched him in stunned silence. Even Stacy, who had not gone to sleep as easily as she thought she would have, sat up and stared at him. "I'm sorry," he continued in a choked voice. He looked like he was on the verge of tears.

104

"We're all in this together now," Cyndi said. Brad looked up at her shocked. "We didn't have to come, but we did. So..." she trailed off, finishing her sentence with a shrug. Brad looked down again, even closer to tears than before. Zack immediately got up and sat down next to him.

"She's right, man," he said to Brad, putting an arm around his shoulders. "Don't worry. We'll find the road in the morning."

Stacy got up out of the raft and Cyndi quickly followed. Stacy took Brad's other side and kissed him on the cheek. Cyndi sat close to her.

"We're gonna make it, okay?" Stacy said, pulling his chin up with her fingertips and looking into his eyes. He nodded at her. His eyes filled with fresh tears and he lowered his head again. Zack held his arm out and looked at Cyndi. She met his gaze and came around, putting her back to the fire, and letting him put his other arm over her shoulders.

After a minute of silence Brad sniffed and looked up at Cyndi. "I can hear your music," he said, his voice still a little choked but stronger now. "I hate the Go-Go's." They all began to laugh.

The four runaways sat there in a circle, hugging each other, cementing the bonds of friendship between them forever. None of them would ever forget that moment, sitting out in the woods in front of a tiny campfire, in the wake of one of the biggest acts of disobedience Camp Kikawa had ever known. They sat knowing their situation was desperate and there would be hell to pay once they got home, and took the only comfort they could in each other.

Twenty minutes later, the fire was dying down. They had all drifted over to the raft and fallen asleep next to one another. Just as Cyndi was dozing off, letting the music of the Go-Go's help carry her away to sleep, she thought she saw the shadow of a man standing back in the woods staring at them. Her heavy eyelids opened a little wider and she tried to sit up, but the figure suddenly moved back into the woods stealthily. She laid her head back down. The last thought she had before sleep took her was, *It's probably just a deer.*

Chapter Ten:

The Rapids

Cyndi woke up to the sound of birds and trickling water. She opened her eyes and saw leaves and tree limbs overhead, blocking out the sun. It was already late morning. She felt disoriented and tried hard to remember where she was. She sat up and looked around, breathing in the fresh forest air. The woods surrounding them were very thick, but she guessed by the sunlight shining through little bare patches in the trees, that it was about ten thirty or eleven in the morning. She could see water from the creek trickling past their little campsite. It looked clear and peaceful, and the sound of it was soothing. She could get used to waking up to that sound.

Her headphones had slipped off her ears sometime during the night (as they did nine out of every ten nights) and hung crookedly around her neck. Her Walkman had reached the end of Side A of her mix tape hours ago while she slept, and it was now still and silent. She took the headphones off, turned back to the other side of the raft to pick up the Walkman, and was startled to see that she had been lying next to a boy all night. Zack was still conked out, sleeping with his mouth slightly open and his legs sprawled over the side of the raft. His arm was out where her shoulders had been.

Did I fall asleep on his arm last night? she thought excitedly.

Seeing him sleeping there made it all come flooding back. Her memories played backwards, putting the pieces together as they went along. Falling asleep in the raft on the shore in between Zack and Stacy, floating down the river in the darkness with the animal eyes glowing back at them, the lake at night, Stacy and her running through the dark, deserted camp. She remembered it all, and now that it was daylight again she felt an immediate wave of nauseous regret deep in her stomach. In the harsh unforgiving light of day she knew that she was in deep trouble. What would her parents say when they found out that their thirteen-year-old daughter had run away from camp, spent the night in the woods, and slept next to a boy all night: a *fourteen*-year-old boy? Not that they had done anything, but he was cute and she couldn't deny the thrill of knowing they had slept together in the raft the whole night. Even though Stacy and Brad had been right there--

Wait! Where were Stacy and Brad? They weren't in the raft, or in the clearing. They weren't anywhere in sight. Cyndi felt herself start to panic. They wouldn't have gone off and left her and Zack to fend for themselves, would they? Or what if Sheehan and the other counselors had captured them? They were undoubtedly searching for them, but why would they leave Cyndi and Zack? Stacy and Brad had to be nearby.

Cyndi was about to get up when she saw a tan leg slide up behind some of the trees, and heard a very quiet sigh of ecstasy. It was Stacy. She quickly put the pieces together in her mind. Stacy and Brad had woken up early and snuck off into the woods to have a little "alone time." She immediately felt guilty for having overheard them. Whatever they were doing, she didn't want to hear it.

She felt for her Walkman, which she remembered laying next to her in the soft bottom of the raft, and couldn't find it. She followed the length of the headphone cord with her eyes up over the edge of the raft and out onto the grass. There was her Walkman sitting there with its tape deck open, but how did it get out here? She slept with it every night, and sometimes if it slid under her back or dug into her skin in an uncomfortable way, she sat up and moved it. She didn't remember sitting up last night at all. In fact, she had slept like the dead after their exhausting trip through the woods.

Cyndi picked up the Walkman and examined it. The open tape deck was empty, her mix tape was gone. She looked around their little campsite for the tape. She leaned over the edge of the raft to see if it had fallen out and lay on the ground somewhere. It was nowhere to be found. Maybe she could have pushed the Walkman out of the raft in the middle of the night, or maybe Zack or Stacy had moved it. But why would the tape deck be open and her tape missing?

She looked over at her backpack. She had dropped it and left it in the grass when they had arrived. She clearly remembered getting her Walkman out of her backpack, then zipping it tight again, thinking that she didn't want bugs, or water, or one of those sparks from their little fire to get in and burn up her tapes. During the night, someone had opened her pack and left it lying askew in the grass.

Getting out of the raft as quietly as she could, she went over to look into the pack. Someone had been in there all right. The neat little stack of tape cases had been toppled, and lay scattered throughout the pack. The clothes, which had been neatly folded, were now crumpled and tossed haphazardly around. She rummaged through the bag herself, taking an inventory of her stuff. There were the fourteen of the fifteen tapes she had brought, plus the empty case for the mix tape that had been in the Walkman. There were the three T-shirts she had packed, the extra pair of shorts, the two pairs of socks, two pairs of underwear...

Wait. Didn't I pack three pairs of underwear? She could have sworn that last night she had packed one striped, one yellow, and one pink pair of underwear, but the pink pair was gone. Maybe she hadn't packed the pink pair after all. She had been in a mad dash to get out the door, or rather out the window, with Stacy.

One of the tape cases fell inside with a loud plastic clatter. Stacy gasped from behind the trees, it was clearly audible to Cyndi.

"What was that?" Stacy whispered.

"Huh?"

"I think they're awake."

"Shit."

Then Cyndi heard the sound of clothes rustling. She ignored them and continued to inventory the stuff in the pack. Stacy came through the trees a second later, her cheeks red and flushed. She combed her hair straight with her fingers.

"Morning, Cyndi," she said smiling.

"Morning," Cyndi said. "Hey, did you, uh, need something?" She pointed to her pack.

"What?"

There was a sharp intake of breath behind them as Zack woke up. He sat up in the raft, rubbing his eyes and scratching his head through his greasy black hair.

"Were you looking for something in my pack?" Cyndi repeated.

Stacy shook her head and Brad came through the trees, looking more disheveled than Stacy.

"What's going on?" he asked.

"Did one of you guys go through my pack last night or this morning?" she asked Brad and Zack.

"Hm'Mmm," Zack mumbled, stretching.

"I didn't touch it," Brad said honestly.

"Are you missing something?" Stacy asked.

Cyndi continued to rummage through her pack. "I'm pretty sure someone went through my stuff last night. It's all messed up inside my backpack, and one of my tapes is missing." She almost added, *I think a pair of my underwear is gone too*, but decided against it. Too embarrassing.

"Cyndi, you have, like, a million tapes. You probably just left it back at camp," Stacy explained smiling.

"I fell asleep listening to it last night," Cyndi said holding up her tape player. "And I found this open when I woke up a minute ago." Stacy and Brad looked at each other, shrugged, then looked at Zack suspiciously. He stopped stretching and looked at them, honestly surprised.

"What?"

"Was it you?" Stacy asked.

"I just woke up. And I slept like a rock."

She turned back to Brad, putting her hands on her hips.

"Don't look at me," he laughed. "You had your clingy legs wrapped around me all night. Besides, what would I want with her tape? I hate the Go-Go's, remember?"

Stacy turned back to Cyndi, shrugged, and looked around their little campsite. "Are you sure you didn't see it anywhere? I mean, maybe it just popped out of your tape player and it's on the ground somewhere."

"But what about my pack?"

"Maybe it was a g-g-g-ghost," Brad shuddered sarcastically. Zack snorted laughter.

"Shut up, you guys," Stacy snapped. Brad and Zack ignored her, letting their giggles die down. As Cyndi searched the grass, a thought suddenly occurred to her.

"You guys think there might be anyone out here?" Cyndi asked a little hesitantly.

The smiles on Brad and Zack's faces instantly faded.

"No, these woods are way too thick," Zack dismissed.

"Yeah, and why would they steal one tape and nothing else? Why not the whole tape player?" Brad reasoned.

"Or the whole backpack?" Zack added.

"Well...I guess that makes sense," Cyndi shrugged. She agreed with their reasoning, but something didn't feel right here. She simply felt like someone had invaded her stuff. Despite their logical arguments, there was no explanation for the missing tape and open pack.

"I don't know, maybe you were sleepwalking, and you were looking for something in your pack in your dreams," Stacy suggested, sounding unconvinced.

"Me? Sleepwalking? I've never done that before."

"That you know of," she still sounded unconvinced. Cyndi frowned skeptically.

"Hey, maybe in your sleep you came to your senses and threw that Go-Go's shit into the river," Brad joked.

Zack added a "HEYO!" like Ed McMahon, and they gave each other a high-five.

"You guys are so immature," Stacy complained. "This is serious. Someone might be out here."

They all looked around the woods suspiciously. The woods seemed so bright and nonthreatening in the daylight. It was hard to believe they had even been so scared riding down the river last night.

"I don't know what to tell you guys," Brad finally said with a shrug. "If there was someone here last night, which I doubt, they're gone now."

"You probably just went through your backpack last night without remembering it," Stacy said. "It was like, four in the morning, remember? We were all half asleep." Cyndi said nothing, she was still unconvinced.

Brad opened his own pack and tossed Twinkies to everyone.

"Breakfast," he announced. Stacy caught hers and looked down at it with disgust.

"Is this all you guys brought?" she asked.

"Well we wanted to bring the Thanksgiving turkey and stuffing, but you know, the Lobster dinner took up too much room in my backpack," he said sarcastically.

"What did you bring?"

"Well, there's some chips, Twinkies, Ring-Dings, some sodas, some candy..."

"Ugh," she said handing the Twinkie back.

"Hey, I thought we'd be in town by now waiting for a ride, okay? Just eat it, and let's get moving. I don't think we're far from the road now."

They ate their Twinkie breakfast and joked a little. They were all in better moods after their rest, and much more comfortable with each other after going through all of last night's unpleasantness. Even Cyndi joined into the conversation a lot more than she ever did back at camp. Afterwards, the girls began gathering up their stuff, and the boys took turns re-inflating the raft. It had deflated noticeably since last night. Cyndi took one last look around for her tape and wrote it off as lost.

Brad and Zack waded into the river and pulled the raft out, holding it there against the current as the

113

girls stepped in. Brad looked around the bend of the river, hoping desperately for some sign of the road, almost imagining he could hear a car drive by. They had better be close to the road, or he knew they would be in deep trouble.

The boys climbed in with dripping legs, picked up their paddles, and continued their trip down the river once again.

*   *   *

It didn't take long for tensions to rise again. Brad expected the river to turn around one bend, then flow peacefully alongside the road. They would then get off the raft, walk for about fifteen minutes, be picked up by a friendly farm truck, head to town, call their parents from a payphone, and be home before dinner. He had gone to sleep thinking they were right around the corner from salvation. Plus, he was actually glad they wouldn't have to hitchhike at night. In retrospect, it was an extremely stupid and dangerous idea. Who knew what crazy, filth covered man would come by, offering them a ride at gunpoint? He was just beginning to realize how his impulsive ideas mixed with his unflinching drive would get him into trouble, but he was still only fourteen years old and had a long way to go.

They came around the first bend in the river and saw no sign of the road. Well, that was okay, it would probably be right around the next corner.

Brad had turned back to the others. "It'll be around this next corner, watch," he assured them. They looked at him hopefully, but were still mostly unconvinced. The next corner came and went with no sign of the road. "Okay, we're getting close now, did you guys hear that car just now?" None of them had heard it, Brad honestly wasn't convinced he had heard it himself.

When he turned his back to them, they gave each other skeptical worried glances.

The trip went on like that for the next hour and a half. The farther they went, the more panic rose in their minds. Brad's insistence and assurances of how close they were to the road began to dwindle. Cyndi empathized with Brad and actually hoped that he was right, even though she heard nothing herself. She needed someone to look toward.

Zack and Stacy began to openly disagree and argue with Brad.

"There. I think I heard another car."

"I didn't hear anything," Stacy argued.

"Well, maybe you need to have your ears checked," he snapped.

Twenty minutes later, "Listen, that was a semi."

"Come on, man. We haven't heard anything all day," Zack reasoned.

"Brad, you're imagining things," Stacy said softly to him.

"Well, at least I'm trying. You three are just sitting on your asses!"

"What does that even mean?" Stacy asked.

"Everybody just shut the fuck up, okay?"

They all did, including Brad.

The current began to pick up speed, and the river began to widen. They passed several trickling streamlets that emptied into their river. The woods around them were still as thick as they had been last night. Most of the large trees growing on the banks had long limbs stretching overhead, blocking out a lot of the sunlight. Brad and Zack found themselves struggling to keep up with the increased amount of paddling. If they didn't keep it up at a steady pace, the raft would turn and spin them in a slow, dizzying circle.

Brad had now given up on the facade that he

knew where he was going. He scanned the woods, looking for landmarks or holes in the foliage where he could see a road or a building, anything that wasn't simply untamed wilderness.

Zack tried to formulate a plan. He needed to figure out just what the hell they should do to survive if they were really lost in the woods. Their makeshift leader, Brad, was pretty much shutting down, and Zack knew that regardless of how little he wanted the position, someone was going to have to step up and do something. He sure as hell didn't want to stay on this river all the way out to the Gulf of Mexico or who knew where. With as little food as they had packed, they probably wouldn't make it that far anyway. He knew it wasn't going to be easy to convince Brad of anything. Brad was a great guy, one of his best friends. Brad was the type of guy that could get focused on something and hammer away at it until the hammer broke. But Brad was not very good at thinking around problems. That's where he and Brad differed, Brad's weakness was Zack's strength. He would have to do something quick if they wanted to stay alive.

He finally gathered up his confidence. "Hey man, I really don't think we're near the road anymore."

Brad heard him loud and clear but ignored him. Zack waited a moment, Stacy and Cyndi glanced back at him in anticipation.

"Hey, Brad," he said again.

"What?" Brad didn't turn around.

"Look man, we gotta talk about this. Why don't we get off the river and just try to figure out where we are?" Brad still ignored him. "Come on, man. Let's just face the fact that we're not anywhere near the road any--"

"You think I don't know that?" Brad snapped. "I have no fuckin' idea where we are! Okay? We're fucking lost! You happy now?"

"Brad, calm down," Stacy said timidly.

"I *am* calm!" Brad yelled in a voice that was anything but calm. Without warning, he began to laugh. Zack, Stacy, and Cyndi let him laugh out his tension. The girls felt like they were on the verge of tears. Zack brought his dripping paddle out of the water and laid it down on the seat. He stood up on wobbly legs and began moving toward the front of the raft. Brad was still chuckling.

"All right, move over, man. We gotta--"

The raft suddenly stopped and jerked to the right. If Brad had been paying attention, he would have seen the huge, slimy, moss-covered rock jutting six inches out of the water. They all jerked forward, Zack toppled over and landed on Brad's left shoulder. Brad's laughter immediately stopped as he flew forward and came within inches of hitting his head on the rock. The water between the raft and the rock splashed up over Brad's head, wetting his hair and most of his back. Cyndi and Stacy let out short surprised screams as they flew forward and cold water splashed up into the raft.

Zack's paddle bounced out of the raft and dropped into the water with a dull *plunk*. The current swept it out of sight before they even realized it was gone. Luckily, none of their packs fell out, though Cyndi's came close. Only her cat-quick reflexes sent her hand flying out at the last second to smash it back down to the bottom of the raft.

The current grabbed hold of the back of the raft and spun them around backwards. Brad coughed and choked on the river water that had gone up his nose. Zack pushed himself up and yanked Brad's paddle back from the edge of the raft where it teetered precariously. He stuck the paddle down three feet into the water, scraping it along the muddy bottom of the river, and tried to turn the raft back around again. The current pulled hard at the paddle, trying to pry it from his hands. He kept his grip tight and could only manage to turn the raft sideways.

"Oh my God," Stacy mumbled as she looked up saw the river ahead, it was full of rocks and white water. In several spots the whole river dropped two or three feet, then splashed up in a huge spray. The biggest drop-off was around a sharp bend, and it was coming up quick.

"Everybody, hang on!" Zack screamed. He shoved the paddle to the bottom and yanked with tremendous effort. The raft spun forward another forty-five degrees. It was the best they were able to do before they hit the first drop.

Stacy and Cyndi picked up their packs and clung to them. Cyndi desperately hoped that she and her pack wouldn't fall out. The water would ruin her tape player. Stacy's thoughts were remarkably similar, except instead of a tape player, she thought of the makeup she had stowed away in her pack. Brad had shut down and let Zack take over. He clung to the side of the raft with wide eyes filled with terror. Zack had no idea how to navigate past these rocks and steep drop-offs. He was on full autopilot, standing with his knees bent at the front of the raft. There was no more time for thinking, only time for surviving.

They went over the first drop and the raft tipped forward crazily. With the two boys in front, outweighing the girls in the back by nearly seventy-five pounds, the raft plunged down into the drop. To Cyndi, it felt dangerously close to flipping over and dumping them all out into the river. They all screamed and leaned backwards, staring down at the rushing white water.

The nose of the raft dipped under the surface as they went over the drop, but the current pushed it forward. With its own buoyancy, the raft bounced up again, sending a huge gush of cold river water on board.

Brad and Zack were instantly soaked and gasped for air. The girls got some of it too, but they somehow managed to keep their packs mostly dry.

The current shoved the raft forward. Zack choked on water that had gone up his nose and stung his sinuses. He looked up to see that they were heading for a sharp dangerous looking rock that lay dead ahead.

Zack paddled like a madman away from the rock, and the raft slid smoothly past it. Brad stared at the rock as they passed close enough for him reach out and touch it.

A number of jagged rocks and low splashing drops lay in the river ahead. Zack saw these, and turned back to warn everyone. Brad, Stacy, and Cyndi clutched the sides of the raft with wide eyes and tensed shoulders. Brad was still too close to the front, that last drop had been too close for comfort and Zack didn't want to risk having them fall out onto the rocks. If that happened, they'd be killed.

"Brad! Get to the back! We need more weight back there!" he shouted over the roar of the rapids. Brad nodded without hesitation, and began crawling to the back of the raft. "Brace yourselves!"

Cyndi looked over and met Stacy's eyes. Her mascara had begun to run, making dark black circles around her huge eyes. Several black tear marks ran down her cheeks. Stacy saw Cyndi's eyes, just as wide, and noticed just how young she looked. She felt an instant of guilt for getting her into this. Without thinking, she held out her hand for comfort, like a big sister would do for her younger sister before going down the first steep drop on a roller coaster. Cyndi grabbed it, and they clasped their hands together tightly. Even though their hands were cold and wet, the strength and comfort was there.

The raft tilted forward again as it went through

three small drops in a row. Zack stood at the front with his paddle up, his feet spread apart and tilted sideways as if he were on a surf board. With Brad now in the back, the weight was evenly distributed and it handled the drops a lot more easily. Each time they went down a drop, they tilted forward and came down with a bump, and white water splashed up on all sides of the raft as they hit the surface.

Zack bent his knees accordingly and surfed his way down the three drops. It was one of the most thrilling things he had ever done in his life. He was still terrified but on the third drop-off he had an uncontrollable smile on his face and screamed out in exhilaration.

"WOOOOO!!!" he screamed, holding his clenched fist high.

Stacy and the others looked up at him shocked. Stacy stared at him in disbelief. They were all holding on for dear life, but Zack was actually cheering. It was insane, but there was something undeniably powerful about his cheers. The tension had been broken, and despite the terror they all felt for their lives, they began to grin helplessly.

Brad, who had all but shut down emotionally, emulated Zack, letting out his own triumphant yell.

"FUCK YEAAAAH!!!" he screamed.

Zack turned and glanced at him, feeling a bit plagiarized, but grinning nonetheless.

Cyndi and Stacy burst out laughing as the water splashed up around them. Off the last drop they lifted their hands up, still clasped together like champion boxers, and gave their own cheer.

In no more than thirty seconds, they had all forgotten the danger, and given in to their sense of adventure.

The raft bounced up off the last drop, and

followed the swiftly flowing current in a slithery S shape around several low rocks. Some bumped under them, scraping against the bottom of the raft with a plastic *zzzzzz* sound. Zack paddled furiously, trying to keep them away from the bigger rocks. He was running on pure adrenaline now.

Cyndi noticed that the surrounding woods were still as thick as they had been last night. If they had been on foot, the woods would have been nearly impenetrable. They also seemed to be sloping and going downhill. Huge rocks and boulders jutted out between the trees. This rocky area must have accounted for all the drops and rapids they were going through.

She looked ahead and saw a large rock straight in their path, the river itself curved around it in a sharp bend to the right. On the right side of the river there was a low spot where the water seemed to get sucked around the corner. Zack saw this and stuck his paddle off to the left so they wouldn't crash into the rock and fall out. He struggled as hard as he could to get the raft to the right, but the current was too strong.

Brad leaned to the right side of the raft, knowing that if they hit the rock, they would hit hard. He might fly off the raft and go rolling off into the woods. Everyone braced themselves, leaning to the right and waiting for the hard bump against the rock.

The water whipping around the side of the rock suddenly grabbed hold of the raft, flinging it forward and pulling them away from the rock at the last possible second. The raft swung within inches of its smooth surface, and they all let out sighs of relief.

They entered a narrow part of the river, a steep downhill stream with low branches drooping down over the water. Zack had to duck down low and still managed to feel the leaves and knobby branches scrape across his shoulders and upper back. The girls leaned away from each other in a V shape and the branches went right between them. With quick reflexes, Brad ducked his head.

At the end of this steep downhill stretch there was another one of those sharp bends around a huge rock. This time the river bent to the left almost a full ninety degrees. They were still picking up too much speed. This time there was no avoiding it, they were going to hit the rock. Zack crouched low and clung to the opposite side of the raft. They all saw it coming and braced themselves.

The raft hit the rock with a thud and bounced back. All four of them were flung to the right, and they let out a singular painful grunt as they hit. Brad felt his jaws clack shut when they hit, and silently thanked God that his tongue hadn't been out. The collision had taken away most of their speed and left them dazed.

The next downhill stretch wasn't nearly as steep, but was maddeningly rocky. Dozens of rocks lined the river, and as the raft went over them they all bounced and jostled. Brad was reminded of the baseball-player bobble-heads he had lined up on his dresser at home. Cyndi and Stacy felt like their brains were being rattled.

This is getting too rough. We're not gonna make it if we keep this up much longer, Zack thought.

Another one of those sharp river bends came up, but none of them had time to see it or prepare for it as they went bumping down the rocky part of the river.

They came racing down at incredible speed and slammed into a huge boulder. Stacy was thrown violently into Cyndi, and the bones in their arms and ribs knocked together painfully. Brad felt his elbow fly out of the raft and crack against the rock. He screamed aloud. Zack was thrown so violently he almost fell off the side. The paddle flew out of his grasp, but he still had enough adrenaline in him to reach out a clawed, desperate hand and hold it down.

The river had smoothed and straightened. They seemed to be on a straight stretch instead of downhill. They were slowing, but still going too fast for comfort.

Cyndi groaned in pain. When Stacy had slammed against her in that last bend, her elbow had rammed against her funny bone, sending maddening tingles up her arm. She clutched her elbow grimacing. Stacy struggled to pull herself off of Cyndi. They both looked forward, wanting to prepare for the next treacherous stretch of river.

Zack struggled to get a grip on the paddle. He pulled it back up into the raft as Stacy began to scream.

"Zack! Do something!"

Cyndi had been the first to see it. Ahead there was a dark cave, at least that was her first impression. A cave of black darkness that opened up in the side of a steep hill and swallowed the entire river. Then she noticed the wooden frame that squared off the opening. It was made of three solid beams that held up the opening like an old mine tunnel. The opening was about ten feet higher than the surface of the river, and spanned ten feet across forming a wooden square. Cyndi was suddenly reminded of an amusement park ride she had ridden as a child, the Haunted Mine, where you sat in a fake log and floated through a dark fun house filled with eerie sounds and cheap thrills. She couldn't really believe what she was seeing. They were in the middle of nowhere, how could the Haunted Mine be way out here?

Stacy had seen it next and began to scream. "Zack! Do something! Do something!" Her screams echoed hollowly from the darkness inside tunnel.

She caught Brad's attention. He looked up from his injured elbow, it was sure to bruise and lump up if it wasn't broken. He stared into the blackness that seemed to be pulling them straight in, and sat frozen, feeling sick terror deep in his guts.

Zack stared at the mine tunnel opening and couldn't believe what he was seeing. *Is this some kind of joke?* Stacy's screams pierced his eardrums and he jumped in panic. He looked around for something to grab as the dark opening loomed ahead, but they were stuck in the dead center of the river. They were too far out of reach to grab onto the mine tunnel's wooden beams.

He looked up and quickly scanned the overhanging branches, but they were too high out of his reach. He stared ahead at the dark mine tunnel and tried to force his brain to work faster. Survival in the woods was one thing, but this? Well, he didn't exactly know what to make of this, and everything was happening too fast. He instinctively began to paddle for the sides, but they were weak strokes. He was too confused and terrified by what he was seeing.

They were almost up to the opening now and Stacy's panicked screams echoed in the darkness ahead.

"Zack! Brad! What do we do?! Do something! Do something, Zack!"

A panicked voice somewhere deep in Brad's mind suddenly spoke up. *Jump out! Do it! Just jump out!* He was frozen and didn't take his own advice, something he would later deeply regret. Cyndi clung to her backpack as they passed under the beams, her eyes wide with terror.

The river carried them in, and the darkness swallowed them whole.

Chapter Eleven:

The Park

Cyndi strained her eyes to see forward in the dark. They had gone about fifty feet into the tunnel, and the little light coming in from the opening was fading fast. All four of them craned their necks around, frantically trying to see as much as they could before they went in too far and the light faded out completely. The walls looked just like they'd expect the walls of a mine tunnel to look, rocky and chiseled, held up by thick wooden beams every ten feet. Zack's eyes landed on one of these beams and it hit him all at once. *Whatever those beams are made of, they sure aren't wooden. They look more like--*

"Zack! DO something!" Stacy interrupted his thoughts, grabbing him by the shoulder. Her panicky screams reverberated off the walls of the tunnel. "Brad! Zack! Are you listening to me?"

"Yes! What?" Brad snapped back at her.

"Paddle! Get us the fuck OUT of here! Do something!" she demanded.

"I can't. The water's going too fast!"

"Well...TRY! Do something! Anything!"

"Like what?" Brad yelled matching her tone.

"Anything! I don't care!"

Zack looked back as the light began to cut out on one side of the tunnel. "Fuck! It's curving!"

They all turned back, watching helplessly as the current pulled them around a slow corner and into complete darkness.

"No. *NO!*" Stacy whimpered, then her voice rose to a scream. She scrambled toward the edge of the raft. She swung her left leg up and over, splashing down into the water. Her leg extended down into the cold water up to her mid thigh, but she still couldn't feel the bottom.

Cyndi heard the splash in the darkness and knew what Stacy was doing.

"DON'T!" Cyndi yelled, instinctively raising her voice to the loudest level it had reached in the last year. Her hands flung out and awkwardly grabbed hold of Stacy's forearm. She began to yank Stacy back into the raft before she could flip over the side into the dark water.

"Let me go! I gotta get outta here!" Stacy said through clenched teeth.

"Stacy, stop it!" Brad shouted at her. He and Zack leaned toward her and also tried to pull her back into the raft. She struggled and thrashed against all three of them. "Quit it! Stace!"

"We don't know what's down there!" Zack yelled at her.

"Stacy! STAY – IN – THE – RAFT!" Cyndi said in a loud, concise voice, putting emphasis on every word. Something about hearing Cyndi speak in such a commanding, authoritative voice shocked her into giving up her struggles. Brad and Zack felt her give up the fight, and they heaved her all the way back into the middle of the raft.

"We have to get out of here," Stacy choked, close to tears. As she lay in a heap in the bottom of the raft, Cyndi put her arms around Stacy's shoulders. Brad awkwardly put his hand on Stacy's shoulder as she cried softly. He wanted to comfort her, but didn't really know how to. Her short gasps and sobs echoed through the dark tunnel.

Zack peered ahead into the darkness the best he could. He felt his eyes adjusting slowly, and thought he could make out shapes, but maybe it was only the reflection on his retinas from the bright sunlight they had been in only a minute ago. He could feel the river curving around again, but this time it was going in a different direction. He tried to peer around this new bend, desperately looking for any sign of light or an opening.

There was a soft scraping sound to the left of the raft only a yard or two from Cyndi. She jumped and tightened her arms around Stacy's shoulders. Zack heard it too and whirled. It had sounded like a shoe or pants scraping across rough gravel.

Stacy hitched in breath, "What? What?" she whispered. Her tears were replaced by a fresh, sickening wave of panic.

"I heard it too," Brad mumbled. In truth, he had only half-heard the sound, it caught his attention just as he had started to zone out.

"What? Heard what?" Stacy asked frantically.

"Shut up," Zack whispered.

The echoes of their voices lingered for a few seconds, then faded out. Cyndi's eyes hadn't fully adjusted either, not that there was any light in the tunnel, but she thought maybe she could see a person standing back in the shadows above the level of the water. She leaned closer to Stacy and felt her heartbeat thumping furiously, as fast as her own.

Zack strained his eyes as hard as he could, trying to make out shapes in the darkness. He thought he saw a man-shaped silhouette standing back on some narrow ledge at the water level, but it was too dark to tell. It was only a dark black shape among slightly darker black shapes. Sometimes he would think he could see something, then it would fade into darkness. His eyes locked onto the shape and he had a startling clear image of the man shape. He jumped back in surprise and the raft bobbed, causing him to lose the image altogether.

"Hello?" Zack said out loud, his voice echoing off the walls. To his own ears, he sounded very young, and very afraid. He instantly wished he had used a deeper voice.

He struggled to see the dark image again and thought, *Damn, if only I had a flash-- Wait! We do have a flashlight!*

"Get me that flashlight out of the pack," he whispered. He felt like kicking himself. Why hadn't he thought of grabbing it in the first place? The more he thought about it, it really made sense. In the panic they had all been through within the last fifteen or twenty minutes, it was no wonder they had forgotten all about the flashlight.

Without a word, Stacy yanked open the pack and rummaged through it, probing through the junk desperately for the unmistakable hard, metal cylinder shape of the flashlight. She felt her way down to the bottom of the pack, then dug her arm along the sides, rummaging through the junk. She wondered why Zack and Brad had brought so much crap. She could not feel the flashlight anywhere.

"It's not in here," she whispered.

"What?" Zack whispered.

"What do you mean it's not in here?" Brad asked, the panic in his voice rising.

128

"It's not *IN* here!   See for yourself," she whispered angrily, shoving the pack into Brad's arms.

Cyndi reached down and searched through her own pack on the off chance that she might have put the flashlight in there by mistake, even though she highly doubted it.   Cyndi thought she remembered Stacy holding it last, while they built the fire last night.   But maybe she had taken it and forgotten about it, she did not want to cause any trouble over a stupid mistake.   The panic level in the raft was rising, if only she could help stop it.

Suddenly, there was a loud metallic clunk and an electric whirring sound from up ahead.   This time the sounds were undeniable.

"WHO'S THERE?!" Zack screamed, whirling around.

He fumbled frantically in the dark for the paddle, and raised it up defensively.

Stacy and Cyndi clutched each other.

"What is that?" Stacy whimpered.

Brad quickly wrapped his arms around Stacy's waist.   He wasn't trying to comfort her though, he was scared out of his mind.   That electric whirring made him feel like he was caught in a gigantic machine, slowly being pulled into a crushing death under greasy gears.

There was another loud CLUNK and blinding light came spilling into the tunnel in a thin expanding vertical line.   All four of them squinted, holding their hands in front of their faces to shield their eyes.   They only squinted for a second, then their eyes widened despite the pain of the sudden dilation of their pupils.   The view ahead took them all by complete and utter surprise.

Two thick metal doors swung open in front of the raft on some sort of automatic hydraulic system.   The river water swirled past the doors, creating small whirlpools on either side. The river had slowed down considerably, reverting back to the same lazy speed it had been last night as they entered the woods.

They were still in thick woods. The trees mostly hung over the river as they had before, but a lot of the trees and shrubbery had been cleared out and cleaned up. In fact, it didn't look wild at all anymore, it looked manicured and landscaped. The grass on either side of the river's edges was neatly trimmed. It reminded Brad of the edges of the creek that ran through the golf course he and his Dad played back home. A few feet farther up the riverbank, the ground leveled out and there were thick flowerbeds filled with white, purple, and red petunias. Interspersed between the petunias every four feet were wild grasses that looked anything but wild in their patterns of strict uniformity. Spread among the flowers were low lights encased in colorful plastic shades of red, green, blue, yellow. The lights were all dark in the daylight.

On the left side of the river, the ground was flat for about fifty yards, then rose in a steep hill covered in foliage. On the hill, they could see white water slides meandering downhill and emptying out in a pool somewhere past the line of sight. The slides snaked around wildly under tree branches.

They all sat slack-jawed, gazing at everything.

"What the hell is this place?" Zack mumbled, lowering his paddle.

The only sounds in the area were the trickle and splash of water flowing down the slides, the soft gurgle of the river, and the chirping of birds. The place seemed to be utterly deserted. None of them added their own noise to break the silence (except for Zack's question), and none of them noticed the metal doors swinging slowly shut behind them as they continued down the river.

The silence was broken as the metal doors shut and locked with two CLUNK noises, one soft then another much louder. They all jumped and spun around to see the river water swirling in front of the closed metal doors and settling. The doors were just inside another mine tunnel entrance, or exit. They were painted black except for a large yellowish-white smiling face painted across the middle. It was three feet in diameter and had laughing oval eyes. To Cyndi, the eyes looked less like human eyes and more like the dark eyes of a dog or a cackling hyena. It had exaggerated yet realistic human features, and a disproportionately wide grinning mouth filled with huge perfect white teeth. The teeth looked very realistic against the simplicity of the face. They jutted forward, seeming to be the driving force of the entire face.

The laughing grinning face gave all of them the creeps. It looked like something old, designed in the thirties or forties, that had been meant to inspire other smiles, but had lost its charm over time. Cyndi thought it looked more apt to inspire screams than smiles. Something was very unsettling about the way it sat back in the shadow of the mine tunnel on those closed doors. It seemed to say, *Welcome to my home. Kick off your shoes because you're going to be here for a while. You're going to be here forever.*

The river curved and the smiling face disappeared behind the neatly manicured riverbank and flowerbeds. They looked at each other with awestruck and wary expressions, each of them wondering just where in hell they were? What had they gotten themselves into? No one asked each other any questions, they all knew no one had any answers.

The raft came around a corner and a wooden deck surrounded by a railing jutted out on their left, coming right up to the river's edge. The wood had a fresh unblemished coat of dark red paint. As the raft passed the deck, they looked up and saw a half a dozen picnic tables neatly arranged and painted the same fresh coat of dark red. Zack was reminded of the picnic tables back at camp.

The picnic table area was completely clean and silent, and it unnerved them all, Cyndi especially. It looked like the sort of place that should be crawling with people and activity, yet it was quiet as a tomb.

She thought, *Where are the voices of people talking? Where's the sound of some radio playing that song from Flashdance for the hundredth time? Where are all the lawnmowers, or tools, or cars on the nearby road?* It was as if the place had been suddenly abandoned.

"Guys? What the hell is this place?" Zack asked again. Cyndi and Brad turned to look at him.

"You tell me," Stacy mumbled without looking away from the picnic area.

Brad was the first to look forward and they all followed suit. The river ahead was split in two. The larger of the two forks continued to the right on its slow meandering path through the woods. It curved out of sight past some cottonwood trees that had grown high above the river. The smaller of the two forks was man-made, branching off to the left up a concrete slope that went up out of the water and onto a smooth cement path. At the top off the slope, and off to the right, was a neat stack of clear blue inner tubes.

"You guys wanna check it out?" Zack asked warily. Stacy and Cyndi shrugged.

"Might as well. Wherever we are, there's probably a road nearby," Brad replied, a smile working its way onto his face. "I mean, there's gotta be one, right?"

"Shit, you're right!" Zack exclaimed.

Zack paddled hard toward the slope. Stacy shared grins with Brad and Cyndi. When they got close enough to the concrete, both Zack and Brad jumped out of the raft and splashed down into the water, it almost came up to their ribs. They each took a side and guided the raft up the slope. They gave it a final shove and its front end slid onto the concrete with a plastic hiss. Stacy and Cyndi jerked forward as it came to a sudden stop.

Zack walked up out of the water and held out a hand to the girls to help them out. Both Cyndi and Stacy were grateful for the gesture. Stacy felt a mild irritation with Brad as he ran up the slope without even looking back. His swimsuit dripped as he ran, leaving a long, wet trail of river water on the dry concrete. He was convinced he had successfully navigated them out of the woods and back to civilization. He had found redemption. Brad ran into the park full of hope and relief, but the feeling was short lived.

Chapter Twelve:

All To Themselves

"Hellooooo?" Brad yelled with a hand cupped to his mouth. His voice echoed back. Off to the right, he saw a medium sized pool about fifty yards away. The water in the pool was light blue, crystal clear, and even from this distance Brad faintly smelled chlorine.   A steady stream of water splashed into the pool from four white water slides that meandered out from the thick surrounding trees and emptied there.

Brad looked back and forth from the water slide pool to the picnic area, searching for something, any sign of life, and saw none.

Zack, Stacy, and Cyndi dragged the raft up to the top of the concrete slope and dropped it there. As the raft plopped down, Zack looked over at the stack of tubes and immediately gave a startled jump.

A man stood next to the stack of tubes dressed in a sea captain outfit. The man's face was the same grinning face they had seen painted on the metal door inside the mine tunnel. Zack sighed with relief as he realized it wasn't a real guy. It was only a painted, wooden cut out shaped like a man and attached to the edge of a blue metal hand railing that was set into the concrete. They hadn't been able to see the wooden figure from the river because the stack of tubes had been blocking it.

"Jesus!" he sighed and laughed at himself. He turned to the girls and pointed back at the cut out. "That thing scared the shit out of me." Cyndi and Stacy both gave polite insincere laughs, the smiley face captain creeped them out too. To Cyndi, it even seemed to be painted in a creepy, shadowy way. It looked more forbidding than welcoming. They stared at it warily for a second, then grabbed their packs out of the raft.

"Hellooooooo?" Brad called again. Stacy, Cyndi, and Zack walked up to him, dropped their packs on the concrete path, and looked around in amazement.

The park seemed to be built on the hill, and the entire place was immaculately landscaped. There were neat flowerbeds everywhere, just like the ones lining the river's edge, and not one had a single weed or dead flower. There were several concrete paths that wandered up the hill and curved out of sight behind thick groves of trees. All of the paths had those multicolored lights planted near the ground. They could also see at least two more wooden decks like the one at the picnic area, only these were smaller and higher up on the hill.

They saw what looked like half a dozen rides and slides swinging in and out of the trees. One large slide seemed to careen down the hill and disappear behind a stand of thick trees and bushes somewhere behind the picnic area. The four slides that emptied out into the pool to the right of the picnic area seemed to be the centerpiece to the park. Stacy was the first to see a wooden rustic looking sign in front of the pool that the slides emptied into. The sign had the words *the RAGIN' RIVERS* painted on it in blue sloppy handwriting that looked like something you would see on the credits of that corny show *Hee Haw*. Next to the sloppy letters, there was a small cartoon painting of that Smiley-Face-Man grinning and paddling down a river churning with white rapids. The sign was made to look like a ragged, splintery old driftwood board, but it was obviously intentional.

Brad turned back to them and shrugged his shoulders. "Where the hell is everybody?" he asked.

"Your guess is as good as mine, man," Zack said.

"Is this some kind of a joke? I mean, I feel like I'm on *Candid Camera* or something," Brad said laughing. He suddenly turned around, yanked on the drawstring of his swimsuit, pulled it down and mooned the trees. "Hey, Dorothy Collins! You like my ass? You can come on out now!"

"Brad!" Stacy yelled in a shocked, scolding tone. She couldn't help but burst out laughing, they all did.

"Well, I guess we can rule out that one," he said and pulled up his swimsuit. He began tying the drawstring knot again.

"Why don't we walk around and see if we can find anyone?" Stacy asked. "There's gotta be *some*one."

"Probably. And I bet we're really close to a road," Brad said.

"You think it'll be okay if we leave our stuff here?" Stacy asked.

"I don't see why not," Zack said.

They walked to the closest picnic table and set their backpacks down. Cyndi almost put hers down when she suddenly felt a wave of nervous tension. She remembered falling asleep last night listening to her mix tape, the one with the Go-Go's, and that new song that she loved. Then this morning she had woken up to find the tape missing inexplicably. What would happen when

136

they came back for their stuff this time? What would be missing?

"Hey, you okay?" Stacy asked her.

"Uh...Yeah, I'm okay," Cyndi said, pulling herself away from her own distracted thoughts. "You really think our stuff will be okay here?"

"It's fine," Brad said dismissively. He was already walking toward one of the paths that wound its way up the hill.

Stacy and Zack nodded in agreement, and Cyndi put her bag down reluctantly. She couldn't help feeling like she was making another wrong decision.

They followed Brad up the nearest path as it wound its way up the hill. There were metal handrails painted bright blue on either side of the path. Beyond the handrails were lots of trees with thick overhanging branches that shaded most of the park. To the right, they could see under two of the four white slides. They looked like giant white crazy straw tubes cut in half and held up by concrete pillars. Underneath the slides was thick green grass that looked mowed and well maintained. To the left, the ground had been left as a natural wild forest floor covered with ferns and low bushes.

"This place is fucking incredible!" Brad said. "Have you guys ever seen anything like this?"

"What I want to know is, where are all the people?" Stacy asked. "Shouldn't there be like, tons of people walking around and riding these rides?"

"Maybe there was a gas leak and they cleared everybody out," Zack suggested.

"I don't smell any gas. Do you?" Brad said sniffing the air. "Oooh, what is this?" A short set of wooden steps broke away from the path and ascended to the left. Brad ran up them two at a time and the others followed him.

They reached the top of the steps and walked out onto another wooden deck. This one had been painted that same dark red as the picnic area deck, but it wasn't as big. Across from the steps were two tall stacks of tubes in the corner, they were a light tan color and looked big enough to hold three or four people. Next to the tubes, a small pool was cut into the deck where you could put the tube into the water to get on the ride.

At the top of the steps, there was another sign designed in that same rustic wooden look, labeling the ride as *DEAD MAN'S DROP*. It showed another cartoony painted picture of one of the rafts going almost straight down. The raft on the picture was filled with three screaming kids, their hair flying out behind them, their eyes bugging out and their heads covered with grotesque veins. That smiley faced Sea Captain sat in dead center of the raft. His arms were wrapped around the kids shoulders and his bony fingers almost looked as if they were painfully digging into their skin.

"Oooh, the Dead Man's Drop, moo-wa-ha-ha-ha!" Brad said in his low, late-night-horror-movie voice. "You guys wanna get on?"

"Yeah!" Zack blurted and immediately went for the stack of tubes.

Cyndi and Stacy looked down at the steep slide and shared the same thought, *something about this ride doesn't look safe.* Low tree branches hung over the ride, giving it a shadowy look. It curved off out of sight halfway down the hill. Stacy felt nervous just looking at it.

"Come on, you guys. Let's find someone first," Stacy protested.

"Aww come on, Stace!" Brad whined. "Don't you wanna have some fun? Ride some rides?" He grabbed the tube at the top of the stack and began to try to yank it down.

"What *I* want is to take a shower and get out of this wet swimsuit," she said.

As they argued, Cyndi wandered out to the edge of the deck and looked down. From this vantage point, the trees were so thick that she had trouble making out the picnic area. She could see just a few small sections of the river they had ridden in on. She happened to glance over at one of the tall poles holding up the deck and saw a large white speaker mounted eight feet off the deck surface. She wondered what the speaker was connected to and why it wasn't playing any music.

"We'll have time for rides later, you guys. Right now let's just find someone so we can figure out where the hell we are," Stacy said, and began walking down the wooden stairs alone. Cyndi saw her leaving and quickly followed.

"Come on, man. We can't let them go off on their own," Zack said reluctantly and began following the girls.

"What? Are you guys too chicken?" Brad yelled. He made several chicken noises but when no one laughed or even turned around, he let go of the tube and quickly followed them down the steps.

"Helloooo? Anybody?" Stacy called cupping her hands over her mouth. She stood at the bottom of the steps, listening for signs of life. Brad came clunking down the wooden steps in his flip-flops, drowning out any noise she might have heard. She glared at him and he grinned. Ignoring him, she looked left and saw that the path ended a little farther up. It seemed to just trail off into thick, untamed woods as if it wasn't quite finished. She decided to walk back down the path again to see what was on the right side of the park. Cyndi followed closely behind her.

Brad put his arm around Zack's shoulders.

"Next ride we come to we're getting on whether

139

you like it or not," Brad called out to Stacy.

"That's right!" Zack agreed. Cyndi glanced back at them, looking slightly annoyed. Zack felt a pang of regret seeing her expression. Stacy never even turned around. Brad and Zack looked at each other shrugging.

"Women," Brad said dismissively.

"Can't live with 'em..." Zack began.

"Can't kill 'em!" Brad retorted immediately. Zack broke into laughter. That was one of those phrases Brad had introduced him to that never failed to crack him up. Brad followed up with an imaginary shotgun, complete with sound effects, pretending to blast the girls away. Then he gave Zack an utterly confused look as if to prove his point that you indeed *couldn't kill 'em.* This made Zack laugh even harder and Brad clapped him on the back once before continuing down the path after the girls. Zack followed him down, chuckling the whole way.

When they reached the bottom of the hill, Cyndi looked over at the picnic table. Their stuff was still all there just as it had been, completely untouched. She felt relieved, but as they started away again, that bad feeling returned. Someone *was* here, and they were going to take all their stuff. All her tapes, her Walkman, her extra clothes, everything.

Stop it, she forced her paranoid thoughts away. *Nothing is going to happen to the stuff. And even if it does, who cares? You ran away from camp and you're in the middle of some weird empty water park miles from home, I think you have bigger things to worry about.*

They walked past the picnic area and down a slight slope to the pool at the bottom of the Ragin' Rivers. Stacy stood in front of the Ragin' Rivers sign and stared at the picture of the grinning smiley face captain paddling his way down a treacherous river filled with white water rapids. It reminded her of their frightening trip down the river just outside this place.

"If you'd been on the river we were just on, it would wipe that stupid smile right off your face," Stacy said out loud. Cyndi started giggling next to Stacy, and she turned startled. "Did I just say that out loud?" Cyndi nodded. Stacy began to giggle herself. "I thought I was only thinking it."

There were two concrete paths leading up the hill on either side of the Ragin' River slides.

"Okay, you take that side, I'll take this one. We'll race down," Brad said in a hurried tone.

"You're going *down*, man," Zack laughed.

"Will you guys knock it off?" Stacy said.

"What is your problem, Stace?" Brad asked. "We're just tryin' to have a good time--"

"Have you guys ever thought that maybe we're not supposed to be here?"

"What do you mean?"

"I don't know, like, what if this is some rich millionaire guy's backyard, and we're trespassing?"

"Hey, Rich Guy!" Brad yelled out, cupping his hands to his mouth. "That cool if we ride your rides? No? Tough shit, 'cuz we're going on 'em anyway!" Zack broke out into gales of fresh laughter. Brad turned back seriously to Stacy. "No one's here. We have this whole place all to ourselves. Lighten up a little, will ya?"

Stacy glared at him for a moment, then glanced over at the other rides. She had to admit that the clear blue water and the smell of the chlorine were pretty inviting.

"Okay," she gave in. "But first we have to look around. We have to figure out where we are and where everyone else is."

"Fair enough, fair enough," Brad said, holding his hands up defensively. "I'm just sayin' you've already run away from camp, you're already in deep trouble.

Might as well have a little fun before we get back to civilization and have to start doin' time. What's the worst that could happen?"

Brad began to walk forward, leading them again. Cyndi watched him distrustfully. She wanted to say, *A lot worse could happen. We've been lucky so far, but it could get a lot worse. You should not be leading us. Either Zack or Stacy should lead us, not you.* She kept her thoughts to herself.

Just past the Ragin' Rivers ending pool, was another smaller pool, where two large slides set into the ground converged. These slides seemed to be built out of smoothed concrete, unlike the plastic tube slides that were smooth and symmetrical. Another rustic looking sign proclaimed: *the DUELIN' RIVERS*. The cartoon picture this time was the smiley face captain in a cowboy hat and cowboy boots. He held two old fashioned six-shooter pistols in his hands.

"Well, lookee here, it's the Duelin' Rivers, y'all!" Zack shouted in a high pitched twangy western voice.

"How-DEEE?!" Brad added in his own western voice, and they all laughed.

"You guys are so stupid," Stacy laughed.

"Why, thank you," Brad joked. "Come on now, li'l ladies. Let's mosey on over past these here Duelin' Rivers, y'all!" Brad waved them along and lead the way down the path.

They walked past the end-pool of the Duelin' Rivers and passed by another long, perfectly manicured flowerbed.

"Whoever owns this place sure does a good job of keeping it up," Zack said.

"It is pretty gorgeous," Stacy agreed.

"All the little helper elves come out at night and do the yard work," Brad said.

"Yeah, and they all wear little smiley face

masks," Zack joked.

"What is *with* all those face things?" Stacy burst out.

"Ugh, those things creep me out," Cyndi said softly.

"Me too," Zack said. "Why are they everywhere?"

"Oh, come on, they're not *everywhere*," Brad said contemptuously.

"Oh no?" Zack began pointing at random spots all around them, accentuating every point with a "There, there, there." There was a small sign in the flowerbeds saying PLEASE KEEP OUT OF THE FLOWERS, with a picture of a smiley face in the middle of a budding daisy. Another sign said, STACK YOUR TUBES HERE, and had a smiley face and a white gloved, Mickey Mouse type hand pointing just to the right of the sign itself. A trashcan had a big crazy smiley face painted right on the lid. Tall umbrellas that stood open at the edges of both the Ragin' and Duelin' Rivers end-pools had the same grinning face painted on the tops.

"And look at those black ones," Zack added. "There, and there, and there."

Zack pointed out a black grotesque smiley face that had been sloppily painted on one of the rocks near the river's edge in black dripping paint. Another was on the side of the trashcan with the same drippy craftsmanship.

Zack had spotted more than Brad, but he was far from the most observant person in the group. Cyndi had spotted half a dozen more crude faces that Zack had overlooked. A rough smiley face carved into the bark of a tree. Another one dripped down the bottom of one of the white Ragin' River slides. Another had been painted low on the side of the Duelin' River slides, and was now fading. They really were everywhere, and she felt more and more uneasy with every face she noticed. The black ones seemed crude and unprofessional. They looked obsessive, as if they had been created by a child with a smiley face fixation running rampant with a can of spray paint.

Brad shrugged, taking Zack's point. "I guess you're right."

"Spooky," Cyndi muttered. Stacy gave her a worried glance, thinking the exact same thing.

"Whatever, let's just get on with it so we can get on the rides," Brad said, dismissively waving his hand and continuing down the path at a brisk walk. The others picked up their own paces to keep up with him.

Another twenty yards farther down the path, they reached another ride. It was a meandering, blue, chlorinated imitation of a river encased in smooth whitewashed concrete. Another faux-rustic sign called this ride *the LAZY RIVER,* and was accentuated by a cartoon of the infamous smiley face captain lounging in an inner tube. He wore a pair of sunglasses in this one and held a drink in his hand, complete with ice cubes and a little pink umbrella.

A few dozen of those same clear blue tubes they had seen near the natural river were floating along in the Lazy River at a slow steady pace, bumping into each other softly. Several wooden posts surrounded the river and the path curved left and went up the hill alongside them. Fishnet held up by a thick yellow rope was draped between the posts, adding to the whole maritime motif. There was an opening in the netting, directly in front of them, forming a front entrance to the Lazy River. Beyond that, a set of concrete steps descended into the clear, blue water.

"A-ha, The *Lazy* River," Brad announced.

"I think I'm sensing a theme here," Zack said sarcastically. He cradled his chin between his index finger and thumb and pretended to be thinking very hard.

"Do they have signs over the bathrooms that say Shit River?"

They broke out into more laughter. Stacy gave Brad a playful shove. "Oh my God. Gag me with a spoon!"

"Yeah, I'd like to see them paint a picture of the smiley guy taking a dump!" Zack added, then did an imitation of a highly constipated smiley face grin. The boys howled with laughter.

"Okay, I think I've had just enough Boy-Potty-humor. What do you think, Cyndi?"

"More than enough," Cyndi said, although she was still laughing with the rest of them.

They began up the hill, looking down at the Lazy River as they ascended. On the other side of the ropes and fishnet, sharp rocks set in rough porous concrete went down a steep hill to the smooth edge of the lazy river. Once they walked twenty feet uphill, the ropes and netting ended and there was a high cliff. A wooden lifeguard's chair and umbrella sat on this cliff, looking out over the Lazy River and the island in the middle of it. Thick willow trees and cottonwoods covered the little man-made island, and their branches hung over a lot of the river, shading it from the bright sun. Just past the cliff was a steep waterfall that cascaded over the rocks and became white foam in the Lazy River.

"Oh my God, it's so beautiful. I call Lazy River next," Stacy said.

"I second that, Lazy River," Cyndi agreed.

"What's this? Is Stacy actually suggesting we ride something?" Brad asked in mock amazement. He ran up and put his arm around her. "There's hope for you yet, Babe." He gave her a big kiss on the cheek. She didn't argue with him. She was beginning to forget the fact that they were all alone in this mysterious water park. The fun atmosphere, combined with Brad and Zack's high spirits, were slowly winning her over, and she couldn't help but feel like she was having a good time. Even Cyndi seemed to be lightening up and coming out of her shell.

Past the cliff, the Lazy River was blocked out of sight by more trees. They turned to their left and saw the beginning of a white slide and a stack of bright green tubes poking out of the foliage thirty yards farther up the hill. Cyndi assumed it was the start of one of the Ragin' Rivers. The boys wanted to cut through the foliage and get on, but Stacy and Cyndi argued to keep following the path and see what was at the top.

The path curved around to the left past some jungly looking ferns and came to another dead end. The four of them stopped and stared into the thick woods.

"And...More...Woods," Brad said, emphasizing each word. "Okay. Rides anyone?" He immediately turned and began walking back down the hill toward the ride entrances.

"I'm with you, dude," Zack said, slowly turning away from the girls.

Stacy peered into the woods. She just couldn't accept the fact that there was this big fancy water park in the middle of the woods, but no people. She turned to Cyndi, who shared her puzzled, contemplative look.

"Something just doesn't feel right here," she said softly, Cyndi nodded in agreement. "I just can't...describe what it is, y'know?"

"It feels like there's a catch," Cyndi filled in without hesitation at all.

Stacy snapped her fingers and pointed at her immediately. "That's it, thank you. It's like, what's the catch here?"

"You guys coming or what?" Brad yelled back.

146

He was already almost at the bottom of the hill. Stacy rolled her eyes, and she and Cyndi rushed after the boys down the hill.

*   *   *

Less than ten minutes later, they were heading up the path between the Ragin' Rivers and the Duelin' Rivers. There was a wooden staircase built just past the end pools of the rides, where the hill became too steep. Each step was covered with a fresh layer of soft green AstroTurf. A little stream trickled underneath the stairs and flowed off into the landscaped underbrush.

At the top of the wooden steps, the path continued in an S-shape under the giant white curving tubes that made up the Ragin' Rivers. A huge, colorful bed of wildflowers sat next to the path, giving off a fragrant summery smell that they all enjoyed.

"Oh man, when I become a millionaire, this is what my backyard is gonna be like," Zack fantasized. "And you guys can come party at my house whenever you want."

"I would but, uh, I'll be too busy in my own water park backyard, thank you very much," Stacy said. Brad put his arm around her shoulders.

"Oh, so we're gonna have a water park mansion then?" Brad asked.

"Yep," she smiled at him.

"And all our kids are gonna play on all the slides and stuff?"

"Sure."

"At least until we ship them off to camp to torture Sheehan." They all laughed and Brad kissed her on the cheek. She turned to face him and they both kissed a little more. Zack and Cyndi didn't mind. They continued on up the hill, giving them space.

"You'll come hang out at *my* water park backyard, won't you, Cyndi?" Zack asked.

"If you want me to, sure," she replied, smiling.

On a sudden unexpected impulse, his hand reached out and lightly held hers. It sent her heart into a wild flutter, and she felt her face turning red. She looked down at the ground to hide it.

Zack was first shocked and worried about potential rejection. For an instant, he was sure that she would yank her hand away from his and say something like, *Umm, what the hell are you doing?* He looked over at her in spite of the fear, and saw Cyndi's blushing cheeks and the wide smile that had spread across her face. She was cute. Hell, she was gorgeous. Her ears were poking out from her hair in an almost elvish way that he loved. There was still some of the crimp left in her light blond hair, and it had that sexy, slightly messy look. He suddenly realized that he had been staring at her for too long and forced himself to tear his gaze away. He focused his eyes on the wildflowers, but didn't see them at all. He was still focused on her face, only instead of seeing it with his eyes, he saw it in his imagination.

Brad glanced up the path at Zack and Cyndi. He saw them holding hands and walking up the hill together, and he felt a surge of pride for Zack. His best friend had finally gotten himself a girl.

"Look," he whispered to Stacy and he pointed at Cyndi and Zack.

Stacy wasn't very surprised. She formed an O with her mouth, and held her hand up, giggling a little. Brad nodded at her, made a kissy face, then stuck his tongue out in sloppy make out motions. She laughed and pushed him playfully.

She felt the same pride for Cyndi that Brad felt for Zack. The timid little girl she had met on the bus just a week ago was coming out of her shell more and more, and Stacy knew she had a lot to do with that. Also, within the last twenty-four hours she had found a new level of respect for Zack that she had never known. He had taken her completely by surprise the way he took charge and led them to safety on the raft. Big Bad Brad had all but curled up into a little ball and stuck his thumb in his mouth. A day ago she would have been mistrustful and a little disgusted at the sight of Zack with one of her friends. Now, because of his kindness and loyalty to their group, he had earned her blessing.

At the top of the hill, the path forked. In the center of the fork was another of those faux-rustic signs, designed to look like a backwoods road sign. One board directed them to take a sharp right towards two of the Ragin' Rivers (the other two presumably started elsewhere), while another board pointed dead ahead toward another wooden foot bridge that rose over one of the Duelin' Rivers. Zack and Cyndi were so lost in their thoughts that they practically walked right into the sign.

"Wait! Stop. Back up," Stacy yelled up to them. They looked up startled and their hands broke away from each other.

"Take a left, love-birds," Brad said.

"Shut up," Zack laughed.

Cyndi looked down at the ground again, blushing harder than ever, and they hurried up onto the AstroTurf steps of this new bridge.

From the bridge, Zack looked over and got his first glimpse of the entrance of the Duelin' Rivers. Both slides started at the foot of a man-made waterfall that gushed out from under a three foot high rock overhang. The water splashed down and foamed in a slow moving river that looked a lot like the Lazy River at the bottom of the hill. After about fifty yards, the river split in two and each end went splashing down fast-paced, bumpy looking concrete slides. The river on the left went under the bridge beneath their feet just after it began to pick up speed.

Brad rubbed his hands together anxiously and took off for the entrance.

"Come on, you guys," he yelled eagerly.

At the front of the ride, there sat another tall stack of large green tubes that looked like they could comfortably seat two or three people. Brad was the first to arrive. He yanked one tube off the top of the stack and it came bouncing down onto the concrete. It rolled in a small diminishing circle like a giant coin before finally settling. He picked up one of the six black handles along the sides of the tube, and dragged it toward the concrete steps that led down into the cool, blue water. The tube made a harsh plastic sliding noise as he dragged it over the concrete.

"Uh, Brad I don't think we're all going to fit in these things," Stacy said.

"Well, then get another one-- Hey!" he stopped, abruptly snapping his fingers. His eyes lit up with an idea. "Why don't we each take a river and race down? I mean, they don't call these the *Duelin' Rivers* for nothin' right?"

"I guess," Zack said, shrugging his shoulders. Stacy pulled weakly at the next tube on the stack. It was heavy and bulky and she had to struggle to get it down. Zack saw this, walked over, and offered to help. "Here, I got it." He took the tube by the handle and yanked it down.

"Thank you for your help, *Zack*," Stacy said with an edge of bitterness, staring at Brad the whole time. She hoped Brad would take the hint, but he was oblivious to her icy stare as he dropped his tube down into the water with a splash. Zack didn't notice Stacy much either. His eyes had met Cyndi's again and they smiled at each other briefly.

"All right, Zack. You're coming with me, man," Brad shouted over the noise of the waterfall directly behind him. "Dudes versus Chicks. I'm gonna need your weight if we wanna win."

Zack dragged the girls' tube to the water's edge. Once it was in the water, he quickly dropped his chivalry and became the immature prankster from back at camp. He stepped down into the water and waded toward Brad's tube, which was already slowly floating away. Brad and Zack hoisted themselves into their tube and fell in clumsily.

Stacy crouched down, held their tube against the top step, and waited for Cyndi to get in. Cyndi looked down at her cautiously.

"You sure we can do this?" she asked, raising her voice over the crash of the waterfall.

Stacy shrugged and looked over at Zack and Brad who were laughing and splashing each other with water. "Those two are as good as gone already."

"Yeah, gone in the head," Cyndi said, and Stacy burst out laughing. It surprised Cyndi. It was one of those rare times you made a joke that got much more laughter than you expected, and it felt good.

Stacy's laughter trailed off to chuckles, and Cyndi glanced around the surrounding woods one more time before stepping into the tube. Stacy got in awkwardly after her, and fell down on her butt.

Both tubes floated slowly along the first part of the Duelin' Rivers. All four of them looked around with wide eyes at the woods and the artificial river stretching out ahead of them. The river was shaded from the sun by thick overhanging branches from the trees. There was another one of those perfect flowerbeds along the right side of the river filled with some exotic looking yellow flowers. Stacy couldn't help but reach out and pick one.

She pulled her blond hair back and tucked the flower stem behind her right ear.

"You want one?" she asked Cyndi.

"Sure," Cyndi replied.

As she reached over to pick another flower, she heard Brad call out, "Hey, Stace!" and her face was suddenly drenched with water. She gasped in shock, and the boys laughed hysterically. A lot of the water splashed onto Cyndi too.

"You said you wanted a shower!" Brad joked.

"HEYO!!!" Zack yelled, then screamed laughter.

"Brad, I swear to God!" she yelled at him. She furiously splashed back at their raft.

"Better hurry if you want to beat us to the bottom, Stacy! Paddle, dude! Paddle!"

Both he and Zack leaned low on the sides of their tube and dog paddled it faster toward the river on the right.

"Oh, I don't think so!" Stacy yelled. "Come on, Cyndi."

They copied the boys, leaned low, and paddled toward the river on the left as fast as they could.

"You girls are goin' down! WOOO!" Brad screamed back as they hit the drop-off edge onto the steep, fast part of the ride. Stacy and Cyndi ignored them and paddled hard, they were slightly behind the boys as they neared their own drop-off point. When the girls reached the drop-off point, they stopped paddling and stared down at the splashing, surging water rushing down the slide.

"You ready?!" Stacy yelled over at Cyndi.

"Ready!"

"Okay! Here's goes nothing!"

Stacy and Cyndi got back up and hunkered into braced sitting positions. They both held onto one of the black handles as the tube tipped forward and almost stopped. Then the current pushed it over the edge and it went sliding its way down the Duelin' River.

The boys yelled and cheered in triumph as their tube cleared the drop-off and began to pick up speed. As they neared the bridge, they both stood up, reached out, and tapped the bottom of it as they went by, like all teenage boys are urged to do whenever they pass under a bridge or a doorway.

They hit a bunch of hard bumps in the slide and they fell over into the tube, bumping and jostling around. Water splashed up all around them, wetting their hair and shoulders.

On the other river, the girls hit a similar patch of bumps and they bounced in the air laughing and screaming.

The boys' tube cleared the bumps and picked up more speed. Up ahead, a tight curve to the left loomed.

"Uh-oh! Here we go!" Brad yelled.

They rounded the curve, tilting at a crazy, frighteningly steep forty-five degree angle. Zack's side of the tube went high up in the air and he had to lean low to keep from falling out. They laughed and hollered with excitement.

The girls went around a similar curve (not as high as the other) to the right, and spun around backwards. Stacy screamed as she went high up on the curve. They had to shift positions in the tube to stay facing forward. They quickly went around another curve next to a willow tree with branches that hung so low they could reach out and grab them.

The sides of Brad and Zack's river began to rise higher above their heads, forming into a small canyon. Up ahead, they saw the ride flowing into a short tunnel covered by boulders. It had been smoothed out above their heads, but left jagged on top. The tunnel curved off to the right, but it was short and they could still see a lot of light coming from the other side. They sped into the low tunnel and quickly went around the corkscrew curve. Before they even had time to realize what was going to happen, they had been drenched and sped off into the sunlight again. The ride had a small waterfall over the exit of the tunnel meant to soak the riders as they passed underneath it.

"Aww!" Brad and Zack cried out as the cold water soaked them.

Stacy and Cyndi passed by a small trickling waterfall that dripped and splashed them lightly. They were having a blast on the ride. The sides began to rise up as they had on Brad and Zack's river, and they saw another one of those sharp curves ahead.

"Oh no!" Stacy yelled.

They went around the curve and down into a short tunnel just as the boys had. There had been no waterfall at the end of their tunnel, but they wouldn't escape being drenched that easily.

Both tubes came out into wider rocky canyons as they neared the end of the ride. They passed under several rock archways. The boys' river had several vines hanging down from the rocks and Brad reached up and yanked one down as they passed.

On the girl's river, a waterfall splashed down from one of the rock arches. Stacy screamed and leaned as far off to the side as she could, trying her best to avoid the steady stream about to splash down on their heads, but she had no chance of walking away dry. They got soaked.

"Oh my God!" Stacy screamed in a shocked tone. Cyndi coughed and laughed.

Another patch of those rough bumps hit the bottoms of both of their tubes and they bounced along for a bit.

The ride finally came to an end at a rushing current of water that was being pumped uphill to slow them down. Both tubes hit the reverse current almost one after the other. The boys beat the girls to the end by a just a fraction of a second. Water splashed into both of their tubes, drenching them all over again.

All four of them got their bearings as they slowly floated toward the metal grate at the end of the ride. The tubes slid to a stop as the water underneath them drained into the grate below. Brad and Zack began to laugh in a worn out, adrenaline rushed way.

"Fuck yeah!" Brad half yelled, half sighed.

"Oh my God. I am *soaked!*" Stacy laughed.

"You guys like it?" Zack shouted.

"I loved it!" Cyndi said grinning.

They awkwardly got back up on their feet again, splashing into the end-pool, and talking excitedly amongst themselves about the rides. In all the splashing around, Cyndi and Stacy had lost the flowers they had put behind their ears. They pulled their tubes out of the end-pool and had to flip them over to drain out the three inches of water that had collected inside them.

"All right," Brad said. He dropped the tube off to the left of the ride and began walking back up the hill toward the entrance again. "Come on, guys."

"Again?" Stacy asked, bewildered.

"Uh, yeah. That was only half the ride. We went right last time, gotta go left this time."

Zack followed him laughing, and soon Cyndi was following close behind him. She turned back to Stacy and shrugged her shoulders. Stacy stood back for a second.

"You guys, we shouldn't..." she trailed off, trying to think of a way to finish the sentence. *Brad's right, we have this whole place to ourselves. Screw it.* She jogged to catch up as they went back up the hill to

155

ride the opposite Duelin' River.

The second time down was even more fun than the first. They laughed and screamed the whole way down. As Brad and Zack went down the fast drop-off point for the left Duelin' River, they pretended to whimper and cry as if they were terrified. Then with exaggerated blood-curdling screams they sped off down the slide, the girls laughed hysterically as they went. They were all familiar enough with the layout of the ride, but were surprised with the differences between the two rivers. Towards the end of the ride, Brad stood up underneath the rock archways and almost fell out as they hit the first of the hard bumps near the end. All thoughts of camp, running away, and the trouble that they were in were completely thrown out the window.

Both tubes splashed into the end-pool again and they cheered loudly.

"DUELIN' RIVERS! YEAH!!!" Zack screamed, throwing his fist into the air. "Let's go again!"

"No, we can't," Brad said solemnly as he splashed into the water and dragged the tube out.

Everyone stopped and looked at him surprised.

"What?"

"What do you mean we can't?" Stacy asked.

"Because now we gotta go do the *Ragin'* Rivers," he said with a sly grin, clasping his hands together in excitement.

"Yeah!" all three of them exclaimed at the same time. They quickly tossed the other tube to the side and splashed out of the end-pool. They ran toward the Ragin' River entrance chattering and giggling. The water from their suits dripped off them, leaving a wet trail on the concrete.

All four of them walked up to the end-pool of the Ragin' Rivers, scoping it out tentatively. Brad looked at the faux-wooden Ragin' Rivers sign and saw two white arrows below the little picture pointing in either direction. There were also two stacks of bright green single-person tubes on either side of the concrete steps leading out of the Ragin' River end-pool.

"Okay, it looks like we can either go up this path on the right again or that one on the left. I'm guessing these two are up this way," he pointed to the right up the same path they took for the Duelin' Rivers, "and those two go up that way," he pointed to the other path on the left. "So which two do you girls wanna take?"

"I don't know. I guess we'll take left again," Stacy shrugged.

"All right. Let's do it." He snagged one of the green tubes and charged back up the path. Zack grabbed his own tube and struggled to keep up. Stacy watched the boys go, then turned to Cyndi who had a strange worried look on her face.

"What's wrong?" Stacy asked.

"N-nothin.' I'm fine."

Watching Brad go, Cyndi had a momentary gut feeling that they should stick together, that maybe splitting up wasn't the best idea. But it was stupid. Besides, she wasn't about to try to start an argument with Brad, who was quite possibly the most hardheaded person she had ever met.

"Come on then." They each grabbed themselves a tube and started up the path on the left.

The girls' path wound around a big curve. Cyndi quickly lost her breath jogging up the hill and carrying the tube. She panted heavily but didn't slow down. Stacy raced ahead, figuring Brad would be in another one of his racing moods. She didn't want to give him the satisfaction of winning again.

Cyndi looked over as they went up the hill and had an awesome high view of the picnic area and the river behind it. She looked at the picnic table where they had dropped off their stuff and saw that it was all still untouched. She allowed herself to relax a little.

Both girls were out of breath once they reached the start of the slides. They were mounted ten feet away from each other at the edge of a large round concrete pad surrounded by woods and trees. Each slide began as a low tub, about as big as a hot tub, with water bubbling in from built-in jets underneath the surface. The whitish-tan sides of the slides then rose until they formed a half circle. A thin stream of water rushed down the middle and quickly curved out of sight. Stacy went to the slide on the right, Cyndi walked over to the left.

"STACY! CYNDI!" Zack's voice echoed from the other entrance. "YOU GIRLS READY?"

"YEAH!" Stacy yelled back, cupping her hand over her mouth. Unlike Cyndi, she could scream as loud as an air horn.

"OKAY!"

Stacy stepped down into the tub and let her green tube smack down onto the water's surface. "See ya at the bottom." She hopped gracefully onto her tube, sending out waves across the small pool. She adjusted her butt comfortably down into the middle, and hung onto the two handles.

Cyndi tried to get onto her own tube as easily as Stacy had, but the tube slipped out from under her and she almost fell into the water. Soaked to her shoulders, she got up again and slowly worked her way up onto the tube. She had to shift and squirm a little to get into a comfortable position, and then she was off.

Her tube got caught in the current of the flowing water and she began to pick up speed. She could already feel a cool breeze against her wet skin as her tube began to race down the river. Swinging around the first curve, she left the entrance behind.

Brad and Zack giggled, taunted each other, and shoved the tubes at each other as they ran up the hill. Near the top of the hill, they took the right fork in the path toward the Ragin' Rivers, instead of continuing straight to the Duelin' Rivers. There was a little stream dotted with cattails that ran alongside the path toward the entrance. The concrete ended up ahead and another wooden bridge continued the path off to the left. They stood on the bridge and looked down over one of the Duelin' Rivers passing swiftly by underneath them.

"Oh, so this is where that bridge was. I was wondering that when we were down there on the ride," Zack said looking down.

"Dare you to jump," Brad said.

Zack climbed up on the wooden railing on the side of the bridge and stuck his foot up on the side. He stopped and made a mocking surprised falling face at Brad.

"Aaaah," he said in a stupid sounding monotone voice. One of his hands held the side of the bridge, the other was braced on his upturned tube.

"Woops," Brad said as he kicked the tube out from underneath Zack's hand. Zack stumbled and had to swing his arm wildly over to the bridge to keep from falling over. His tube rolled for a few feet, then tipped over.

"Dude! What the fuck?!" Zack screamed outraged. Brad only laughed and went ahead to the Ragin' Rivers' entrance. Zack got down from the bridge awkwardly and immediately felt the pain from where he'd slapped his legs and arms against the wooden sides of the bridge. "Seriously, man. That was not fuckin' cool."

"Oh relax. You didn't fall in. You're fine," Brad

159

replied in a patronizing tone.

The bridge ended at the other concrete pad entrance to the Ragin' Rivers, identical to the one on the other side where Stacy and Cyndi were. On this side the concrete pad was surrounded by tall, blue spruce trees. Across from the bridge there was a steep six foot drop-off to the underbrush below. That side was blocked off with wooden beams, thick rope, and fishnet, just like the path that went up the hill alongside the Lazy River.

Brad had already thrown his tube down into the water on the right slide and waded in after it.

"Hang on. Shouldn't we, like, signal the girls or something?" Zack asked.

"Why?"

"So we can race 'em down."

Brad shrugged. "If you want to."

Brad waited as Zack called out to them. After a second they heard Stacy's faint reply. Zack yelled back an *Okay* and walked over to his slide. Brad hoisted himself into his tube backwards and was floating slowly toward the fast part of the slide. As Zack walked past, he stuck out his foot and kicked water up into Brad's face. Brad was taken by surprise and immediately jumped out of his tube to go after Zack.

"I don't think so, fucker!"

"Race you to the bottom!" Zack yelled running toward his slide. He jumped onto his tube face first and splashed into the water, coming very close to smacking his face on the rounded bottom of the slide. He flipped himself over in his tube as Brad kicked water at him repeatedly.

Zack held his hands up, choking and coughing on the water. He finally caught his breath and yelled to Brad, "Oh, you're dead, man. You're fuckin' dead!"

He feebly reached down and tried to splash Brad but his tube was already beginning to pick up speed.

Brad made a mocking scared face at him and flipped him off. Laughing to himself, he walked back to his slide. He picked his tube up off the concrete where he had dropped it while going after Zack, and dropped it down into the water with a small splash. He sat down in his tube, adjusted himself, then reached down to try to paddle himself along faster.

With a rubber squeak, the tube got stuck on the slide and stopped altogether.

"Come on, asshole." He made little scooting movements and felt the tube start to slide along onto the faster part. The tube finally let go and began to slide but it turned sideways. "Aww, dammit!" He made more scooting movements to turn himself forward, but the tube turned again and now he was facing backwards toward the entrance again. He looked up at the entrance and his breath caught in his throat.

There was a man standing on the side of the slide. He leaned in and watched Brad, cocking his head slightly. Brad only caught a brief glimpse of the man's black clothes and pallid white face before the slide curved and the entrance was swept out of sight.

Brad froze. *Caught. We're caught,* was all he could think over and over in his head. *Someone else is here and we're caught. Oh shit.* His tube turned around again and he was finally facing forward. He felt the same light breeze going down that Cyndi had felt. He barely noticed the ride. His mind was racing, trying to think up excuses to explain to that guy, whoever he was, as to why they were in his water park.

Another thought flashed through his mind, *What's wrong with that guy's face?*

The slide swung to the right and Brad looked up to see low branches hanging over the slide. He whipped around the curves and drops, going faster and faster.

Frantically, he tried to think of what to do before the guy inevitably caught up to them. The slide curved again, so violently that he thought he would tip out of his tube. The curve had even been built up so that it hung overhead three-quarters of the way to the lip on the other side. It tore Brad away from his frantic thoughts.

Just past the curve he saw the dark tunnel he was racing toward. The slide had been built up as a full closed tube here. It was pitch black inside and seemed to echo eerily like a ghostly train whistle. Brad suddenly got a strong sense of eerie foreboding from the tunnel.

I don't want to be on this ride. I have to get off this ride, he thought for no good reason. That tunnel was dark, that tunnel was evil, and he did not want to go into it.

The current swept him into the black depths anyway, and Brad never saw the sun again.

Chapter Thirteen:

The Missing

The wind whipped through Cyndi's blond, crimped hair as she flew around the curves down the Ragin' River. Despite her anxiety with letting the volume of her voice become louder than a mumble, she felt herself uncontrollably whooping and screaming out loud as her tube ripped around the curves and splashed water up over the sides. The farther down the slide she went, the faster, and wilder, the curves got.

She rounded the last curve and the end-pool came back in sight. She flew down the last long slope, feeling exhilaration and a slight disappointment that it had to end so soon. Her tube splashed down into the foaming churning water at the bottom of the slide, sending up large waves in a circle all around her.

Stacy came screaming down into the end-pool half a second later and the waves that burst up from her tube made Cyndi's bob up and down wildly. They both looked at each other and laughed as the rolling waves pushed them slowly toward the steps leading up out of the pool at the other end. They looked around the pool expecting to see the boys.

"Oh my God, did we actually beat them for once?" Stacy asked amazed. "Did the twins really just lose, or am I dreaming?" Cyndi laughed and grinned at her, then saw a flash of green coming down the slide on the far right.

"Here he comes."

Zack came careening down his slide backwards. The moment his green tube hit the still water in the end-pool, it flipped over backwards. Zack's body went with it, tumbling into the water like a goofy rag doll. Cyndi and Stacy burst out laughing at his awkward dismount.

He suddenly sprang up out of the water with his fists held triumphantly in the air.

"Yeaaaaaaah! That was *so* awesome!" he shouted slamming his fist down into the water. "That was even better than the Duelin' Rivers. What'd you guys think?"

"I don't know. It's a tough decision," Cyndi said.

"Where's Brad? Did we really all beat Mister Competitive?" Stacy asked.

Zack spun around, facing the slides again and punching the water aggressively, sending up fans of water toward Brad's slide. "Oh, we've got a score to settle."

They waited for Brad to come flying down the slide, his feathered hair whipping back from his forehead. And they waited... And waited...

"Jeez, where the hell is he? I didn't get that good of a head start on him."

Zack looked at the girls and they shrugged. They had both gotten down off of their tubes, and now stood in the waist deep water alongside Zack.

"HEY, BRAD!" he shouted, cupping his hands around his mouth. "YOUR FAT ASS GET STUCK OR WHAT?"

As if in response to his call, an empty green tube came around the corner on the slide. The three of them watched it slide down and bump softly off the slide into the water. They glanced back and forth from the slide, still devoid of everything but water, to the empty tube as it slowly floated past them.

"What's he gonna do, *surf* down?" Zack asked jokingly. No one laughed. Cyndi and Stacy shared a wary suspicious look.

"He's probably just hiding on the slide, holding himself up or something," Stacy said.

"You're right. He always does shit like this. Remember two years ago when he hid in a tree and had Sheehan and all the other counselors looking for him for, like, an hour?"

Stacy smiled. "I hate to admit it, but that was pretty good. Sheehan was totally freaking out."

"Hang on, I'll go get his ass," Zack sighed. He started toward the slide, struggling through the surging water at the bottom. He grabbed onto the slippery, smooth edge of the slide and lost his grip. He tried twice more to hold onto the sides and finally had to stretch his shaking, straining arms wide and palm the sides to hoist himself up. He lifted himself up with a great effort and put his right knee down on the edge. It held for only a second, then let go with a rubbery slipping sound. Zack cried out and crashed down onto the edge before sliding fully into the water. Stacy and Cyndi both grimaced as he crashed down.

Zack came back up, shaking water out of his eyes. "Okay, now I'm starting to get mad."

"Okay, WE GET IT. VERY FUNNY, BRAD," Stacy yelled.

No answer.

"BRAD!" Zack screamed, sounding more angry and afraid than ever. "IF YOU DON'T COME OUT

RIGHT NOW, YOU'RE A DEAD MAN!" Once the words were out of his mouth, he immediately regretted them. They brought images of Brad's twisted, broken body into his mind, and he felt his heartbeat speed up. He suddenly remembered that those were the same last words he had said to Brad before taking off down the slide, and he immediately wished he could take them back.

Stop it. Just stop! Zack thought to himself, quickly suppressing his dreadful thoughts.

"Okay, that's it," Zack said, suddenly wading his way toward the steps leading out of the end-pool.

"Where are you going?" Stacy asked.

"Out for a pizza," Zack said sarcastically. "Where do you think I'm going? Back up to the top. See if he's still there."

"Well, hold on," Stacy said.

"Yeah, we're going with you," Cyndi said.

They all waded to the steps and left their green tubes drifting around in the end-pool. Cyndi looked back and saw her tube bump into Brad's empty one just to the right of the steps. At the sight of it, she felt that nervous tension worming its way into her stomach again.

Cyndi and Stacy hurried closely behind Zack as they stepped out of the end-pool. He walked at a rushed, frantic pace, unsuccessfully trying to keep his cool. He was half convinced that Brad was just playing another one of his pranks and that he'd be a fool to believe anything was wrong. But... There was an undeniable feeling in the air that something *was* wrong.

"I swear I'm gonna kil--" he trailed off briefly, choosing his words carefully. "I'm gonna kick his ass if he jumps out and scares us."

"Yeah, you think he'd grow up. It's like, we don't even know where we are, and he's joking with us like this," Cyndi said.

"Yesterday I would have said that *you* were the least mature person in this group," Stacy said pointing to Zack. "Now I'm not so sure."

Zack looked at her insulted. "Is that supposed to be a compliment?"

Stacy was taken aback. She honestly had not meant to offend him. "No, I didn't mean it like that. It's just... He's been acting like such a jerk."

"Yeah, what else is new?"

A harsh crackle of static and high pitched feedback suddenly exploded in their ears. They all jumped and cried out in surprise. One of those white speakers, mounted high up on one of the concrete pillars holding up the far right Ragin' River slide had come to life. After a second of jagged electronic noise, a song began to blast from the speakers. Cyndi recognized it immediately, "Vacation" by the Go-Go's.

Cyndi, Stacy, and Zack stared at the speaker in wonder, then looked at each other.

"What the hell is that?" Zack asked, having to yell over the loud music.

"Is that...the Go-Go's?" Stacy yelled looking over at Cyndi, who nodded hesitantly.

The unmistakable Go-Go's sound of the synths, driving beat, and Belinda Carlisle's voice poured out of the speaker, but the copy of the song was badly garbled. The pitch kept dipping to a lower register, then spiking back up to normal as if it couldn't hold on. It sounded like it was coming from either a warped record or a battered old tape.

The wavering music was so loud that they couldn't really do much but stand there, listen, and wait for it to pass like a storm cloud. Cyndi's ears picked up a lot of reverberation from the music, the way it sounded at a loud rock concert. She looked around and saw another speaker mounted near the picnic tables, and another on the other side of the Ragin' Rivers.

"It's playing everywhere. It's all over the park," Cyndi shouted out to Stacy and Zack, pointing at the other speakers.

"Yeah but who?" Stacy asked.

"What?" Cyndi asked, not understanding the question.

"Who's playing the music?" she screamed.

"I don't know."

The song began its last chorus, and Stacy started to look around anxiously at them.

"How long do you think this is gonna go on?"

Cyndi shrugged. Zack put his hands up and yelled, "How should I know?"

"Should we keep looking?"

"What?" Zack asked.

"Should we keep looking for Brad?" she screamed even louder at him.

The music cut out abruptly in the middle of one of the last lines of the chorus. There was another static blast, a ring of feedback, and a clunk as the speakers turned off. It cut off as Stacy was in mid-sentence, leaving her awkwardly yelling the last two words over silence. They remained tensed, listening and looking around for any new noise or signs of life. The entire park was now as dead silent as it had been before. The sounds of the slides splashing and churning down into end-pools seemed to slowly rise again in their ears.

Cyndi, Stacy, and Zack all let out sighs of relief. They all felt their eardrums thrumming and beginning to ring.

"What the hell was *that* about?" Stacy asked in confusion.

Cyndi shook her head and shrugged.

"Brad?" Zack suggested. "You think it was him just messing around with us?"

"My tape!" Cyndi suddenly blurted out. "He must've stolen my tape last night. I fell asleep listening to my mix tape, the one with "Vacation" on it, and when I woke up someone had taken it."

Zack's face lit up with realization, "That sneaky son of a bitch!" He turned toward the speakers and yelled out. "OKAY, BRAD! NICE ONE! WE WERE REALLY SCARED! SO COME ON OUT NOW!"

"I don't know, you guys," Stacy said hesitantly. "I don't think he had your tape with him."

"Why not?" Zack asked.

"Because he would've had to have that tape with him the whole time we've been here." Cyndi knew instantly that she was right.

"Maybe he kept it in his swimsuit," Zack offered.

"We would've seen it or it would have fallen out or something. And on those rides? No way. It would've been gone."

"Yeah, but who else could it be?"

"I don't know. What if we're not the only ones here?"

Zack was caught off guard and stood silent. He had no argument against her. The thought sent a shiver down Stacy's spine, and she looked around nervously. Cyndi saw her and did the same. Zack repressed the urge to look around. He felt eyes watching him, but he refused to acknowledge them. In broad daylight, it was much easier to be rational rather than scared.

"Whatever. Look let's just go up to the top of the ride and see if Brad's there, okay?"

He turned and began walking back up the hill. Cyndi and Stacy glanced at each other nervously, and followed him up.

*   *   *

They reached the top of the hill, took the right fork in the path, and crossed the bridge over the Duelin' River where Zack had pretended to fall. The entrance to the Ragin' Rivers looked just as it had when Zack and Brad had been up here fifteen minutes ago. Zack pointed out the slide on the right.

"That's the one he got on." They all looked down the slippery slide and saw nothing out of the ordinary. They turned and looked deep into the surrounding trees, searching for Brad's laughing eyes peering out.

"BRAD?" Zack cried out, and again got no answer. He thought for a moment, turning over the last time he saw Brad in his mind. "There's only one other thing I could possibly think of. Maybe he didn't even get on the ride."

"Why would he do that?" Stacy asked doubtfully.

"He was on the ride. Then I kicked water in his face and he got all pissed. I got on this one, and he got off to go kick water back in my face, but I never actually saw him get on again. Maybe he just threw his tube on and went off to play a trick on us."

"That still doesn't explain the music though," Cyndi added.

"What do you mean?" Zack asked, a little hurt.

"Isn't it a little convenient for Brad to just steal my tape, keep it with him all day, then go find wherever it is they have their speakers hooked up, and play my tape?"

"Well, fuck, I don't know. I'm just trying to figure out what the fuck's going on, okay?"

"Zack! Calm down," Stacy said in a low, controlled voice. "If this is just another one of Brad's stupid pranks, which I honestly think it is, then let's just go wait for him. If we just ignore him, he'll come out."

Zack shrugged his shoulders, giving up. He sighed, "Okay. But I just wanna check one more thing." He grabbed a green tube off the stack and walked toward the slide Brad took. "If he's still hiding somewhere on this slide, I'm gonna catch him red-hand--"

Stacy rushed forward and grabbed his arm, holding him back. "Don't!" she interrupted.

"What?"

"Please don't get on that ride," she pleaded. "What if something happened to him on there? How do we know the rides are even safe?"

Zack's pride told him that he could handle anything, that he should yank his arm away from her and get on the ride, but his reasoning was stronger. He knew Stacy had a point. It seemed all too plausible that maybe there *was* something wrong with this ride. Brad may have been hurt, or even (he hated to even think the word) killed. He suddenly felt so stupid for even getting on any of the rides in the first place. What the hell had they been thinking?

"Okay," he said shakily, dropping his tube.

Cyndi sighed with relief. *Thank God he's not as stubborn as Brad,* she thought.

As they walked back over the bridge, Zack looked back at the slide where he had last seen his best friend and thought the same thing all three of them were now beginning to think, *I don't trust that ride.*

171

Chapter Fourteen:

The Lazy River

Zack, Stacy, and Cyndi went back to the picnic tables to wait. As they passed the front of the Ragin' Rivers, they all looked up at Brad's slide distrustfully. The rides didn't seem so inviting anymore. In fact, none of the park seemed inviting anymore.

As they approached the picnic tables, Cyndi saw, to her satisfaction, that their stuff was still untouched. This time it didn't relieve her nerves much. They sat down at the table uncomfortably, and Zack finally broke the silence.

"Do you guys feel like...?" he struggled with the words, "like we're...unwelcome here?"

Cyndi and Stacy looked at each other cautiously, then nodded at Zack.

"A few years ago me and Brad went out to TP this girl's house," Zack began in a low solemn voice. "Once we got there, we were about to start TP-ing it, y'know, but we saw these flashing cop-car lights. So we took off and ran down this cul-de-sac, but the cops followed us. I was hiding under this car in some random guy's driveway, Brad was across the street. I heard the cops get out of their car and start walking up the street towards us. They got close enough so I could see their flashlights pointing at the house next door to me. And at that point I was totally freaking out. So I, like, crab-walked to the back fence and jumped over into the backyard. I tore up my hands jumping over the fence and they were all bleeding and stuff. I went around the corner of the house and they had this hammock hanging up. So I sat down, y'know, and just, like, waited for the cops to leave. The way I felt sitting in that stranger's backyard, I feel that same way now. I feel like I jumped over the fence into someone's backyard and started messing with their stuff. It feels like we're...I don't know, trespassing or something."

"I feel it too," Stacy said, looking around suspiciously.

"How did you guys get out of that?" Cyndi asked.

Zack shook his head and gave a bitter little laugh. "Brad left me behind and went home. And the cops wouldn't leave. On the other side of the backyard, the fence was really tall because it was behind this busy street. There was no way I could jump over it without breaking my ankles. So I looked around and saw this little concrete drainage gutter that went under the fence and out to the sidewalk. I squeezed through there and got away. I got my shirt all nasty with mud too." Cyndi imagined a muddy Zack climbing through a drainage gutter under a fence.

Stacy shook her head. "Typical Brad," she muttered.

The three of them sat mostly in silence, waiting for Brad to come out. Stacy and Zack figured he would come out after about twenty minutes of silence. He would hold out for a while, but if no one was humoring him, looking for him, or calling out his name, he'd come right out. Zack and Stacy agreed he'd make some snappy, sarcastic comment like, *jeez, so if I was really dead, I guess you assholes would be just fine. Glad to know you really care about me.*

Twenty minutes passed as they listened to the water rushing down the Ragin' and Duelin' River slides. There were no other sounds, no other signs of life. The picnic area was mostly shaded, but it was a hot day and they were in the hottest part of the afternoon. Zack figured it must be at least ninety-five degrees out. This close to the river, the air was muggy and filled with mosquitoes and gnats. Cyndi pulled her Walkman out of her backpack and rummaged through to find a tape. She settled on another mix tape and listened to some Billy Idol.

Stacy crossed her arms on the picnic table and put her head down. Her arms smelled so strongly of chlorine and river water that she immediately put her head back up.

"Ugh, I'd kill for a shower right now," she complained.

"Me too," Cyndi agreed.

"He probably won't be long now, then we can get out of here," Zack said. To Cyndi, he didn't sound very confident about it.

Another twenty minutes passed by. And another. And another. Zack stared at the sun dismayed. It was beginning to set now, casting long afternoon shadows through the trees. He sat shirtless, and his skin felt tight and dried out from the chlorine and the sun. His throat was achingly thirsty.

"God, I wish he would just get the fuck out here," Zack said, putting his hands to his mouth to yell for Brad again.

Stacy cut him off just as he drew in breath, "Don't! If you call him, he'll never come out. You know

174

how he works."

Zack exasperatedly sighed out the breath he had taken in for his yell.

"Well, I gotta go get in the water or something. I'm fuckin' dyin' out here in the heat. You guys wanna try out that Lazy River?"

"I don't think it's a good idea, Zack," Stacy said.

"Stacy, it's fine. You saw how slow it goes, and we don't even have to get separated. We'll just hang on to each other's tubes."

Cyndi and Stacy shared another of their doubtful looks.

"Come on, you guys. Aren't you hot? It's gotta be like a hundred degrees out here. Besides, the fuckin' bugs are starting to drive me nuts."

Stacy and Cyndi looked to each other for approval again, and Cyndi shrugged. "It *is* pretty hot out here."

"Okay, I guess we can go," Stacy said. "But if anything starts to seem dangerous about it, we're all getting right off. You got it?"

"Thank you," Zack said, jumping up from his spot at the picnic table.

Cyndi stopped her tape in the middle of The Go-Go's "Fading Fast," and stood up, stretching her creaky arms and legs. She felt sweaty and sticky all over. It would be good to wash some of that off in the Lazy River. She put her Walkman into her backpack and zipped it up tight, as if pulling the zipper tighter would make it more secure. She gave it a little pat for good measure and walked away feeling that nervous tug at the back of her mind that someone might try to mess with her stuff. She forced herself not to look back at the picnic table and forget about it.

As the three of them walked past the end-pool of the Ragin' Rivers again, Zack cupped his hands up against his mouth and inhaled deeply, getting ready to scream for Brad again. Stacy saw him and grabbed his forearm just in time.

"Zack, come on," she urged, shaking her head.

He sighed with exhausted frustration and they continued on in silence.

They walked up to the entrance of the Lazy River. Zack glanced at the sign with the smiley faced captain lounging in his tube and felt an uncontrollable twinge of hatred for it. He gave it a contemptuous look, then stepped down into the water.

The water felt like ice as it splashed up onto their feet, shins, and thighs. They each made their own sounds of shock and relief from the baking heat. Zack stood on his tiptoes, being careful to keep the water level below his crotch.

Stacy sunk down to her neck and immediately bounced back up. The water splashed and poured off her shoulders. "Oh God, it's freezing."

Cyndi sunk down to her shoulders and crossed her arms over her chest. She felt her previous stickiness turn to a slippery sheen and disappear as she rubbed her arms and chest.

"Okay, okay. Just do it. Gotta take the plunge," Zack said aloud to himself. He relaxed his tensed shoulders and let himself collapse all the way into the water. He bounced back up, shaking off water like a dog, and pulled his black hair back. "Oh man, that feels good."

All three of them reached out for the clear blue tubes that were floating along slowly past them and they each snagged one. They hoisted themselves up into the same lounging position as the Smiley Sea Captain on the sign. The tubes were warm from sitting face up in the sun all day.

"Oh yeah," Zack sighed, laying his head back

and letting only his hair and the top of his head dip down into the water. "This is the life."

"Well, it's a hell of a lot better than sitting at the tables," Stacy said, dipping her own light blond hair back into the water like Zack. Her floating hair fanned out behind the tube, looking soft and light as a feather. She pulled her head up again, letting the water slick her hair back. It darkened to a sandy blond color.

Cyndi ducked her head underwater and came up through the hole in the middle of her tube. She leaned forward on her chest and let her arms dangle up to her elbows in the clear, chlorinated water. Her dripping hair cooled her shoulders and back. She looked over at Zack and caught him staring at her from his upside-down vantage point. He wasn't looking at her eyes. He noticed that she was watching him and quickly looked away, pretending to notice something else off to the side of the river. She looked down and saw that the tube had been pressing her cleavage up, giving Zack a seductive view. She self-consciously adjusted and lowered herself farther down into the tube so that she wouldn't look and feel so revealing. Still, she couldn't keep a little satisfied smile off the corner of her mouth.

Nervous as they all were about the rides, and the place in general, they all felt wonderful to be out of the heat and back in the water. They idly sat back and let the Lazy River slowly take them around its easy curves. Thick trees and bushes covered the island formed in the middle of the Lazy River. Zack and Stacy both peered into the trees hopefully, then caught each other doing the same thing.

"You thinking what I'm thinking?" she asked.

"Perfect Brad-Hiding-Place?"

"Mmm-hm," she nodded in agreement.

They floated along on the sunny side of the river without saying much. As Stacy's tube spun around slowly toward the west, she could see just how low the sun was setting. She figured it must be five or six o'clock now. That orange afternoon glow shimmered on the water, and cast longer shadows through the trees. She normally loved the afternoon, but today the long shadows darkened her thoughts. They made her realize just how long Brad had been gone and she felt uneasiness growing deep in her stomach.

The sun went behind the tops of the tall trees on the middle island as the Lazy River began take a wide curve. They had come to the rounded edge of the Lazy River's long oval shape and were curving around. Off to the east, there seemed to be nothing but more thick woods and trees. Cyndi stared down at her hand and the small ripples her fingers made as they poked into the water.

"So, is this it? I mean, is this the whole park?" Cyndi asked the others.

"Beats me," Zack replied.

Stacy seemed to be off in her own world, lying back in her tube with her eyes closed. Cyndi worried about her, but decided to give her space.

The river followed the long slow curve around and straightened out on the other side of the island. This side had tall cottonwood trees on either side with low branches draping over a lot of it, blocking out the sky. Way down at the far end, they could see the rocky slope, the cliff, and the path they had walked up earlier.

Farther down the river, they passed a waterfall that cascaded down into the right side of the Lazy River. Bubbles foamed up from the churning waterfall and spread into the river. As they approached the waterfall, they saw an old decaying wooden paddle boat, complete with a warped paddle, tipped over on its side for decoration. The splintery wood of the boat was so old it looked like it would crack and puff dust if you tried to touch it. Cyndi felt like it gave the Lazy River a comforting, rustic look. She felt the first cold drops of water splashing on her from the waterfall. Stacy gave a little scream as they hit her, and she paddled to get to the other side of the river. Zack just smiled, put his hands out, and let the water wash over them. The slow current carried them away from the waterfall along with the bubbles as they popped and dispersed.

"Why couldn't we just stay here forever?" Zack asked smiling.

Cyndi smiled at him and nodded, "I know." Stacy, lying back in her tube, was drowsing in and out of sleep and didn't hear them.

They came to the end of the long stretch and began around the curve that would take them back to the sunny side of the river. The rocky slope ascended on their right, and a big willow tree on the island draped down near the river on their left.

A hollow whirring sound like a huge fan drifted toward them and Cyndi looked up. She saw a big yellow grate on the right side of the river, just to the right of the steps that led down into the water. She figured it was some kind of filtration system or something. Looking inside the grate she saw concrete pillars holding up the sidewalk above, and only darkness behind them. An echoey hollow sound from the water drifted back from that darkness.

A flash of white caught Cyndi's eye and she noticed the man standing far back in the darkness. He was all dressed in black and had been almost indistinguishable against the darkness behind him. His shoulders were hunched and his head lowered and tilted so he could stand in the waist-high water. He could have gone totally unnoticed or been mistaken for another concrete pillar, but his face gave him away. The movement of the man tilting his head just slightly, as if

179

examining her, was what caught her eye. In her short glimpse of him, she noticed he had some sort of white mask on. It was hard to make out its shape, but it almost looked like one of those smiley face drawings. This mask wasn't a bright sunshine yellow like on the drawings though, it was a faded ghastly white, like the color of dead skin.

Cyndi abruptly sat up in her tube, her heart hammering in her chest. The tube bobbed and threatened to turn over. She was forced to look down and get her balance before she toppled over into the water.

The waves roused Stacy and Zack out of their dazed lounging states.

"You almost fall out?" Stacy asked.

Cyndi sat back in her tube and looked into the grate again. The man was gone. Her eyes searched for him desperately. He must have known she had seen him and moved. She could only see the concrete pillars and darkness. Had she just imagined the whole thing?

"Cyndi?" Zack asked. He whistled two notes at her to catch her attention. "You okay?"

Cyndi looked over at them, her face white and scared.

"I-uh...I thought I just saw..."

She debated with herself. *What could I tell them? Am I just being a baby? Am I just imagining things? Why would anyone be standing back there anyway?*

"Nothing. It was nothing. Never mind."

"Sure?" Stacy asked.

Cyndi nodded, sighing. "Just my imagination."

Stacy and Zack gave each other a curious look, then forced themselves to turn away and look at other things, so Cyndi wouldn't feel like they were staring at her.

Cyndi glanced back at the grate as they floated

away from it. She listened to that hollow echo fade, and wondered....

*   *   *

They rounded the corner and came out on the straight side of the river again. Stacy was getting anxious. It had been too long since they had seen or heard anything from Brad. She couldn't put it off any longer. She had to say something to Cyndi and Zack. She had to try to convince them to do something.

"You know what?" Stacy began. "I gotta be honest with you guys. I feel like there's something wrong, like this isn't just another one of Brad's pranks."

Zack and Cyndi looked at her and said nothing. They had both been thinking similar thoughts of their own, especially Zack.

"I mean, what if he's actually hurt somewhere, and we've just been sitting around doing nothing about it?"

"She's right," Cyndi muttered.

Zack looked down at the water. *I do not want to be hearing this. I can't accept any of this. Brad is fine. He'll always be fine. All of us, including Brad, are practically untouchable. Aren't we?*

"He's probably fine, you guys," Zack said, dismissing his own thoughts.

"Do you really believe that?" Stacy asked. "Yes, I'll admit that Brad's pulled some really big pranks in the past, and if we were still in camp, I wouldn't put this past him at all. But this is different. I don't think he'd leave us hanging for this long. Not in this situation."

"What situation?"

"In case you've forgotten, we are still lost in the woods."

181

That one hit Zack like a slap in the face. He stared down at the water ashamed. Cyndi gave him a pitying look, but he was too lost in his own turbulent thoughts to notice it.

"Zack, I'm sorry, okay?" Stacy continued in a softer tone. "I'm just tired, and scared, and all I want is a shower and some real food. So let's just find Brad and get the hell out of here, all right?"

Zack nodded. "Okay, let's go."

He jumped out of his tube and splashed down into the water. Stacy and Cyndi quickly followed. Their tubes floated away, quickly getting lost in the crowd of other tubes floating slowly around the endless circle of the Lazy River. The three of them waded against the current back to the steps leading out of the water. After a moment, Zack turned back to Stacy with a smile on his face.

"Stace, remind me to kill him as soon as we get back to civilization," he joked, trying to brighten her spirits. For Stacy, the word *kill* had an ugly resonance in her mind about Brad's possible demise, and she could only manage a tiny, strained smile. Cyndi wasn't smiling at all. Zack immediately wished he had kept his stupid mouth shut.

Chapter Fifteen:

The Fence and The Showers

"Okay, you guys, here's the plan," Stacy said as they stood outside the entrance to the Lazy River, their swimsuits still dripping. "We'll go back up the hill to the start of the Ragin' Rivers. Zack, you're the loudest, so you yell for Brad every, oh I don't know, let's say thirty seconds."

"Whoa, whoa, whoa, hold on. What do you mean *I'm* the loudest? *You callin' me a loud-mouth?*" he joked in a voice loud enough to echo back through the trees.

"A loud job for a loud mouth," she fired back at him. "Cyndi, you've got the best hearing so you listen for him, okay? If you hear anything, and I mean *anything* at all, you tell us and we'll all go check it out."

"Right," Cyndi said, feeling a little flattered that Stacy thought she was *the best* at something.

"I'll keep my eyes open for any little signs of him," Stacy continued. "You guys keep your eyes open too, but I'll pay especially close attention to the visual details. You guys got it?"

"You got it, chief!" Zack said, saluting her.

"Zack, come on. Be serious for once," Stacy sighed. "Brad might be hurt and I don't want you missing anything because of stupid jokes."

"You're right, sorry," he said, his voice dropping back to a serious, resigned tone.

So it was back up the slope again for the three runaways. They trudged uphill, keeping their eyes peeled on the grass and shrubs for any sign of Brad; a torn piece of his swimsuit, a Twinkie wrapper, anything. Zack bellowed out Brad's name every thirty seconds, his voice echoing back and scaring flocks of birds out of the trees. Cyndi listened hard for a slight whimper, a tiny gasp, or a rustle of clothes in the bushes. All she heard were their own footsteps, Zack's echoing cries, and the birds. Her imagination left her alone and didn't play any tricks on her. Except for their own noises, the place remained eerily silent.

Their pace was slow and methodical, but they saw no sign of Brad. Stacy impatiently asked, "You guys see anything yet?"

"Nada," Zack replied. Cyndi shook her head.

Stacy suppressed the urge to speed up. She half expected Brad to jump out and yell *Boo* any minute now. They would all hit him and scold him, then they could all go home. She also half expected to find him off in the woods, dead, bloody, and pale white, with a cloud of flies that incessantly landed on his glazed, open eyes. She told herself that idea was ridiculous, but the image of it kept creeping back into her mind like a stubborn weed.

After twenty minutes of thoroughly searching the path and the surrounding woods, they made it to the east entrance of the Ragin' Rivers again.

"HEY BRAAAAD!" Zack yelled out louder than any of his previous calls. His voice was beginning to sound hoarse. They all listened for any sound. "God! Where the *fuck* is he?!" Zack said clenching his fists in frustration.

Stacy walked around the edge of the concrete circle, peering into the trees. *He's gonna jump out any second now,* she thought. *Come on Brad, please jump out. I'm sick of this game.*

"BRAAAD!" Stacy yelled. Her impatience was reaching its boiling point. She felt tears of fear and frustration gathering inside her head. If he didn't come out soon, she would have to let them loose. *I'm not gonna cry, I'm not gonna cry, I'm not gonna cry,* she repeated to herself.

Cyndi was scared and frustrated too. She could sense Zack and Stacy tiptoeing along the edge of completely losing it. Stacy looked like she was about to burst into tears, and Zack looked like he wanted to hit something. She desperately looked around the concrete circle like Stacy. She needed to find something, anything, even if it was something terrible, because her friends needed it. If she couldn't do something for them, then what was she? Dead weight?

She stood at the opposite end of the concrete from the slides, scanning the tall evergreens that stood a few feet away in the grass. Nothing. She took a few steps out into the grass and looked between two of the trees. Nothing but more trees, low lying bushes, and a speck of blue metal...

Wait! What was that? There was something high up, just barely poking out from behind more evergreens off in the distance. It was another building. It sat back behind another low hill, almost totally blocked out of sight.

"You guys! I see something!" Cyndi yelled. In her excitement she completely forgot to keep her voice low. Zack and Stacy rushed over.

"What is it?"

"Where? I don't see anything," Stacy said.

Cyndi pointed past the trees to the building. "There. You guys see that blue metal? Just past that little hill. I think it's a roof on some building."

Stacy squinted her eyes and finally saw the corner of the building just past a big pine tree that stood at the top of the small hill.

"Oh! I see it!" Stacy cried out. "Damn, you've got good eyes, Cyndi!"

"What? Where? I don't see it," Zack said.

He came up behind Cyndi, put his hands on her shoulders, and leaned down close to her head. She felt butterflies stirring in her stomach. She lined up her arm as close as she could with his eye level and pointed to the blue corner of roof.

"Right there, just past that tree," she said, turning to face him. He squinted his eyes, and after a moment, finally saw it.

"Oh yeah! You *do* have good eyes," he said turning to her. They stared at each other, close enough to kiss.

"Come on, you guys," Stacy said impatiently. "Maybe Brad's over there." She grabbed Cyndi's arm and yanked her away from Zack and past the evergreen trees. They both felt a pang of disappointment as they were pulled apart. Zack followed the girls closely.

"What do you guys think it is? Maybe it's a house or something," Stacy babbled. "It reminds me of this cabin my father rents in Colorado. It has a metal roof like that, only it's green." They trampled over some low lying vines and came to the concrete edge of one of the Duelin' Rivers (the first one Stacy and Cyndi had taken). The water was rushing by quickly, and the smooth slide's surface looked too slippery to cross in their flip-flops. Zack saw one of its high curves nearby on their right.

"Look, we can go around it," he said pointing.

He lead the way around the ride. Cyndi almost lost her footing on some wobbly cobblestone just near the high point of the curve. Stacy gripped her hand tight at the last second and held her up for support.

"Whoa, you okay?" Stacy asked quickly. Cyndi nodded and they continued on.

They passed the slow-moving entrance to the Duelin' Rivers. Their feet crunched on the river rock just next to the full flowerbed that lined the edge of the ride. Cyndi watched the water of the Duelin' Rivers glistening and reflecting beautifully in the orange afternoon sunlight.

Zack's right, she thought, *it really would be nice to stay here for a while.*

Once they passed the large rock waterfall at the start of the Duelin' Rivers, they crested a hill and their view became a lot less obstructed. They could now see two buildings instead of one. The other building was closer and larger, but not as tall. It sat in a low spot between the hill they were standing on and the next hill about a hundred yards away. It was rectangular and stretched back about thirty yards. Its wooden walls were freshly painted white with blue trim. A row of metal lockers lined one of the outside walls underneath the low overhanging blue metal roof. Near the closest side of the building was an open doorway leading inside and they could see the brick tiled floor within.

Just beyond the long locker building, and standing a little higher up on the far hill, was the tall building with the blue metal roof that Cyndi had spotted. It had high concrete walls with vertical ridges. High up on the second story, two dark tinted glass windows looked out over the park. No windows or doors were visible on the ground level. The trees behind the building shaded the roof and the surrounding sidewalk. A smooth concrete sidewalk surrounded both buildings, and connected the two by a short path.

"Oh my God, look at this," Stacy exclaimed.

"I can't believe we were this close to these buildings and didn't see them before," Zack said.

"Well, how could you see them past the hills and the trees?" Stacy said. "And with you and Brad rushing us to get on those Duelin' River rides, no wonder we missed them."

"That's true. I guess we were so excited I never thought to look back this way."

The three of them hurried over to the buildings, getting dirt and pine needles in their flip-flops. Stacy felt sure that Brad was somewhere inside one of these buildings. Her imagination effortlessly unraveled a story explaining Brad's disappearance. *Of course he never came down the slide, he had seen this place through the trees and walked over to check it out. Then, he met someone inside one of these buildings, probably the owner.* She pictured a kindly, rich, suburban family: a mom, a dad, and two kids roughly their own age, the kind of family that you'd see on one of those old corny TV shows like *The Brady Bunch*, or *Leave It To Beaver. They probably welcomed Brad as they sat around in comfortable padded deck chairs, and offered him lemonade as he told them the story of how they had gotten lost in the woods.*

Great explanation, but why didn't they come down and get us? For Christ's sake, we've been waiting around for at least two and a half hours, a skeptical part of her mind challenged.

Stacy didn't want to hear *that* voice. *Everything is going to be fine.*

It's more likely that the father of that kindly family pulled out a big, expensive hunting rifle and shot Brad, the trespasser, right between the eyes. He's going to shoot us too if we don't get the hell out of here right now. She tried to squash the voice but it was too reasonable, too logical. Her caution got the best of her and she slowed down as they came close to the first building.

"Hello?" Stacy called out, more as a warning for the possible gun-toting owners than an actual question.

"HEY, BRAD!" Zack bellowed. "WE FOUND YOUR HIDING SPOT! COME ON OUT, YOU ASSHOLE!"

Ah, this is it, Stacy thought. *This is where he's gonna jump out from.* She halfheartedly braced herself for the scare, looking ahead at the lower building. They had come up to an open hallway that went all the way through the building to the other side. The setting sun reflected a yellow glow against the brick floor tiles. Inside this hallway on the right, there was another open doorway. She could see dim, artificial light spilling out from inside.

"Hello?" she called again, hearing her voice reverberate hollowly on the tiles.

She looked back at Zack and Cyndi who stood behind her, letting her lead. Her position made her very nervous. She shrugged questioningly back at them, *Should we go in?* They shrugged back, *How the hell should we know?* They had to find Brad, and if he was going to jump out and scare them, so be it.

Stacy led them cautiously onto the smooth tiles inside the strange building. It was perfectly clean. They still had at least an hour or two of daylight left, but they found it strange and a little scary to have a roof over their heads again. They saw that the other doorway in the middle of the wall was actually two corridors split down the middle by a dividing wall. As they approached the corridors, Stacy noticed the little plastic sign mounted halfway up the wall. The sun glinted off the shiny smooth plastic, and she had to walk up close to see what it said. The familiarity of it dawned on her at once. The sign had a rudimentary stick figure picture of a person, with a head, two arms, and a lower body that fanned out. It was the universal symbol for a Ladies Restroom. She sighed with relief and turned to Zack and Cyndi.

"Ladies room," she laughed and walked in. Cyndi and Zack let out their own sighs of relief and followed her. The corridor walls were lined with brick and curved around in an S-shape to block any outsiders from looking in. They followed it around and stepped into the large ladies room. Along the right wall was a long line of white porcelain sinks, each with little soap dispensers full of pink liquid soap. Paper towel dispensers were mounted right into a huge mirror above the sinks. Along the back wall were toilet stalls all painted white with their doors closed uniformly. The left wall was comprised of four white tiled shower stalls, each with a little curtain in front.

"Thank God! My prayers have been answered," Stacy gasped, her voice bouncing and echoing off all the tile. She went into the first shower stall, yanking the curtain back. Inside, she saw no knobs for water control, there was only a large silver button. She pushed it and immediately got a stream of warm water pouring out from the shower head above.

Zack looked around with wide eyes. "Whoa, so this is what it's like inside the Girls' Bathroom," he said, his reverberating voice filled with awe. Cyndi turned to him and couldn't help but laugh. It was really no different from any ladies room she had ever been in, but Zack looked as if he had just stumbled into the Land of Oz or something.

Stacy whipped around, suddenly remembering that Zack was there. "Hey, what do you think you're doing?"

"Huh?" he asked, sincerely puzzled.

"Uh, this is the *Ladies* Room. Get out," she shooed him back with her hands.

"But--"

"Out, out, out!" She pushed him back so fast he couldn't even gather his words.

"Uh, I'll just wait for you guys out here then," he said awkwardly.

Cyndi couldn't help but put a hand up to her mouth and giggle. Stacy came back in and went straight for the shower.

"I've been waiting for this all day. You gonna take one, Cyndi?"

"Well...shouldn't we keep looking for Brad?" The reverberation in here gave her that same nervous twinge she always got when her voice became too loud.

"I don't know about you, but this can't wait." Stacy pulled the shower curtain closed with a harsh rattle and a second later the water was on.

"Okay, we'll wait outside." Cyndi walked past the shower stall as the two pieces of Stacy's hot pink swimsuit flipped over the top of the stall. She walked out through the brick-lined S-shape and saw Zack leaning against the wall outside, looking down at his feet. They could hear Stacy back in the shower starting to hum something way off key, that Cyndi couldn't quite place.

"What the hell is she doing?" Zack asked in a low voice.

"Taking a shower," Cyndi mumbled.

"What the--? We're supposed to be looking for Brad. We don't have time for this shit."

Cyndi shrugged. "She said it couldn't wait."

Zack sighed in exasperation, threw up his hands, and began walking off. "Screw it. I'm gonna keep looking for Brad. You coming?"

"You're just gonna leave her?"

"She'll be fine. Right now I just wanna find Brad. We can take all the showers we want after we find him. You gonna wait for her or are you coming?"

Cyndi looked back at the entrance to the Ladies Room reluctantly, feeling the same way she did about leaving her backpack on the picnic table. She really didn't want to split up, but she had left her backpack several times today, and it had remained untouched. Zack stood there holding out his hand toward her with that cute smirk on his face. Cyndi took his hand, leaving the sound of Stacy's humming behind. Suddenly, Cyndi figured it out, Stacy was humming the theme to *The Brady Bunch*.

*   *   *

Cyndi and Zack walked hand in hand around the building and examined the lockers. Their metal silver fronts were all so polished and shiny that Cyndi and Zack could see their reflections in them. Zack noticed that they all had built-in combination locks, like the lockers he had back at school, and all the locks were turned with the number zero facing perfectly straight up, as if they had never been touched. *Maybe some obsessive-compulsive nut had turned them all that way.* He reached out and pulled a few of the levers to open them, but they didn't budge.

"What do you think these are here for?" he asked Cyndi, who shrugged. "I mean, this place can't just be some rich guy's house. Why would he have a bunch of lockers?"

"Maybe they're for the servants," Cyndi suggested.

"Couldn't be. There's too many. No, I'm thinking that this place is either open already or about to open."

192

"Yeah, but why are all the rides running? Wouldn't they, like, shut them down if they weren't going to have any people here?"

"I don't know. Hey, what's that?"

Zack pointed back in the direction of the entrance pool of the Duelin' Rivers. There was a neon sign mounted up on wooden posts. It stood across the path from the bathroom building in front of a thick patch of bushes. Neither of them had noticed it before. The left side of the neon sign looked smashed and broken. The neon tubes were all dark and the sign looked as if it hadn't been turned on in a while, if it even *could* turn on. Cyndi noticed the shape of that same strange smiling face formed with neon tubes near the middle of the letters. At the bottom of the sign on the right, the word RIVER in a broad, wavy font was about the only word that remained intact.

"Something, something RIVER," Zack read. "Can you make any of the rest of it out?"

"Something, something *RIVER* is all I can see," Cyndi said squinting. "Is that the name of this place or something?"

Zack shrugged. He gave the sign one last look, then gave up on it.

"Let's check that other building. Maybe someone's there. Maybe even Brad."

Zack and Cyndi picked up the pace and jogged over to the second building. Zack felt very conflicted. He was thrilled and excited to be holding hands this casually with Cyndi, and the more time they spent together the more he felt his crush for her deepen. On the other hand, he felt guilty and afraid since Brad was still missing. He tried to deny it, but he knew that there was something very wrong and unsettling about Brad's sudden disappearance. He knew Brad very well, better than Stacy. Brad was his best friend and they had been through a lot together. Zack knew Brad's pranks and jokes, had even come up with the ideas for more than a few of them, then let Brad take all the credit, he didn't mind. But this just didn't fit with the Brad he knew. This had gone too far, and gone on for too long. Something was wrong, but what?

"Hey, Brad! Get out here! I'm getting sick of yelling for you!" Zack yelled, clearing his throat which was starting to sound and feel raw. He raised his hand to his eyebrows to shield the glaring setting sunlight, and peered up at the smooth glass windows for any sign of movement inside. They were tinted a dark black and he couldn't see a thing. They reminded him of the dark windows of a limo he had once seen while looking out the bus windows on the way to camp a few summers back. He and Brad had seen the limo on the side of the bus and began pounding on the windows and mouthing, *HELP! PLEASE HELP US!* Whoever was in the limo hadn't been very impressed because it sped up abruptly, leaving the bus behind.

Cyndi suddenly pulled on Zack's arm and pointed forward, yanking him back from his memories.

"Look! Stairs!" she said excitedly.

Zack looked forward and saw the first few neat wooden steps, and the railing around the far corner of the building. He imagined the steps leading up along the side of the building to a deck or a door or something. His heart sped up with excitement and curiosity.

"Come on!" he shouted as he took off running. She ran with him and their hands parted. It was just too hard to run and hold hands at the same time.

They came around the corner and looked up the stairs. Thick evergreen trees were up against the railing at the top of the stairs. Underneath the steps, a bed of large cobblestone had been spread out all the way to the building.

At the top of the stairs, there was no deck, and no Brad. Zack saw only a closed metal door at the small top landing that led into the building. He bounded up the steps two at a time, while Cyndi struggled to keep up behind him.

Zack reached the top and immediately tried the thick metal doorknob. It was locked tight. His thoughts darkened with disappointment. He had been sure that he would be able to open the door and Brad, or someone, would be there. Cyndi had reached the top landing as Zack pounded his fist on the door.

"Hey, Brad, open up," he shouted at the door. He waited a second, then pounded again. "Hello? Anybody in there?" He waited for a second, then put his ear up against the door. Cyndi also listened for movement from inside.

"Hear anything?" she asked.

"Not really." Cyndi and Zack shared a look of disappointment. Zack slammed his fists against the door even harder. "HEY! IS ANYBODY IN THERE? CAN YOU HEAR ME? WE NEED HELP!"

"Zack, I don't think--" she trailed off. No need to tell him what he already knew. He ignored her, pressing his ear against the door again.

Cyndi looked out over the railing absentmindedly. Just past the big pine tree that was up against the deck, she saw the hill sloping back down again. On the downslope, the ground became wild underbrush again. In the midst of all the trees and wild vegetation, she suddenly noticed something that blended in, but didn't quite fit. It stood only about ten yards from where they were now. It was tall, black, and had such a uniform symmetrical shape that it was impossible to have occurred in nature. It was a wrought iron fence.

"Zack, look down there!"

Zack turned and squinted into the woods, after a

moment he saw it. They gave each other a knowing look, then immediately started down the stairs toward the fence. Zack took his usual two at a time, while Cyndi took each small step as quickly as she could. Zack jumped from the last four steps and landed hard onto the concrete.

They ran through the underbrush and stopped just in front of the fence. There were vines growing all over the lowest three feet of it. The bars were evenly spaced six inches apart from each other and stood seven feet high. Each bar ended in a sharp, wicked looking point. Zack cringed at the thought of climbing to the top and getting snagged on one of those deadly points.

"Well, I guess we found the end of the park." Zack said. Cyndi nodded, looking from side to side for a gate or an opening, and couldn't find one. The fence stretched as far as her eyes could see, which wasn't very far through all the trees.

"There's gotta be a gate or a road or something around here," she said.

"Yeah, but what if it's locked?" He turned back to the fence and leaned forward, lifting his hands as if to grab the bars. Cyndi looked out at his hands and noticed the thin metal wires running horizontally along the outside of the fence. He was about to wrap his fingers around one of those wires.

The words tangled awkwardly in her mouth and all she could manage was a choked *w--* sound. His hands wrapped around the bars and the thin metal wire slipped between his middle and third fingers.

Zack immediately felt an electric jolt blast through his hands and up his arms painfully. It felt as if tiny air bubbles were torpedoing through his muscles. In the first instant of the shock, he was confused. He thought, *why can't I move? What's happening?* In milliseconds his brain put the pieces together and he panicked. *Oh God. I'm being electrocuted. I have to let go. Letgoletgoletgo.* He could feel the wires growing hot underneath his hands.

Cyndi reached out instinctively to yank him back but hesitated, knowing that she would also be shocked if she touched him. She stood there helplessly watching as his jaw clenched and his body went rigid. Chords stuck out in his neck. She couldn't move, she couldn't think. She had no idea what to do. She began to shriek in sheer panic.

Zack was aware of nothing. He struggled with all of his willpower to let go of the bars. The shock suddenly gave out for a split second and his hands unclamped. He dimly felt himself flying backward and everything went gray.

Cyndi watched in terror as Zack was suddenly jerked off his feet. His body limply flew back ten feet like a rag doll. He crashed into the pine needles and dirt on the ground and settled like a bag of bones. She ran over to him as tears began to stream out of her eyes uncontrollably.

What do I do? Oh God! I need an adult! What the fuck should I do? she thought desperately. She did the only thing she could think to do. She began to scream for Stacy.

*   *   *

Stacy thought she heard a noise in one of the bathroom stalls, a metallic click. Hadn't Cyndi said she would wait outside? Maybe she came back in, that girl could be as quiet as a damn mouse.

"Cyndi?" she asked softly.

Stacy waited for a response and heard none. *Oh well. It was probably nothing. Cyndi's probably outside, making out with her new boy-toy.* She went back to

197

relishing her shower.

Under the warm stream of water she felt the dirt and sweat slide off of her body as if she were a snake shedding skin. The soap from the dispenser wasn't the best smelling soap in the world. It reminded her of the generic kind of soap she would find in the school bathroom, but it was better than continuing the day covered in filth. Stacy wasn't the kind of girl who could just go through the day being sweaty and dirty. It would nag at her constantly. She felt the layer of oil and dirt caked on her skin with every movement she made, rubbing against her clothes and staining them. She would brush up against something dirty and feel more dirt sticking to her, piling on top of the dirt she already accumulated. She wouldn't call herself a germ freak, but she hated being dirty. Besides, she came from money. Her world was clean, neat, and expensive. When you needed something, you got it, no problem. When you wanted something, that was usually also no problem.

Stacy's thoughts wandered back to Brad. This little expedition that he had gotten them into was a big eye opener for her. Before last night, Brad had seemed like the perfect guy for her. He came from money like herself, and would likely have no trouble staying in the land of the upper class for the rest of his life. He also had a wild side that could get her heart racing. He could make her laugh until her sides hurt.

This time he'd gone too far though. This time he had gotten them all in real danger and had completely folded up when it came time to do something about it. Then he had acted so childish when they found this place, all he wanted to do was ride the rides. She still loved him and cared for him as a friend, but she wasn't sure she could ever look at him with desire again, at least not until he grew up a little. Right now she only could see him for what he was, a spoiled bratty boy. Sure, she still wanted to find him so they could get out of this place and go home, but when they did finally make it home again, she wouldn't be all that excited to see him anymore.

Stacy looked around the shower stall for shampoo and saw none. There was only the single soap dispenser with its milky pink school-bathroom soap. She debated whether putting the soap in her hair would be a good idea or not, it would surely dry it out and give her major split ends. She ran a hand through her hair and it felt stiff and greasy. She decided to risk it, pumped out a handful of soap, and lathered her hair up. She dug into her scalp gently with her hot pink painted nails.

Without thinking, she began humming *the Brady Bunch* theme again, then stopped herself. *Ugh, I gotta stop that crap. It's gonna be stuck in my head for the next few days if I don't stop.* She decided to hum something, anything, else and settled on that new song "What A Feeling" from that movie *Flashdance* that had come out a few months ago. She had twisted Brad's arm to sneak in to see *Flashdance* after they had already snuck into a bloody movie he wanted to see called *The Final Terror. That was only a month ago*, she realized. Now here they were in the woods, just like the people in that creepy movie. *Stop it. I will not think about scary movies right now.* She forced herself to concentrate on the song she was humming.

Her mind stubbornly drifted back to the movie theater, and she remembered the preview for the upcoming movie *Psycho II*. Brad had turned to her and whispered, "Oooh, we're seeing that!" She had whispered back, "No way, Jose!" The thought of watching more women getting butchered in showers by some freaky guy made her stomach turn. *Here you are in a shower though, just like in the moooovies,* the morbid part of her mind insisted. *This is the part where he GETS ya!*

The soap ran down her forehead and over her closed eyes now. Her imagination had run away with her and she had to get the shampoo off. She had to open her eyes and turn around, had to make sure no one was there. In a hurry, she wiped soap off her eyes and opened them.

The shadow of a tall man stood silhouetted outside the shower curtain with his long bony fingers turned up, reaching out for her. She saw him for only a split second before water and soap ran down into her open eyes, burning them and temporarily blinding her.

"Ah, shit!" she hissed.

Stacy jumped back and tried to look forward at the shower curtain again, but only saw a wild blur and felt the sting of the soap in her eyes. She turned her face into the water again, rubbing her eyes with the palms of her hands. *There's no one there. It's just your imagination.* Yet she felt the presence of someone right behind her again reaching forward. *Come on, come on. Get this shit out of your eyes.*

"Zack! Cyndi!" she called out, her voice echoing loudly against the tiled walls. Maybe Zack was standing there trying to scare her, or maybe it was Brad. There was no response. "You guys?!" No one there.

Someone was there. Suddenly, she was afraid to turn around. If she made a sudden move, he might lunge forward and grab her. She stopped rubbing her eyes and blinked the soap out furiously, it was almost all out anyway. She listened carefully and could hear faint shallow breathing behind her. It sounded muffled, like breathing from behind a rubber Halloween mask.

Her heart thumped wildly in her chest. *Oh come on, Stacy,* a more rational voice finally spoke up. *Haven't you been around these guys long enough to know their tricks? They must have found Brad and this is his way of coming back out of the woodwork, by scaring the living shit out of you while you're in the shower. The jokes just keep on coming today. Well, we'll just see about that.* She waited, tensing her shoulders. She got ready to spin around, reach through the gap in the shower curtain, and slap whoever was standing out there in the face with her wet hand. That would give them a shock. Next time they'd think twice about scaring old--

A scream rang out. It was Cyndi, but it sounded far off, somewhere outside. She spun around. There was no one there. She poked her head out from behind the shower curtain and glanced around the room. No one there.

Cyndi continued shrieking outside and now it sounded serious.

"STACY! STACY! OH MY GOD! HELP!!!"

Stacy's heart leaped back to its frantic pace. She reached behind her and grabbed her bathing suit. She had it on in seconds, and sprinted out the bathroom toward the sound of Cyndi's screams.

*   *   *

Still dripping wet, Stacy practically flew out of the ladies room. She glanced left and right wildly and saw Cyndi kneeling next to Zack way over by the edge of that far building. Her first thought was that Zack was dead. She ran over to them, getting dirt and pine needles stuck to her wet feet and legs. *So much for the shower*, she thought.

She skidded to a stop in front of them and looked down at Zack's upturned head. All the color had drained out of his face, his skin looked white and waxy. His eyes were rolled back in his head showing the whites, and he was twitching and jerking. There was dirt and needles in his hair. The sight of him like that made

201

her feel sick with dread. She knelt down awkwardly, afraid to touch him, afraid to get too close.

"Wh-what happened?" she stuttered breathlessly. She looked at Cyndi with wide frightened eyes and a trembling jaw that didn't comfort Cyndi in the least bit.

"H-he touched that f-f-fence," Cyndi choked out in hitching tear-filled breaths. "I-it's e-el-electric."

Stacy looked up and saw the wrought iron fence behind them. Her mind put the pieces together sluggishly. She couldn't think, her brain struggled to wade through all those thick waves of panic as if it were walking through mud.

"What?" she asked again.

"It *shocked* him!" Cyndi blurted in a loud shout. She didn't mean to yell at Stacy but she had to make her understand what the hell was going on. "Oh God, Zack! What do we do?"

Stacy shook her head, this situation was beyond her fourteen years of experience. This was grownup territory. Hell, this was dial 911, call for an ambulance territory. Even under calm circumstances, if someone were to ask her what she would do if someone got electrocuted out in the middle of nowhere, she would promptly respond with 'uhh....'

Cyndi caressed Zack's cheek softly.

"Cyndi, don't touch him!" Stacy shouted too late.

His cheek felt hot. With a sudden harsh intake of breath, his eyelids flew up like window shades and he looked around wildly.

"Wh-what the fuck?" he mumbled in a shaky voice. He sounded as if he had just woken up from a nightmare. "What the fuck happened?"

"Zack! Oh my God!" Cyndi cried out, letting out another fresh burst of tears. She hugged him.

202

"Are you okay?" Stacy asked timidly.

"What the fuck happened?" he repeated, his eyes glancing around quickly. He looked as if he were desperately trying to figure out where he was.

Cyndi was so overwhelmed with relief that she unthinkingly leaned down and kissed him on the lips. After a moment, she lifted her head back up and Zack just stared at her with a bewildered expression.

"You were unconscious," Stacy explained.

"You touched that fence and it shocked you," Cyndi said. "I wanted to warn you but I was too late. Oh my God! You flew like, ten feet!"

"Are you all right?"

Zack took a deep breath and sighed it out. He seemed to be getting his bearings.

"Shit!" was all he could manage to exhale. "How long?"

"What?"

"How long was I out?"

"Just a minute. Zack, talk to me. Are you okay?"

He exhaled again deeply and shakily, considering the question. "I guess so. Holy shit." He tried to sit up, but only got his head a few inches off the ground. Cyndi put a hand behind his dirt covered back and helped him the rest of the way up. Stacy helped too.

Zack stared blankly into space, looking dazed. His greasy black hair was all tangled up in the back and clumped with dirt, but he seemed not to notice. Stacy saw this and guessed that someone who had just faced potential death didn't seem to care about such trivial things as hair. Cyndi examined his eyes, trying to make sure he didn't have brain damage or some other catastrophic side effect to the electrocution he had just suffered.

Stacy stood up and walked over to the fence.

She stopped four feet in front of it, and saw the thin electric wires that crisscrossed the iron bars on the outside of the fence. Their small size made them look deceptively harmless. She listened and thought she could almost hear the strong electric current buzzing through the wires.

"Who the fuck did this?" she asked angrily. "Who would put these things up? I mean, he could've been killed." Zack looked over at Stacy, her comment seemed to finally capture his full attention.

"I'm okay, I'm okay," he said quickly swallowing. He said it more for his own comfort than for the girls.

Stacy stared at the wires, they seemed to be mocking her. She began to feel very caged in and claustrophobic.

"We're getting the fuck out of here right now!" Stacy declared with a burst of determined anger. She walked past Cyndi and Zack.

"What about Brad?" Zack asked dreamily.

"The hell with Brad!" she shouted. "We're leaving. I'm going to go down and get the raft and stuff ready. Then we can get back on the river and get you to a doctor as fast as we can. I'll wait for you guys at the raft."

Stacy took off jogging toward the path near the entrance to the Duelin' Rivers without looking back.

"You think you can walk?" Cyndi asked him softly.

He nodded. "I think so." With Cyndi's help, he got to his feet on wobbly legs and they turned to slowly follow Stacy.

"I thought you were dead," Cyndi whispered bitterly, feeling fresh tears well up in her eyes.

"I thought I was too," he said and laughed a little. He offered her a thin smile as tears began to roll down her cheeks. She turned away from him embarrassed. He reached out and pulled her chin back toward him.

"Hey," he soothed. He sounded like his old, normal self again. "Everything's gonna be okay." She nodded, half laughing half crying. He leaned down and kissed her passionately, without holding anything back. He could say one thing for almost dying, it sure gave a guy confidence. His kiss was more comforting and distracting to Cyndi than she could have hoped for. The terror and tension seemed to roll off her shoulders. After a long sweet minute, they finally broke apart, and held each other as the sun set below the trees.

*   *   *

Stacy's jog down the hill past the rides helped get her back under control of the storm of emotions raging in her head. It hadn't been a hard jog, it was almost ninety percent downhill, and it was so steep in parts that she had bounced down on pure forward momentum. She was breathless just the same, and she could feel her heartbeat pounding in her temples. She had a high level of endurance after four years of tennis lessons paid for by her mom and dad. During some of those lessons, she had played so hard and so long that her instructor had to give up and demand that she take a break. The fact that her instructor was only twenty years old and pretty cute also had more than a little to do with that.

She jogged past the Ragin' River's end-pool and stared at the horizon. As she watched, the last sliver of sun dipped below the treetops in the west. Seeing that sunset did nothing for her nerves. It was getting too dark and shadowy in this place already, and she would be damned if she was still here after dark. This silent water park with all its smiley faces was getting creepier by the minute. To Stacy, those ghoulish faces looked more at home in the shadows of twilight than they had in daylight.

She glanced over her shoulder, hoping to see Cyndi and Zack jogging down the hill after her. They were still nowhere in sight, which was pretty much what she expected. She sympathized with Zack, but really hoped he had the energy to hurry up so they could get the hell out of here.

Her foot struck something small and she slowed her pace to look down. It was a familiar black cylinder. She bent down, picked it up, and examined it. It was a tube of her lipstick lying open without its cap, slowly melting from the heat of the concrete. Its keen edge that she had obsessively tried to preserve was now blunt and scratched, as if someone had used it as a crayon.

Stacy looked up again and the sight in front of her made her mouth drop. Thirty feet ahead stood the picnic area with all of their belongings strewn wildly around. Someone had rummaged through their backpacks and touched all of their belongings with filthy groping fingers. Her own thin, pink cheerleading pack sat upside down on the ground next to the table.

"No," Stacy exhaled, as the gravity of the situation slowly dawned on her. *"No!"*

All at once a sick feeling of dread and violation filled her stomach. She sprinted over to the table and looked down at her scattered possessions. All four of their packs had been rudely ripped open and their clothes had been thrown around the picnic area. One of the straps on Zack's backpack had been ripped off and stuffing spurted out of the seam. Several of Cyndi's cassette tapes and cases had been scattered. Cyndi's Walkman lay on the ground looking scratched but intact. Stacy picked up one of Brad's sleeveless muscle shirts that had been savagely ripped open at the armpit. Looking around the picnic area, she couldn't see a single pair of either Cyndi's or her own underwear. Whoever had done this had taken them with him as a perverted prize.

Suddenly, she remembered the shower. She was so sure it had been her imagination when she had seen that silhouetted man-shape reaching for her, but the truth smacked her across the face. There *had* been someone in the shower with her.

Oh dear God, there was some crazy man standing there with only a thin shower curtain between his dirty hands and my naked body. Cyndi's screams must have scared him away.

"Oh God," Stacy choked out, cupping her hand over her mouth.

She bent down, picked up her backpack, and quickly looked through it. Most of its contents had been tossed out. There were black smudges on the opening as if some brutish man with dirty hands had held it open and felt around inside. She looked down and saw a skimpy pink pair of shorts on the ground underneath where the backpack had been. Filthy fingerprints covered the surface, especially around the crotch area. She turned them over in her hands and gasped as she saw a jagged, dark red rendition of that smiley face drawn rudely across the butt with her lipstick. She dropped the shorts in utter revulsion and the smiley face, now crumpled, stared up at her with blank, stupid joy.

Several of the other objects had rough crooked smiley faces drawn on them as well. The front of Stacy's backpack, a white sock, and one of Brad's shirts had them. They were all scribbly child-like imitations of the face on all the painted signs.

"Jesus Christ," Stacy whispered. "We're not alone here. Dear God, help us. We are *not* alone here."

207

A shiver of dread wormed down her spine, and she felt eyes on her, all around her. She spun around looking left and right into the trees and the shadows. She saw no hint of a man's shape anywhere, and no movement behind the trees. There were too many damn shadows. It was getting too dark to see clearly. Whoever did this would be able to move around in the dark more freely. They had to get out of--

"Oh shit, the raft!" she cried with a fresh new wave of dawning horror. She whispered to herself as she ran toward the ramp where they had stupidly left the raft. "Please God, let the raft be okay. Please, please, please." She ran around the corner away from the picnic tables, glancing around nervously, expecting some strange dirty man to pop out at any second.

The ramp area came into view, it was covered by overhanging trees and was darker than the picnic area. Despite the darkness, the flattened, lumpy orange hulk on the concrete was unmistakable.

"Son of a bitch," Stacy muttered, looking down at the useless shredded mound of plastic that had once been their raft. Someone had viciously slashed the hell out of it with some deadly sharp object. It had jagged cuts all over the sides and bottom. Several chunks of orange plastic were lying uselessly on the concrete next to it. In the center, where they had sat only six hours ago, was another one of those crude psychotic imitations of the smiley face, this one stretching across the whole bottom of the raft.

Stacy slowly backed away from the raft. She suddenly realized how alone she was, and felt stupid for leaving Zack and Cyndi behind. It seemed like they were miles away from her. She felt surrounded by predatory, hungry eyes gazing down at her from the darkness of the woods. If she ran, the owner of those eyes would surely jump out after her and make chase.

She had to get back to Cyndi and Zack, but not make it too obvious.

She had backed up almost to the picnic tables, when a loud bark of static and feedback from only a foot or two above her head ripped into her ears. She jumped and screamed aloud in stark terror as the music started and the park was suddenly filled with bright colored lights.

*   *   *

Cyndi and Zack were just stepping onto the path near the Duelin' Rivers entrance, and when the music roared to life, they also jumped and screamed. Another one of those speakers had been placed only three feet behind them, and the ear shattering break in the silence had all the shock and surprise of a slap across the face.

Next to Cyndi's leg one of those low sets of garden lights flashed on with a spark of electricity. She jumped away from it as two puddles of light, one blue and one yellow, lit the path in front of the Duelin' Rivers. Cyndi and Zack whirled around and saw sets of those lights flashing on near the paths all over the park.

Once again, music started playing in that warbling, pitch fluctuating sound that reminded Cyndi of old, warped vinyl. The music blasted in their eardrums and she and Zack stared at each other, intensely worried. Cyndi recognized the song almost instantly, and remembered that it had been on one of her tapes also. The lyrics of the song were eerily fitting. The song was "I Know There's Something Going On" by Frida.

Chapter Sixteen:

Trapped

It was the music pounding in his head that made Zack start puking. It was so ear-splittingly loud he could feel his eardrums vibrating. He clapped his hands over his ears and grimaced at the resonating ringing in them. He still felt the weird vibrations of the music surrounding him, moving up through the concrete, rattling his bones, and making his stomach churn.

It was too much. His knees went weak and trembly, and he had to drop his hands from his ears to try to hold himself up. He felt his gorge rising and tried to force it back. Then he toppled over, losing control of his legs. Cyndi looked down and saw him collapse. She reached down to help keep him up, but his clammy arm slipped out of her grasp.

Zack dropped down into the bushes near the stack of tubes at the entrance to the Duelin' Rivers. Cyndi heard his knees thunk on the river rocks underneath the thin bushes and winced. He hadn't felt a thing. Hot puke bubbled up his throat and he involuntarily heaved forward. A liquid stream and a few chunks splattered out onto the bushes. His stomach lurched again and pushed forward, but there was nothing left to spew out. He dry heaved several times, involuntarily making harsh gagging sounds that hurt his raw throat. From what seemed like somewhere far away, he felt Cyndi rubbing his back, it didn't help at all. He wished she would just get the hell away from him and let this pass. He threw an arm behind his back and waved her away like a fly.

Cyndi stepped away from Zack and watched helplessly as he gagged roughly, his body trying to force out nothing. The music blasting in her ears was too loud and she involuntarily reached for her Walkman to turn it down, but after a confused moment she remembered it wasn't there. God, if only she could turn that chaotic shit down. It was so loud it filled the air, making it hard to breathe, adding to the panic that was already there.

Wow, I'm really in Bizarro World now, she thought. *I'm with friends and I'm kissing boys, but I want the music to just stay off so I can get some peace and quiet. What an upside-down day this has been.*

The music was grinding against her nerves, she had to shut it off. She looked up at the off-white plastic speaker mounted in the tree, then turned and looked down at the rock bed that Zack was puking into. That was it, she could throw a rock at the speaker. It wouldn't cut the music out completely but it was a big step towards cutting the ear-shattering volume down. She reached down next to Zack, being careful not to touch him or any of his puke, and picked up an oval shaped rock the size of a baseball. She looked back at the speaker, carefully aimed, and threw it as hard as she could. She felt it tumble and wobble awkwardly as soon as it left her hand. It flew a foot under the speaker and tumbled off into the woods. She reached down and grabbed for a second and third rock, knowing she would probably miss again. The second bounced back off the

211

tree trunk, flying dangerously close to her left shin. The third rock was smaller and its aim was true, but it ineffectively bounced off the plastic covering.

There was a final, hard dry-heave and then the sick spell passed, leaving Zack gasping for air. The music was still blaring through what he hoped was the last chorus of the song.

What if it doesn't end after this song? What if it keeps going? He didn't know how much more he could take of this. He looked over and saw Cyndi weakly throwing rocks at something, and it took a moment for his brain to register that she was throwing them at the speaker. She threw another one and it bounced off its bottom right corner.

Suddenly, with that harsh rip of static, the music cut out again and they were plunged into blessed silence. He leaned his arms on one of the Duelin' River tubes and hung his head down in relief, trying to catch his breath.

"Thank *GOD!*" Cyndi exclaimed in an uncharacteristically loud voice. "Are you all right?"

He nodded. The world was ringing, but the quieter ambient noises slowly crept back into his consciousness. Zack's skin was alarmingly pale and there was a sheen of sweat on his arms and neck.

"You're sick. You need water. And food. We gotta get you to a doctor." He didn't reply. "You stay here and I'm gonna go down and get you what I can, okay? Then we'll go home. Just stay right here."

He nodded again and exhaled shakily.

She felt the urge to kiss him again before she left, but thought better of it. He was in bad shape right now. None of them had really eaten in almost a full twenty-four hours and they were all pretty dehydrated. After the shock he had gotten from the fence, his body was rapidly shutting down. If she didn't do something quick, he might--

Oh just shut up and get going, her mind interjected.

"Don't go anywhere." She got up and ran for the hill. She went over the bridge above the right Duelin' River and looked back over her shoulder one more time at Zack. He didn't look back, he only leaned there on the tubes with his head down. She ran on.

Cyndi ran down the hill, taking long wild strides and short panicked breaths. She only thought of Zack, she had to do something for him. She looked back over her shoulder at the shadows as she went around the corner past a concrete pillar that held up one of the Ragin' Rivers. She turned her head forward again and crashed into Stacy's back. They both screamed in surprise.

Stacy spun around, thrashing her arms as if she meant to hit Cyndi. Her eyes were wild with terror. Cyndi grabbed her arms and held them.

"It's me! It's just me!" Cyndi repeated, and Stacy stopped screaming. She was trembling all over.

"S-s-suh-home-one's i-in here w-w-with us," Stacy stammered between mad, frightened sobs. Her wide eyes kept glancing around at the woods. "H-he's s-somewhere in here. We g-gottagetout! Wegottagetout!"

"What? Stacy! Stop! Slow down! What happened?!" Cyndi grabbed Stacy's head. She forced Stacy to look her into her eyes. "What happened?"

"He c-cut the raft up. He got all our stuff. He drew s-s-smiley faces on it," Stacy whispered in a tiny, terrified voice.

"What?" Cyndi said, feeling her panic level rise even higher. "Show me."

"No! We gotta get *out* of here!"

"Zack needs water and food. He needs help. Come on."

Cyndi dragged her by the arm, leading her back

down the steps toward the end-pool of the Ragin' Rivers and the picnic tables. Stacy protested the whole way.

The girls finally came into view of the picnic tables and even from thirty feet away Cyndi could see the mess that someone had left of their stuff. Her mouth dropped open and she ran toward the tables. She remembered the constant nagging feeling she had earlier about leaving their backpacks unguarded and out in the open.

"I knew it," she whispered.

She surveyed the disaster area and found her pack upside down on one of the benches among her scattered clothes. She picked the backpack up and saw a red smiley face scribbled down the back of it.

"I knew this would happen. I knew it!"

"You knew it?"

"I had this bad feeling all day. Every time we left our stuff it felt like someone was gonna...touch it or something."

"Let's just get out of here!" Stacy pleaded. She grabbed Cyndi's arm and began to actually pull her toward the river in desperation.

"What about Zack?"

"Let's just go!"

"We can't just *leave* him!"

"You left *me* back at the showers," Stacy blurted. The thought had only crossed her mind briefly in the showers before more urgent matters pushed it aside.

"What are you talking about?" Cyndi asked.

"Why were you two way the hell over by that fence, huh? I told you to wait for me for *ten* fucking minutes! And what did you do? You *left* me!"

Stacy's words hit Cyndi like a slap on the face, and she could do nothing but stare down at her feet in total shame. The distractions of their situation had made

214

her forget her anxiety, but the realization of her own betrayal of Stacy shoved her all the way back down the hill of progress she'd been climbing steadily all day. She was utterly speechless.

"Cyndi, there's something very wrong in this place! Can't you feel it? There was someone in those showers with me. I could almost feel him standing behind me, waiting for me to come out. And it never would've happened if you and your *boyfriend* hadn't left me." The word *boyfriend* came out dripping with disdain and sarcasm. "First Brad left me, then you two did. So I'm sorry, but I'm getting the fuck out of here with or without you guys. Are you coming with me or not?"

"Stacy...I'm sorry," Cyndi stammered in a tiny voice. "I just—we...we gotta stick togeth--"

"Sorry, Cyndi. I gotta go before it gets too dark," Stacy interrupted and began walking towards the river's edge. "Once I get far enough away from here, I'll call out for you and wait for five minutes. If I don't hear from you..." Stacy shrugged and turned away from her.

"Stacy, wait!" Cyndi called out, and Stacy slowed her pace just slightly. "Don't touch the fence!"

"I won't!"

Stacy disappeared behind a tree. A million confused thoughts and emotions whirled around inside Cyndi's head.

We can't just leave Zack. He needs help.
She's right. Zack will just slow you down.
How can she just leave us like this?
We're not supposed to be here.
We need to stick together.
We need to get out of here now!
Go get Zack!
And GET OUT!
NOW!!!

Cyndi came back to reality with her mind made

up. She would go after Zack first. She would not just leave him to die up on that hill. Glancing back at their scattered belongings, she saw her Walkman on the ground. On impulse, she bent down, picked it up, and examined it. It looked a little scratched but it was still intact. She tried pressing the play button, and The Go-Go's "Fading Fast," the last song she had listened to before they went over to the Lazy River, resumed in her headphones. The Walkman still worked just fine. She wrapped the headphones around the back of her neck. The Walkman, or at least the music it played, had always given her strength whenever she felt alone, and if there was ever a time that she needed strength it was now.

Cyndi spotted a pair of her white shorts lying on the concrete. They had been mostly untouched by whoever it was that had ransacked their little base. She brushed the shorts off, slipped into them, then clipped the Walkman to her waistband.

Now she was ready. She jogged up the hill towards Zack.

*   *   *

Zack faded in and out of consciousness. His head and eyelids felt too heavy, and he felt a sick, feverish heat throughout his body. He knew he had to stay awake, it was his only chance. He forced his head up and his eyes open, but within a few seconds they were drooping back down again.

God, I am so thirsty, he realized. *When was the last time I had any water? This morning? I can't remember.* His throat felt sticky and rough, and he could still taste lingering bile from when he had puked earlier. Even his eyes and sinuses felt hot and dried out.

Where the hell is Cyndi? She's been gone too long. He turned his head to look down the path for her.

His vision was too blurry, and it felt like the moisture in his eyes was starting to get gummy. He raised the palms of his hands to his eyes and rubbed them vigorously, then looked up again blinking. He saw only darkness down the path, no sign of Cyndi, no sign of anyone.

Maybe they left without you. You would only slow them down. He seriously doubted Cyndi would do that, Stacy maybe, hell Stacy probably. She might not have done that before, but things had changed since they went on this little adventure. The real people behind the outer layer they normally presented in public had come out. Now that he thought of it, maybe Brad had even left them behind hours ago. He doubted it, but at the same time he wouldn't put it past Brad.

The thought of slowing Cyndi and Stacy down didn't sit right with him. Like it or not, he had reluctantly become the leader of their little group and he knew it. Brad was persuasive, but he had been in over his head on this one. Then he disappeared off the face of the earth, leaving it up to Zack to give the girls some kind of direction.

Zack knew he had to get moving. He had to get down the hill and get back to the girls, but first he needed a drink of water. He turned his head to the water in the entrance-pool at the Duelin' Rivers. The tendons in his neck creaked like an old door. The last lingering shreds of daylight shone just enough for him to see the clear blue water slowly rippling. He could smell the summery inviting scent of chlorine from where he sat.

Zack shakily tried to put one foot firmly on the ground and stand up. As he started to push forward, his stomach gave a sickening lurch and he collapsed back down again. He did not want to start in with the dry heaves again and fought them back mentally for a full minute. Once his stomach slowly settled, he sighed with relief.

Looking up at the water again, he began to crawl toward its ripply surface on his hands and knees. As he got closer, he listened to the water at the edge of the pool bouncing and lapping against its concrete sides. It sounded like something out of a sweet dream. His mind focused in on the sound of the water, tuning everything else out.

It only took a minute to crawl over to the pool's edge. Zack had time to think that he was lucky he'd collapsed this close to the water and not farther down the hill. As he reached the concrete lip at the edge of the pool, he hooked his fingers over the side and stared directly down into the water. It had a hypnotic effect on him. Before he even realized what he was doing, he had leaned down, his face only an inch away from the water's rippling surface. He was bent precariously forward with his butt in the air. He could practically feel the water's cool temperature, and the moisture rising up off the surface, evaporating in the air in front of his face. He stretched out his legs and laid down on the concrete. His stomach gave an initial twinge in protest, then it reluctantly settled.

Zack took a deep breath and dunked his whole head right in. He immediately felt more refreshed and awake as his body temperature rapidly cooled. He opened his mouth and felt the water flow over his tongue and into his throat, wetting everything, setting his mouth back to normal. He swallowed a mouthful of chlorinated water and stopped himself.

You're gonna get yourself sick if you drink that chlorinated pool water. Forget it, he was already sick and dying of thirst. A little chlorine wouldn't kill him.

Zack gulped down the two more huge mouthfuls. The bitter chlorine taste made him want to gag at first, but once he felt the cool water cascading down his desert dry throat he couldn't stop. He chugged the water like a camel and came up gasping for air. He felt so much better than he had just a minute ago. That old phrase popped into his head, *water, water everywhere, but not a drop to drink*.

The water dripped off his face and he felt the sting of chlorine in his eyes, he hadn't bothered to close them. He blinked away the pain and lowered his head again, stopping when his lips reached the surface. He let more cool water flow smoothly into his mouth. He drank deeply, only mindful of how good it felt to moisten his throat and lips again.

You'd better stop before you make yourself puke again. The thought of those painful heaves sobered him and he opened his eyes. He raised his head and saw a dark reflection of his own face on the water's surface staring back at him. Occasionally, a small wave would roll by, distorting the image and his eyes would have to work to reconcile it again. Then, he noticed something else in that reflection. Something behind him. The water settled and in the reflection he saw the dark figure of a man standing above him looking down. He was only a foot away.

Just as Zack realized with horror that someone had silently crept up on him, a rough hand crashed down on the back of his skull and shoved his head underwater again.

Zack thrashed. His first instinct was to gasp in surprise, and he inhaled water. He began to cough and huge bubbles full of his air supply rolled past his face to escape to the precious surface. He raised his hands and tried to push himself up, but the man's knee came down hard in the middle of his back, pinning him roughly to the concrete. He kicked his legs wildly, the man's iron grip on his head was unrelenting. He tried to yank his head to the side quickly and roll his body over, but the man jammed his head down even deeper and he began to scream and panic under the water.

Zack bucked his body with as much desperate strength as he had, and the man lost his balance. The man's knee buckled and the pressure on Zack's spine was relieved. The man loosened the death-like pressure from the hand on the back of his head. With the pressure off, Zack tried to turn his head up out of the water to gasp for air.

Suddenly, Zack felt another strong hand on his shoulder, then the top half of his body was being lifted. The fingers on the back of Zack's head hooked into his hair, yanking him up. His head was out of the water, but all he could do was cough and choke on the water that he had inhaled. He couldn't get a decent breath.

The man pulled Zack's head to one side, then slammed him face first into the concrete at the edge of the pool. A white hot lightning bolt of pain shot through his entire head. His nose broke with a brittle crunch. It felt like it was on fire, and the warm blood that immediately began to flow from it caused him to choke even more.

The pain registered and he had barely begun to scream as his head was shoved down into the water again, the scream became a muffled, useless set of bubbles. He didn't have time to think, he didn't have time to plan. He tried not to breathe, though his lungs wanted to force him. He struggled to move, and that knee was instantly back, pinning him down again. The pain in his forehead and nose made it hard to think. He could taste his own blood in his mouth.

He desperately needed air and began to twist his legs around wildly to shake the man off. His knees beat down on the concrete and scraped the skin. It didn't seem to loosen the man's hold on him very much, he was far too strong. The hard knobs of his fingertips cruelly dug into his scalp as he held Zack's head underwater.

Zack gave in and inhaled water. He was starting to see bright pinpoints of color in his vision.

All at once, the pressure let go, and Zack had only the briefest moment of relief before the hands were on his shoulder and in his hair again, yanking him up. Just like before, they lifted him out of the water, turned him, and slammed his head down on the concrete. This time, Zack's lips mashed against his teeth and he felt his two front teeth chip and break against the concrete. *My teeth*, he thought between agonizing waves of pain.

His head was shoved into the water again. He bucked and flailed his arms feebly. He was now so weak he didn't stand a chance against the man. It was hard to think straight, he felt as if he were helplessly falling asleep.

Oh my God, he thought, falling into a wave of blackness for a second. Then he was awake again and thinking, *Oh God, I think I'm dying. But* (black) *what about my Mom* (black) *and Dad?*

He inhaled a large breath of water and coughed.

He was being lifted up again, this time farther than before. His back was bent back too far and he groaned. The man pulled Zack by the hair and twisted him around, bringing Zack face to face with him. Zack was barely coherent and could only blearily blink away water and blood running through his eyes. Zack sputtered and coughed up water, trying desperately to breathe. The man's head tilted to the side oddly, as if examining Zack in his last moments. His eyes cleared enough just at the last second to make out the white, grinning, exaggerated features of a mask, and a set of stony black eyes peering out from behind it.

"*P-please,*" he coughed.

The word was barely out of his mouth before he was flung back to the concrete and his face crunched one last time. Zack felt like he was half asleep. He couldn't open his eyes all the way, and could only take the most shallow breaths. He barely even felt it when the man stood and picked him up by his armpit and one of his thighs. He clutched at the man's strong long-fingered hands without any real effort. The man lifted him high off the ground, then sent him flying through the air. Zack splashed down into the shallow pool at the start of the Duelin' Rivers, and his knees clunked against the bottom. He was too weak to move and was still breathing in more water. His last thought was how nice the water felt cooling his hot skin, before his mind went into the darkness forever.

Chapter Seventeen:

The Girls Alone

Out of the four of them, the person who's body was physically handling this whole situation best was Stacy. To most people, she gave the impression of a lazy, rich, spoiled girly-girl. Yes, she would admit her family was very well off, she was spoiled, and she was as girly as they come, but one thing she definitely was not, was lazy. Her years of tennis lessons and mall-walking had strengthened her legs and given her incredible stamina. Furthermore, after years of eating only the tiniest portions in an attempt to lose weight (if anyone told her she didn't need to lose any more weight she would've laughed in their face), she felt only mildly hungry and would last a while longer before she would have to break down and eat something. She was awake, alert, and prepared to run fast for a long time if she saw...well, whoever it was that was in this freak-show water park with them.

Stacy moved along the river's edge over the manicured grass and neatly tended flowerbeds they had seen earlier this morning. The riverbank rose four steep feet above the river, then the ground flattened, making the walk easy.

Glancing back at the park, she could see a long slide winding down the hill behind trees. This must have been that first ride they had seen, the one called Dead Man's Drop. She looked back, scanning the picnic table area for Cyndi and Zack, but saw no signs of life. The thought of Cyndi brought a wave of guilt.

How could you just leave her in here by herself? That poor timid little girl looks up to you like you're the big sister she never had. At that thought, Stacy stopped walking and almost ran full speed back up the hill after Cyndi.

"No, no. She can handle herself. Plus her boyfriend can take care of her. I'll wait for them on the outside," she reasoned aloud.

Her boyfriend is in no condition to help her, and you know it. She'll be taking care of him. And what about him? Zack has been one of your closest friends throughout all these years. Sure he's annoying, and he's a geek, but he's done a lot for you, maybe even more than Brad ever did for you. And what about Brad? We still never found him...

"Just shut up," she snapped at the voice in her head. She picked up her pace and began to jog. The added speed and effort to see where she was going in the dark drowned out the voice enough to keep her resolution strong.

After a few minutes, she looked up and saw the place she was heading towards, the place where the trouble really began this morning. The big smiley face painted on the metal door hung back like a spider in the dark exit from the fake mine tunnel. At the sight of it, Stacy felt her heart begin to pound. The last thing she wanted to do was go back into that dark tunnel where God knows what lurked. She stood directly in front of it across the curving river and gathered up her nerve.

224

This is the worst part. Just get through this and you'll be out of this fucking place, okay? Besides, maybe the doors won't even open anyway, and you'll have to just go back along the river and see what's on the other side of the park.

Stacy took a deep shuddering breath and said, "Okay, let's just get this over with." She started forward, taking cautious steps down the riverbank. Once she had made it down the steep slope, she braced herself and stepped into the cold river water once again. "So much for that shower," she muttered regretfully. She had to sit down on the edge of the bank and lower herself down into the water. It was deeper than she'd expected, rising nearly to her waist. She felt the soft squish of mud underneath her flip flops and cringed, she had reached the bottom.

As Stacy crossed the gently flowing river, she looked over to her right at the little stream that joined the main river. It seemed to be flowing down from somewhere else in the park. She hadn't even noticed this stream earlier. She and the others had been too busy adjusting their eyes to the sun after the darkness of the tunnel, and adjusting their minds to try to figure out just what the hell kind of place they had stumbled into. She speculated that this little stream was most likely runoff from that Dead Man's Drop ride.

A wave of some rotten, gassy smell drifted its way down that stream at Stacy. She took one whiff and wanted to gag. She held her breath and covered her nose and mouth with one hand.

"Oh God, what died up there?" she muttered to herself, but her poor choice of words shocked her. They gave her an all too plausible image of dead bloated bodies floating in some putrid pool somewhere along that little stream. She literally shook the image out of her head. "Just stop it. Okay? Just fucking quit it.

You're not helping," she said to herself.

She turned back to the task at hand, moving toward that grinning, beckoning face in the darkness. The water level had risen up past her waist as she waded towards the fake wooden beams of the mine tunnel opening. The mine tunnel thankfully blocked out that horrible dead smell and she could lower her hand again. She peered around the corners of the tunnel, looking for anyone that may be creeping along the walls, waiting to jump out and grab her. It was dark, but there was still enough light to see the rough rocky walls along the sides of the tunnel. She waded in.

Stacy stopped an arm's length away from the doors, she couldn't make herself go any closer. Her heart thumped frantically in her chest as she stared up at the white grinning painted face. It looked like it wanted to open its huge grinning mouth and bite her. She wanted to turn and bolt, but instead lifted her hand and reached toward the door. She lightly pressed her fingertips against the cold metal door on the right and pushed forward. The door moved forward an inch, then stopped, clunking loudly against something. She reached out, planted her other hand on the left door, and gave both doors a stronger push. They rattled and clunked hollowly, but wouldn't budge more than an inch. River water sloshed up on both sides of the doors, echoing in the mine tunnel.

There was a dark slit down the center of the face, a small half-inch crack between the two doors. She would have to try to get her fingers in there and pull them open. She peered into the darkness behind the doors. She felt hot, humid air gently blowing out through the crack. She thought she caught a whiff of that rotting dead-body smell again, but it was there and gone in a second. That nasty smell was probably still stuck in her nostrils from earlier.

Stacy wondered if it was safe to put her fingers through that crack between the doors. There was only one way to find out. She slid the fingertips of her right hand into the crack just above the smiley face's painted teeth. On the other side of the doors, her middle fingertip barely poked out. She tried to pull the doors open but they only gave that measly inch. She had no leverage standing at this angle, with her hand shoved awkwardly in the middle of the doors.

She slid her right hand down to the water's edge and stuck her fingers in, then put her left hand up high above the smiley face's wide eyes, and began to pull. She yanked on the doors in three quick bursts. *Clunk clunk clunk.* The metal doors were fastened tight. River water sloshed up against the doors even more violently than before. She was about to give them another yank, when something squishy and unmistakably hairy bumped into her fingertips just above the water level.

Stacy gasped and yanked her fingers out of the crack, taking a huge step back. She examined her fingers, expecting to see them covered with a nasty slime, but they were only wet. There was nothing nasty on them, at least nothing that she could see. She lifted her fingers to her nose and sniffed them, they reeked of that gassy dead body smell. Gagging, she yanked her fingers away from her nose and threw them into the water to wash away the smell. She looked back at the doors and realized that the dead smell wasn't just lingering in her nostrils, it was coming from behind the doors.

The smiley face seemed to mock her. *Come on in Stacy. I was only messing with you before. If you try to open me up now, I'll let you. I'll let you come see what nasty dead things I have waiting for you back in the dark.*

"No, no, fuck this. I'm not going that way," she

told to herself, on the verge of hysteria. She wanted to scream, she wanted to laugh. "Just go back and find Cyndi and Zack. We'll find some other way out, okay? There's nothing there. You didn't see anything. It's okay, you're okay. This was just a stupid idea."

Stacy waded out of the tunnel as fast as she could, paddling against the current with her hands to speed herself along. She continuously scrubbed her fingertips in the water trying to wash away every molecule of whatever dead thing she had touched.

She reached the other side of the river and scrambled up the bank. Her entire body was tensed, wanting to take off frantically, but her mind kept her body in check. *Don't let him see that you're afraid. If you do that, he'll chase you.*

Who was *he*? She didn't know. It was just a crazy thought. She got back up onto the grass and walked as fast as she could back toward the hill where Cyndi had gone. Just before Stacy was out of sight of the tunnel, she thought she heard a clunk and the metallic whirr of the doors opening up behind her. She hurried away, refusing to look back.

*   *   *

As Cyndi began to climb the hill, she put both headphones on and pressed play on her Walkman, keeping the volume low. She tried to listen to the music for a few seconds, but it seemed to limit her outside hearing too much. She wouldn't be able to hear anything else, not some unknown stranger's footsteps, snapping twigs and crunching around in the underbrush, or the shallow breath of someone slowly creeping up behind her. At that thought, she immediately took one orange cushioned headphone off her right ear and looked over her shoulder. No one crept up behind her. She placed the headphone below her right ear, that ear would remain alert. The other ear would listen to some random Go-Go's song she had heard a million times to distract her, to keep her intense fear at bay.

"There's nothing to be nervous about," Cyndi whispered to herself. She stopped, realizing that somewhere during the last day she had found her voice again. Stacy and Zack had brought it out of her. She was still addicted to music, but she didn't feel so nervous about speaking out loud anymore. "Just go back up the hill, get Zack, and go back down again to find Stacy. That's all. It'll only take five minutes." But Cyndi had that same sinking feeling deep down in her gut that Zack would be gone, just like she had felt about their backpacks. She tried to forget it and concentrated on the lyrics as she went up the wooden steps yet again.

How many times have I gone up this hill and back down again today? She honestly couldn't remember. It was beginning to take its toll on her body, her legs were exhausted and sore. Her stomach was getting that starved pinched feeling that she had once heard Zack comment on back at camp, saying: "I'm so hungry, my stomach's starting to eat itself."

"Don't focus on it, just get Zack and we'll get out of here. Get Zack, get out. Get Zack, get out," she repeated.

Cyndi passed the sign at the fork in the path and went straight toward the Duelin' Rivers entrance where she had left Zack. The bridge over the Duelin' River was already in sight. She was close enough that she would almost be able to see him again, and she felt her heart beat faster in anticipation.

Zack was essentially her boyfriend now, a thought that continued to amaze her. *Who would've thought that quiet old Headphones-Girl-Cyndi would make friends and get a boyfriend?* She imagined all four of them back at home, walking down the street in front of her ex-best friend Jennifer's house, Cyndi holding hands with her boyfriend. Cyndi walking next to her new best friend Stacy, who was much prettier and much more popular than Jennifer, who would be at her own front window seething with jealousy. It would be so sweet to see the look on her stupid face.

Cyndi came up the steps over the bridge and peered across to the spot where she left Zack. Just as she suspected, he was gone.

"Shit," she said out loud. She took off her other headphone, letting them both drape around her neck, faintly blasting music into the air. "Shit, shit, shit!" It was the first time she had ever used that word, and it was as appropriate a time as ever. Her mind flooded with panicked thoughts full of dread.

That guy that Stacy was talking about, the guy on the Lazy River. He got Zack.

No, Zack went back down the hill already, found Stacy, and they left without you. Now you're all alone in this creepy place. All alone except for some stranger lurking in the shadows.

"Zack?" she called out, running across the bridge to the spot where she left him. She spun around, looking into the trees, listening for him. Even the faintest response from him would do. There was only the whisper of music still coming from her headphones, the crickets, and the trickle and splash of the water that ran on endlessly in this lonely place. "Zack? Where are you?" No response. She found it increasingly frustrating to call for someone and not get any answer back. They had been doing it all day.

Zack was nowhere in sight, but she didn't feel like she was alone at all. She felt eyes on her wherever she went now, watching her from the darkness and waiting.

230

"ZACK!" she shouted, cupping her hands over her mouth. She looked around for a response and found none. "Where the *hell* could he have gone?" she asked herself. The last time she saw him he had been puking and was so out of it he could barely move.

Someone got him. First Brad, now Zack. You're next. You or Stacy. So get OUT. Just get the hell--

No! She couldn't think like that. She looked around wildly, searching desperately for a possible answer. She just couldn't leave yet, not without searching for him at least a little bit. He needed help, and she wouldn't be able to live with herself if she just abandoned him.

Cyndi wasn't like Stacy. She couldn't just say, *screw you, you're on your own*. Within the last ten minutes, she had lost a lot of respect for Stacy, but Cyndi always tried to give everyone the benefit of the doubt. She repeatedly told herself that Stacy would get out of this creepy park and wait right outside the gates for them, ready to run back in at the first sign of trouble. Now it was getting harder and harder to believe that.

Where the hell had Zack gone? Had he somehow found his strength and gotten out of here too, leaving Cyndi all friendless and alone? She thought back to her last fleeting glance back at Zack. He had been slumped on the ground with his head down, sick and dehydrated, barely able to walk. She knew it couldn't be true, he couldn't have left without her.

Her eyes stopped on the buildings where the bathrooms had been and another possibility presented itself. *Maybe he went to use the bathroom.* It wasn't as far-fetched as him getting up and just walking out of the park without even trying to find Cyndi and Stacy. That idea just didn't make sense to her at all, he would never do that. But the bathrooms? Well, it wasn't the greatest explanation, but it was at least something. She had to go check it out.

Cyndi walked quickly toward the bathrooms, peering around defensively. It was a dark stretch between the entrance to the Duelin' Rivers and the bathrooms, and it did nothing for her nerves. As the bathrooms came into view, she saw that they were now dark. Why would Zack go in there without at least turning on the lights?

Maybe Stacy had the right idea after all, and Cyndi should just turn and run. She looked back in the direction she had come, it looked much more inviting than the dark bathrooms ahead. The urge to run was strong, but the thought of Zack, of her "boyfriend" as Stacy now called him (even though they hadn't made anything official yet), continued to hold her back. She had to know, had to see that he wasn't there before she could walk away.

"Damn it," Cyndi said, continuing on towards the bathrooms. "Just run in and see. And if he isn't there..." She trailed off, trying to keep her mind focused on the task at hand.

Cyndi's footsteps crunching softly in the underbrush, were replaced by the sounds of her own soft steps on the smooth concrete. She had made it back to the paved path and slowed down as she approached the bathroom building. She stood outside the open hallway with the brick tiles, looking through to the other side. Bright moonlight shining down on the other side made the inside of the bathrooms look like a black pit.

"Zack? You in there?" she called. Her own voice echoing back on the tiles served as her only response. She began to step slowly forward into the dark bathrooms, heading toward the other side this time, the Men's side. There must be a light switch in there. What if he was in there, passed out on the floor or something?

Something Stacy said instantly came back to her. *There was someone in those showers with me. I could almost feel him standing behind me, waiting for me to come out.* It stopped Cyndi cold. Someone *in* there. Maybe *still in* there. Hiding behind a shower curtain in the darkness. Yes, she could feel someone's presence too, just like Stacy had said, and it sure as hell wasn't Zack.

Cyndi slowly backed away from the dark hole of the bathrooms, wishing she hadn't called out Zack's name and given herself away. If there was someone in there, now they knew she was just outside. If she didn't come in soon, they would come out after her. She backed away slowly, stepping as softly as she could, trying not to give away her position. She tensed her leg muscles, listening for a quick scampering set of footsteps to come echoing out of the darkness. She watched, waited for some predatory figure to run out, grab her, and drag her away, screaming into the night. If she heard anything from that bathroom, at least anything except Zack's voice, she would turn and sprint away.

As Cyndi backed away from the bathroom, she noticed another noise behind her, a sporadic electric fizzling. She turned around partway, careful not to completely turn her back on the bathroom, which seemed like some dangerous animal's den now.

The broken neon sign they had seen earlier was on now, just like the rest of those low colorful lights that surrounded the rides. Some of the smashed neon tubes were flickering and struggling to remain lit. A few of the letters still remained intact, glowing brightly. At the top, she could now make out what the smaller letters were supposed to say: *Kaptain Smiley's.* They were almost all dead or flickering weakly. Only the big K was left untouched, and was glowing a fierce red. The other wavy blue bubbling letters on the bottom were meant to say *Thrill River*. They were mostly still intact except for a few broken letters on the left side. That ugly smiley face in the middle was also still working, eerily glowing white. She stared at the letters transfixed, noticing that they spelled out a new message, one that she didn't care for at all. Surrounding that mocking face and flickering mess of smashed letters, two words were spelled out:

K ill River.

* * *

  Stacy's skin broke out in the biggest goosebumps she had ever had. The water down in the river had been cold as usual, but somehow seemed warmer at night. It was getting out of the water that chilled her skin. All day she had been perfectly comfortable whenever they had gotten wet. It had been hot, probably close to one hundred degrees. After sitting at the picnic tables waiting for Brad to show up and baking in the sun, she hadn't honestly felt cold again until now. She let her bottom half drip dry in the chilly night air, raising goosebumps on her legs and sending them all the way up to her shoulders. The thought of that unthinkable, squishy, dead thing behind the door, and the constant feeling of eyes watching her sent shivers down her back that only perpetuated the problem. She desperately wished she could towel off the cold water that dripped down her legs.

  Speed-walking past the picnic tables, Stacy noticed a few scattered remnants of her belongings. The pair of shorts that had the vulgar smiley face painted on were directly in her path as she cruised by. She kicked them out of the way. They flew up into the air, fluttered back down on the top corner of a picnic table, and slid off the edge back down to the ground. She felt an urge to gather up her stuff and take it all with her, but she knew there wasn't enough time. Someone was following her, she was sure of it. If she hurried, she might be able to either lose him or meet up with Cyndi and Zack. She felt like such an idiot for going off on her own. That was exactly what *he* wanted, whoever *he* was. It wasn't too late to meet back up with Cyndi and Zack though. They would probably just be coming to the bottom of the hill now, maybe at the bottom set of wooden stairs taking a rest.

The picnic table area and the woods beyond were silent and still. She half wished those stupid colorful garden lights would turn off. They helped only a little bit by vaguely lighting up scattered areas in the park, but they hurt matters by causing all the surrounding woods to look darker. Moonlight was rendered ineffective because of the lights, and she wouldn't be able to see a dark figure shift among the shadows in the trees. She kept her eyes locked on those trees.

Turn around, he's right behind you. She whipped her head to the other side and jumped prematurely. No one was there. She sighed in relief and frustration.

"Stop doing that to yourself!" she scolded. "There's no one. Just get to Cyndi and Zack. Keep your eyes and ears open, but get to Cyndi and Zack." Her little self-pep talk did not make that feeling of watchful eyes go away.

Still shivering, she rubbed her legs with her hands, trying to wipe away some of the water that was making her cold. It only spread the water to places that had dried already and made her colder.

She shuddered, *"Fuck! It's so cold."*

It occurred to Stacy that she could towel off with that pair of shorts that she kicked, or some other pair of clothes. She immediately vetoed that idea though. First off, they seemed soiled after being manhandled by some unknown assailant. Secondly, she just wanted to get the fuck out of this creepy area. During the day, the picnic table area had seemed like the safest spot in the park, it was their home base. Now that night had fallen and it had been invaded while they were away, it felt like a shadowy snake pit. She hurried away from the picnic area, taking a last glance at the shorts that were now underneath the table.

Walking down the short slope toward the Ragin' River end-pool, Stacy looked for Cyndi and Zack coming down the path. She still couldn't see them. She wanted to call out to them, but knew it wouldn't really do any good. She felt nervous about raising her voice, as if the noise would stir up something or someone that was better left alone.

She was so focused on looking for Cyndi and Zack that she didn't even notice what was floating in the pool until she was almost directly in front of it. Its slow movement caught her eye and she stopped dead in her tracks.

A person was floating on a tube near the corner of the pool, spinning in a slow circle. They were sprawled out on top of the tube, lying flat on their stomach. The head was down low, either touching the surface of the water or down in it. She couldn't tell because long, sandy-blond, feathered hair hung down covering the face. Arms and legs dangled off the tube, bobbing up and down in the water. She recognized the white football jersey and the neon green and blue swim trunks before she recognized the hair.

"Brad?" Stacy whispered.

He didn't respond, didn't give even the slightest twitch. Stacy swallowed, her heart hammering.

"Brad?" she repeated in a louder, shakier voice. He continued to float in that endless circle, caught in some whirlpool current. She wanted to ask him where the hell he had been all day. She also wanted to turn and run. She did neither, and felt her feet carrying her over to the edge of the pool, seemingly of their own accord.

Why was he just lying there on top of the tube with his face in the water? *You know why. He's dead.* No, she couldn't accept that. It was unbelievable, it was impossible. How could someone she knew and grew up with be dead? How could someone who was only fourteen years old be dead? It had to be a trick.

Stacy's feet carried her closer, now she could see that his skin looked pale and waxy. Surely that was just a trick of one of the underwater lights shining up from the walls of the pool. That pool light gave off a ghostly blue campfire glow to everything. The water was clear blue except for a thin pink cloud around the tube he was floating on.

No, no, NO! I don't want to see this. Her feet stopped at the edge of the pool. She was only four feet away from him and could clearly see how unmistakably pale his skin was. His hands and feet had the thick pruny wrinkles of being in water for a long time. His head was coming around to her and she could feel her hand uncontrollably reaching out across the water for it. Her heart thundered in her ears, drowning out everything else. She breathed in shallow, whispery breaths.

She put her hand out and the weight of his head bumped into it. The circle he had been turning in stopped, and the current sent up larger ripples in resistance to his lack of movement. She dug her fingers into his hair feeling his scalp, it was cold and rubbery. She pulled his head up, slowly revealing the face that had been down in that water, and felt a sick scream building in her throat.

Brad's eyes had rolled up high, only the bottom of the irises showed at the top of his eyelids. His skin looked wrinkly and bloated, and was beginning to take

237

on that pruny look that Stacy only thought you could get on your hands and feet. Water dripped lazily from his pruny skin back down into the pool. His mouth had been slashed open on the sides all the way to his jawbone. Jagged, meaty flaps of what were once his cheeks hung down dripping pink water, losing the last bits of blood they had. His jaw had been rudely yanked down and broken, forcing his mouth open to a grotesquely wide angle. His jaw was broken in several places and his teeth gathered in crooked clusters. Water poured out of his mouth like it would from a pitcher as she pulled his head out of the water.

She saw all of this in terrifying vividness and detail in only a second or two. She could feel a raw powerful scream building in her throat when the ripping static sound blasted into her eardrums again. An impossibly loud alien sound battered her eardrums and the music from the speakers began once again.

Stacy dropped Brad's head back down into the water and began to shriek.

*   *   *

Cyndi was unable to hear Stacy's shriek standing in front of the neon sign because the music drowned it out. It drowned out everything, and once the song was over it would be another ten minutes before the ringing in her ears would subside. She screamed aloud as that rough static barked out like a fire alarm. Something that sounded like a short electronic scream blasted out. Then the music began, and she instantly recognized the song. She put the pieces together in her mind, realizing what that sound was.

It was a rushed synthesizer keyboard slide at the beginning of a brand new song she had only heard once on the radio the day before she left for camp. She had been taping another song when her mom came in and told her to start packing her clothes for camp, distracting her from hitting the stop button on the tape recorder. After she had successfully gotten her mom to say her peace and leave her alone again, the song had started and already caught her ear. She had never heard of the artist before, but she was captivated.

Cyndi knew better than most people how some songs just hit you the first instant you hear them. You sit there listening, completely swept up in them, every note feeling perfectly in place and sounding sweet, like destiny. You know that this song is going to be an instant classic, one you will listen to for the rest of your life. You'll always remember where you were the first time you heard it. Once the song ends, all you want to do is rewind the tape, or pull the needle on the record player back to the start, and play it over and over again. This song locked a tiny piece of time forever in her mind, sitting in her room on her bed on a summer evening. Her mom had left her room, and she stared out the window at the setting summer sun as the song held her captive.

Now a new piece of time was being locked into her memory, one filled with terror and death. The notes pounded into her ears so loud that her eardrums vibrated painfully. She clapped her hands over her ears and screamed again. The song was called "Girls Just Wanna Have Fun," and yet again, it was so frighteningly appropriate. Zack had disappeared, Brad was still gone, and the girls were left alone for whoever the real owner of this dark paradise was.

*   *   *

"CYNDIEEEEE!!!"

Stacy sprinted up the hill screaming for Cyndi. She knew she had to reach Cyndi and Zack before someone else did. She ran with the image of Brad's ruined face burned into her mind. Someone had killed Brad, had actually brutally *murdered* him. Now she had seen the killer's twisted handiwork, and he would come after her next. She could feel eyes on her all the time now, and could sense that *he* (it was definitely a masculine presence) knew she had found Brad's body. Hadn't he left it there for her to see?

"CYNDI! ZACK! HELP!!!" she shrieked at the top of her lungs. It only sounded weak and small, drowned out by the music. She stopped halfway up the hill and could see no one coming down at all. The warped music was unbelievably loud in her ears, deafening her. The total loss of one of her senses made her easier prey.

"CYNDI! ZACK! WHERE THE HELL ARE YOU?!" This time she screamed more out of terror and frustration than for any solid purpose. The blasting music completely robbed her voice of all its force and power.

She thought she heard a *snap-pop* from behind her, and whirled around. Was it Cyndi coming back up the hill toward her, or was it the man from the showers, the man who killed Brad? Her eyes scanned the dark path frantically, but she saw no one and no movement. In fact, she didn't even see where the noise could have come from. It had sounded like a twig snapping in the underbrush, but there was no underbrush behind her. There was only grass on the left and flowerbeds on the right. Maybe she hadn't even heard anything. With this music still blasting out her ears who could tell? She reluctantly turned back around and continued to hurry up the hill.

*   *   *

Cyndi was just about to turn around and sprint down the hill after Stacy, but the light caught her eye. She hated to leave Brad and Zack behind, but this was getting too creepy. As much as she hated to admit it, she knew she should have left Zack and gone with Stacy. The thought made her feel dirty, as if she were mentally betraying Zack, the first boy she ever kissed. This whole damn situation was dirty. It seemed unbelievable that the events of her recent past had led her to this frightening alien present. One day, she was safe, living a normal life and thinking that she had only moderate problems, the next she was alone, trapped in some water park in the middle of nowhere, and holding her hands over her ears to block out that thunderous pop music.

The music was giving her a headache even through her hands. She was starting to feel dizzy. Somehow it seemed much louder at night than it had during the day.

I'll just take one last long look for Zack, then I'm dust. She scanned the dark surrounding woods slowly. The music was so loud it almost made her vision vibrate. She felt her brain thumping in her head every time the bass hit. The world started to sway. She blinked her eyes furiously, trying to clear her vision.

I'm so sorry, Zack. Cyndi turned to leave but a pool of light that she hadn't seen before caught her eye. This wasn't one of those strange decorative colored lights that only lit select spots and gave the whole place that weird tribal look. This light was warm and natural. It was the comforting light you would see from the front door of your house as your Mom called you to come in after a long day of playing outside.

She saw the light clearly at the end of those steps that lead up to the locked door in that far building. It came from somewhere up beyond those steps, from whatever was behind that door. Someone had the door

241

open up there, and the lights were on.

Cyndi ran over to the steps. *Could Zack be up there? Or Brad?* Maybe this whole thing was just some trick made up by the both of them to scare her to death. If so, it was pretty damn elaborate, and she didn't really believe that Brad or Zack were clever enough to pull off something of this magnitude.

But they might be up there. And if they're not, then someone has to be.

She looked up at the tinted windows, but still couldn't see anything inside that mysterious room at the top of the stairs. She had to go up and see who or what was in there.

Moonlight shined down on the concrete path as she walked towards the wooden stairs. Every so often one of those low lights would flood it out, but another ten feet farther and it was back to that ghostly pale blue moonlight reflecting off the concrete.

As Cyndi approached the far building, she kept her hands jammed over her ears. She looked up at a speaker that was mounted high up on the building, blaring that strange music throughout the park. She stared at it with disdain. Then she noticed something she hadn't seen on any of the other speakers. The wire that fed the speakers with power and music was strung out behind the speaker and ran along the wall below the tinted windows. Her eyes followed the wire along its path to a tiny hole drilled into the building.

The music's coming from up there, she realized. She ran to the steps which seemed to be glowing with warm comforting light.

Cyndi peered around the corner of the building. The bright light coming from the top of the stairs made her squint briefly as her eyes adjusted. At the top, there was a porch light mounted high on the wall. Next to the porch light, the metal door that Zack had pounded on earlier stood wide open. Its white paint reflected the light down the stairs and onto the concrete below. The light's warm yellow glow reminded her so much of home.

"Hello?" she called, lowering her hands from her ears. On this side of the building the music wasn't nearly as loud. She listened for a response and only heard more of the music coming from somewhere inside the room. There was no reply to her call, and it didn't really surprise her. If anyone was up there, she would have to go up and meet them face to face.

Cyndi slowly began walking up the wooden steps.

*   *   *

Stacy passed the fork in the path and quickly ran onto the bridge toward the Duelin' Rivers entrance.

"CYNDI!" she screamed, expecting to find her there struggling with Zack. Several of those low colored lights lit up the path. Cyndi and Zack weren't there. She ran over to the end of the path, spinning in a slow circle and looking for any signs of them. She was alone.

Did they leave without me? Did Cyndi and Zack go down to the path and make it all the way to the other end of the park without me? She felt like an idiot for coming back up this way all alone. *But how would they have made it that far so fast? I would have at least seen them heading toward the picnic area. Or maybe they went the other way, toward the Lazy River. Maybe.*

Stacy stopped spinning around as her eyes locked on some movement from out in the woods to her left. Branches swung wildly as someone brushed past them. A man was running toward her. For a brief moment she felt relief, thinking it had to be Zack. She put her hands up to call out to him, but then she saw his dark figure more clearly. He was much taller than Zack and wore all black. He had his head down as he ran, but she could see his face was white. He wasn't just running toward her, he was running *at* her.

Stacy felt her feet sluggishly start running, giving the man chase. She let out a low, guttural, terrified scream, completely unlike the shrieks she heard in movies whenever a girl was being chased by some killer. This scream was one of raw, primal terror.

She took off in a diagonal direction, going around the waterfall entrance to the Duelin' Rivers and into the woods toward the lazy river. She sprinted, pumping her strong tennis legs as fast as she could. No matter how fast she ran, she still seemed too slow, as if she were running in water.

Glancing back she saw the white faced man still chasing her, gaining on her. She could only take quick glances at his misshapen face. He bounded along behind her, slowly gaining, getting dangerously close.

Low branches slapped her face as she turned forward again, she slapped them away. The music continued to blast in her ears, warbling and droning, making it hard to hear the footsteps behind her. Nevertheless, she felt him closing in. He had to be only fifteen feet behind her.

She suddenly zigzagged to the right, like a frightened jackrabbit being chased by a wolf. She wanted to throw him off and put some more distance between them. She felt like a rabbit, utterly helpless. She darted between two huge pine trees and came out at the far entrance to the Ragin' Rivers, the last place Brad had been seen alive. Two of those low lights shined down on the concrete giving it a chaotic red and green glow.

Looking back between the pine trees, she lost sight of the man. Her eyes darted back and forth but she couldn't see him anywhere. She didn't want to slow down though, he couldn't be too far away. Should she dart in between the two Ragin' River slides and hide? No, he's too close. He would see where she went and she'd be cornered. She looked over her shoulder and spun around in a panic.

Where the hell is he? She couldn't hear him over the ear shattering music, and couldn't see him in all the darkness. She felt blind. *But he can see you*, she thought, and it was enough to get her sprinting again.

She took a huge leap off the concrete pad over the ropes and sailed through the air. She crashed down in the underbrush past the steep six foot drop-off beyond the concrete pad. A jolt of pain shot up through her feet, forcing her to roll on the ground. Pine needles and dirt caught in her hair and clothes, poking her and drawing tiny bits of blood. She rolled to a stop on her hands and knees. She looked back up at the Ragin' River entrance just in time to see the man's white face whirl away from the edge. He had gotten there just as she jumped, and now he was going back to find another way down after her.

She scrambled to her feet and took off into the woods.

*　　　*　　　*

Cyndi had seen rooms like this on TV before, but never in real life. She stood in the doorway, staring into a control room that she guessed was as big as her living room back home, although it was so cramped and full of equipment it looked smaller than the living room. It was fully lit with several florescent tubes behind large plastic grids in the ceiling, just like the lights at her school. There was a dark rust-red carpet on the floor, and more carpet halfway up the walls. It was also like the carpeting at her school, extremely thin and tight, as if it was only put there to cover up the wood floors.

Along the wall on the right side of the room were half a dozen filing cabinets, then massive black electric panels with blinking red and green lights. Next to them were several electric switchboards. Along the back wall and left side of the room were long desks covered with huge control boards filled with dials and switches. These desks were pushed up against the wall below dark tinted windows. Several crumpled papers and legal pads were left strewn over the control boards. There were also several Styrofoam coffee cups sitting in front of the control panels. One of them had spilled and congealed into a solid dark brown puddle on the desk.

There were two wooden office chairs with thin red cushioning. One office chair was neatly pushed up against the desks, the other lay overturned in the middle of the room.

On the left wall nearest her, there was a round card table, complete with a pack of cards that had been left scattered on the table, abandoned in the middle of some game. There were several more coffee cups, a few Styrofoam plates, and an ashtray with a Budweiser logo full of crushed cigarette butts. Most of the cups were at least half-full with old black coffee that looked more like black syrupy sludge now. Also on the table was a pile of papers that looked like a stack of blueprints and schematics. Resting on top of one of the blueprints was a petrified, half-eaten bagel that looked hard as a rock. Behind the table was a small cabinet with warped faded wood, and an old relic of a coffee maker sitting on top.

Cyndi heard that strange music coming from somewhere in this room, and her eyes locked onto the source in the back left corner. There was an old, clunky Teac Reel-to-Reel, and a cassette player below it. She recognized the Teac only because her dad had one just like it at home. To the left of the cassette player, there was a disorganized box of reels and tapes. To the right, there was an old speaker, blaring out the "Girls Just Wanna Have Fun" in a tinny, distorted squawk.

She saw a cassette tape's reels spinning behind the plastic view-window in the tape deck.

So this is it. This is where the music has been coming from all along, she thought. Question answered. But the answer had only led to another more disturbing question. *Who has been up here pressing play? And where is he now?*

*　　*　　*

Stacy ran for her life. Her lungs felt like they were on fire. She had an insane urge to scream for a timeout, but this wasn't a game of tag in the school yard, this was life and death. She ran through the bushes, glancing back every two seconds and not seeing the man. She was starting to feel sick from all the running, panic, and music pounding through her head, but she couldn't stop. She sensed him back behind her somewhere, chasing her through the darkness.

The bushes and underbrush ended and she found herself on a concrete path again, the one that went up the slope past the Lazy River. She was winded and had to find some place to hide quick, she couldn't keep this chase up much longer. She turned and ran down the path, maybe she could hide somewhere on that island in the middle of the Lazy River. At least the path was smooth and she could run a lot faster without worrying about stepping in a strange divot and spraining her ankle.

A flash of white and red stripes caught Stacy's eye as she glanced back to look for the man. It was an umbrella somewhere off to the left. She almost ran right past it, but curiosity got the better of her and she slowed down.   Then it hit her, this was the umbrella on the wooden chair   that was up on that lifeguard's lookout cliff above the Lazy River.

I could hide by that chair and he wouldn't be able to see me, she thought.   It took only a split second to make her decision.   She took a long look behind her, saw that the coast was clear, and bolted for the cliff.

Stacy brushed past some low hanging limbs that obscured the view of the chair from the path.   As she approached the chair, she saw something that made her stop dead in her tracks and cover her mouth with her hands to stifle a scream.

Someone was sitting in the chair.   Stacy's first thought was that the man had somehow gotten around her and sat down in the chair.   Then she realized that it couldn't be him, he would be breathing hard from the long chase.   This man sat as perfectly still as the wooden planks on the chair.   His head tilted back as if reclining, a head with greasy black hair.

*   *   *

Cyndi stood in front of the cassette player.   The music coming from the speaker blasted in her ears.   She didn't know if she dared turn it off, as much as she wanted to.   She would be giving herself away to whoever was out there.   She stared down at the cassette player and saw audio cables coming from the back of both the cassette player and the Teac to the control panel to the left.   The panel looked like an audio-mixing board with a dozen volume bars, and VU meters above them with needles bouncing along to the beat of the music.   The needles bounced along in the high-volume red zone of the VU meters.

That tape in the tape deck had to be hers.   She just knew it.   The pitch of the music struggled and wavered, going flat then sharp. It gave the singer of the song a demonic low voice at certain points, and a freakish chipmunk voice at others. This old cassette player was broken and it was ruining her tape.

Cyndi's finger moved toward the stop button just below the cassette deck, but she hesitated.

Don't give yourself away. He'll know you're here.

"He already knows we're here," she reasoned aloud.

She held her breath and pressed the stop button under the cassette deck. The music abruptly stopped. The needles in the VU meters instantly dropped back and lay still.

Cyndi immediately wished she hadn't stopped the music as a complete, overwhelming silence fell over the entire park.

*   *   *

Right as the song reached its loudest peak, it was abruptly cut off, leaving the entire park in a state of stunned silence. A lingering echo of the last dismal note pounded back in the still air. Stacy felt naked and vulnerable without the weird music crushing out the rest of the noises.

She looked around quickly, listening for a rush of footsteps crunching through the underbrush. All she heard was the ringing in her ears left over from the pummeling they had taken from the music. She didn't want to move, if she moved she would step on a branch and give herself away. She didn't want to breathe, her harsh gasping breaths seemed much too loud. She cupped her hands over her mouth to stifle the sound. The man with the weird white face was laying low somewhere in the shadows, waiting for her to make a move, waiting for her to do something stupid and give herself away.

Where did he go? He can't be too far away. And who's sitting in that chair?

She turned back to the chair, the guy sitting there hadn't moved. It couldn't be the guy chasing her. No way. She had to see who it was. Maybe this person was hiding t--

Suddenly, she recognized the hair. It was Zack. She knew those greasy black curls anywhere. He had to be hiding here too, keeping still. Maybe he even thought she was that man. He must have come to hide over here when the music began. He probably saw that white-faced man and ran from him, just like she had.

Stacy took a careful step forward, putting her foot down ever so lightly, feeling for brittle twigs that would give her away to the killer, wherever he was. She silently prayed that Zack would move or breathe or do something. Stacy tried to peer around the back of the chair, hoping Cyndi was with him, but she couldn't see around to the other side.

"Zack," she whispered in a voice that was just barely audible. She doubted the man would be able to hear her through that white mask thing that he was wearing. Zack didn't move or respond.

He's probably dead, she realized, *just like Brad. Go ahead and see what grisly nasty things that psycho did to Zack.*

No. She didn't want to see his face. Brad had been too much. Seeing the back of Zack's head like this made her want to turn and run, but where could she go? Wherever she went, *he* would be right behind her, chasing her down until he got bored with the game and made her the next victim in his collection.

I'll just tap on Zack's head. If he's alive, he'll turn around, he'll have to. But if he doesn't move, I'm not gonna stick around to see his face. Okay? That's the deal, just tap his head. That's all.

Stacy took one last step forward, now she was only an arm's length away from him. She lowered one of her hands from her mouth and slowly reached toward his head. It looked wet.

Oh God, please don't be dead. Please don't be dead. Her heart continued to thud in her chest, not slowing down at all from the frantic pace it had when she sprinted through the woods. Her fingers inched forward. *Just do it. Come on, just do it. The sooner this is over, the sooner I can get away from here.*

Stacy forced herself to push forward, and her finger connected with his wet hair. His head moved a little when she touched him, and she instantly yanked her hand back to her chest. She wanted to scream and run away. Had he moved on his own or had it just been the force of her finger?

She had to tap him again. *Shit shit shit! Don't be a baby. Just do it, it's easy.* She swallowed and braced herself again to tap his head. Leaning forward, she reached out and tapped his head again, more lightly this time. He didn't move. She pushed forward more solidly, and his head slumped to his right shoulder.

Stacy instantly saw the red bloody scrape marks all over his face. She gaped at the mashed, mushy quality of his shattered nose and cheek bones. The glazed, tired expression on his face and in his eyes was the worst. He looked as if he had died moaning in agony.

Stacy gave a horrified gasp and turned to run. Something swung out and slammed into her head. She heard the splintery crack of old wood as fresh pain exploded in her head. She saw white, then a wave of brightly colored stars that dissipated as her blurry vision tried to clear itself. She smelled a strange ozone smell that seemed to come from somewhere inside her head. She remembered that same smell from one time when she had accidentally hit herself in the nose with her tennis racket.

The masked man had crept up behind her so silently that she never had a chance. When she had turned to run, he had swung an old wooden rowboat paddle at her head with full force. She spun and collapsed on her stomach next to the lifeguard's chair. Half of the paddle clattered on the rocks next to her.

The man stared down, studying her as she weakly struggled to get her bearings and get back on her feet. He looked down at the splintered half of his broken paddle and tilted his head. It now had a jagged, deadly edge that hadn't been there before. The weapon had been broken, but now it had become a new weapon, one far more deadly.

Stacy struggled to breathe and pull herself away from the man. She tried to turn herself around and look up at him, but it was hard to see. He had hit her so hard with the paddle that even thinking was a challenge. The inability to do something as easy as thinking caused a new blind terror that she had never felt before. She had to move, but where could she go, how could she get away now?

She looked over her shoulder and saw him staring down. Her vision was blurry but she thought his face resembled the white face from all the signs. In real life the three dimensional white face seemed even more grotesque than when it was just a painted cartoon image.

The man ran a finger over the sharp edge of the paddle then examined his finger. He looked back down at her and rotated the paddle in his hand, turning the sharp end down towards her. He raised it up, clasping it in both hands.

"No," she managed to mutter, holding her hands

up defensively.

The man raised it over his head slowly, savoring the moment. She tried to scoot back, but it was too late.

The sharp end stabbed down into her abdomen on her left side just below her rib cage. She felt it crush downward, cutting open something inside her that popped like a small balloon bursting. She shrieked in agony and horror. She clutched at the thick piece of wood jammed deep in her stomach. She tried desperately to yank it out but she had no leverage. The man pushed the broken paddle down farther and lightning bolts of pain shot through her entire body.

He held the paddle down, pinning her to the ground like a bug. She screamed over and over, her voice became hoarse. She felt her own blood running down the sides of her stomach and flowing freely inside her body.

Suddenly the man shifted his hands on the paddle, lowering one while raising the other. The weight that had been holding her down now began to yank her up. She felt the wooden thing in her stomach shift and rip something else. A fresh sheet of agony made her bark out another short scream. The wood caught on the underside of her rib cage and scraped against the bone sickeningly.

The man began to lift her up off the ground. She held onto the wood with her hands trying to pull herself off of the dreadful skewering stick. Her feet slid around uselessly in the dirt. He lifted her up into a leaning back position with her body at a forty-five degree angle. Her feet stamped down on solid ground and she tried to pull herself off the impaling end of the paddle. She felt her body begin to slide off of it. The man realized what she was doing and twisted the paddle cruelly, sending sharp new jabs of pain through her body. She cried out and stopped struggling to pull herself off.

He lifted her up into the air, her feet dangling. Only her toes scraped the rocky overhang. Then he took a step forward, pushing her towards the edge of the cliff. She held on to the paddle with both hands trying desperately to keep it from driving up farther into her body. Her mind was in a blind panic, thinking only: *Get it out, get it out, get this thing out of me!* She felt the wood scrape against the bottom of her rib cage, and the blood trickling down her stomach and legs.

He took another step forward, her feet now scraping only six inches from the edge of the cliff. Now the fear of heights flooded into her mind as well. She dangled dangerously close to the edge. The only noise she could manage to utter was a guttural *ug, ug, ug*, filled with pain and desperate terror.

The man took a final step forward, pushing her out over the edge of the cliff now. She hung over the water, held only by the wooden paddle and her clutching hands. Her feet swung madly out in the open air, desperately trying to feel the edge of the cliff again. She let out only short hitching breaths and stared at her killer with wide pleading eyes. Her hair hung haphazardly over one side of her face and a mixture of drool and blood trickled from the corners of her mouth.

He gazed at her for a moment, as if her death were the most fascinating thing he had ever seen. He appeared to be completely unsympathetic to her agony.

Please just let this end, she thought. *Why won't he let me go? I want it to be over.*

For some strange reason her thoughts turned to Cyndi. She sensed that Cyndi was still alive and still in the park somewhere, and she would be next. She would be the last one alive after Stacy. If only she could warn her....

Stacy sucked in air, mustering all the strength she could. The man watched what she was doing and cocking his head in that odd, puzzled way.

"CYNDEEEEEEE!" she wailed with all of her remaining effort. Her cry echoed into the night and the man jumped as if waking up out of a doze.

He suddenly lashed out with a heavy booted foot, kicking into her lower abdomen. She felt her body slide off the paddle, the skin splitting in one final tear below her rib cage. The man's kick knocked the wind out of her, cutting her scream off abruptly. She felt thick splinters from the wood rip into her palms as her hands slid off the paddle and clutched thin air.

Stacy tumbled silently through the air, her arms and legs pinwheeling in mad unfocused circles. The man watched as she fell straight down twenty feet, then splashed into the Lazy River. Her back sent up a huge cannonball wave and she sunk into the bright blue water. Blood seeped out of her gaping wounds in thick red clouds, the entire Lazy River seemed to be slowly turning pink.

A single drop of blood fell off the tip of the paddle all the way down to the water below. The man watched the Lazy River's endless current carry Stacy's body and the clouds of bloody water away until she was out of sight.

Then the masked man turned and walked toward the control room. There was one more intruder left, and she had been tampering around in his control room. For that, he would make her suffer the most.

Chapter Eighteen:

The Man in the Mask

Cyndi waited in the thick silence, feeling like she had just stepped on some tripwire in a faraway jungle deep in enemy territory. Like Stacy, she felt like someone was behind her watching and tiptoeing up, ready to grab her and make her pay for trespassing and messing with their controls. She looked over her shoulder, fully expecting to see some hulking man with a raging red face standing there, but she was alone.

She peered out the dark tinted windows. Only portions of the concrete paths were visible from the colorful low garden lights. She also saw the dim flicker of the broken neon Kaptain Smiley's Thrill River, now K ill River, sign. The rest of the view was darkness. Cyndi supposed if some hulking, red-faced man were to come through the woods to get her, she would either see him through the windows, or hear his footsteps crunching through the underbrush. She was probably safe in here for now, but she didn't have much time.

I have to find out more. If any of these papers say anything about what this place is, or where it is, I can give myself some direction as to where to go, and which part of the park I should try to leave through.

She took another careful glance out the window, saw that the coast was still clear, then went back to what she assumed was the break area table to look at those blueprints again. There had to be a map of the park on one of them. There just had to be something on how to get in and out of the park. She refused to believe that everyone who came into the park rode a raft down a white-water river into a mine tunnel to get in. People worked here, this control room was proof of that.

With two fingertips, she delicately picked up the petrified half-eaten bagel by one stale corner, and wasn't surprised to find that it actually was hard as a rock. She tossed it aside, and it gave a clunk that sounded more like a piece of thick plastic than a bagel. An oily transparent grease spot in the shape of the bagel stained in the corner of the top blueprint where it had sat for weeks.

Cyndi flipped through the stack of papers. She recognized a few of them, the Duelin' Rivers and the Ragin' Rivers were both in the plans, meticulously drawn to scale by someone with professional drafting skills. All of the designs were labeled with the word *Prototype* along the top of the page. There were other ride designs in the plans that looked completely unfamiliar, one had some kind of Egyptian pyramid in the middle of the ride that the riders would presumably float through.

The designs were impeccable, but the designer's handwriting was a tiny, slanted chicken scratch that was barely legible. She could barely make out most of the words and notes that had been scribbled all over them.

Some of the designs were specific to the plumbing system that had to be buried underneath the park. Cyndi glanced at them only briefly, most of them looked highly technical and didn't make a whole lot of sense to her. There were several drawings of intricate web works of pipes, pumps, and tubes. On a larger drawing, she recognized the winding curve of the real river they had ridden in on. Another even more convoluted drawing came up and she figured it must be the park's electric grid.

Cyndi reached the bottom of the pile and found what she was looking for. It was folded in thirds. She tossed down the other papers and unfolded it, revealing a giant detailed map of the park. Each ride was labeled in that scribbled handwriting. She recognized the thin Ragin' Rivers, the Lazy River, the Duelin' Rivers, and the Dead Man's Drop, even though none of them had ridden that one. Near the upper middle of the picture were the bathrooms, and above that the control room. She imagined a star sticker on the control room and the words *You Are Here* next to it.

On the left side of the map, she spotted the mine tunnel they had ridden through earlier. It was labeled *Gold-Mine River Prototype 7483* in pencil. It looked like a full ride starting from somewhere farther up the path past the Dead Man's Drop.

She remembered walking up that path earlier, but there had been nothing but woods past the Dead Man's Drop. She read that mysterious number again. *7483*, was that just some technical jargon? It was scribbled as big as the name of the ride. She figured it must be important, but it meant nothing to her.

Did they mean 7 4 83? As in July 4th, 1983? A few weeks from now? she asked herself. *Maybe that was the day the ride was supposed to be finished.*

This is all very interesting but what about the entrance and exit? Cyndi's impatient inner voice chimed in suddenly. She scanned the edges of the map. There was no visible entrance or exit labeled on the map at all. *You must be missing it. There's got be something. Anything!*

Suddenly, there was a high pitched animal cry from somewhere nearby. Cyndi gasped in shock and dropped the blueprint, whirling toward the door. Her heart was trip hammering and her breath came in small panicked gasps. There was only darkness outside. The cry must have come from a loon or some kind of other nocturnal animal. She had heard similar sounds back at camp as she and Stacy had walked back to their cabin every night.

Cyndi was relieved to still be alone up in the control room, but alarmed at the fact that she had focused in on the blueprints so hard and forgotten to mind her surroundings. Someone was still out there, and they could be coming back any minute. How could she be so stupid?

"You've got to be more careful," she scolded herself aloud. She turned back toward the windows, thinking that it would be a good idea to look out and see if anyone was coming. After another thorough scan, her eyes revealed nothing new. She felt satisfied that she had a bit more time to look around before she would have to leave.

Cyndi glanced down at the cassette player and remembered the tape in the cassette deck. Was that really her tape? It could have been anyone's tape really.

"Only one way to find out," she mumbled to herself as she pressed the Stop/Eject button below the cassette deck. The deck popped open and the tape rattled as a bundle of unspooled ruined tape bounced out. This old broken cassette player must have ruined her tape. She turned the tape over and saw the Memorex tape label and the words New Radio 5-15-83 in her own distinct loopy handwriting.

It was her tape without a doubt, the one she had fallen asleep to last night and gone missing this morning. How the hell had it turned up here? She thought back to last night. She had been drifting off in the raft, thinking how the flickering shadows thrown off by their dying little campfire made it look like someone standing in the woods only ten feet away. There *had* been someone there after all, and he was now in this park.

But who is this person? Is he one of the construction workers that built the rides? The architect who drew all those designs? Or was he someone else entirely?

Cyndi's eyes drifted up to the reel-to-reel and saw the word *52083-* labeled on the left reel in that same scribbly chicken scratch. *May 20th, 1983?* she wondered. That had been her last day of school before summer break. She set her ruined tape down on the desk in front of the Teac and reached out to touch the Play button. She suddenly stopped herself.

"What is *wrong* with you?" she scolded herself again. If she pressed play, whatever was on this audio reel would blast out on all the speakers throughout the whole park. She had to figure out how to turn off the outside speakers.

She looked over at the volume bars on the mixing board. Above each bar were thin pieces of paper covered by Scotch Tape. Each volume bar was labeled by which speaker it controlled. *Picnic, Duelin, Dead M, Ragin1, Ragin2, LazyW, LazyE, GoldM, RRIn, RROut, CRIn, CROut.* All of the volume bars were cranked to the highest volume level. Did RR stand for Rest Room? She had seen restrooms labeled as RR on maps before. Then CR had to stand for Control Room.

Cyndi quickly slid the volume bars all the way down except for the one labeled *CRIn.* She turned that one down to a quarter of the maximum volume level, then turned back to the Teac. She pressed play, bracing herself for a loud blast.

The reel began to turn slowly, but the only

sound that came out of the speaker was the thin hiss of blank unrecorded tape. She waited for a second, then pressed stop. She hit the rewind button and the reels quickly spun counterclockwise. The old machine didn't rewind nearly as fast as her Walkman did so she gave it a minute before pressing the stop button again. When she felt satisfied that she had rewound the reels far enough to hear anything, she pressed play again.

Cyndi braced herself, half expecting that same weird music to come blasting out again, half expecting to hear some low demonic voice whispering the words "GET OUT!" What actually came out was neither.

It was a man's nasally, droning voice speaking mostly in technical jargon. Just based off of his voice, Cyndi guessed that he had to be somewhere in his mid-forties. His tone was dry and had no enthusiasm whatsoever. She thought it was a voice that was born to make sarcastic remarks, complain about the government, and recite statistics.

"--usion things seem to be moving along steadily towards our projected date of July fourth. As long as the rest of the crew shows back up tomorrow, we'll be right on schedule. Over." The two VU meters near the bottom of the Teac bounced along with the man's voice, then the needles fell back to the left as the man went silent for a few seconds.

Cyndi glanced out the windows and over her shoulder at the door again while she waited out the silence. There was a click and a low pop. Then the man sighed out the beginning of a new speech.

"Progress Report June 3rd. Four more people were no-shows today. Juarez, Stein, Wistrand and uh, Michaelson. None of the others have seen or heard from them since yesterday at quittin' time. I honestly don't know what the hell is going on, I mean, this is...absolutely ridiculous." The man sighed, seeming to try to gather his composure. "At any rate, we had to postpone the Night-Light tests until tomorrow night. The downslope for Gold Mine is being poured by Nunez's team, but they're only about halfway to where they need to be. Uh, what else? Oh, Berens, who was on night duty last night, claims the place is haunted." The man began to chuckle, then gave off another exasperated sigh. "Oh, God. So in conclusion, we're about four days behind, but should be able to close that gap to about one day once the crew comes back. Over."

The audio went silent again.

"Haunted?" Cyndi whispered aloud. Hadn't they all felt something similar when they first arrived here? Even in broad daylight there had been something spooky about this place. It felt as if all the rides and bright happy colors were a front for some deep terrible--

A click and another low pop sounded off. Now the man's voice came back on, but it had changed. He had given up his dull lifeless drone. He sounded controlled, but afraid.

"Okay, I wanna get this down for the record, I don't know what the fuck is going on here. It's about two-thirty in the morning now. We're in the middle of our Night Light test and all of sudden I can't get anybody on the radio. Nobody. Then Nunez finally radios in and he's screaming something about a bunch of blood or something. Then, and I quote, I heard him say the words 'everybody killed.' I don't know if this is a joke or... Oh, God." The man now spoke in a shuddering terrified voice. "I'm locked...in the control room. I can't see shit out the windows. I don't know if I should go out there or-- What the fuck?! Who's there?"

The man's voice moved away from the microphone, she could imagine him facing the door. After a short moment, the man shouted out again, "*Answer me! Who the fuck is there?*" His voice sounded high-pitched and full of panic.

Then there was a loud reverberating stomp noise. It made her jump a little at its raw powerful force. "Hey! This is company property asshole!" There was another loud stomp. "Hey! Knock it off!" There was one more stomp and a splintery crack. "Hey!" the man screamed again. It seemed to be all he could think of to yell out anymore.

There was a final stomp, a loud crack, and a rattle. The man began to scream, a deep, guttural scream from down in his belly. Cyndi could hear the sounds of a struggle, the clang of a coffee cup turning over. The man continued to shriek and Cyndi put her hand to her mouth in horror.

"Oh my God," she whispered uncontrollably. Her eyes were fixed on the spinning tape reels playing out the horrific scene that had taken place in this office only a few weeks ago. The man's screams became gurgly, as if he were choking on his own blood and trying to gasp for breath at the same time. It was a terrible, ugly sound that made her feel dirty and ashamed to hear it.

Cyndi noticed another sound, a man's muffled ragged breathing. She remembered hearing breathing like that last year on Halloween when a kid in a creepy rubber mask came running up to her door for candy. The breathing on the tape wasn't full of good-natured Halloween cheer though. It sounded like something out of the slobbering mouth of a wild animal. It sounded predatory, like it was enjoying the taste of blood from a fresh kill. She could practically hear the smile on his filthy lips, behind some horrible mask.

It was too much for Cyndi. She frantically reached out and pressed the stop button with a shaking hand. She couldn't listen to any more. Murder had taken place right where she now stood. She couldn't see any stains on the carpet because it was already a dark rusty red color, but she could sense it underneath her feet. Did the carpet feel crusty with dried blood underneath her shoes, or was it just her imagination?

Cyndi had to get out of the room quickly. She glanced up at the window, meaning to turn right around and walk away, but what she saw made her blood run cold.

A man was walking down the path toward the control room. His legs and feet, clad in black pants and heavy black boots, were visible as they passed the low colored lights. Cyndi saw only the slightest glimpse of his white face through the tint of the windows and the darkness outside. He was coming down the path for her.

Her stomach dropped and she felt sick with terror. She knew she had to move quickly but her feet felt glued to the floor. Alarm bells were going off wildly in her head, but her slow, stupid body would not move.

The man looked tall and he walked at a brisk pace, full of purpose. He knew exactly where she was and he was coming for her. Judging by the way he was walking out in the open, he didn't really seem to care if he was seen anymore.

After what felt like a full minute (it was actually only about ten seconds), Cyndi yanked herself away from the window and figured out what to do. She knew she had no time to run, and without the music covering the sound of her footsteps, he would easily be able to find her. God, how she wished she had just kept the music on.

She frantically looked around the room for a good hiding spot. Under the desks? No, he would see her the second he walked in, plus there was no escape route from inside the control room. Maybe under the break table near the door? Still too risky. What if he walked in, closed the door behind him, and locked it?

Then she had it. The door. She could hide behind the door on the landing outside as he came up the stairs. Once he was in the control room, she could make a run for it. She would have to move fast though. If he came around the corner and saw her as she crept around the door, it would all be for nothing.

Cyndi carefully ran for the door, trying to be as light on her feet and make as little noise as possible. She poked her head out and looked down the stairs. He hadn't arrived yet. The porch light on the wall above her would make a shadow on the ground below if she passed too close to the right. She knew she would have to do this carefully or she might as well forget the whole thing.

She moved to the left side of the door frame and flattened her back up against the door. She side-stepped along the door just like she and Stacy had done along the side of the main lodge last night. From this spot, she only cast a small shadow underneath her feet and on the wooden boards of the landing at the top of the stairs. So far so good.

Now came the tricky part. In order for Cyndi to get behind the door, she would have to close it slightly and sneak behind, without letting any of the shadows reach the path below. She pulled the door slowly and its hinges gave off a rusty squeak. She flinched and stopped immediately. Taking a deep breath, a feeble attempt to calm her screaming nerves, she tried again. She pulled the door forward in tiny increments, the hinges only made small creaks. She rolled around the edge of the door with barely enough room.

Behind the door she was under the blessed cover of darkness again. If this didn't work, her only alternative would be to jump over the railing and drop at least twenty feet down onto hard river rocks below. She faced forward again, waiting for the man's boots to come bounding up the staircase. She kept her hand over her mouth to stifle the sound of her own breathing.

Her eyes popped open as she noticed the two inch gap underneath the door and her bright pink flip-flops fully visible underneath it. If she didn't pick up her feet, he would see them as soon as he came up the stairs. She quickly put her hands on the wooden railing and hoisted herself up, just as she heard the first sounds of footsteps on the concrete below.

The man slowed to a stop as he approached the stairs, as if he were calculating his own plans on what would be the most effective way to get her. She waited through an extremely long pause and began to wonder if he had decided to check around the building. Then she heard it, a soft step on the first stair, just barely audible in the still night. As he proceeded up the stairs, he seemed to be making as little noise as possible.

He thinks he can surprise me, her mind analyzed with dread. *And he would have too, if I hadn't seen him coming down the path. God, how can he be so light on his feet?*

Soft creaks in the wood underneath the man's weight gave him away as he continued up. If she hadn't noticed him in the window a few minutes earlier, she surely would have heard him by now. A man his size, in boots, could only be so quiet on a wooden staircase. Cyndi braced herself, praying that he wouldn't see or hear her.

He reached the top landing and stood there for a moment looking into the room. He placed a big hand on the edge of the door, his long filthy fingers snaked around the door two inches from Cyndi's face. Her eyes opened wide in front of them as they drummed slightly, then they slipped away. He stepped inside the room and began looking around for her. She silently sighed with relief to the fact that he hadn't thought to look behind the door.

The man suddenly tossed one of the plastic break table chairs away, and it clattered on the other side of the wall right next to where she was. She winced at the sheer rage and raw insanity that seemed to emanate from the man.

Not yet, she thought to herself. *Wait until he's farther inside.*

The man's boots clomped on the thin carpet. He shoved one of the electric boxes to the side. It teetered up on two of its stubby bottom wheels for a second, then crashed back down to the floor. The man glanced behind the boxes, hoping to find Cyndi hiding there. He gave the huge box a shove and it crashed into the wall. A huge hand smashed down on the top of one of the file cabinets, and its sheet metal sides clanged hollowly.

He was in a full rage now, shoving papers around and kicking the overturned chairs.

Now! a voice screamed in her mind. *It's now or never! Go while he's distracting himself.* She stood there frozen. As soon as she passed the doorway she would be in plain sight to him unless his back was turned. She had no choice.

The man threw silverware wildly against the wood-paneled walls and they rang out with jangling clarity. Cyndi peeked around the corner of the door and saw him standing there with his back to her. He looked tall, maybe six-foot-five or six-foot-six. His shoulders heaved with his raspy breathing. He picked up one of the legal pads and threw it against the wall, the pages fluttered and flapped wildly as they flew through the air.

Cyndi snaked around the doorway, moving with cat-like grace. Her years of being known as "the quiet girl in class" seemed to be finally paying off. By coincidence, the man turned around a split second after she was out of sight of the door frame and creeping down the stairs. He hadn't noticed her. She slid along the wall

267

and took each step with as light a foot as she could possibly manage. The man apparently hadn't heard a thing, he was too busy throwing stuff around upstairs.

She reached the bottom of the stairs and took off into the woods. She stayed away from the path, knowing that the lights would give her away just as they had given away the man. Her footsteps crunched in the pine needles and underbrush, but compared to the racket going on in the control room, she didn't think he would hear her. She had a head start now, and that was all that mattered. If he chased her, she would run. If he didn't see her, she would find a good place to hide.

*   *   *

Breathing heavily behind the white mask, the man turned and saw the old Teac. He bounded over to it, meaning to throw it at the dark tinted window. He put two hands on its sides, and felt his strength go out as he noticed something lying on the desk in front of it. It was small, made of plastic, and was overflowing with bunches of wrinkled dark brown tape.

It was the girl's cassette tape, the one he had put in the stereo. He examined it for a second, realizing what it meant: she had been here, and she had gotten past him. The tape disappeared into his huge fist, and made splintery, plastic cracking sounds as he crushed it.

*   *   *

Cyndi had made it to the far side of the Duelin' Rivers entrance when all the lights suddenly went out, leaving the park in a state of darkness that she hadn't yet experienced. He was onto her, but what was he planning?

Originally, she meant to go all the way down the

path to see if she could find Stacy. She hadn't gotten far enough away from the control room when the lights went out. Now she had to find a place to hide. She knew the darkness would make it harder to run, but easier to hide.

She glanced over at the Duelin' Rivers entrance, a plan forming in her mind. This plan would either prove to be horrendously stupid or totally brilliant. She went to the edge of the water, sat down, and put her feet in. It felt surprisingly warm after she had gotten used to the cool night air. Just as she was about to lower herself into the water, she suddenly remembered her Walkman clipped to the waistband of her shorts. She unclipped it and carefully held it up above the water in her right hand.

That was a close one, she sighed mentally.

She lowered herself in slowly, being careful not to make any extra splashing sounds or make more ripples in the calm surface than necessary. She was also careful to keep her Walkman above water. The bubbling waterfall fountain was still on and water surged down into the entrance pool. She recognized the dark curve in the rock formation behind the fountain.

Just like I remembered, she thought. Even in the daylight it had looked so dark back there, and with the noise of the fountain covering any little noise she might make, it would be the perfect hiding spot. She might just make it through the night in there. She headed toward the dark opening, then stopped herself. Another idea had formed in her head.

If I can send one of those tubes down the ride, it'll send him on a wild goose chase after it. It was so simple, yet so brilliant. She knew she would have to move fast before he got too far out of the control room and saw her messing around with the tubes.

Cyndi set her Walkman down near the fountain, being careful to keep it safely away from any water. Then she waded across the entrance pool, leaning against the current. She slowly walked up the concrete steps leading out of the pool. She didn't want to make a lot of splashing noises and drip all over the concrete, those would be dead giveaways. Keeping her shoulders low, she craned her neck towards the control room building, scanning the area for any signs of the man coming down the path straight towards her. He was nowhere to be seen, but that didn't calm her nerves. Not being able to see him only meant that she couldn't be sure where he was.

Cyndi turned back to the tubes and reached out for one. She had to lift her body almost all the way out of the water to actually reach the stack of big green tubes. Earlier today, when the stack had been full, it had stood over six feet tall. They had used up all but three of the tubes on the stack to ride down twice. She reached for one of the handles and her foot slipped on the smooth step beneath her. She nearly went face first into the concrete but caught herself with her hands. Her knee scraped painfully against the top concrete step. The chlorine stung her skin and she hissed in pain. She wanted to cry out, a rare thing for her, but held her tongue.

You're getting nowhere, just step out of the pool and grab the stupid tube already.

"Screw it," Cyndi whispered out loud. She had fought with that inner voice enough for one day.

She lifted one dripping wet foot on the concrete and carefully grabbed the tube. She yanked it down as quietly as she could. The gushing water fountain was good cover, but not good enough to mask that sliding wheeze of tube against tube. She checked for any signs of the man, the coast was still clear. The tube rolled down into the water, wanting to spin on its rim like a coin, but it was too heavy and collapsed flat onto the face of the water with a smack and a light splash. She winced at the noise. In her imagination, she saw the man prowling around out in the woods somewhere and hearing the sound of the tube, instantly changing directions and heading right for her.

Cyndi stepped back down into the warm water again and gave the tube a gentle push. *I hope I didn't just do this for nothing*, she thought. As the tube floated slowly toward the Duelin' Rivers, she turned around and went back to the fountain. Up close it seemed to roar in the still silence of the night.

She pressed her hands down firmly on the rocks to the left of the waterfall. As she hoisted herself up, the rough porous surface of the rocks dug into her hands. She clenched her teeth as her body, heavy with dripping water, seemed to weigh her down even more. She swung her right leg up and stepped down on the rock next to the fountain. Little drops of water from the fountain splashed onto her as she lifted her other leg up. She managed to get herself into a stable crouching position on top of the rocks and relieved the pressure from her hands. Upon examination, her hands looked like they were full of craters. No time for the hands. She had to get behind the fountain and out of sight before the man came by. He would be here soon.

Cyndi crawled back behind the fountain. It was a tight squeeze even for her, and there wasn't anywhere she could comfortably sit. She would have to crouch low and stay still if the man came by. She sat on another porous rock that dug into the bottom of her swimsuit. The last thing she needed now was a ripped swimsuit, but she didn't care, she had to sit somewhere. She settled and looked out just in time to see her tube drift around the corner out of sight, heading toward the river on the right. From this spot she couldn't see either of the fast parts of the rivers.

Cyndi sat there for what felt like twenty

271

minutes, peering out from her dark cave like a defensive animal, waiting for the moment the man would come into view. After her quick dip in the warm water of the pool, she could really feel the chill of the night air. The droplets that constantly rained on her from the fountain didn't help. Goosebumps stood up on her arms and legs.

"Where the hell is he?" she whispered aloud. Her skin felt freezing cold and she rubbed her arms and legs.

Maybe I would be better off finding another place to hide. Anywhere as long as it's dry. I've had enough water to last me a life--

There he was. Her eyes caught the movement of his legs walking slowly along the path dangerously close to her right side. His walk was so stiff and lifeless. If she saw someone walking that way down the street in broad daylight, she would probably still get the creeps. She bent down even lower behind the fountain and peered out at him with wide eyes. The top overhang covered his face from view, she still hadn't gotten a clear look at it yet. Although she couldn't see his face, it was obvious that he was wearing some kind of white mask covered with long black hair.

He had some kind of heavy metal stake in his hands. As he walked down the concrete path he used it as a kind of walking stick, lifting it and setting it down with a thudding clink. The stake had notches all the way down one side, and was covered in rust and dirt except for the end closest to his gloved hand. That end had been filed clean at an angle, forming a wicked-looking point which glinted into the moonlight. She held her breath as she watched him walk down the path, handling that ugly piece of metal very delicately.

The man suddenly stopped and Cyndi's heart skipped a beat. *He saw me! Oh God, he saw me!* But he didn't turn towards her, he was looking down at something.

After a moment, she realized what he was doing. He was counting the tubes. *He must be trying to remember how many we've used so far. Is he about to fall for it?* Then he took a step backwards and crouched down, seeing something on the pavement. He reached down and touched the concrete. *My footprint. My wet footprint!* The man looked over at the Duelin' River's entrance pool as if he were tracking her movements, imagining where she went. She was still unable to see his face. She didn't dare move a muscle and attract his attention.

Then he stood up, and she heard that whispery rasp of a tube being dragged off the stack. He tossed the tube down into the water, sending up large waves that lapped against the concrete sides of the pool. He walked down the steps into the water, holding that metal stake partially up above the surface. The water came up to his waist. He placed his free hand on the bright green side of the tube and slowly walked with the speed of the current down the river.

It worked. I can't believe it. He fell for it, Cyndi thought with growing relief as she watched him go.

The man delicately placed the wicked looking metal stake on top of the tube and waded through the river in that stiff, slightly slouched posture. He didn't turn his head, he seemed to have his eyes dead set on the two rivers ahead of him. He moved slowly through the water, barely disturbing the calm surface.

Cyndi's legs and arms began to ache as she held herself in that low position waiting for him to leave.

Just hurry. Please, I don't know how much longer I can sit like this, she thought.

The man stopped, almost as if he heard her thoughts.

273

What are you doing? GO! She screamed at him mentally.

The man's head turned slowly to the right, paused, then to the left, and paused again. He was deciding which river to take. The man held his gaze on the left river for an agonizingly long pause.

Cyndi's arms and legs began to shake with the strain of holding herself down low, but she refused to move until he was out of sight. She knew the second she moved, it would be just her luck that he would suddenly decide to spin around and see her.

He finally came to a decision and waded toward the river on the right. *Thank God!* She waited until the man waded around the corner and was fully out of her line of sight before she lifted herself up again. As soon as she sat up, the porous rock she sat on dug into the skin of her butt again painfully. Despite the pain in her butt, she sighed with relief and rubbed her aching arms. Her hands were cold and clammy and a fresh batch of goosebumps rose up all over. Her body had conveniently forgotten about trivial things like temperature as soon as the masked maniac had shown up.

"Okay, I gotta get the hell out of here. Any hiding place would be better than this," Cyndi whispered aloud. She sat and waited for a few minutes, knowing that he might not be gone. She gritted her teeth against the pain in her butt. She listened for the scrape of a tube beginning its fast journey down the right Duelin' River, but couldn't hear anything over the roar of the waterfall.

After a few minutes, Cyndi felt satisfied that the man had gone down on the ride and she crept out of her hiding spot. She crawled over to the edge of the rock, trying to peer around the corner and see if the man had actually gone down the ride or not, but the angle from this spot made it so she could see even less than she had when she was behind the fountain.

Cyndi grabbed her Walkman and held it high as she dropped down into the blessedly warm water again. She relished the warmth of the water on her cold legs. She wanted to drop her head down in it, but knew she couldn't because of the Walkman in her hand. Besides, the wetter she got, the colder she would be once she got back out of the water. She waded across and began up the first few steps, crouching down and looking over to her left to see if the man was still there waiting for her. She peered over the tall grasses and flowers that lined the edge of the Duelin' Rivers pool and saw nothing. The man had apparently gone down, probably holding that weird sharpened stake the whole time. She allowed herself to take another deep sigh of relief and relaxed the tension in her shoulders. She had made it through another close encounter with the man, but she wondered what would happen when he began to catch on.

What happens next time, what happens when he hides out in a spot waiting for me? What then?

Cyndi walked out of the pool dripping on the concrete. She looked down at the puddles forming at her feet with regret. *If he comes back here, he's gonna see that and he'll know you were here again. He's not gonna fall for the ole' send a decoy tube down trick again.* Oh well, there was nothing she could do about it now. She would have to just find--

Something caught her eye as she looked down at the concrete. It was a dark puddle on the edge of the pool, a bright reflection of moonlight against it had caught her eye. There were a few little clumps of something in the dark liquid.

"What the hell is that?" she whispered to herself. She hadn't noticed that dark puddle when she came up here to grab her tube. She had been frantically looking around to see if the man was coming then, and hadn't had time to spot any abnormalities on the sides of

275

the pool. It was also very dark now with all the lights off.

Cyndi cautiously walked over to the dark puddle, staring down at it, trying to figure out what it was. It looked like something nasty, something she would later regret looking at when it haunted her dreams, but she still couldn't look away. She crouched down at the edge of the pool. The clean water dripping off her swimsuit diluted the dark liquid in the puddle, causing tiny red streams to flow into the pool. With horror she realized the dark liquid was blood. Her mouth hung open in shock and she leaned down closer to see what those little white chunks were. She recognized the curvature of one of the chunks and figured it out, they were fragments of someone's teeth.

Wasn't this the last place you saw Zack?

"Oh my God," she whispered, clasping a hand over her mouth. She felt fresh tears welling up in her eyes.

A shadow moved down in the water, and Cyndi looked down into the dark depths. Under the rippling surface she saw a black cloud and a white face in the middle of it, peering up at her.

The sharp stake shot up out of the water only an inch from her head. She screamed out in surprise and ducked back, falling on her butt. The Walkman flew out of her hand and went skidding along the concrete behind her. The man hadn't gone down the ride at all. *He* had used the old tube decoy trick on *her*. Cyndi scrambled backwards in a panic.

One dripping white hand shot up out of the water and came down on the concrete with a wet smack. The other hand holding the stake came down in front of it, slamming the stake down with a loud clang. Then his head came up, a horrible white mask with those same detailed grinning features that were on all the signs

276

around the park. Unlike the pictures, the mask hung down on the man's face with the weight of the water like dead skin. The black eyes pulled down giving it a sad, suffering look. The real eyes behind the mask were lost in total darkness. The open mouthed toothy smile looked like a hideous grinning maw. Long black hair hung down in sopping wet strands and tangles on the backside of the mask. She shrieked as she caught her first up close glance at the murderer whose park she and her friends had trespassed into.

The man brought his huge black boot down on the edge of the pool and stepped out of the water. He lifted himself to his full height of six foot five. The rusty stake scraped along the concrete as he stood, sending up a few sparks that flashed brightly in the darkness. Pool water poured off of him onto the concrete as he began to walk toward Cyndi. She crawled away in total terror, gasping for breath and staring up into his masked face as he glared down at her.

Cyndi flipped over into a crawling position in a desperate attempt to get to her feet. The man stomped heavily down onto the back of her left calf, crushing it against the pavement. She cried out in desperate agony as his foot smashed her leg against the rough concrete. Fresh tears of pain and terror streamed down her cheeks. She screamed and twisted around to face him again, knowing that she had reached her own terrifying end.

The man clenched the stake in one wet fist, the sharp end pointing down at her throat. He began to raise the stake.

"NO! Please! NO!" Cyndi screamed out holding her hands up defensively. Her head tilted away from the man, but her wide eyes stared up at him intensely. She cringed and cried, waiting for the pain that would be the last thing she would ever feel.

Suddenly, the man stopped. All of the force and

intensity seemed to leave him. His shoulders slumped and he leaned forward staring down at her. His head cocked to the side as if he were thinking intensely or as if she reminded him of something. The hand holding the stake lowered distractedly.

Cyndi panted and looked up at him. He seemed to be just staring at her now. It was as if he had completely forgotten where he was. She watched him lower the stake and felt the pressure of his heavy booted foot come off of her leg. She didn't know what to think.

Do something. You can get away from him, that voice in her mind suddenly spoke up. Her eyes darted back and forth frantically as he stared down at her. He tilted his head to the other side now. She glanced down and saw the Walkman only about a foot away from her right hand. Its scraped tape deck hung open like a mouth.

She kept her eyes on the mask, but her hand crept to the Walkman on her right. She felt it, pulled it a bit closer, and got a good firm grip on it.

The tape deck snapped shut and broke the man out of the trance. He looked down at the Walkman. In one quick motion, Cyndi lifted the Walkman and hurled it at his head. The man turned to duck but his reactions were too late. The solid Walkman connected directly with his left temple and she heard a dull clunk against his skull, muffled behind the mask.

The man took two stumbling steps backward, clutching his head. The stake dropped out of his hand and landed only inches away from Cyndi with a deafening clatter. She turned back around as she had been before the man stomped down on her leg. The raw skin on her shin and knee screamed as they scraped against concrete again but she barely noticed. She was running on full adrenaline now.

Screaming, she quickly scrambled to her feet

278

and began to run as fast as she could in the direction of the control room. She glanced over her shoulder and got only a fragmentary view of the man as he struggled to get his bearings.

The masked man shook his head quickly as he tried to focus again. He looked down at the Walkman that had broken when it fell to the concrete after hitting him in the head. Its open tape deck hung askew and a few of the buttons along the top had fallen off. The man stomped his heavy boot down on the tape player, shattering it into dozens of tiny plastic and metal fragments. He kicked what was left into the Duelin' Rivers pool, and it sank slowly.

He picked the sharpened stake back up and clenched his furious fist around it as he began to chase her back toward the control room.

Cyndi glanced back again as she passed the bathrooms and saw the man sprinting after her with long furious strides. She screamed again, her heart pounded with fresh terror, and pushed her legs to move faster. She was sprinting for her life, but felt like she was running through water.

The man seemed to move with unnatural speed as he gained on her. He was closing the distance much too fast. He smacked low hanging tree branches away from his face with hard, rage-filled swings of his heavy arms.

All thoughts left Cyndi's mind. She only knew blind panic and fear as she ran from the awful death in human form that chased her, gaining on her every second. She was just outside of the control room building now. If only she could make it up the stairs and lock herself inside....

She looked back. The man was just passing the bathrooms now. He was coming too fast. She wouldn't have time to make it up the stairs, but there was nowhere else to go.

Cyndi hit the staircase, ramming into the banister as she quickly changed direction. Fresh pain flared up all along her side as a metal bolt on the side of the banister jammed into her lowest rib. She flew up the stairs as fast as she could.

The man came around the corner and slammed into the banister, it gave a splintery crack and hung crookedly. She could hear his harsh muffled panting behind that white smiling mask. He sounded like some kind of wild animal. His heavy boots clomped up the stairs behind her.

The metal stake slashed forward. Its sharp end snagged her skin on her left side as it flew past and stuck into the wooden step ahead of her. She cried out in pain and grabbed her left side as fresh blood began to pour through her torn skin.

She felt long, strong fingers close tightly around her left leg. She shrieked and stumbled forward as the man yanked her leg back. With her other foot she kicked out desperately and felt it connect with the man's chin. His head flew back and he let go of her foot. He struck the wall next to the staircase.

Cyndi got to her feet and scrambled onto the banister. It wobbled underneath her feet. She held on for a second, her feet beginning to slip on the smooth wood. She looked down, bracing herself for the fall. The man reached up, grabbed for her again.

She jumped. His arms closed over empty air inches behind her. She sailed down eight feet to the ground below. Her feet hit the hard ground first and lightning bolts of pain jammed into her heels and shot up her legs. She remembered a similar pain whenever she jumped over the fence from her backyard to her front yard, but this was much more intense.

The man yanked the metal stake out of the step,

and the wood gave a slight groan of protest. He began to climb up on the banister.

From the ground, Cyndi looked up and saw the man looking like a black grinning gargoyle crouching on the banister. His boots clung to the smooth wood much better than her flip-flops had, but the banister wobbled even more with the man's extra weight balancing on it.

He jumped holding his stake pointed down ready to stab out at her. She rolled out of the way as he came crashing down to the ground. She felt the spray of dirt and pine needles as he landed hard.

Cyndi hurriedly got to her feet and backed away from the man. He stood up slowly, his lowered head rolling up to face her once he had reached his full height. His shoulders heaved as he rasped breath behind the mask. He raised the stake and rearranged it in his hands, making it now look like he was about to throw it like a javelin. He stepped towards her slowly. She didn't want to make any sudden movements, knowing that they would surely set him off. He took another step forward, she took another step back.

He suddenly lunged toward her right side, and she sidestepped to the left, but it was only a fake. He quickly changed directions and stabbed to her left with the javelin. She pivoted right and dropped to her knees. The metal stake missed her by inches, and slammed into the metal fence behind her.

Sparks flew as the metal stake connected with the electric wires. She stared up as the man clung to the stake and shook uncontrollably. He was being electrocuted just as Zack had been earlier, except Zack hadn't been holding a huge rusty piece of metal.

The man abruptly let go of the stake and shot backwards, just like Zack had earlier. He flew through the air and his back slammed into the wooden banister. He made a muffled OOF noise as he hit, and the banister tilted with another splintering crack. He landed in a heap on the rocks below the stairs.

Cyndi yanked her legs away just as the stake fell to the ground in front of her. She stared at the man in shock. Her mind raced to put the pieces together and figure out what had just happened. She glanced up at the fence, then down at the stake, then back over at the man lying motionless on the rocks. There were two charred black spots where the skin of the man's hands had burned on the stake, thin wisps of smoke rose from the spots. She could smell an ozone smell that reminded her of the train tracks on the electric train set her dad liked to put up around the Christmas tree every year, except this smell had a nasty burned hot dog undertone to it.

Nervously, she watched the masked man, waiting for him to suddenly jerk and move again. For a full minute he lay still. He had received a much nastier shock than Zack had, but she knew he wasn't dead. The shock hadn't killed Zack, and it probably wouldn't kill the man either.

Cyndi cautiously kept an eye on the man as she leaned forward to examine the stake. If only she could take it, she would have something to defend herself with. She reached out, meaning to touch it, but saw that it was still resting on one of the lower electric wires. She pulled her hand away defensively.

"Gotta be more careful," she whispered to herself. She stood up and looked back at the man. She had no idea when he might wake up, it could be hours, or it could be any second.

What should I do with him? she asked herself. She had no weapons to use against him, and even if she had weapons would she be able to use them? She would surely have to kill him, but she didn't think she had the ability to actually kill another human being. On the other hand, if she just left him here, he might wake up and come after her again.

His smiling mask crumpled against the ground. She tried to peer into the open eye-holes, but could only see darkness inside. He was out cold.

Well, use the opportunity. Get away from him while you've still got the chance. Go find a hiding spot. Or better yet, get out of the park. Maybe Stacy made it out and she's waiting for you right now. It was a comforting thought, but she seriously doubted it was true. She felt in her heart that all of them were dead now: Brad, Zack, and Stacy. She was the last one left.

Cyndi began to walk quickly away from the man. She headed toward the Dead Man's Drop and the Gold Mine Tunnel rides. According to those recordings, that was the last place the construction workers had been working on when they were all killed. It was also the only place where she and her friends hadn't really spent much time on this dark day. Maybe there would be some clue as to how to get out of here.

As Cyndi walked away from the control room building she took another long look at the man. He hadn't moved at all. She would keep an ear out and pray that she didn't hear a bunch of rustling footsteps coming toward her in the darkness again.

After five minutes of walking, the man's body was completely out of view. Had Cyndi stayed near the control room, she would have seen his fingers start to twitch.

Chapter Nineteen:

The Dead Man's Drop

The far corner of the park was not how Cyndi had imagined it would be. In her paranoid walk through the woods, a walk in which she looked over her shoulder roughly every thirty seconds, she desperately clung to the hope that there would be some easy or convenient way out of the park. Every time she tried to picture a gate at the end of the fence or the daylight she wanted to see tomorrow, a dark image of a stunned electrocuted killer in a white grinning mask getting up and dusting himself off intruded into her mind.

She half jogged half ran with tense light footed steps along the black wrought iron fence. The woods in this back corner of the park were thick and had been mostly untouched by the workers and landscapers that had been here. A few times she lost sight of the fence and had to wander back in the direction she thought it was in. Then she would stop herself within inches of walking right into it and getting a nice electric shock to the face. The black iron bars blended in with the shadows of the forest too well.

"Come on, get it together, Cyndi," she mumbled

to herself after skidding to a stop only a few inches from the fence. "Just slow down and watch where you're going."

She hurried on, knowing that in her panic she would likely run into more trouble, but there was absolutely nothing she could do about the panic. She was trapped in this electrified cage with a psychopath in a mask. In a situation like that, panic was as plentiful as air.

The fence seemed to continue on forever. She looked back into the park to try and get her bearings, but saw only thick woods and hills. What little moonlight there was got blotted out by the treetops. She faintly heard the sound of running water about thirty feet away and realized that it must be the sound of one of the rides. She figured she must be near that ride they had first seen, the Dead Man's Drop, an ominous name considering there were probably dozens of dead people stashed around here somewhere, including the bodies of her friends. God, how she hoped Stacy had gotten out of the park all right.

Up ahead, Cyndi spotted a bunch of tools and shovels sticking out of a large hole in the ground and her heart fluttered with anticipation. She hoped whatever the workers had been doing would lead her to some clue as to how to get out of here. She looked back for what felt like the hundredth time, confirmed that the man was still nowhere in sight, and proceeded over to the hole.

As she approached the hole, it became clear that they had been digging a trench and laying down some big pipe. The ground underneath her feet began to slope back downhill, and gradually became thick dried mud, packed down by dozens of worker's footsteps in heavy boots. The hard mud made little or no sound under her feet and that was good. If the man was coming after her, he wouldn't be able to hear her footsteps crunching in the underbrush. She hoped she would be able to hear his.

Twenty feet of thick black pipe lay outside the long rectangular hole, waiting for workers that would never come to finish their jobs and put it into place. Peering down into the hole, she saw pipe jutting up out of the ground, coming from somewhere farther down the hill. She presumed it was near the river since it seemed to supply the rides with all of their water. It looked like some of the dirt had been shoveled back in, though the hole was still about two feet deep. One of the shovels was tossed in the hole haphazardly, unlike its counterparts which stood neatly upright along the edges of the hole.

Off to the right, she saw a small Compact Loader machine with yellow paint peeling off its rusty sides. Its front bucket had been left with a full load of dirt and the driver-side door hung askew. She walked towards the machine, peering inside. A horrible rotten smell came from somewhere inside and she saw dark reddish-brown splatters that had dripped down the windshield and dried. She backed away from the machine, having no desire to see what other horrible surprises were inside it.

Just beyond the machine was another hole in the ground, and several wooden boards covered it up. This hole was round and Cyndi guessed it was about ten feet wide. It was framed with a familiar porous looking rock that she recognized as the same rock used around the fountain at the Duelin' Rivers. It was also the same rock used around openings to the mine tunnel that they had gone through earlier that day.

This must be where they are building that Gold Mine Tunnel ride, she realized. *Maybe it connects with the mine tunnel where we came in. Maybe that's where I'm supposed to get out of the park.*

Beyond the boards she saw only darkness. She

could practically hear a ghostly echo reverberating off the rocky walls. There was no way she was going down in that hole. She had no idea how far it dropped down but it looked deep. For all she knew it might not lead anywhere at all. It might only lead to a dead end that hadn't been dug out yet. Then she would really be trapped. Also, the mine tunnel they had traveled through had been dark and scary enough in broad daylight. She decided to leave this as a last resort and focus on finding a way out somewhere along the fence.

Cyndi spotted the fence and followed it with her eyes, searching for some kind of gate. It ran along where she had been walking, turned at a ninety degree angle, and continued on down the hill. It disappeared into more thick woods with no visible breaks at all. This corner of the park was a dead end.

But this has to be it! There has to be a way out somewhere up here!

"No!" Cyndi whispered in frustration. She slapped her hands on her bare legs hard enough to make them sting. How could she have come this far only to be stuck up here at a dead end? She began to walk over to the fence and stopped cold.

There was the sound she had been dreading, footsteps crunching through the woods with slow, deliberate determination. The man in the mask was awake.

Cyndi spun around to face the woods. He wasn't close enough to see through the thick trees yet, but he was close enough for her to hear his approach. She glanced around frantically for a hiding place. In this mud-flattened clearing, where the construction workers had begun the Gold Mine Tunnel ride, she felt completely exposed. Her eyes fixed on the trench they had been digging and she found her answer.

Moving with as much cat-like silence as she

could manage, Cyndi ran toward the hole and jumped in. The soles of her flip-flops made wet slapping sounds as they touched down. Her feet landed in soft mud, and began to sink slowly. She crouched low and kept her head down.

The man's slow footsteps came close as they crunched through the underbrush. He seemed to be following the same path she had taken along the fence. His footsteps slowed as he got to the point where she had turned toward the trench.

My footprints. What if he sees my footprints in the mud? Her heart beat so loud and fast that she was sure the man would be able to hear it. She crouched down lower into the hole. Her butt went all the way to the bottom of the hole, and she felt a cold hand cup around it.

She jumped startled, lifting her butt away defensively and whirled around. There was a human hand sticking out of the dirt in the hole. It was so covered with filth that she had not even noticed it when she looked down into the hole. It had been a beefy man's hand with stubby, thickly calloused fingers. The skin on it was now a dead gray color, almost the same color as the killer's mask. Just below the wrist, the skin looked frayed, like a hole in a sweater. There were several white maggots wriggling around on its rotting skin.

Cyndi turned away from it and gagged silently. The sight of the dead hand crushed down on her stomach like a dead weight. She had sat on a dead man's hand. It had practically touched her bare butt. She struggled against the urge to vomit right there and then.

The killer stopped. Silence.

Cyndi held her hand over her mouth waiting, trying to force her gorge back. She began to notice the dark, dead-animal smell the hand gave off.

The killer's feet slid in the underbrush as he

turned to look in a different direction.

God, please let me get out of this hole. Please.

He spun again and waited, looking around in a different direction.

She could feel the bile rising in her throat, and the familiar surge of saliva rushing forward just before throwing up.

Thankfully, the man began walking again, moving back in the direction he came from.

Thank God! She waited in disgusted agony as the man slowly walked back toward the control room.

After what felt like an eternity, she flew up out of the hole and frantically brushed off her butt with her hands. She felt massive chills rush up and down her spine and she shivered all over with revulsion. She could still feel the hand on her, as if it had never left. The filth of it seemed to permeate her hands after she had brushed her butt off. She wanted nothing more than to just run back to the showers and wash off every trace of that dead hand. She guessed that if Stacy had been in her place, she would have promptly jumped up and let the man kill her.

Cyndi noticed the sound of running water from the Dead Man's Drop ride again. It sounded like clear, clean heaven. She began to hurry back toward the sound of the running water. She kept an eye out for the man, but he was completely out of sight and earshot. She dangled her hands out in front of her, they felt like there were covered in dead germs. She could not wait to rinse them off in the clean water.

Once Cyndi passed a familiar stand of thick bushes, she had reached the concrete end of the path at the top of the hill again. Yes! She could walk flatfooted on the concrete without worrying about the man hearing her soft crunching footsteps. She took another look toward the control room, saw that the coast was still clear, and continued down the path at a hurried pace.

She reached the wooden steps leading up to the Dead Man's Drop quickly. Remembering the creakiness of the wooden steps and the deck above, she tried to stay light on her feet. She heard water rushing down the ride more clearly now, and could even smell the faint bleachy scent of the chlorine again.

At the top of the deck, the entrance pool came into view. The rippling surface of the water glistened in the moonlight, beckoning to her. The tubes, stacked neatly near the pool, looked orderly and perfect. The deck was devoid of trees so the moon shone its soft silvery light down on the boards without a shadow.

As she crossed the deck to get to the entrance pool, she glanced out at the view down the hill. She could see the tops of trees down the hill and hear the crickets. The night sky was cloudless, clear, and full of stars. Despite all the terror she had experienced in the last twenty-four hours, she couldn't help but marvel in the beauty of the view from up here. Maybe someday this place would open for real and it truly would be a paradise. A touristy paradise, but a paradise all the same.

Creeeeaak! A warped board under her foot protested loudly as she stepped on it. She winced at the loud noise. She looked down and saw that her foot was still pressing down on the board, when she lifted it up again, it would give another loud squeal. She turned back nervously, fully expecting to see the man standing there at the end of the deck, ready to take another run at her. He wasn't there, but had he heard the noise out in the woods? Was he somewhere close enough to hear the noise? He hadn't sounded like he had gone off in this direction, but that didn't mean a thing. He was too tricky. She knew she had to get out of this park fast.

First thing first, she had to rinse off the residue of the dead hand that had touched her skin. She lifted her foot off the board and it gave a smaller squeak, one that was still too loud for comfort. She kept her eyes down the rest of the way across the deck, carefully avoiding any boards that looked even slightly less than solid.

Finally, she made it across and stepped down into the water. It felt so warm and slippery, just like it had in the entrance pool back at the Duelin' Rivers. The water was only a foot deep in the entrance pool so she waded in and crouched down, letting the warm water wash away the rotting remnants of the dead hand. The second she put her hands down into the water and sloshed them around, she felt instantly relieved. She could almost feel the water washing away the putrescence of that dead hand.

Some soap would be really nice right now, Cyndi thought, *but hey, beggars can't be choosers. Of course you can always go back to the dark creepy bathrooms.*

"No, thank you," she whispered out loud.

She pulled her hands up out of the water and flicked the water off her fingertips, just like she did every single time she washed her hands. It was a trait she had inherited from her mother. Her father, on the other hand, never used a towel on his hands and simply flung them around wildly in the air. Her mother hated it. Cyndi couldn't believe it, but she wished she could be home with them right now. Not up in her room like she usually was, but actually with her mom and dad at the dinner table, or in the living room watching TV.

With a small breeze, a wave of nauseating stench swept past her suddenly. She took one sniff and gagged. She immediately stood up, letting the water drip down her legs. The smell had come from somewhere down below, maybe at the end of the ride. Whatever it was, it smelled like something dead. She had been thinking that maybe she would ride down, then head for the mine tunnels and try to find her way back out to the river in the dark. Now she wasn't so sure.

Cyndi peered down the slide, seeing only darkness below. It seemed ominous and potentially threatening. They hadn't ridden this ride earlier for that same reason, she and Stacy had both felt it. In the light it didn't look safe, in the dark it looked downright dangerous. She backed out of the pool and stepped up onto the deck without looking forward. She stood staring down into the darkness, trying to see where that smell came from.

Crreeeaak! It came from behind her. She whirled.

The killer lunged at her with a huge curved knife, the kind she had seen her father use to gut fish. The grin on his mask seemed to be laughing cruelly.

Cyndi screamed and stumbled backward. Her heel caught on the edge of the pool and she fell in.

The long knife jammed into one of the tubes up to the hilt, just past where she had been standing. It sliced into the plastic and the air inside immediately began to seep out with a hiss.

Cyndi hit the water directly on her back, and it splashed up around her. She was completely submerged and felt her butt bump softly on the bottom. Water went up her nose and stung her sinuses. She sat up in the water choking and coughing. It ran into her eyes and everything in her vision became a dark running blur except for the bright white flash of moonlight reflected off the man's grinning mask.

The knife was stuck in the plastic side of the tube he had stabbed. He yanked the knife hard and the stack of tubes tumbled. One rolled down and fell into the water next to Cyndi. She saw it coming and ducked out of the way just as it splashed down into the pool.

The man turned toward her, the knife turned up in his hand. With a smooth twist of his fingers he had the knife pointing down in a stabbing position again. Her vision cleared and she backed away from him, stumbling and slipping on the smooth bottom of the pool.

Her shoulders bumped against the edge of the connecting slide. She was trapped. The man stepped down into the water, his heavy boots making dunking sounds as they splashed in. She glanced around frantically for a way out and saw the tube floating next to her. She reached out and yanked it towards her.

The man lunged forward, stabbing down at the tube, but the knife only cut through the surface of the water. Cyndi jumped up, planted her butt on the side of the tube, and kicked off with her feet as hard as she could. She leaned back precariously in her tube as it began to slide backwards.

Grabbing another tube that leaned against the steps, the man gripped the handles and lunged down the ride after her, masked-face first.

They careened down the ride as if they were on bobsleds. The breeze picked up and blew against her skin, chilling her hair and shoulders though she barely noticed it. Her attention was fixed on the masked murderer riding on the tube only ten feet behind her. He had gotten a stronger start, was heavier, and was gaining fast. She flew blindly backwards down the slide, but didn't dare turn away from him.

He leaned with the curves of the ride and lifted himself up. His legs dragged behind the tube, the tips of his boots squeaking as they slid against the smooth slide. He bent his knees, pulling them forward, and positioned them on the sides of the tube.

Cyndi pulled herself back on her own tube, trying to get herself centered so she would have more control as she flew backwards. In front of her the masked maniac was closing the distance and hoisting himself up on his knees. She looked over her shoulder and saw only darkness ahead.

He was now only three feet away. He slashed sideways at her, the razor sharp tip of the knife whistling through the air in front of her face. She shrieked and leaned back.

They both flew up on a high curve and held on to the handles of the tubes. The slide straightened again and he slashed out at her in an upward motion. The knife tip sliced through the air inches from her chin. She wailed in terror.

He stabbed down at her legs and she spread them apart. The knife came down between them, gutting the side of her tube like a fish. She felt the rush of air against her legs as it whistled out from the gaping wound in the side of the tube.

Another curve came up and they were whipped around. The man's knife held the tubes in the center and they spun around like a record. Now Cyndi had the upper ground and the killer was flying backwards.

The knife came down again toward her left side, going straight for her heart. She rolled out of the way, uttering a short panicked scream. She was now teetering on the edge of her tube and could feel it leaning to one side. It would have flipped over if it hadn't been stabbed and started deflating.

Cyndi rolled onto her back again as the man reared back to stab down again. She kicked out and her foot planted directly in his chest. He bent forward, making a muffled woof noise as most of the air ejected from his lungs.

He cut down and the knife dug a long, thin diagonal wound across her shin. It was so sharp she barely even felt it.

Suddenly, Cyndi saw only blackness beneath

her tube as the slide's surface disappeared out from under her. Cyndi and the killer tumbled through the air in a jumble of legs, arms, tubes, and water. She completely lost her sense of direction as they fell through space.

The drop at the end of the ride was a full five feet into a deep pool. They crashed down into the water and Cyndi felt her arms collide with his legs, his elbows connect with her head, his knees connect with her back, his head connect with her ribs.

Something was not right. She hadn't sunk down more than a foot into the water. And there were far too many limbs. Instantly, that gaseous smell she had caught a whiff of a minute ago was all around her. The water felt brackish and slimy, and all at once she realized what was happening.

She was floating in a pool full of corpses.

A man's pained face with bloated cheeks and gray-green skin floated up to meet her own. Its eyes looked like rotten grapes. Its throat was a frayed gaping mess of dark brown and black. She was caught in a tangle of dozens of fish-white arms, clammy hands, boots, legs, and ratted clumps of hair. The bodies were lifeless, but they held her down just the same.

Cyndi began to shriek in hysteria. She turned away from one face and looked straight into another one with long strands of hair hanging down over its forehead and eyes. Its mouth hung open in a grimace with yellow crooked teeth and dark gray gums.

She thrashed and tried to pull herself away from the dead bodies, but they surrounded her everywhere she turned. They were underneath her, to her left, her right, some were on top of her. Their dead weight held her down. She was trapped floating in a maze of wet rotting bodies and body parts.

The water was dark brown, and had a nasty foam build-up that was greasy to the touch. The killer was also caught under the dead weight of several of the bodies. He had lost the fishing knife in the drop, it had sunk down underneath the bodies somewhere. He had gone down face first and his mask was full of slimy water. There were heavy legs over his shoulders weighing him down.

Cyndi spun around wildly in the tangle of bodies and finally regained her sense of direction. She was crouched on top of a huge mass of bodies and the edge of the pool was about fifteen feet away, surrounded by bushes and beds of crushed lava rock. She began to scramble and crawl through the bodies toward the edge. Their skin was slimy like the skin of a fish, except it didn't feel completely solid. It felt as if it were stretching and beginning to dissolve as it decomposed.

Several times her hands and feet slipped off the skin of one of the bodies and her chin fell down into the dark putrescent water. She whimpered and kept her lips tightly shut. If she tasted any of that dark liquid she would probably die of revulsion.

After a full minute of struggling and wading through the bodies, Cyndi's hand reached the blessedly cool, clean concrete. She yanked herself forward and collapsed on her filthy stomach at the concrete edge of the pool. She turned, rolled, lifted her legs up out of the putrid pool, and she was free.

Cyndi got up onto her hands and knees and looked back. There were probably three dozen bodies floating in the water. They all wore dark gray jumpsuits like the one the masked man was wearing. Most of them had been severely mutilated, and some were only pieces. A few of them seemed to still be fully intact, but they had all been dead for weeks. The gassy, rotten stench rising from the pool was overpowering.

The man was thrashing around wildly under a thick tangle of bodies near the middle of the pool, working his way toward the edge. He seemed to be in some wild rage and it was only forcing him to sink deeper into the water.

This is where he dumped the bodies, she thought. *And why not? This is the Dead Man's Drop isn't it?*

She couldn't hold it back any longer. She leaned forward and puked out a thin stream of liquid onto the concrete. She felt her stomach heave several times, but she had nothing left to throw up. She had barely eaten a thing in the last twenty-four hours. Her stomach gave a final lurch and she sat there crouched and gasping for breath. The killer was getting closer to the edge. She had to run and find somewhere to hide.

Cyndi weakly got to her feet and ran across the concrete toward a thick stand of bushes that lined the path. She didn't look back to see if the man was following her yet. The image of all those dead men floating in the pool was enough to haunt her nightmares forever.

Chapter Twenty:

In The Tunnel

Cyndi came around the bushes onto a grassy open stretch. The grass was mainly thick crabgrass, but, like the landscaping around the rest of the park, it had been flawlessly mowed. It was a small open clearing, with no trees and no cover whatsoever. On the other side of the field there was a long rock formation that stretched across the field and disappeared into more thick bushes on either side. She was about to give up and turn around, thinking she might be backed into a corner if the man came running up right now. Then she spotted the door.

She did a double-take and squinted her eyes, trying to make it out in the moonlight. The door was set back in a deep cave-like opening in the rock.

It must be the Gold Mine Tunnel. This might be the way out! she thought. *But it could also be locked.*

Cyndi glanced back and saw that the killer still hadn't gotten out of that putrid pool, she still had time to run. She had to make a fast decision. It might be her only chance.

You're gonna have to get in there somehow, might as well try it now.

She tore across the grass, running for her life, gasping for breath and crying. Her skin was sticky and covered with a thin film of blood and dead matter that had been floating around in that awful pool. She reeked of decomposing bodies. One of her shoes had been lost in her mad struggle to wade through the bodies, and she only noticed it now as the crabgrass scraped and cut into the bottoms of her tender bare foot.

Running desperately fast, she ducked under the low overhang of the cave. She was moving too fast to fully slow down and slammed into the door. There was a keyhole for a lock above the silver vertical handle.

"Please, please God. Please be open," she whispered.

Cyndi yanked at the door and it didn't want to budge.

"No!" she cried. She yanked at it furiously and felt it give a little, then clunk back against its door frame. Something was holding it shut. She looked down and noticed her one remaining shoe pressed up against the bottom of the door. She pulled her foot back and tried the door again. It opened easily.

It was pitch black inside but Cyndi didn't care. She flew in and yanked the door closed behind her.

She was alone in the dark. Her panting panicked breath echoed loudly through the still humid air of the tunnel. She would have to get her own breathing under control if the man decided to come in here.

First she had to lock the door, lock the crazy man out. She turned back around and felt for the door handle. Her hands quickly found it and felt their way up in the dark. A few inches above the handle was the lock. She examined it with her fingers and found, to her relief, that it was a deadbolt turn lock just like the one they had at home. For that she was thankful, it could just as easily have been another keyhole. She turned the lock and the deadbolt slid into place with a solid click. She tested the door again, pushing at the door handle. To her satisfaction, it refused to budge.

Cyndi turned back to the darkness and thought, *What now?* Getting out of this damned dark tunnel was top priority. She took a few blind steps forward with her hands stretched out in front of her. Without warning, half of her bare foot stepped down on empty air and tipped forward, dipping into cool water. Her arms pinwheeled for balance and she managed to stumble back onto the concrete ledge.

Catching her breath, she figured there must be at least two feet of ledge throughout the tunnels. If she could just feel her way around the walls, she might be able to make it out a lot faster than if she went down into the water. She backed up until she felt the rough, rocky concrete beneath her hands, then began inching her way to the right. From what she remembered, the tunnel had felt like it swept to the right just before they had seen the light coming from the crack between the two doors.

Cyndi continued along, taking only small baby steps, afraid to fall off the ledge or make too much noise. Every little scrape of her shoe or breath she took seemed to echo loudly in the tunnel. She knew that if the killer wanted to, he could be as silent as a mouse, she was in his territory.

She took another step and her hip collided with solid metal. A sudden loud buzz and the hum of pumping machinery broke the silence. She gasped and uttered a little scream. An eerie light began to glow from underneath the murky river water that flowed through the tunnel. The light cast odd ripples and low-lit shadows along the ceiling that reminded her of the flashlight under the counselors' faces as they told those spooky stories around the campfire back at camp. Except this light was unlike the warm orange glow from the campfire and the flashlights, it was a witch-green from the dark, murky color of the river water.

Cyndi turned to her right and looked directly into the awful face of a grizzled, toothless old man. He was brandishing a rusty pickax and stood ready to stab down at her. She screamed and fell back along the ledge, almost falling into the water. Directly between her and the old man was a rust-covered mine cart full of obviously fake gold nuggets. Suddenly she realized the truth, the old man was a dummy, and he and the mine cart were only props for the ride. The mine cart also appeared to be blocking an electric control box, the solid metal that she had bumped into. Once again she was reminded of the Haunted Mine Ride that she had ridden so long ago. She let out a short sigh of relief and held her hand over her racing heart.

Cyndi clambered up on her knees and went back to the electric box. Her first instinct was to turn the lights off so the killer wouldn't be able to see her. She bent down and frantically examined the controls on the electric box. There were four buttons labeled: MAIN POWER, the big red button which must have been what she had bumped into, LIGHT OVERRIDE, WATER OVERRIDE, and DOOR OVERRIDE. She held her finger over the red button, debating on whether or not she should push it. She didn't want to give herself away like this.

Water began to trickle and pour into the main river from two different waterfalls that had been built high up the rocky tunnel walls. The splashing, sloshy noises they made boomed in the tunnel. The larger waterfall was a yard or two behind the miner dummy on Cyndi's side of the river, and the smaller one was near the two doors on the opposite side. She realized that the loud echoes of the waterfalls would mask any noises she made as she traveled along the ledges and made her way out of the tunnel. Besides, it was too late to turn them off now, the noise had already been made, the damage had been done. She had to just leave them on and get the hell out of there.

Now that there was light, she stood up and got a good look around the room. Off to her right, just past the old miner dummy, the ledge went behind the larger of the two waterfalls and dead-ended against a solid rock wall. The river continued on into the darkness without any ledge.

Well, so much for that idea, she thought dismally. She looked back behind where the mine cart stood and saw only darkness leading far back into the tunnel.

Cyndi's eyes continued around the room and she saw how the river curved and stopped at the dark metal doors. She was about to turn away from the sight of the doors when she saw something that made her stomach clench. There were bodies in the water in here too.

Three of them were floating face down, bunched up against the metal doors. They wore the same dark jumpsuits and the skin on one of their bald heads looked waxy and gray. Cyndi put her hand up to her mouth in shock, noticed the dead smell that still covered her skin, and yanked her hand away.

That must be why I didn't notice the smell in here. I'm covered in it. They had also been easy to miss at first since the light didn't travel very far underneath the murky water, and the lights closest to the door were at least ten feet away.

A soft sliding noise and a click echoed in the darkness. Cyndi turned and looked into the darkness behind the mine cart. She saw only the flickering, wavy shadows cast by the lights underneath the water. Had the noise been real or had she just imagined it? It had been so faint over the sound of the waterfalls, and her mind was so exhausted that she couldn't tell.

Quit screwing around and get going, she told herself.

She went to the edge and stuck her feet down into the water, it was much cooler than the water had been on the other rides in the park. This was half river water and half heated park water. She glanced over at the bodies and grimaced. She hated getting in the water with those things again, but at least the current would be moving them away from her. Also there were only three of them instead of the thirty or more that had been in that Godforsaken pool.

Only three that you can see. What else is sunken down at the bottom that you're about to put your feet in? She forced the thought away. It seemed like whenever she had to do anything, that negative voice spoke up in her head, trying to freak her out and make her imagine the worst possible things.

Cyndi dropped down into the water, trying to make as little splash as possible. When she touched the bottom, the water came up past her waistline. She crouched down low, let the water come up to her chin, and began wading toward the dark tunnel opening. She dreaded going into the darkness, but knew she would have to do it to get out. She would have to fight against the current and her own fears.

She stopped in front of the large waterfall near the opening, and thought, *I'll just duck back behind the waterfall if he comes in.*

She stared at the dark opening in front of her, trying to work her way up to it, wondering what grisly surprises would be in store for her in there. She rubbed her arms and felt the nasty film that coated her skin begin to wash away in the water. It was only river water, but it felt so clean after the Dead Man's Drop.

Behind her, she was completely unaware that

303

the killer's masked grinning head had suddenly risen up out of the dark area behind the mine cart. The man slowly stepped out onto the ledge, staring at her. The noise of the waterfalls drowned out the sounds of his soft steps.

Cyndi rubbed her body with her hands, feeling the filth melt away and be carried off with the current of the river. As the dead slime washed away, she could almost feel some of her tension and fear washing away with it. She was mentally preparing herself, slowly gaining the strength to go into the pure darkness. She began to sing her favorite song, "Our Lips Are Sealed" by the Go-Go's, to herself in a voice so soft it couldn't be heard over the waterfall. That song always gave her strength and confidence. It made her forget about all the petty stuff in the world and told her that everything was going to be all right. She wished desperately that she still had her Walkman. If only she could listen to that song right now.

The killer slipped down into the water behind the waterfall on Cyndi's right. Only the waterfall separated them like a screen. Small drops of water splashed against the faded white rubber of his mask. He raised his hands out of the water and slowly began to reach for her throat.

Cyndi's head was the only place left for her to wash before she would be completely ready to venture into the dark. She took a breath and slowly let herself sink down.

Under the surface, all was quiet and peaceful. The chaotic roar and echo of the waterfalls was only a soft susurration. Her blond hair floated freely around her head. She grabbed large chunks of it and squeezed the dead slime out. She wiped her face down with her hands and felt clean again. Now she would be ready to--

A strong hand clamped down on her head. She

choked out her breath in surprise and it floated to the surface. The hand held her down, and her screams rose to the surface as a series of bubbles.

He was here. Had been in here. Had found her. Had gotten her.

She thrashed and sank lower trying to pull away from his rough grip. He palmed her skull like a cantaloupe and held her down. Her air was all gone. She had to reach the surface and get more air. Her lungs were beginning to sting.

She kicked out violently and her foot struck the man's knee. He let go of her head and she burst up to the surface.

She came up with a frantic splash, gasping in great gulps of air. The man's rough dirty hands came out from behind the waterfall and yanked her by her shoulders. She felt herself being spun around, and suddenly came face to face with the grinning white mask as it splashed out from behind the waterfall. She shrieked in raw terror and defeat, but it was choked off as his hands closed around her throat and shoved her back under the water.

Water flowed into her nose, stinging her sinuses. It filled her mouth with a fishy, muddy river taste. She gazed up at the white mask grinning down at her from above the rippling surface of the water.

His strong hands tightened around her throat. She began to gag and choke. She clawed uselessly at his hands and sleeves with her nails. He straddled her, holding her down underneath the water as she thrashed violently for her life. She suddenly kicked out fiercely and her foot connected with his groin. He grunted in pain and instantly let go of her, falling back through the waterfall.

Cyndi kicked herself away and burst back up, gasping for air again. She coughed and ran as fast as she could through the water. She paddled furiously with her arms to help move her along faster. The water forced her to move so achingly slow.

She reached the concrete ledge just in front of the mine cart, slapped her hands down, and yanked herself up out of the water. Dripping, she scrambled up behind the mine cart and ran for the door.

Behind the waterfall, the man clutched his aching crotch and saw her running from him. He hoisted himself up onto the ledge and began to chase her.

Just behind the mine cart, he caught her, wrapping his arms around her squirming torso. She kicked back at him, but he stood with his legs to the side. He wouldn't fall for that again. She wriggled as he yanked at her, trying to lift her off the ground.

Desperately, she reached out for anything to hold onto, anything that she could use to pull herself away from this madman. Her flailing hands connected with the electric box and she clung to it as he tugged at her legs. Inadvertently, she pressed down on the button marked DOOR OVERRIDE, and with a familiar clunk and electric hum, the doors began to open. Fresh cool air rushed into the tunnel. The bodies spilled out into the river and were swept away into the night.

The man got a solid grip around her legs and body, and lifted her with a huge surge of strength. He tossed her into the air. She flew over the mine cart and crashed back down into the water.

Cyndi belly-flopped awkwardly, the surface of the water smacking the air out of her lungs. The skin on her stomach stung from the impact. Her kicking feet found the bottom and she stood up, spinning around to face the killer. He jumped down into the water after her, creating a huge tidal wave splash that washed over her face.

She turned and waded away from him, paddling

with her arms again. Her short legs were no match for his long powerful ones as he chased her through the water.

Just as Cyndi reached the open doorway, the killer grabbed her again, one hand painfully pressing the metal band on her headphones down into her neck. He yanked and she spun, slipping out of his grasp and leaving him holding a pair of empty headphones.

She faced him as he tossed the headphones aside and lunged at her again. His fingers wormed around her throat again and he began to dunk her head underneath the water. She scratched and clawed desperately at his arms but it was no use. He had an iron grip on her throat and had let her get away too many times to let the pain get the better of him.

He lifted her up out of the water suddenly, letting her gasp for air briefly as the water fell off her face. He stared into her eyes briefly as she struggled for breath, then dunked her back down again. She tried kicking out at his crotch again, but this time he stood to the side of her legs.

He lifted Cyndi again, giving her only a short breath. He looked into her eyes, then shoved her back under the water. He was playing with her, watching her face as she struggled. The corners of her vision were beginning to cloud. She had to have air, had to get away. Scratching and kicking were ineffective against him. She had to try something else. She reached out for anything around her that she could use. A rock on the nearby ledge, or a piece of driftwood, anything would help. Her hand landed on something floating in the water next to her. Her headphones.

Cyndi grabbed the headphones by the soaking orange ear-pieces. He lifted her out of the water again and she thrust the headphones forward at him. The metal band wrapped around his neck, cutting off his air supply.

He pulled one hand off her throat and attempted to grab the headphones away. Now she had some room to move.

She turned her head and bit down on his wrist hard enough to break the skin. He uttered a muffled cry behind the mask and let go of her throat completely. The hand he used to pull away the headphones immediately clutched the hand she bit.

Cyndi jumped up and gasped for air while kicking him firmly in the stomach. The air flew out of his lungs and he fell backward. Water flowed into his mask through the black open eye holes.

From behind them, the doors began closing with that whirring machine sound again. The little whirlpools swirled around the doors as they slowly closed.

Cyndi saw her chance. She grabbed him by the shoulder and yanked him around, then whipped the headphones around his neck again, just above the bottom of the mask. Then she wrapped the headphone cord around his neck as many times as she could. He noticed what was happening and launched up out of the water. She held the cord tight.

He tried to grab her behind his back but only managed to swipe at her. She yanked the headphone cord with all her strength and held the ends of the mask tight around his neck. She planted a foot in the middle of his back for leverage and pulled even tighter.

The mask was full of water and he was beginning to drown in it. As he struggled and jerked, water sloshed out of the open eye-holes. He desperately tried to untangle the cord around his throat, but kept losing his balance on the slippery floor.

Cyndi pulled him just inside the door frame as the doors closed. He planted his hands on the edges of the metal doors and tried to hold them open. The gears began to grind harder and squeal, but they were ultimately stronger than the man.

Cyndi gave a final yank downward, and he went underwater. The hard edges of the metal doors were now crushing the man's stomach. The gears squealed and began to thrum but the doors crushed down tighter and tighter.

The man's thrashing hands flew up out of the water, grabbing for Cyndi. She let go of him and quickly backed away into the main part of the river. The doors began to tremble with tremendous force as they crushed the man between them. His body was caught beneath the grinning mouth part of the smiling face painted on the doors.

Cyndi waded across the river, coughing and gasping, trying to regain some of the air she had lost. Her throat felt raw and sore. She reached the riverbank across the way and turned back just in time to see the doors close with a final snap and clunk of effort. They hadn't shut right. They were off center, and the face painted on the doors looked divided and uneven. She couldn't see the man. He was somewhere under the water, crushed by the doors and drowning in his mask.

Cyndi scrambled up out of the cool water and stood in the grass. She took a last look at the door with the horrible grinning face and turned away. She clutched at her sore throat and felt the tender spots where the man's fingers had crushed down. There would be dark purple bruises there tomorrow.

She couldn't think. Her mind struggled to reconcile the last few minutes of her life. Horrible images danced in front of her eyes. Had she really just killed a person? It seemed so unbelievable. It seemed like it couldn't have really happened. It sickened her, but she thought that in a way it didn't seem like such a big deal.

"Now what?" she sighed to herself.

Suddenly, she remembered what she had to do,

309

and it filled her with terror. She had to go back in the
tunnel and do what she had set out to do before: get out
of the park.

Chapter Twenty-One:

The Second Escape

By the time Cyndi reached the side door leading into the tunnel again, she honestly could not remember any part of the walk over. The last moment she could remember was standing on the riverbank, shivering and dripping wet in the cool night air, and staring at the metal doors with that ugly grinning face. She had turned away from the doors and began walking over. The next thing she knew, she was standing in front of the side door. She turned around, trying to remember her walk along the concrete path past the bushes and across the grassy field, but it just wasn't there. It was as if she had experienced a hiccup in time.

(She wraps the headphone cord around his throat. He chokes on the water inside his mask.)

There was only one thing she could remember, the song "How Much More?" by the Go-Go's. The stereo in her head had been blasting that song as she walked over, forcing her to half hum, half sing it. It was still playing by the time she reached the door. She abruptly stopped singing when she realized she had experienced a temporary lapse in memory.

(The grinding gears behind the mechanical doors shut themselves on the man's body. Is that the snap of the his ribs breaking? Being crushed....)

Will you forget the memory loss and focus on getting out of here? that forceful inner voice yelled to her.

(The killer springs out from behind the waterfall. His strong fingers wrap around her throat and squeeze.)

She shook away all of her distracting thoughts and clasped the door handle. She tugged at it, but it wouldn't budge.

"What?" she asked, confused. She tugged at the door again, much more forcefully this time, and it still wouldn't give an inch. "Wait."

Her mind had been flashing back useless traumatic images since she left the killer for dead at the doors. Now it conjured up an image that she could use. She saw herself standing on the other side of this door in pure darkness, turning the deadbolt to lock the killer out. She heard the slide-click sound of the deadbolt as she turned it.

"Oh yeah," she muttered, realizing that she had locked both the killer and herself out at the same time. She gave the door another futile tug, then let her hand drop. So much for that.

Wait! The guy! He got in there somehow too. There's got to be another door. Her eyes lit up. Maybe there was still a chance. She stepped back from the doorway and looked at the rocky outside wall of the tunnel ride. The other door had to be farther up the hill, or maybe even on the other side.

Another memory floated to the surface in her mind. There had been another sliding-click sound, she hadn't known what it was at the time. It had sounded like some kind of movement back in the darkness, she barely heard it over the sound of the waterfalls. Now that she could think straight, without being half-crazy with fear, she remembered that noise had sounded a lot like another deadbolt being turned. The killer must have locked himself in too.

But what if he didn't?

(She stands in the water inside the tunnel, peering forward into total darkness.)

Cyndi had to face the facts. Even if there was some other way in, she did not *want* to go back into the tunnel. She had faced a nightmare in that shadowy, humid, stinking tunnel. She had faced death, and by some strange miracle had escaped. Going back in that tunnel would be like tempting fate. She wasn't sure if she would have the strength to face it again.

"There has to be some other way out," she whispered, rubbing her eyes. She looked back in the direction of the rest of the park, going over everything she could remember from the day. She tried to remember Stacy and Zack's smiling faces, and the kind things they had said to her and done for her. Images from the tunnel and the Dead Man's Drop kept rudely popping in and rearing their ugly heads. She thumped the heel of her palm against her forehead, trying to will the bad images away and think.

She focused on Stacy, who may or may not still be alive as far as she knew. Stacy who had befriended, then abandoned her. But hadn't Stacy been right to abandon her? What was the last thing Stacy said to her? She couldn't remember. Something else now bubbled up from her memory banks. It was the story Zack told them while they sat at the picnic tables. The story about how he had snuck into someone's backyard, and how he had crawled under the fence in a drainage ditch.

The river. It had to get out of the park somewhere. There had to be a drainage ditch or something on the other side of the park. Maybe Stacy had even gone down that way. Maybe Stacy was still alive and waiting for her on the other side of the fence.

Do you really believe that?

She *had* to believe that. The alternative was too horrible to imagine. All the dead bodies in that pool were bad enough, but the bodies of people she had cared about deeply were just too much for her to handle right now. She clung to one thought: *Stacy's alive and she's outside the park waiting for me.* Cyndi began to walk.

*   *   *

The river trickled along slowly and quietly beside Cyndi. The flashes of horrific images became less frequent with time and distance from the tunnel. She kept her head low and her ears alert for any sounds of approaching footsteps. As far as she knew the masked man was dead, but she still didn't feel any safer. The entire park was still full of death and corpses, and Cyndi knew she wouldn't feel truly safe until she was miles away.

There was also the possibility that the man she had just killed was not the only other person left alive here. Maybe there were other men in here too, waiting to finish the job that the first one failed to do. That dreadful thought had occurred to her, but she didn't think it was true. If there were other men in the park, they would have gotten her already. You could run and hide from one man, but not two or three. They would've worked together to take her and her friends out more quickly and easily. Still....

As she approached the picnic tables, she looked over at the shredded, scattered remnants of their belongings and saw her backpack lying there. It looked very lonely and forgotten sitting slumped on the ground like that. The idea that she had fully intended to leave the park without even thinking to grab it brought up shameful feelings deep in her stomach. She walked over and picked it up, rummaging through its contents. It was still full of tapes. She seemed to be missing only a few pairs of clothes and the mix tape that the killer had stolen from her last night.

Cyndi looked down and saw the scattered, ripped belongings of Stacy, Brad, and Zack. She had an impulse to pick up their things and take them with her, but hesitated. What difference would it make? They were probably gone. She took a few steps forward, then reached down and grabbed one of Zack's gray T-shirts, the one with the monster truck on the front and the cutoff sleeves. It hadn't been too badly ripped. Then she grabbed one of Stacy's pink shirts that had been flung, but not defiled like the others. She didn't know why she had such an impulse to take them. She stuffed the shirts into her bag, zipped it closed, and continued away.

Cyndi made her way back to the river's edge and continued toward the other end of the park. She passed the shredded raft that had brought them here and also met its untimely end. She caught a glimpse of the primitive, jagged smiley face painted on its orange sides and quickly turned away. The mere sight of that ghastly face made her sick to her stomach.

As she passed the end-pool of the Ragin' Rivers, she heard the sound of water splashing down off the four slides into the pool. She navigated her way around a treacherous looking bush full of thorns and glanced over. There was some dark mass floating in the pool, spinning in a slow circle. She was so startled to see it that she almost cried out. Squinting her eyes, she took a few steps forward to get a closer look. It was a person floating on a tube with their face down in the water. The guy's head came around and even in the dark she recognized the white football jersey and the wet blond hair. It was Brad.

All at once, her worst fears became real. The killer *had* gotten Brad. They had all gone down the ride and the killer had gotten Brad. It could have been any one of them. It could have been her. An image of herself floating face down on a tube in the Ragin' Rivers pool flashed into her head. She had never seen a dead person before today, and didn't want to see Brad's dead face now. She couldn't take it. The bodies in the Dead Man's Drop pool had been strangers, but this was too much. She turned and ran.

Up ahead, Cyndi saw a ghostly pink glow through the trees, and she came to a skidding stop. At first, she thought it was a ghost or some kind of apparition peering at her from behind trees. Then her mind reconciled the image and she realized what it was. The killer had apparently not shut off all the lights in the park. He had missed one of the lights in the Lazy River, the one closest to the real river. The light shining up through the water looked pink. She realized with horror that the water was full of blood.

Cyndi approached the lazy river slowly, dreading what she knew she would see, but forcing herself to see it just the same. The clear blue tubes were caught in a floating traffic jam in the slow current, and underneath them was a shadow, some dark form floating under the surface.

She walked across the grass and stopped at the edge of the Lazy River, watching the shape as it slowly floated closer to her. The tubes and the rippling surface of the water distorted the image, but it was clear enough as it floated along underneath the tubes. The body was floating face down in the darkest pink of the bloody diluted water, about a foot below the surface. A cloud of long blond hair that looked like fine seaweed billowed around its head. The arms were outstretched, and the knees and toes dragged and scraped along the bottom of the river. It was a girl, and she was still wearing the same hot pink swimsuit that Cyndi had seen only a few hours ago.

"Stacy! No!" she cried aloud. Before she even knew what she was doing, she was climbing down into the bloody water. She waded over to the body and wrapped her arms around Stacy's chest. She flipped Stacy over and hauled her head and shoulders up out of the water. Stacy's eyes were open, and the water ran over them, a sight that looked unnatural and disturbing to Cyndi.

Cyndi walked Stacy's body over to the edge of the Lazy River, it was surprisingly light. With one arm holding onto Stacy's chest, she hoisted herself out of the water. It took a few tries before she could actually manage to get her butt up and onto the concrete. She fell back in the water twice, scraping her lower back painfully against the edge. Stacy was much heavier out of the water, and her smooth skin was slippery. The thought of leaving Stacy there to float in the water, going round and round in endless circles as she degenerated into something like what she had seen in the Dead Man's Drop, forced Cyndi to keep moving.

Finally, she got herself up out of the pool. She scooted back into the grass, pulling Stacy's body by the arms. Fresh tears spilled out of her eyes as she looked down at Stacy.

"Stacy, I'm s-s-sorry," she stammered between sobs. "I should have gone with you. We should have stuck together." She burst into a fresh gale of tears, and sat there in the grass with her friend for a long time.

*   *   *

The lonely call of a loon finally brought Cyndi back to reality. She had sat there in the grass calming down. Her mind went over everything that she and Stacy had done together over the past week. It all seemed so unreal now. The bird's cry in the night shocked her and she sat bolt upright. She realized she had to keep moving, the park was still a bad place.

She stood up and looked at Stacy. There was a gaping wound in her abdomen filled with water and dark liquid. Cyndi bent down and placed Stacy's hand over the wound, knowing that it would never heal.

"I have to leave now," she said in a low, calm voice. "But I'll send people back for you. I won't leave you alone for too long. You know that you're the best friend I ever...."

Cyndi felt new tears coming on, and knew that if she didn't get moving soon, she'd be here all night.

"Goodbye, Stace," she managed to choke out. She forced herself to begin walking away. Once she reached the concrete path, she turned and took one last look. Stacy looked like she was sleeping peacefully in the grass under the stars. It was the last time she ever saw Stacy outside of her nightmares.

Cyndi walked back to the river and continued alongside it for another five minutes, mostly looking down to make sure she didn't step in anything or lose her balance. This side of the park remained wild and untouched, with long grass and cattails sprouting up along the sides of the river. Several areas were full of mud and low water. Cyndi had to go back up the slope to get around those mucky spots. A few times she thought she heard someone following her and had to look back into the darkness, her heart pounding. After a thorough look around, she decided that no one was there.

The long grass along the river's edge abruptly stopped, giving way to a concrete wall that jutted two feet out of the water. Cyndi stopped walking and got her first look at the far edge of the park.

As she had walked along the river's edge, she imagined the river going under some chain link fence in a drainage ditch similar to the one in Zack's story, a fence that she could easily swim under. What she actually found was nothing like that. She had been lost in thought, focused on her feet, and the far end of the park had crept up on her. Now she looked up and saw that the river was diverted into a concrete canal for about twenty feet, then it went through a metal grate made of thick vertical bars that were set into the water at an angle. Beyond the bars, the river pooled against a concrete wall, then spun around in a lazy whirlpool before dropping into some unseen tunnel below and exiting the park. Another fifteen feet beyond the grate was more of that same wrought iron fence.

"No," Cyndi said, her heart sinking.

She walked quickly along the concrete wall and passed the grate. Between the fence and the grate there was a flat concrete pad. In the center of the concrete, there stood a thick, two foot tall, metal control valve with a wheel on top. The control valve was painted bright red like a fire hydrant. On either side of the control valve there were manhole covers set into the concrete. Cyndi went straight to the back fence, barely giving any of this a second glance.

There's got to be an opening over here. There's just got to be! She stopped in front of the fence and almost gripped the iron bars as if she were in a jail cell. Luckily, she saw the copper electric wires in time and held her hands back. In both directions along the fence, she saw nothing but more iron bars stretching off endlessly into the woods. She would have to go back into the tunnel after all.

She took a long look at the outside world,

desperately wanting to be out of this prison. Just past the fence, there was a steep drop-off, and the river continued in a deep gully nearly twenty feet below. Water fed into the gully by a large pipe on the right, about three feet in diameter, that jutted out of the hill. Another pipe stretched out high over the drop and went deep into the hill across the way. On the other side of the gully, Cyndi could see another concrete pad like the one she was standing on. The pipe across the gully connected with the far concrete pad. There was another manhole cover on the far side as well.

A plan formed in her mind as she traced the pipe back to where she stood. If she could open the manhole cover on this side of the gully, she could crawl through the pipe under the fence and make it across to the other side. She would get out of here.

Yeah, but crawling through a pipe? Doesn't sound very safe. You'd probably be better off going back to the tunnel.

She had to admit, it did sound less than appealing. It would be filthy, and God knew what bugs or animals were crawling around down there. Why did that negative voice in her head have to be right so much of the time?

A loud crash and a clatter of wood echoed from somewhere back in the park. Cyndi spun around, her heart leaping into her throat. She only could see woods and darkness. The sound had been faint and distant.

Was that one of the picnic tables?

For a moment there was only silence, then came another crash, this one louder and closer.

"Shit," she whispered. The killer was still alive, and coming at her fast.

Time to go.

Cyndi looked around frantically for something to pry up the manhole cover. On the red control valve

320

wheel she saw a long crowbar wedged in between the spokes for leverage. She pulled it out with a dull metal sliding noise. It felt heavy in her hands.

She shoved the hook end down into the small hole in the manhole cover on the left and began to pull. She used all of her strength and barely felt it budge at all, the manhole cover seemed to weigh a ton. *They never looked this heavy when people opened them up on TV.*

She heard the man stomping through the underbrush, snapping off branches and twigs that got in his way. He had to be somewhere near the Ragin' Rivers now.

She tugged and strained, gritting her teeth and yanking at the manhole cover. It lifted up an inch and her strength gave out. It gave a hollow metal clunk as it fell back into place. Her hands were sore from clutching the crowbar so tight. Ignoring the pain, she placed the hook end down and tried a different tactic. She jammed the long end of the crowbar into the hole and pushed down on it, using leverage to lift the manhole cover up. To her surprise, it lifted up much more easily than before. She pushed the crowbar forward and the manhole cover slid to the side with a metal scrape. She had gotten it open.

The noises of rage from the man had gone silent now.

Not good, not good. Hurry.

Cyndi crouched and tossed the crowbar aside. She reached into the small crescent moon shaped opening and tugged at the manhole cover in short bursts. The opening widened an inch at a time.

"Come on. Come on," she whispered impatiently.

Finally the opening was wide enough for her to climb down into the pipe. She looked down and saw mostly darkness. She could hear the echo of a tiny trickle of running water. There was enough moonlight for her to see the first two rungs of a ladder embedded into the concrete leading down. Thick strands of spiderweb blocked the entrance and she brushed them away quickly with her hand.

Cyndi stuck her feet in first and began climbing down into the pipe. The metal rungs were cold on her bare feet and hands. She made her way fully inside the pipe, and the sound seemed to close in around her. Every move she made and every shuddering, fearful breath reverberated against the concrete. With the little moonlight shining in she saw a dead crawdad floating in the shallow puddle of water at the bottom of the pipe.

Oh God, this place is full of bugs. Maybe this wasn't such a good idea.

Without warning, there was a loud series of *CLANGS* as the killer yanked the manhole cover aside.

She looked up just time to see the grinning white mask and the crowbar in his hand as it came smashing down toward her head. She let go of the rungs and fell to the bottom. The crowbar hit the top metal rung and rang out deafeningly loud in the pipe.

Her feet splashed into the water at the bottom of the pipe and she landed in a heap. The ice cold water she sat in was only six inches deep. She looked up and saw the white grinning mask leering down at her. His arm lashed out with the crowbar and swiped down at her. The man seemed more full of rage than ever.

How did he get out of the tunnel? she wondered.

It was about eight feet from the manhole cover to the bottom of the pipe, but the man had a long reach. The crowbar crashed into the concrete inches above her head. Concrete dust fell down into her hair.

Cyndi lowered herself and looked directly into three drooping, rotting faces. She screamed aloud and it rang out hollowly through the tunnel. Three bodies

322

clogged the opening where the water was supposed to come through. They had been the bodies that were in the tunnel. They had floated down the river after the tunnel doors had opened and let them go.

She turned away from their horrible gray faces and looked into the pipe. It looked so narrow. With the little bit of moonlight, she could see the walls were covered with spiderwebs. The man swiped at her with the crowbar again, narrowly missing her head by an inch. He was leaning into the pipe now, slashing at her wildly. She had no choice, she dove into the pipe on her hands and knees.

The pipe was so narrow that Cyndi didn't have any room to turn around if she got stuck. All she could do was turn her head and look back. She felt claustrophobia worming its way into her mind. Her shoulders and backpack scraped the top of the pipe, and she had to keep her head down. Her knees sloshed in the icy water beneath her.

Up above, the masked man could no longer see Cyndi. He looked over at the control valve and stood up. With a harsh metal scrape that Cyndi heard distantly in the pipes, he picked up the crowbar off the concrete pad, went over to the control valve, and jammed the crowbar into the wheel. He struggled against the wheel, yanking and grunting, trying to turn it and divert the flow of river water from the pipe on the right, which fed the riverbed below, to the pipe on the left, which Cyndi was currently crawling through. If he couldn't stab her, he would drown her like a rat.

From behind Cyndi, there was a loud metal groan. She craned her neck to look back over her shoulder and saw something moving mechanically back in the darkness. Water began flowing more freely into the pipe behind her. The current hit her knees and she felt herself being pushed forward. Her hands slipped on the scummy surface of the pipe and she fell into the cold water. It was now a foot deep, and was starting to fill the pipe.

"NOOO!!! STOP IT!!!" she screamed out.

The killer heard her cries from above and yanked the wheel even harder. Suddenly, it came to a shuddering stop.

The valve caught up against the tangle of bodies that were clogging the pipe. Its metal edge pressed against one of the dead men's skulls. The valve squeezed harder, and the dead man's skull crunched, but it refused to give way.

The killer yanked on the wheel again with all his strength. It suddenly turned and spun effortlessly as if some internal gear had come loose. He looked down into the pipe and saw the water still only faintly flowing through. It definitely wasn't up to its full force yet. He knew something was blocking the valve from opening all the way.

He savagely jerked the crowbar out from the wheel and walked over to the manhole cover. Then he began his descent down into the pipe after her.

Cyndi heard a splash behind her and turned her head. The killer's feet were down in the pipe. He crouched down and began crawling his way toward her. The crowbar in his hand and the white smiling mask were the last things she saw before she was immersed in total darkness. She screamed in terror and crawled forward blindly, as fast as she could.

The man's shoulders scraped along the top of the round pipe. He swung the crowbar wildly against the pipe's concrete sides. Cyndi screamed with every hit out of fear and pain for her ringing eardrums. She could feel the vibrations from the crowbar every time it hit the pipe.

Cyndi's hands and knees began to feel numb in the icy water. She continued to slip in the sludge that lined the bottom of the pipe. She felt bugs sporadically crawling on her shoulders and wriggling underneath her hands and legs. The killer seemed to be right behind her. His gravelly panting breath behind the mask echoed throughout the pipe. He seemed to be taking up all of the stale air, yet she still felt the wind from his mad swings with the crowbar.

The killer sensed how close she was, and swung the crowbar too hard, hoping to snag the soft flesh of one of her thighs with its heavy hooked end. He missed her by mere inches and the crowbar stuck tightly into the pipe. He grunted and tugged, trying to free it. Cyndi screamed aloud when the crowbar hit. For a second, she was convinced that he actually hit her with it, and her leg throbbed sympathetically with the pipe. She realized the truth a moment later, and continued away from him, feeling a sliver of relief at the widening distance between them.

As she crawled away, she felt the pipe above her shoulders give way to open air. In her panic, she almost passed right by the opening, but slid to a stop and looked up. She felt her way up the wall and her hand slipped around the familiar shape of another cold metal rung. She had made it across to the other manhole cover outside the park.

"Yes!" she cried aloud as she began pulling herself back up to the surface.

Cyndi scrambled up the rungs of the ladder and hit her head on the hard manhole cover. Ignoring the pain, she clung to the top rung with one hand, and pushed with all her might against the manhole cover with the other. She felt it lifting slightly, maybe a few centimeters, not nearly far enough.

On the other side of the pipe, the dead man's skull that had been holding the valve closed splintered away with a loud, sickening crunch. The river water forced the valve open all the way. A torrent of water thundered into the pipe.

The man yanked at the crowbar a final time, and pulled a thick chunk of concrete out of the pipe as it came free. He started to move forward again but stopped and turned to look back as he heard the flood of water nearly two and a half feet deep rushing toward him. He began to crawl forward as fast as he could.

Cyndi shoved upward with her legs, her shoulders and back felt like they were burning. She felt the manhole cover lifting above her shoulders. She clenched her jaw and screamed, giving it everything she had.

Moonlight and fresh air came spilling through the opening. The cool air on her face seemed to energize her and she pushed even harder. She tilted to the side and felt the cover heavily scraping open, inch by brutal inch.

A deluge of water hit the killer with the force of a strong shove. He slipped forward and felt himself floating, being dragged away. He wildly swung the crowbar, trying to grab hold of anything. It was no use. The water began to fill up inside his mask and his clothes.

Cyndi now had enough room to put her hands on the side of the manhole cover. She tugged on the rusty lip of the cover, forcing it open just enough so that she could squeeze herself out. Beneath her, she heard the loud rush of water gushing through the tunnel. She felt a rush of stale air that had settled in the tube being displaced with water. It blew past her, escaping into the night. She threw out her backpack first, then began squeezing herself out. She slid out from underneath the manhole cover and stood up on the concrete island. Looking down, she saw the black crescent she had just crawled out from, and realized that she had to get the manhole cover closed before the masked man could come crawling out after her.

Cyndi scrambled around to the other side of the manhole cover and began to shove it closed. It scraped and slowly slid shut as she dug her feet into the dirt and put her whole body weight into it. Getting the manhole cover closed was a lot easier than it had been opening it. It finally fell into place with a clang, and spun around briefly like a huge coin. It clanked to a stop and Cyndi stepped down on it for good measure.

She listened to the muffled rush of water below, echoing faintly up from the small hole near the edge of the manhole cover. She hadn't seen or heard what happened to the man. He had to be somewhere down in that darkness, floating and being tossed around like a cork. She knew he had tried to kill her by drowning her in the pipe, but something had happened, something had ruined his murderous plans. Surely he couldn't survive down there in all that water, but where did this pipe go? Did it empty out somewhere further along the river, or did it divert into smaller pipes that led off somewhere else?

Cyndi looked back across the gully and saw the fence to the park.

"So this is what the other side looks like," she said to herself.

She took a deep breath and sighed with relief. She had made it out. She had escaped.

Chapter Twenty-Two:

Coming Home

Cyndi sat on the manhole cover for what felt like an hour. She had no way to tell time, and no idea how long she actually sat there waiting for some sign from the killer. She listened for the sound of him crawling through the pipe, but only heard the steady flow of water and the crickets in the night. She constantly scanned the surrounding woods and the other side of the fence, watching for the man to come climbing out of the pipe back inside the water park. Shivering, she sat long into the night, crouched inside layers of both Zack and Stacy's shirts from her backpack. For extra warmth, she pulled her arms all the way into the sleeves and wrapped them around her chest. The cuts on her legs and left side stung, and the bruises on her neck ached dully.

Finally, she decided it was time to get moving again. She picked up her backpack and took one last look at the fence.

I never want to see this place again. I'm turning my back on it forever, she thought somberly. Although she couldn't help but feel that that wasn't true. She had the strange, inexplicable feeling that she would see it again, somehow, sometime far in the future. Nevertheless, she turned away, and didn't look back.

Cyndi continued following the river along the high ledge of the gully. The river had died down to a small trickle without the surge of river water from the park. It wound around endlessly through the woods. The high sides of the gully eventually began to descend, evening out with the river again. She peered around paranoid, trying to keep her guard up, but felt her eyelids growing heavy. She was yawning too much and her knees ached. She had to face the fact that she was physically and mentally exhausted.

I have to get some sleep. But what if he's still out there? The thought was unnerving. She didn't feel his presence out in the woods like she had back in the park, or like she had felt it the night before as the four of them floated down the river toward their destiny.

She spotted an old tree with a lot of low thick limbs. The image of a black panther she had seen on some nature show, sleeping high up in a tree like this one, popped into her mind. It seemed like a far-fetched idea, but she was much too nervous to sleep on the ground out in the open. If the killer was out there somewhere, he would find her and take care of her once and for all.

She looked around cautiously, searching for any watching faces in the woods. When she was satisfied that she was alone, she began to climb. She climbed up about fifteen feet and settled into a nice crook between three thick limbs. It seemed sturdy enough to hold her, and gave her enough space that she wouldn't fall out of the tree.

Despite her exhaustion, sleep did not come easily. Several times, as she was about to nod off, she felt her body sliding off one of the limbs. Every time this happened, she came fully awake with a jolt of adrenaline. She adjusted herself and settled again, but a knob from one of the limbs she was leaning on became painful, and she had to rearrange her position again. After a half dozen rearranged positions, she finally settled, straddling one of the thick limbs with her arms and legs, and dozed off into a light, unrestful sleep.

She awoke two hours later out of some nightmare of confused images that she couldn't even remember once she was awake again. The only thing she remembered clearly from the dream was the dead face of Stacy. Her mouth was bone dry, and her tongue felt like it was covered with thick, congealing slime. She stretched and felt achy all over. It was still dark out, but she didn't think she would be able to sleep up here anymore.

So she sat in the tree for a while, resting, waiting for the sun to come up, and listening to her stomach growl and gurgle ceaselessly.

Just as Cyndi started to feel tired enough to sleep again, she saw the first shreds of daylight brightening up the horizon. She watched with a growing sense of relief as the sun slowly came up. Never in her entire life had she felt more happy to see the sun. It stood as proof that she had made it through that awful night, and gave the promise of warmth and light. It looked like it would be another hot, sunny day.

Once the sun cast its orange morning rays through the treetops, she slowly climbed back down to the ground. Her legs felt stiff and wobbly. Her feet were too full of blood from hanging for hours. She walked back to the river and picked up where she had left off. As she walked, the morning sunlight seemed to warm everything. She took off Stacy and Zack's shirts and stuffed them back into her backpack.

After an hour of walking, she heard her first car on the road ahead. It was such a strange sound to hear after days in the woods, it made her jump. Her first thought was that the killer had somehow acquired a car and was now driving around and looking for her. Her instinct told her to run deeper into the woods and find a good hiding place. Then her mind began to reason its way back to reality.

"Car. Wait!" she cried out. The car was long gone, but she ran toward the sound anyway. She splashed across the shallow riverbed and stomped past bushes.

Up ahead, at the top of a hill, she saw a flash of metal glinting in the morning sunlight. It was a road sign. Her heart pounded in her chest as she ran toward it. She felt nervous to make contact with the outside world again. Thick, slippery leaves covered the steep hill up to the road, and she had to use her hands to climb up.

Cyndi finally reached the top of the hill and the washed-out gray pavement came into view, sparkling in the sun. She got up off her hands and knees and walked out onto the pavement. Looking back and forth, she saw no signs of cars.

"Now what?" she whispered to herself. The road sign in front of her was only a SPEED LIMIT 45 MPH sign, and gave her no indication of where she was or which direction she should take. The road seemed familiar, and she racked her brains trying to figure out if she had been on this road on the way to camp or not. Which way was camp? She decided to walk down the road. It seemed like the more logical choice since she had been moving that way along the river to begin with.

Soon after she began walking, she heard a car approaching from behind her. From her position, she could see it was an old station wagon, one of the ones that had the fake wood paneling on the sides.

The car approached and didn't slow down. She took a few steps toward the side of the road and the car

331

veered to the left, away from her. As it flew past, the wind picked up Cyndi's ratty blond hair and tossed it around. She saw a fat woman behind the driver's seat with a mass of curly, poodle-like hair. The woman turned and gave her an ugly disapproving frown, but didn't bother to slow down. Cyndi wasn't bothered by this in the least. She was too exhausted to be offended. She began walking again.

Another ten minutes went by, then the rattle of an old truck came up from behind her. She turned around again and saw its rust-flaked tan colored hood. It was slowing down. She stopped and waited for it.

With a squeal of brakes, the truck pulled up next to her. An older guy, he must have been in his late fifties, leaned over and cranked down the window of the truck. He wore a beat-up white and green trucker hat and had big glasses on. His teeth were yellow and horribly crooked.

"You okay, girl? You need a ride?" he asked in a thick southern accent. She studied him for a moment, wondering if she could trust him. He seemed to regard Cyndi with caution, but looked genuine enough.

"Uh, yeah. Yeah I do," she croaked through dried vocal chords.

"Well, hop on eein," he said amiably and pulled the handle. The door sprung open a few inches.

Cyndi climbed up into the truck, took her pack off, and put it on the floor between her feet. She slammed the rusty door shut, and the man began driving again.

As he drove, he studied her cautiously. He noticed the bruises on her throat, the cuts on her filthy legs, and the one on her left side. She was covered in dirt and had a nasty, muddy, rotten smell that he couldn't quite put his finger on. He said nothing about her smell though, he simply rolled down his window a few inches.

She ignored him and looked out the cracked windshield through heavy eyelids. The truck was a mess but she didn't mind. The only thing she could think about was how she was going to explain all this to her parents. What could she possibly tell them? They were going to completely lose their minds as soon as she got home.

"You-uh...If you don't mind me sayin' so, you look like hell. D'you get lost out there?" he asked.

She nodded without turning to look at him.

"You ain't one of those kids from Camp are ya? Holy shit, you are!" he declared. "They've been out lookin' all over for ya! Saw it on TV and everythin.' Say...where're the other ones?"

Cyndi finally turned and looked at the man. She stared at him, her mouth clenched shut and her lower lip began to quiver. Her mind suddenly drew up the images of Brad and Stacy's bodies, and tears stung her eyes. She burst into fresh sobs and buried her face in her hands. The driver was taken aback.

"Hey. Hey now. Just uh-- Oh, Jesus," he stammered, completely at a loss for words. "I-I'll get ya back to camp right away. Okay? Don't you worry. Everythin's gonna be okay. Don't you worry now."

Cyndi didn't look up at all for the next twenty minutes as they drove on in awkward silence back to Camp Kikawa.

*   *   *

Two weeks passed in Cyndi's memory as a blur, only fragmentary images remained. Her arrival back at camp. The staring gaping faces of the campers as she stepped out of the man's truck looking dazed and dirty. The stern, enraged face of Counselor Sheehan taking one look at her, then turning white as a sheet. The frantic questions from the counselors. Sitting in the lodge on the couch waiting for them to do something with her. The nervous stares of the other campers through the windows of the lodge. Counselor Ashley and the nurse helping get her into the shower in the Nurse's office, then cleaning her wounds and bringing her food, which she gobbled down ravenously. Rushing to the bathroom to throw the food back up. The arrival of the big, burly police officer who seemed to know exactly how to talk to her and how to make the whole story come spilling out of her. The arrival of her parents who looked a lot like Counselor Sheehan did when they first saw her. Her mother bursting into tears and repeating, "Thank God. Thank God. Thank God," over and over again. The small handful of reporters standing outside the lodge as she walked out with her parents, shoving microphones in her face and pelting her with a barrage of questions. The ride back home in total, stunned silence.

Cyndi had gone back home, to her room. The next day, she endured a long talk from her parents (they did all the talking) and had been grounded indefinitely. The days passed, she listened to music, remembered that awful night over and over again in her mind. She constantly thought about Stacy, Zack, and Brad. Every now and then, she pulled out Stacy and Zack's T-shirts from her closet, where she kept them folded neatly. She would lay them out on her bed and lose herself in good memories of them.

With each passing day, she slowly began to feel more like herself, except she wasn't really *herself* anymore. The terrible night had left an impact on her without a doubt, but something had changed her even before all that had happened. She had made friends, she had been told she was a valued member of a group of kids, she had broken the rules, gotten a crush on a boy, and kissed that boy. She had lost her Walkman and her headphones on that trip, but she didn't think she actually needed them anymore.

Eleven days into her sentence, something happened that made her realize her own change more than anything else. She sat on the windowsill, enjoying the fresh summer air. The song "Caught Up In You" by . 38 Special was playing on the radio behind her as she flipped through a teen magazine with a picture of Joan Jett on the cover.

The sound of a lawnmower started up and caught her ear. She looked down into her front yard. That cute boy with the surfer-look was back and was mowing their lawn again. His blond hair was flipped over again, and he had developed a darker tan since the last time she had seen him. His lean, toned arms came out from the sleeves of a blue Hawaiian shirt he wore now, unbuttoned halfway down, and tucked into his acid-wash jeans. His grass-stained high-tops looked greener than ever.

The boy looked up at her again, just as he had last time, and flashed her that crooked smile. Cyndi didn't turn away from him at all, didn't even flinch. Instead, she held up a hand and waved at him, giving him her own smile. He raised his own hand in return, his smile brightening, then turned back to his mowing. She watched him as he continued his work and noticed how he kept glancing up at her bedroom window.

I'm not turning away from him. I'm not embarrassed, she thought with amazement.

Why should you be embarrassed? He's cute, and he obviously likes you, another voice spoke up in her mind. It was Stacy's voice.

The boy had moved on to the other side of the yard where she couldn't see him now. She sat there stunned, thinking how just a few short weeks ago she would have only given him a glance, then turned away embarrassed like a little girl. Things had changed. She felt glad, confident, and strong.

Maybe the little smile that they shared and their wave of acknowledgment was nothing. After all, she knew nothing about him. He probably had a girlfriend, or was in college or something. But just maybe, the two of them waving at each other was just the start of something special.

When I get out of here, I'm gonna go talk to him, she thought, nodding her head. The song ended and a commercial came on the radio, rudely pulling Cyndi out of her thoughts and back to the real world. She walked over to the radio and began flipping through the stations, searching for a new song.

Epilogue:

The leaves began to turn in late August, and over the last few weeks they had gotten nothing but clouds. Cyndi went with her mother to run some errands across town. Her mother didn't trust Cyndi to stay home alone anymore after the events of the summer, and wanted to take her everywhere. She viewed Cyndi as some kind of unpredictable troublemaker now. She also thought Cyndi was getting much too friendly with that kid that mowed their lawn. She could see her little girl growing up before her eyes, and it terrified her.

She looked over at her daughter, seeing the pink bow tie in her hair, the plethora of bracelets around her arms, and the silly mismatched leg warmers she had on below her frilly skirt. She simply did not understand her daughter or her fashion choices at all.

Cyndi's mother was in the middle of a lecture about something or other, she had tuned her out a while ago. Judging by the somewhat bored tone in her mother's voice and her frequent pauses, she must have been boring herself as well.

Cyndi reached over and clicked on the car radio. It was set on some jazz station and she immediately turned the dial over to the pop station she liked the best.

The radio squawked with static as she carefully tuned it over to her station. She caught the tail end of "We Got the Beat" by the Go-Go's and settled on it. Her mother looked over at her with a disapproving glare but didn't touch the radio.

The car began up a steep hill, and Cyndi glanced out the windshield at the stream and wild open area that they were passing on the left. The stream was full of trees and cattails, and something about the area seemed dark and wild. She was about to turn to the passenger's side window when something caught her eye that made her blood run cold.

The grinning white face loomed ahead on the left side of the road. It was huge, plastered onto a billboard that stood in the middle of a hilly dirt lot. It was painted just like the signs had been inside the water park that day, showing a cartoon drawing of the smiley face captain riding a tube down a water slide. Big blue curls of water splashed up on either side of him. In wavy, watery letters were the words COMING NEXT SUMMER: THRILL RIVER!

Cyndi's mouth dropped open as she read the words. All of the color drained from her face. Her mother had thought of something new to say and drew in breath to begin again. She turned to her daughter, saw the horrified expression on her face, and almost choked on her own breath.

"Cyndi, honey. What's wrong?" her mother asked immediately.

On the radio, a familiar synthesized keyboard slide rang out loudly and Cyndi jumped and shrieked aloud, deafening and shocking her mother next to her. The song that began to play was "Girls Just Wanna Have Fun."

Afterword:

I was a little kid, maybe only four or five years old, when I first discovered horror novels. In the downstairs bathroom in my house, there was a little closet where the furnace and water heater were tucked away. Along the back wall were shelves with random things: wrapping paper, boxes of Christmas ornaments (my dad *loves* his Christmas ornaments), and a cat door set low in the wall where the litter box for our recently departed cat, Tony, had been. But along the wall to the left, I found a treasure trove.

My dad had built a simple wooden bookshelf and kept all of his old paperbacks in this secret room. They were all stored alphabetically and most of them had a thick black mark along the top left corner, Dad's way of keeping track of what he has and hasn't read. One shelf about midway up contained a bunch of paperbacks with black scary looking covers, all written by some guy named Stephen King (my future idol). I picked up one with an evil monkey on the cover called *Skeleton Crew* and flipped through it, wishing I was old enough to be allowed to read it.

Naturally, my mom did not want me reading Stephen King, or any other adult horror for that matter.

She always tried her best to keep me away from the really adult stuff, which only made it that much more attractive. A year or two later, the Goosebumps series started up and would tide me over for the next few years while I waited to be allowed to read the hard stuff. Thank God for R.L. Stine. Luckily, I didn't really have too long to wait, I ended up reading *'Salem's Lot* at age nine.

That musty little room has always stuck with me. I almost feel like there's a little closet in my mind, identical to the original, with a homemade bookshelf full of story ideas. Some of those ideas will probably never see the light of day, but I think the strongest of them will, God willing.

The idea for *Kill River* has been with me since I was seventeen. It came from a nightmare where I was sliding down a water park ride in the middle of the night. A masked killer dressed in black was swinging a knife and standing dangerously close on another tube behind me. I've thought about the story almost everyday since then, but it wasn't until few years ago that I had the courage to finally take it off the shelf.

I had such a blast writing *Kill River.* For about a year I sat at the table in my apartment, looking out the window at the pool downstairs, blasting some Go-Go's albums, and just enjoying escaping to the '80's, Camp Kikawa, and Kaptain Smiley's Thrill River. I hope this book allowed you to go back to the '80's and escape the repellent aspects of modern times: facebook, smart phone apps, dub-step music.... (I could keep going but don't get me started.)

For anyone with extensive '80's music knowledge, I do admit that Cyndi Lauper's "Girls Just Wanna Have Fun" technically wasn't released until late 1983, a few months after this story takes place, but it was too good to resist. I apologize for that and for any other inaccuracies that I may have written.

I have to acknowledge my friend, and fellow 80's horror lover, April Martin. In high school, I worked with April at a grocery store when I first got the idea for the story. She was probably the first person who really encouraged me to write it. Thanks April, wherever you are. I also have to thank my friends and family who test-read and helped me edit the early drafts: Alex Wheeler, Tim Taylor, Kyle Doran, my Dad, who's unflinching criticism always pushes me harder, and last but not least my wife Darla, who puts up with my "insanity" and was the first person to read this book.

If you liked it don't be shy, email me at cameron@killriver.com. Also keep your eyes peeled for the upcoming sequel to *Kill River,* it wouldn't be an 80's slasher story without sequels, right? Thrill River will be opening up in Cyndi's hometown in 1984, and as Brad would say, "what's the worst that could happen?" Until then, go enjoy your local water park (for me its Hyland Hills Water World, my Happy Gilmore "Happy Place"), crank some Go-Go's tapes on your Walkman, and keep it old-school.

Cameron Roubique
Westminster, Colorado
March 20, 2014

Soundtrack:

The following is a list of songs that are either prominently featured in this book or inspired me as appropriate background music in some of the scenes. You really don't have to listen to these songs to enjoy *Kill River,* but all of them are excellent and if you're not already familiar with them, I highly recommend checking them out.

Cameron Roubique

1. "Our Lips Are Sealed" - The Go-Go's
2. "We Just Don't Get Along" - The Go-Go's
3. "Girl of 100 Lists" - The Go-Go's
4. "This Town" - The Go-Go's
5. "Tonite" - The Go-Go's
6. "Vacation" - The Go-Go's
7. "I Know There's Something Going On" - Frida
8. "Girls Just Want To Have Fun" - Cyndi Lauper
9. "How Much More" - The Go-Go's
10. "Caught Up In You" - 38. Special

About the Author:

Cameron Roubique lives in Thornton,
Colorado, with his wife, Darla, cat, Penny,
and pug Vader. He is an avid 80's slasher
movie, superhero, and water park fan.

You can follow him on his website
at www.killriver.com
on twitter at twitter.com/lil_cam_ron
and on instagram at instagram.com/cameronroubique.

He can also be reached through email at
cameron@killriver.com.